WORLD OF WARCRAFT®

ARTHAS

RISE OF THE LICH KING

CHRISTIE GOLDEN

POCKET STAR BOOKS

New York   London   Toronto   Sydney

Pocket Star Books
A Division of Simon & Schuster, Inc.
1230 Avenue of the Americas
New York, NY 10020

This book is a work of fiction. Names, characters, places, and incidents either are products of the author's imagination or are used fictitiously. Any resemblance to actual events or locales or persons, living or dead, is entirely coincidental.

First Pocket Star Books paperback edition February 2010

POCKET STAR BOOKS and colophon are registered trademarks of Simon & Schuster, Inc.

For information about special discounts for bulk purchases, please contact Simon & Schuster Special Sales at 1-866-506-1949 or business@simonandschuster.com.

The Simon & Schuster Speakers Bureau can bring authors to your live event. For more information or to book an event contact the Simon & Schuster Speakers Bureau at 1-866-248-3049 or visit our website at www.simonspeakers.com.

Cover art by Glenn Rane

Manufactured in the United States of America

10   9

ISBN 978-1-4391-5760-2
ISBN 978-1-4391-5938-5 (ebook)

U ther was the most controlled man Arthas had ever known, and yet his eyes were bright with unshed tears as he placed the armor on Arthas's broad shoulders. He spoke in a voice that was both powerful and trembling with emotion.

"By the strength of the Light, may your enemies be undone." His hand lingered a moment on Arthas's shoulder, then he, too, retreated.

Archbishop Faol smiled at the prince kindly. Arthas met the gaze evenly, no longer worried. He remembered everything now.

"Arise and be recognized," Faol bade him. Arthas did so.

"Do you, Arthas Menethil, vow to uphold the honor and codes of the Order of the Silver Hand?"

Arthas blinked, momentarily surprised at the lack of his title. *Of course*, he reasoned, *I'm being inducted as a man, not a prince.* "I do."

"Do you vow to walk in the grace of the Light and spread its wisdom to your fellow man?"

"I do."

"Do you vow to vanquish evil wherever it be found, and protect the innocent with your very life?"

"I d—by my blood and honor, I do." That was close, he'd almost messed up.

Faol gave him a quick wink of reassurance, then turned to address both the clerics and the paladins. "Brothers and sisters—you who have gathered here to bear witness—raise your hands and let the Light illuminate this man."

The clerics and paladins all lifted right hands, which were now suffused by a soft, golden glow. They pointed at Arthas, directing the radiance toward him. Arthas's eyes were wide with wonder, and he waited for the glorious glow to envelop him.

Nothing happened.

This book is dedicated to all the Warcraft lore lovers out there.
I hope you enjoy reading this as much as I enjoyed writing it.

Acknowledgments

Special thanks to Chris Metzen (yet again) for his passion for the game and its lore, and to Evelyn Fredericksen, Micky Neilson, Justin Parker, and Evan Crawford at Blizzard for their diligent aid and help in research. So big a book with so many details could not have been written without their cheerful and accurate help and support.

THE EASTERN KINGDOMS

THE SUNWELL

SILVERMOON

QUEL'THALAS

STRATHOLME

HEARTHGLEN

LORDAERON

BALNIR FARMSTEAD

CAPITAL CITY

ANDORHAL

LORDAMERE LAKE

DALARAN

DURNHOLDE KEEP

KHAZ MODAN

STORMWIND CITY   IRONFORGE

FROSTMOURNE CAVERN

FORGOTTEN SHORE

DAGGERCAP BAY

NORTHREND

PROLOGUE: THE DREAMING

The wind shrieked like a child in pain.

The herd of shoveltusk huddled together for warmth, their thick, shaggy coats protecting them from the worst of the storm. They formed a circle, with the calves shivering and bleating in the center. Their heads, each crowned with a massive antler, drooped toward the snow-covered earth, eyes shut against the whirling snow. Their own breath frosted their muzzles as they planted themselves and endured.

. . . In their various dens, the wolves and bears waited out the storms, one with the comfort of their pack, the other solitary and resigned. Whatever their hunger, nothing would drive them forth until after the keening wind had ceased its weeping and the blinding snow had worn itself out.

The wind, roaring in from the ocean to beat at the village of Kamagua, tore at the hides that stretched over frames made of the bones of great sea creatures. When the storm passed, the tuskarr whose home this had been for years uncounted knew they would need to repair or replace nets and traps. Their dwellings, sturdy though they were, were always harmed when *this* storm descended. They had all gathered inside the large group dwelling that had been dug deep into the earth, lacing the flaps tight against the storm and lighting smoky oil lamps.

Elder Atuik waited in stoic silence. He had seen many of these storms over the last seven years. Long had he lived, the length and yellowness of his tusks and the wrinkles on his brown skin testament to the fact. But these storms were more than storms, were more than natural. He glanced at the young ones, shivering not with cold, not the tuskarr, but with fear.

"He dreams," one of them murmured, eyes bright, whiskers bristling.

"Silence," snapped Atuik, more gruffly than he had intended. The child, startled, fell silent, and once again the only sound was the aching sob of the snow and wind.

It rose like the smoke, the deep bellowing noise, wordless but full of meaning; a chant, carried by a dozen voices. The sounds of drums and rattles and bone striking bone formed a fierce undercurrent to the wordless call. The worst of the wind's anger was deflected from the taunka village by the circle of posts and hides, and the lodges, their curving roofs arching over a large interior space in defiance of the hardships of this land, were strong.

Over the sound of deep and ancient ritual, the wind's cry could still be heard. The dancer, a shaman by the name of Kamiku, missed a step and his hoof struck awkwardly. He recovered and continued. Focus. It was all about focus. It was how one harnessed the elements and wrung from them obedience; it was how his people survived in a land that was harsh and unforgiving.

Sweat dampened and darkened his fur as he danced. His large brown eyes were closed in concentration, his hooves again finding their powerful rhythm. He tossed his head, short horns stabbing the air, tail twitching. Others danced beside him. Their body heat and that of the fire, burning brightly despite the flakes and wind drifting down from the smoke hole in the roof, kept the lodge warm and comfortable.

They all knew what was transpiring outside. They could not control these winds and snow, as they could ordinary such things. No, this was *his* doing. But they could dance and feast and laugh in defiance of the onslaught. They were taunka; they would endure.

The world was blue and white and raging outside, but inside the Great Hall the air was warm and still. A fireplace tall enough for a man to stand in was filled with thick logs, the crackling of their burning the only noise. Over the ornately decorated mantel, carved with images of fantastical creatures, the giant antler of a shoveltusk was mounted. Carved dragon heads served as sconces, holding torches with flames burning bright. Heavy beams supported the feast hall that could have housed dozens, the warm orange hue of the fires chasing away the shadows to hide on the corners. The cold stone of the floor was softened and warmed by thick pelts of polar bears, shoveltusk, and other creatures.

A table, long and heavy and carved, occupied most of

the space in the room. It could have hosted three dozen easily. Only three figures sat at the table now: a man, an orc, and a boy.

None of it was real, of course. The man who sat at the place of honor at the table, slightly elevated before the other two in a mammoth carved chair that was not quite a throne, understood this. He was dreaming; he had been dreaming for a long, long time. The hall, the shoveltusk trophies, the fire, the table—the orc and the boy—all were simply a part of his dreaming.

The orc, on his left, was elderly, but still powerful. The orange fire- and torchlight flickered off the ghastly image he bore on his heavy-jawed face—that of a skull, painted on. He had been a shaman, able to direct and wield vast powers, and even now, even just as a figment of the man's imagination, he was intimidating.

The boy was not. Once, he might have been a handsome child, with wide sea green eyes, fair features, and golden hair. But once was not now.

The boy was sick.

He was thin, so emaciated that his bones seemed to threaten to slice through the skin. The once-bright eyes were dimmed and sunken, a thin film covering them. Pustules marked his skin, bursting and oozing forth a green fluid. Breathing seemed difficult and the child's chest hitched in little panting gasps. The man thought he could almost see the labored thumping of a heart that should have faltered long ago, but persisted in continuing to beat.

"He is still here," the orc said, stabbing a finger in the boy's direction.

"He will not last," the man said.

As if to confirm the words, the boy began to cough. Blood and mucus spattered the table in front of him, and he wiped a thin arm clad in rotting finery across his pale mouth. He drew breath to speak in a halting voice, the effort obviously taxing him.

"You have not—yet won him. And I will—prove it to you."

"You are as foolish as you are stubborn," the orc growled. "That battle was won long ago."

The man's hands tightened on the arms of his chair as he listened to both of them. This had been a recurring dream over the last few years; he found it now more tiresome than entertaining. "I grow weary of the struggle. Let us end this once and for all."

The orc leered at the boy, his skull-face grinning hideously. The boy coughed again, but did not quail from the orc's regard. Slowly, with dignity, he straightened, his milky eyes darting from the orc to the man.

"Yes," the orc said, "this serves nothing. Soon it will be time to awaken. Awaken, and move forward into this world once more." He turned to the man, his eyes gleaming. "Walk again the path you have taken."

The skull seemed to detach itself from his face, hovering above it like another entity, and the room changed with its movement. The carved sconces that a moment before were simple wooden dragons undulated and rippled, coming to life, the torches in their mouths flaring and casting grotesque dancing shadows as they shook their heads. The wind screamed outside and the door to the hall slammed open. Snow whirled about the three figures. The man spread his arms and let the freezing wind wrap about him like a cloak. The orc laughed, the skull floating over his face issuing its own manic peals of mirth.

"Let me show you that your destiny lies with me, and you can only know true power through eliminating *him*."

The boy, fragile and slight, had been knocked out of his chair by the violent gusts of frigid air. Now he propped himself up with an effort, shaking, his breaths coming in small puffs as he struggled to climb back into his chair. He threw the man a look—of hope, fear, and odd determination.

"All is not lost," he whispered, and somehow, despite the orc and the skull's laughter, despite the shrieking of the wind, the man heard him.

PART ONE

THE GOLDEN BOY

CHAPTER ONE

"**H**old her head; that's it, lad!"

The mare, her normally white coat gray with sweat, rolled her eyes and whickered. Prince Arthas Menethil, only son to King Terenas Menethil II, one day to rule the kingdom of Lordaeron, held fast to the bridle and murmured soothingly.

The horse jerked her head violently and almost took the nine-year-old with her. "Whoa, Brightmane," Arthas said. "Easy, girl, it'll be all right. Nothing to worry about."

Jorum Balnir grunted in amusement. "Doubt you'd feel that way if something the size of this foal was coming out of *you*, lad."

His son Jarim, crouching beside his father and the prince, laughed and so did Arthas, giggling uncontrollably even as hot and soggy foam from Brightmane's champing mouth dropped onto his leg.

"One more push, girl," Balnir said, moving slowly along the horse's body to where the foal, encased in a shiny shroudlike membrane, was halfway through its journey into the world.

Arthas wasn't really supposed to be here. But when he had no lessons, he often sneaked away to the Balnir farmstead to admire the horses Balnir was known for breeding and to play with his friend Jarim. Both youths were well aware that a horsebreeder's son, even one whose animals were regularly bought as mounts for the royal household, was not a "proper" companion for a prince. Neither cared much, and thus far none of the adults had put a halt to the friendship. And so it was that he had been here, building forts, throwing snowballs, and playing Guards and Bandits with Jarim, when Jorum had called to the boys to come watch the miracle of birth.

The "miracle of birth" was actually pretty disgusting, Arthas thought. He hadn't realized there'd be so much . . . *goo* involved. Brightmane grunted and heaved again, her legs held stiff and straight out, and with a sloshy wet sound her baby entered the world.

Her heavy head thumped down into Arthas's lap, and she closed her eyes for a moment. Her sides heaved as she caught her breath. The boy smiled, stroking the damp neck and thick, rough mane, and looked over to where Jarim and his father were attending to the foal. It was chilly in the stables at this time of year, and steam rose faintly from its warm, wet body. With a towel and dry hay, father and son rubbed off the last of the foal's unsettling shroudlike covering, and Arthas felt his face stretching in a grin.

Damp, gray, all long tangled legs and big eyes, the foal

looked around, blinking in the dim lantern light. Those large brown eyes locked with Arthas's. *You're beautiful,* Arthas thought, his breath stopping for a moment, and realized that the much touted "miracle of birth" really *was* pretty miraculous.

Brightmane began to struggle to her feet. Arthas leaped to his own and pressed back against the wooden walls of the stable so the great animal could turn around without crushing him. Mother and newborn sniffed each other, then Brightmane grunted and began to bathe her son with her long tongue.

"Eh, lad, you're a bit worse for wear," said Jorum.

Arthas looked down at himself and his heart sank. He was covered in straw and horse spittle. Arthas shrugged. "Maybe I should jump into a snowbank on my way back to the palace," he offered, grinning. Sobering slightly, he said, "Don't worry. I'm nine years old now. I'm no longer a baby. I can go where I—"

There was a squawking of chickens and the sound of a man's booming voice, and Arthas's face fell. He squared his small shoulders, made an intense but ultimately ineffectual attempt at brushing off the straw, and strode out of the barn.

"Sir Uther," he said in his best *I am the prince and you had best remember it* voice. "These people have been kind to me. I pray you, don't go trampling their poultry."

Or their snapdragon beds, he thought, glancing over at the snow-covered piles of raised earth where the beautiful blooming flowers that were Vara Balnir's pride and joy would burst forth in a few short months. He heard Jorum and Jarim follow him out from the barn, but did not glance behind him, instead regarding the mounted knight, fully clad in—

"Armor!" Arthas gasped. "What's happened?"

"I'll explain on the way," Uther said grimly. "I'll send someone back for your horse, Prince Arthas. Steadfast can travel faster even with two." He reached down, a large hand closing on Arthas's arm, and swung the boy up in front of him as if he weighed nothing at all. Vara had come out of the house at the sound of a horse approaching at full gallop. She was wiping her hands off on a towel, and had a smudge of flour on her nose. Her blue eyes were wide, and she looked over at her husband worriedly. Uther nodded politely to her.

"We'll discuss this later," Uther said. "Ma'am." He touched his forehead with a mailed hand in courteous salute, then kicked his horse Steadfast—armored as his rider was—and the beast leaped into action.

Uther's arm was like a band of steel around Arthas's midsection. Fear bubbled up inside the boy but he pushed it down even as he pushed on Uther's arm. "I know how to ride," he said, his petulance covering up his worry. "Tell me what is going on."

"A rider from Southshore has come and gone. He brings ill news. A few days ago, hundreds of small boats filled with refugees from Stormwind landed on our shores," Uther said. He did not remove his arm. Arthas gave up that particular struggle and craned his neck, listening intently, his sea-green eyes wide and fastened on Uther's grim face. "Stormwind has fallen."

"What? *Stormwind?* How? To who? What—"

"We'll find all that out shortly. The survivors, including Prince Varian, are being led by Stormwind's onetime Champion, Lord Anduin Lothar. He, Prince Varian, and others will be coming to Capital City in a few days. Lothar has warned us he bears alarming news—obvious enough if something has destroyed Stormwind. I was sent to find you and bring you back. You've no business playing with the common folk at this moment."

Stunned, Arthas turned and faced forward again, his hands gripping Steadfast's mane. Stormwind! He had never been there, but had heard tales about it. It was a mighty place, with great stone walls and beautiful buildings. It had been built with sturdiness in mind, to withstand the buffeting of the fierce winds from which it had taken its name. To think that it had fallen—who or what could be strong enough to take such a city?

"How many people came with them?" he asked, pitching his voice louder than he really wished to in order to be heard over the drumming of the horse's hooves as they headed back toward the city.

"Unknown. Not a small number, that much is certain. The messenger said it was everyone who had survived."

Survived what?

"And Prince Varian?" He'd heard of Varian all his life, of course, just as he knew all the names of the neighboring kings, queens, princes, and princesses. Suddenly his eyes widened. Uther had mentioned Varian—but not the prince's father, King Llane—

"Will soon become King Varian. King Llane fell with Stormwind."

This news of a single tragedy hit Arthas harder some-how than the thought of thousands of people suddenly rendered homeless. Arthas's own family was close-knit—he, his sister, Calia, his mother, Queen Lianne, and of course King Terenas. He'd seen how some rul-ers behaved with their families, and knew that his was remarkable in the degree of closeness. To have lost your city, your way of life, and your father—

"Poor Varian," he said, quick tears of sympathy com-ing to his eyes.

Uther patted his shoulder awkwardly. "Aye," he said. "It is a dark day for the boy."

Arthas shivered suddenly, and not from the cold of a bright winter's day. The beautiful afternoon, with its blue sky and softly curving snow-draped landscape, had suddenly darkened for him.

A few days later, Arthas was standing up on the castle's ramparts, keeping Falric, one of the guards, company and handing him a steaming hot mug of tea. Such a visit, like the ones Arthas paid to the Balnir family and the castle's scullery maids and valets and blacksmiths and indeed nearly every underling on the royal grounds, was not unusual. Terenas always sighed, but Arthas knew that no one was ever punished for speaking with him, and indeed he sometimes wondered if his father secretly approved.

Falric smiled gratefully and bowed deeply in genu-ine respect, pulling off his gauntlets so the mug would warm his cold hands. Snow threatened, and the sky was a pale gray, but thus far the weather was clear.

Arthas leaned against the wall, resting his chin on his folded arms. He looked out over the rolling white hills of Tirisfal, down the road that led through Silverpine Forest to Southshore. The road along which Anduin Lothar, the mage Khadgar, and Prince Varian would be traveling.

"Any sign of them?"

"Nay, Your Highness," Falric answered, sipping the hot beverage. "It could be today, tomorrow, or the day after. If you're hoping to catch a glimpse, sir, you may be waiting awhile."

Arthas shot him a grin, his eyes crinkling with mirth. "Better than lessons," he said.

"Well, sir, you'd know that better than I would," Falric said diplomatically, clearly fighting the impulse to grin back.

While the guard finished the tea, Arthas sighed and looked back down the road as he had a dozen times before. This had been exciting at first, but now he was becoming bored. He wanted to go back and find out how Brightmane's foal was, and began wondering how difficult it would be to slip away for a few hours and not be missed. Falric was right. Lothar and Varian might still be a few days away if—

Arthas blinked. He slowly lifted his chin from his hands and narrowed his eyes.

"They're coming!" he cried, pointing.

Falric was at his side immediately, the mug forgotten. He nodded.

"Sharp eyes, Prince Arthas! Marwyn!" he called. Another soldier snapped to attention. "Go tell the king that Lothar and Varian are on their way. They should be here within the hour."

"Aye, captain," the younger man said, saluting.

"I'll do it! I'll go!" said Arthas, already moving as he spoke. Marwyn hesitated, glancing back at his superior officer, but Arthas was determined to beat him. He raced down the steps, slipping on the ice and having to jump the rest of the way, and ran through the courtyard, skidding to a halt as he approached the throne room and barely remembering to compose himself. Today was when Terenas met with representatives of the populace, to listen to their concerns and do what he could to assist them.

Arthas flipped back the hood of his beautifully embroidered red runecloth cape. He took a deep breath, letting it escape his lips as soft mist, and nodded as he approached the two guards, who saluted sharply and turned to push open the doors for him.

The throne room was significantly warmer than the outside courtyard, even though it was a large chamber formed of marble and stone with a high domed ceiling. Even on overcast days such as this one, the octagonal window at the apex of the dome let in plenty of natural light. Torches in their sconces burned steadily on the walls, adding both warmth and an orange tint to the room. An intricate design of circles enclosing the seal of Lordaeron graced the floor, hidden now by the gathering of people respectfully awaiting their turn to address their liege.

Seated in the jeweled throne on a tiered dais was King Terenas II. His fair hair was touched with gray only at the temples, and his face was slightly lined, with more smile lines than the creased frowns that etched their marks on souls as well as visages. He wore a beautifully tailored robe in hues of blue and purple, wrought with gleaming gold embroidery that caught the torchlight and glinted off his crown. Terenas leaned forward slightly, engrossed in what the man who stood before him—a lesser noble whose name Arthas couldn't recall at the moment—was saying. His eyes, blue-green and intent, were focused on the man.

For a moment, knowing whose coming he was about to announce, Arthas simply stood looking at his father. He, like Varian, was the son of a king, a prince of the blood. But Varian had no father, not anymore, and Arthas felt a lump rise in his throat at the thought of seeing that throne empty, of hearing the ancient song of coronation sung for him.

By the Light, please let that day be a long, long time away.

Perhaps feeling the intensity of his son's gaze, Terenas glanced over at the door. His eyes crinkled in a smile for a moment, then he returned his attention to the petitioner.

Arthas cleared his throat and stepped forward. "Pardon the interruption. Father, they're coming. I saw them! They should be here within the hour."

Terenas sobered slightly. He knew who "they" were. He nodded. "Thank you, my son."

Those assembled looked at one another; most of them, too, knew who "they" were and they moved as if to end the meeting. Terenas held up a hand. "Nay. The weather holds and the road is clear. They will arrive when they do, and not a moment before. Until then, let us continue." He smiled ruefully. "I have a feeling that once they come, audiences such as this will need to be tabled. Let us finish as much business as we can before that moment."

Arthas looked at his father with pride. This was why people loved Terenas so much—and why the king usually turned a blind eye to his son's "adventuring" among the common folk. Terenas cared deeply about the people he ruled, and had instilled that sentiment in his son.

"Shall I ride out to meet them, Father?"

Terenas scrutinized his son for a moment, then shook his fair head. "No. I think it best if you do not attend this meeting."

Arthas felt like he'd been struck. Not attend? He was nine years old! Something very bad had happened to an important ally, and a boy not much older than he had been rendered fatherless by it. He felt a sudden flash of anger. Why did his father insist on sheltering him so? Why was he not allowed to attend important meetings?

He bit back the retort that would have sprung to his lips had he been alone with Terenas. It would not do to argue with his father here, in front of all these people. Even if he was totally and completely in the right on this. He took a deep breath, bowed, and left.

An hour later, Arthas Menethil was safely ensconced in one of the many balconies that overlooked the throne room. He grinned to himself; he was still small enough to hide under the seats if anyone poked their nose in for a quick perusal. He fidgeted slightly; another year or two and he wouldn't be able to do this.

But in a year or two, surely Father will understand that I deserve to be present at such events, and I won't have to hide.

The thought pleased him. He rolled up his cloak and used it as a pillow while he waited. The room was warm from braziers, torches, and the heat of many bodies in a small space. The heat and the soothing murmur of voices in normal discussion lulled him, and he almost fell asleep.

"Your Majesty."

The voice, powerful, resonant, and strong, jerked Arthas awake.

"I am Anduin Lothar, a knight of Stormwind."

They were here! Lord Anduin Lothar, the onetime Champion of Stormwind . . . Arthas edged out from under the seat and rose carefully, making sure he was hidden behind the blue curtain that draped the box, and peeked out.

Lothar looked every inch the warrior, Arthas thought as he regarded the man. Tall, powerfully built, he wore heavy armor with an ease that indicated he was well accustomed to its weight. Although his upper lip and jaw sported a thick mustache and short beard, his head was almost bald; what hair he had left had been tied back in a small ponytail. Beside him stood an old man in violet robes.

Arthas's gaze fell on the boy who could only be Prince Varian Wrynn. Tall, slender yet but with broad shoulders that promised the slim frame would one day fill out, he looked pale and exhausted. Arthas winced as he regarded the youth, a few years older than he, looking lost, alone, and frightened. When addressed, Varian recovered and gave the polite requisite replies. Terenas was an old hand at knowing how to make people feel comfortable. Quickly he dismissed all but a few courtiers and guards and rose from his throne to greet the visitors.

"Please, be seated," he said, choosing not to sit in the glorious throne as was his right but instead perching on the top stair of the dais. He drew Varian down beside him in a fatherly gesture. Arthas smiled.

Hidden away, the young prince of Lordaeron watched and listened closely, and the voices that floated up to him spoke words that sounded almost fanciful. Yet as he regarded this mighty warrior of Stormwind—and even more, as he studied the wan visage of the future king of such a magnificent realm—Arthas realized with a creeping feeling that none of this was fantasy; all of it was deathly real, and it was terrifying.

The men gathered spoke of creatures called "orcs" that had somehow infested Azeroth. Huge, green, with tusks for teeth and lusting for blood, they had formed a "horde" that flowed like a seemingly unstoppable tide— "Enough to cover the land from shore to shore," Lothar said direly. It was these monsters that had attacked Stormwind and made refugees—or corpses, Arthas realized—of its denizens. Things got heated when some courtier or other clearly didn't believe Lothar. Lothar's temper rose, but Terenas defused the situation and brought the meeting to a close. "I will summon my neighboring kings," he said. "These events concern us all. Your Majesty, I offer you my home and my protection for as long as you shall need it."

Arthas smiled. Varian was going to stay here, in the palace, with him. It would be nice to have another noble boy to play with. He got along well enough with Calia, who was two years his elder, but, well, she was a girl, and while he was fond of Jarim, he knew that their opportunities to play together were perforce limited. Varian, however, was a prince of the blood, just like Arthas, and they could spar together, and ride, and go exploring—

"You're telling us to prepare for war." His father's voice cut in on his thoughts with brutal efficiency, and Arthas's mood grew somber again.

"Yes," Lothar replied. "A war for the very survival of our race."

Arthas swallowed hard, then left the viewing box as silently as he had come.

As Arthas had expected, a short time later Prince Varian was shown into the guest quarters. Terenas himself accompanied the boy, resting a hand gently on the youth's shoulder. If he was surprised to see his son waiting in the guest quarters, he did not show it.

"Arthas. This is Prince Varian Wrynn, future king of Stormwind."

Arthas bowed to his equal. "Your Highness," he said formally, "I bid you welcome to Lordaeron. I only wish the circumstances were happier."

Varian returned the bow gracefully. "As I told King Terenas, I am grateful for your support and friendship during these difficult times."

His voice was stiff, strained, weary. Arthas took in the cape, tunic, and breeches, made of runecloth and mageweave and beautifully embroidered. It looked as though Varian had been wearing them for half his life, so dirty were they. His face had clearly been scrubbed, but there were traces of dirt at his temples and beneath his nails.

"I will send up some servants shortly with some food and towels, hot water and a tub, so that you may refresh yourself, Prince Varian." Terenas continued to use the boy's title; that would wear off with time, but Arthas understood why the king emphasized it now. Varian needed to keep hearing that he was still respected, still royal, when he had lost absolutely everything but his life. Varian pressed his lips together and nodded.

"Thank you," he managed.

"Arthas, I leave him in your care." Terenas squeezed Varian's shoulder reassuringly, then departed, closing the door.

The two boys stared at each other. Arthas's mind was a total blank. The silence stretched uncomfortably. Finally Arthas blurted, "I'm sorry about your father."

Varian winced and turned away, walking toward the huge windows that overlooked Lordamere Lake. The snow that had been threatening all morning was finally coming, drifting softly downward to cover the land with a silent blanket. It was too bad—on a clear day, you could see all the way to Fenris Keep. "Thank you."

"I'm sure he died fighting nobly and gave as good as he got."

"He was assassinated." Varian's voice was blunt and emotionless. Arthas whirled to look at him, shocked. His features, in profile to Arthas now and lit by the cold light of a winter's day, were unnaturally composed. Only his eyes, bloodshot and brown and filled with pain, seemed alive. "A trusted friend managed to get him to speak with her alone. Then she killed him. Stabbed him right in the heart."

Arthas stared. Death in glorious battle was difficult enough to handle, but this—

Impulsively he placed a hand on the other prince's arm. "I saw a foal being born yesterday," he said. It sounded inane, but it was the first thing that sprang to his mind and he spoke earnestly. "When the weather lets up, I'll take you to see him. He's the most amazing thing."

Varian turned toward him and gazed at him for a long moment. Emotions flitted across his face—offense, disbelief, gratitude, yearning, understanding. Suddenly the brown eyes filled with tears and Varian looked away. He folded his arms and hunched in on himself, his shoulders shaking with sobs he did his best to muffle. They came out anyway, harsh, racking sounds of mourning for a father, a kingdom, a way of life that he probably hadn't been able to grieve until this precise minute. Arthas squeezed his arm and felt it rigid as stone beneath his fingers.

"I hate winter," Varian sobbed, and the depth of the hurt conveyed by those three simple words, a seeming non sequitur, humbled Arthas. Unable to watch such raw pain, yet powerless to do anything about it, he dropped his hand, turned away, and stared out the window.

Outside, the snow continued to fall.

CHAPTER TWO

Arthas was frustrated.

He thought when word had come about the orcs that he'd finally begin serious training, perhaps alongside his new best friend, Varian. Instead, exactly the opposite happened. The war against the Horde resulted in everyone who could swing a sword joining the armed forces, right down to the master blacksmith. Varian took pity on his younger counterpart and did what he could for a while, until at last he sighed and looked sympathetically at Arthas.

"Arthas, I don't want to sound mean, but . . ."

"But I'm terrible."

Varian grimaced. The two were in the armory hall, sparring with helms, leather chest pieces, and wooden training swords. Varian went to the rack and hung up the training sword, removing his helm as he spoke. "I'm just surprised, because you're athletic and fast."

Arthas sulked; he knew Varian well enough to know that the older prince was trying to soften the blow. He followed sullenly, hanging up his own sword and unfastening his protective gear.

"In Stormwind, we start training when we're quite young. By the time I was your age I had my own set of armor specifically designed for me."

"Don't rub it in," Arthas grumbled.

"Sorry." Varian grinned at him, and Arthas reluctantly gave a small smile back. Although their first meeting had been laced with grief and awkwardness, Arthas had discovered that Varian had a strong spirit and a generally optimistic outlook. "I just wonder why your father didn't do the same for you."

Arthas knew. "He's trying to protect me."

Varian sobered as he hung up his leather chest piece. "My father tried to protect me, too. Didn't work. The realities of life have a way of intruding." He looked at Arthas. "I'm trained to fight. I'm not trained to *teach* fighting. I might hurt you."

Arthas flushed. No suggestion that Arthas might hurt *him*. Varian seemed to see that he was only digging himself deeper into a hole with the younger boy and clapped him on the shoulder. "Tell you what. When the war's over, and a proper trainer can be spared again, I'll come with you to talk to King Terenas. I'm sure you'll be handing me my rear in no time."

The war eventually did end, and the Alliance was triumphant. The leader of the Horde, the once-mighty Orgrim Doomhammer, had been brought back to Capital City in chains. It had made a big impression on both Arthas and Varian, to see the powerful orc paraded through Lordaeron. Turalyon, the young paladin lieutenant who had defeated Doomhammer after the orc had slain the noble Anduin Lothar, had shown mercy in choosing to spare the beast; Terenas, who was at heart a kindly man, continued in that fashion by forbidding attacks on the creature. Jeers, boos, yes—seeing the orc who had terrorized them for so long now powerless, an object of scorn and derision, heartened morale. But Orgrim Doomhammer would not be harmed while in his care.

It was the only time Arthas had seen Varian's face ugly with hate, and he supposed he could not blame the other boy. If orcs had murdered Terenas and Uther, he supposed he'd want to spit on the ugly green things, too. "He should be killed," Varian growled, his eyes angry as they watched from the parapets as Doomhammer was marched toward the palace. "And I wish I could be the one to do it."

"He's going to the Undercity," said Arthas. The ancient royal crypts, dungeons, sewers, and twining alleys deep below the palace had somehow gotten that nickname, as if the place was simply another destination. Dark, dank, filthy, the Undercity was intended only for prisoners or the dead, but the poorest of the poor in the land somehow always seemed to find their way in. If one was homeless, it was better than freezing in the elements, and if one needed something . . . not entirely legal, even Arthas understood that that was where you went to get it. Now and then the guards would go down and make a sweep of the place in a desperate and ultimately futile attempt to clean it out.

"No one ever gets out from the Undercity," Arthas reassured his friend. "He'll die in captivity."

"Too good for him," Varian said. "Turalyon should have killed him when he had the chance."

Varian's words were prophetic. The great orcish leader had only appeared to be humbled by the scorn and hatred heaped upon him. It turned out he was far from broken. Lured by his dispiritedness, or so Arthas gleaned by eavesdropping, the guards had grown lax in their care of him. No one was quite sure how Orgrim Doomhammer's escape had been engineered, because no one survived to report on it—every guard he encountered had gotten his neck broken. But there was a trail of bodies, that of guards, indigents, and criminals—Doomhammer did not discriminate— leading from the wide-open cell through the Undercity to the single escape route—the foul-smelling sewers. Doomhammer was captured again shortly thereafter, and this time placed in the internment camps. When he escaped from there, too, the Alliance collectively held its breath, waiting for a renewed attack. None came. Either Doomhammer was finally dead, or they had shattered his fighting spirit after all.

Two years had come and gone, and now it looked like the Dark Portal through which the Horde had entered Azeroth the first time—the portal that the Alliance had shut down at the end of the Second War—was going to be reopened. Or had already been reopened, Arthas wasn't sure which, because nobody apparently seemed to want to bother to tell him *anything*. Even though he was going to become king one day.

It was a beautiful day, sunny and clear and warm. Part of him wanted to be outside with his new horse, whom he had named Invincible—the same foal he had seen being born on that bitter winter day two years ago. Maybe he'd do that later. But for now, his footsteps took him to the armory, where he and Varian had sparred and Varian had embarrassed him. The slight was unintended, to be sure, but it stung all the same.

Two years.

Arthas walked over to the rack of wooden training swords and took one down. At eleven, he had had what his governess called a "growth spurt"—at least she'd called it that the last time he had seen her, when she wept and hugged him and declared him "a proper young man now" and no longer in need of a governess. The little sword he had trained with at nine was a child's sword. He was indeed a proper young man, standing at five foot eight and likely to grow even taller if his heritage was any indication. He hefted the sword, swinging it this way and that, and suddenly grinned.

He advanced on one of the old suits of armor, gripping the sword firmly. "Hoy!" he called, wishing it was one of the disgusting green monsters that had been such a thorn in his father's side for so long. He drew himself up to his full height, and lifted the tip of the sword to the suit of armor's throat.

"Think you to pass here, vile orc? You are in Alliance lands! I will show you mercy this once. Begone and never return!"

Ah, but orcs didn't understand surrender, or honor.

They were just brutes. So it would refuse to kneel and show him respect.

"What? You will not depart? I have given you a chance, but now, we fight!"

And he lunged, as he had seen Varian do. Not directly at the armor, no, the thing was very old and very valuable, but right beside it. Strike, block, duck in under the swing, bring the sword all the way across the body, then whirl and—

He gasped as the sword seemed to take on a life of its own and flew across the room. It landed loudly on the marble floor, sliding along with a grating sound before slowly spinning to a stop.

Dammit! He looked toward the door—and right into the face of Muradin Bronzebeard.

Muradin was the dwarven ambassador to Lordaeron, brother to King Magni Bronzebeard and a great favorite at court for his jovial, no-nonsense approach to everything from fine ale and pastries to matters of state. He had a reputation as an excellent warrior as well, cunning and fierce in battle.

And he had just watched the future king of Lordaeron pretend to fight orcs and throw his sword clear across the room. Arthas felt his whole body break out in a sweat, and he knew his cheeks were pink. He tried to recover.

"Um . . . Ambassador . . . I was just . . ."

The dwarf coughed and looked away. "I'm lookin' fer yer father, boy. Can ye direct me? This infernal place has too many turns."

Arthas mutely pointed to a stairway on his left. He watched the dwarf go. No other words were exchanged.

Arthas had never been more embarrassed in his life. Tears of shame burned in his eyes, and he blinked them back hard. Without even bothering to put away the wooden sword, he fled the room.

Ten minutes later, he was free, riding out of the stables and heading east into the hills of Tirisfal Glades. He had two horses with him: a gentle, elderly dapple-gray gelding called Trueheart upon which he was mounted and, on a training lead, the two-year-old colt Invincible.

He'd felt the bond between them from the moment they had locked eyes, moments after the foal's birth. Arthas had known then that this would be his steed, his friend, the great horse with a great heart who would be as much a part of him as—no, more than—his armor or weapons. Horses from good stock such as this one could live twenty years or more if cared for well; this was the mount who would bear Arthas elegantly in ceremony and faithfully on daily rides. He was not a warhorse. Such were a breed apart, used only for specific purposes at specific times. He'd have one when he went into battle. But Invincible would, and indeed already had, become part of his life.

The stallion's coat, mane, and tail, gray at his birth, had turned white as the snow that had coated the ground on that day. It was a color that was rare even among the Balnir-bred horses, whose "white" coats were really mostly just light gray. Arthas had toyed with names like "Snowfall" or "Starlight," but in the end, he followed the informal tradition of Lordaeron knights and gave his steed the name of a quality. Uther's mount was "Steadfast," Terenas's "Courageous."

His was "Invincible."

Arthas wanted desperately to ride Invincible, but the horsemaster warned that two years old was at least a year too young. "Two's a baby," he'd said. "They're still growing; their bones are still forming. Be patient, Your Highness. Another year isn't that long to wait for a horse that'll serve you well for two decades."

But it *was* a long time to wait. Too long. Arthas glanced back over his shoulder at the horse, growing impatient with the plodding canter that seemed the most that Trueheart could summon. In contrast with the elderly gelding, the two-year-old moved almost as if floating, with hardly any effort. His ears were pricked forward, and his nostrils flared as he scented the smells of the glade. His eyes were bright and he seemed to be saying, *Come on, Arthas. . . . It's what I was born for.*

Surely one ride couldn't hurt. Just a little canter, and then back to the stables as if nothing had happened.

He slowed Trueheart to a walk and tied the reins to a low-slung tree branch. Invincible whickered as Arthas walked up to him. The prince grinned at the velvety softness of the muzzle brushing his palm as he fed the horse a piece of apple. Invincible was used to having a saddle; it was part of the slow and patient breaking process, to get the horse accustomed to having something on its back. But an empty saddle was much different from a live human being. Still, he'd spent a lot of time with the animal. Arthas said a short prayer and then quickly, before Invincible could sidestep out of the way, vaulted onto the horse's back.

Invincible reared, neighing furiously. Arthas wrapped

his hands in the wiry mane and clung like a burr with every inch of his long legs. The horse hopped and bucked, but Arthas held on. He yelped as Invincible tried to scrape him off by running beneath one of the branches, but did not let go.

And then Invincible was galloping.

Or rather, he was *flying*. Or at least so it seemed to the giddy young prince, who crouched low on the horse's neck and grinned widely. He'd never been on an animal this fast before, and his heart pounded with excitement. He didn't even try to control Invincible; it was all he could do to simply hang on. It was glorious, wild, beautiful, everything he'd dreamed of. They would—

Before he even realized what had happened, Arthas was hurtling through the air to land hard on the grassy earth. For a long moment he couldn't breathe from the impact. Slowly he got to his feet. His body ached, but nothing was broken.

But Invincible was a rapidly disappearing dot in the distance. Arthas swore violently, kicking a hillock and balling his fists. He was in for it now.

Sir Uther the Lightbringer was waiting for him upon his return. Arthas grimaced as he slid off Trueheart and handed the reins to a groomsman.

"Invincible came back a short time ago by himself. He had a nasty cut on his leg, but I'm sure you'll be glad to know the horsemaster says he'll be fine."

Arthas debated lying, telling Uther they'd been spooked and Invincible had fled. But it was obvious from the grass stains on his clothes that he'd fallen, and

Uther would never believe that the prince couldn't stay on gentle old Trueheart, spooked or not.

"You know you were not supposed to ride him yet," Uther continued inexorably.

Arthas sighed. "I know."

"Arthas, do you not understand? If you put too much pressure on him at this age he—"

"I get it, all right? I could cripple him. It was just the one time."

"And that's all it will be, isn't it?"

"Yes, sir," Arthas said, sullenly.

"You missed your lessons. Again."

Arthas was silent and did not look up at Uther. He was angry, embarrassed, and hurting, and wanted nothing more than a hot bath and some briarthorn tea to ease the pain. His right knee was starting to swell.

"At least you are in time for the prayer session this afternoon." Uther eyed him up and down. "Though you'll need to wash up." Arthas was indeed sweaty and knew he smelled like horse. It was a good smell, he thought. An honest one. "Hurry up. We'll be assembling in the chapel."

Arthas wasn't even sure what the prayer session was focusing on today. He felt vaguely bad about that; the Light was important to both his father and Uther, and he knew that they badly wanted him to be as devout as they were. But while he couldn't argue with the evidence of his own eyes—the Light was most definitely real; he'd seen priests and the new order of the paladins work true miracles with healing and protection—he'd never felt called to sit and meditate for hours as Uther did, or make frequent references in reverent tones as did his father. It was just . . . there.

An hour later, scrubbed and changed into an outfit that was simple yet elegant, Arthas hurried to the small family chapel in the royal wing.

It was not a large room, but it was beautiful. It was a miniature version of the traditional chapel style that could be seen in every human town, perhaps a trifle more lavish with regard to the details. The chalice that was shared was finely wrought of gold and inlaid with gems; the table upon which it lay, an antique. Even the benches had comfortable padding, while the common folk had to make do with flat wooden ones.

He realized as he entered quietly that he was the last—and winced as he recalled that several important personages were visiting his father. In addition to the regular attendees—his family, Uther, and Muradin— King Trollbane was present, though he looked even less happy than Arthas to be here. And . . . someone else. A girl, slender and straight with long blond hair, her back turned to him. Arthas peered at her, curious, and bumped into one of the benches.

He might as well have dropped a plate. Queen Lianne, still a beauty in her early fifties, turned at the sound, smiling affectionately at her son. Her gown was perfectly arranged, her hair pulled back in a golden coif from which no unruly tendril escaped. Calia, fourteen and looking as gawky and coltish as Invincible had been at his birth, shot him a scowl. Evidently, word of his misdeeds had gotten out—or else she was just angry with him at being late. Terenas nodded at him, then returned his eyes to the bishop giving the service. Arthas cringed inwardly at the quiet disapproval in that gaze. Trollbane paid him no mind, and Muradin, too, did not turn.

Arthas slouched down onto one of the benches against the back wall. The bishop began to speak and lifted his hands, limned with a soft, white radiance. Arthas wished the girl would turn a little so he could catch a glimpse of her face. Who was she? Obviously the daughter of a noble or someone else of high rank, else she would not be invited to attend private family services. He thought about who she might be, more interested in discovering her identity than in the words of the service.

". . . and His Royal Highness, Arthas Menethil," intoned the bishop. Arthas jerked to attention, wondering if he'd missed something important. "May the Light's blessing be upon him in every thought, word, and deed, so that he may thrive beneath it and grow to serve it as its paladin." Arthas felt a sudden calming warmth flow through him as the blessing was laid upon him. The stiffness and soreness vanished, leaving him refreshed and at peace. The bishop turned to the queen and the princess. "May the Light shine on Her Royal Majesty, Lianne Menethil, that she—"

Arthas grinned and waited for the bishop to complete the individual blessings. He'd name the girl then. Arthas leaned against the back wall of the room.

"And we humbly request the Light's blessing on Lady Jaina Proudmoore. May she be blessed with its healing and wisdom, that she—"

Aha! The mystery girl was a mystery no longer.

Jaina Proudmoore, a year younger than he, daughter to Admiral Daelin Proudmoore, naval war hero and ruler of Kul Tiras. What did intrigue him was why she was here and—

"—and that her studies at Dalaran go well. We ask that she become a representative of the Light, and that in the role of a mage, she will serve her people well and truly."

That made sense. She was on her way to Dalaran, the beautiful city of magi not too far from Capital City. Knowing the rigid rules of etiquette and hospitality that were so pervasive in royal and noble circles, she'd be here for a few days before traveling on.

This, he thought, *could be fun.*

At the end of the service, Arthas, already located near the door, stepped out first. Muradin and Trollbane were the first out, both looking slightly relieved that the service was over. Terenas, Uther, Lianne, Calia, and Jaina followed.

Both his sister and the Proudmoore girl were fair haired and slender. But the resemblance stopped there. Calia was delicately boned, with a face right out of old paintings, pale skinned and soft. Jaina, however, had bright eyes and a lively smile, and she moved like someone who was well accustomed to riding and hiking. She obviously spent a great deal of time out of doors, as her face was tanned with a smattering of sprinkles across her nose.

This, Arthas decided, was a girl who would not mind getting a snowball in the face, or going for a swim on a hot day. Someone, unlike his sister, he could play with.

"Arthas—a word wi' ye," came a gruff voice. Arthas turned to see the ambassador peering up at him.

"Of course, sir," Arthas said, his heart sinking. All he wanted to do was talk to this new friend—he was already sure they would get along famously—and Muradin probably wanted to scold him again for the embarrassing display earlier in the armory. At least the dwarf was discreet enough to walk a few paces away.

He turned to face the prince, stubby thumbs hooked into his belt, gruff face knotted in thought. "Lad," he said, "I'll get right tae th' point. Yer fightin' form is terrible."

Again, Arthas felt the blood rush to his face. "I know," he said, "but Father—"

"Yer father has many things on 'is mind. Dinna ye be saying a thing against 'im."

Well, what was he supposed to say? "Well, I can't very well teach *myself* fighting. You saw what happened when I tried."

"I ken tha'. I'll teach ye if ye like."

"You—you will?" Arthas was at first disbelieving, then delighted. The dwarves were renowned for their fighting prowess, among many things. Part of Arthas wondered if Muradin would also teach him how to hold his ale, another thing dwarves were known for, but he decided not to ask that.

"Aye, that's what I said, wasn't it? I've spoken wi' yer father, an' he's all for it. Been put off long enough as it is. But let's get one thing straight. I'll take nae excuses. And I'll be pushin' ye right hard. And if at any moment I say tae mesel', 'Muradin, ye're wastin' yer time,' I stop. D'ye agree, boy?"

Arthas fought back an incongruous giggle at the thought of someone who stood so much shorter than he calling him "boy," but bit it back. "Yes, sir," he said fervently. Muradin nodded and stuck out a large, calloused hand. Arthas shook it. Grinning, he glanced up at his father, who was deep in conversation with Uther. They turned as one to regard him, both pairs of eyes narrowing in speculation, and inwardly Arthas sighed. He knew that look. So much for playing with Jaina—he'd probably not have time to even see her again before she left.

He turned to watch as Calia, her arm around the younger girl's shoulder, swept Jaina from the room. But right before she disappeared through the doorway, Admiral Proudmoore's daughter turned her golden head, caught Arthas's gaze with her own, and smiled.

CHAPTER THREE

"I'm very proud of you, Arthas," said his father. "Stepping up to the responsibility like this."

In the week that Jaina Proudmoore had been with the Menethil family as an honored guest, "responsibility" had been the watchword. Not only had his training with Muradin begun—and it was every bit as rigorous and demanding as the dwarf had warned, the pain of sore muscles and bruises augmented by the occasional ringing cuff on the ear when Arthas was not paying sufficient attention for Muradin's liking—but as Arthas had feared, Uther and Terenas also decided it was time that the prince's training was stepped up in other areas. Arthas would rise before dawn, grab a quick breakfast of bread and cheese, and go on an early ride with Muradin. The ride would end in a hike, and it was the twelve-year-old youth who always ended up shaking and winded. Arthas secretly wondered if the dwarves had such an affinity with stones that the very earth made it easy for them to climb it. Back home, bath, lessons in history, mathematics, and calligraphy. A midday meal, then it was all afternoon in the chapel with Uther, praying, meditating, and discussing the nature of paladins and the rigorous disciplines they must observe. Dinner, and then Arthas stumbled into bed to sleep the deep dreamless sleep of the utterly exhausted.

He'd seen Jaina only a few times at dinner, and she and Calia seemed to be thick as thieves. Arthas finally decided enough was enough, and, taking the lessons in history and politics that were being drilled into his head, he approached his father and Uther with the offer to escort their guest, Lady Jaina Proudmoore, to Dalaran himself.

He didn't bother to tell them it was because he wanted to get out of his duties. It pleased Terenas to think of his son as being so responsible, Jaina smiled brightly at the prospect, and it got Arthas exactly what he wanted. Everyone was happy.

And so it was that in early summer, when the flowers were blooming, the woods were full of game, and the sun danced above them in a sky of bright blue, Prince Arthas Menethil was accompanying a brightly smiling, blond, young lady on a journey to the wondrous city of magi.

They'd gotten a little late of a start—one thing Arthas was starting to learn about Jaina Proudmoore was that she was not exactly punctual—but Arthas didn't mind. He was in no hurry. They weren't alone, of course. Propriety demanded that Jaina's lady-in-waiting and a guard or two ride escort. But still, the servants hung back and let the two young nobles become acquainted. They rode for a while, then stopped for a picnic lunch.

While they were munching on bread, cheese, and watered wine, one of Arthas's men came up to him.

"Sir, with your permission, we will make preparations to spend the night in Ambermill. On the morrow, we can push on the rest of the way to Dalaran. We should arrive there by nightfall."

Arthas shook his head. "No, let's continue. We can camp overnight in the Hillsbrad area. That will get Lady Jaina to Dalaran by mid-morning tomorrow." He turned to smile at her.

She smiled back, though he caught a hint of disappointment in her eyes.

"Are you sure, sir? We've planned on accepting the hospitality of the locals, not subjecting the lady to sleeping out in the open."

"It's fine, Kayvan," Jaina spoke up. "I'm not a fragile little figurine."

Arthas's smile widened into a grin.

He hoped she'd feel that way in a few hours.

While the servants set up camp, Arthas and Jaina went exploring. They scrambled up a hill that gave them an unparalleled view. To the west, they could see the little farming community of Ambermill and even the distant spires of Baron Silverlaine's keep. To the east, they could almost make out Dalaran itself, and more clearly, the internment camp to its south. Since the end of the Second War, the orcs had been rounded up and placed into these camps. It was more merciful than simply slaughtering them on sight, Terenas had explained to Arthas. And besides, the orcs seemed to be suffering from a strange malaise. Most of the time when humans stumbled upon them, or hunted them, they fought only halfheartedly and went into internment peacefully. There were several camps just like this one.

They had a rustic meal of roasted rabbit on a spit and retired shortly after dark. Once he was assured that everyone was asleep, Arthas threw a tunic over his breeches and quickly tugged on his boots. As an afterthought, he took one of his daggers and fastened it to his belt, then crept over to Jaina.

"Jaina," he whispered, "wake up."

She awoke in silence and unafraid, her eyes glinting in the moonlight. He squatted back as she sat up, putting a finger to his lips. She spoke in a whisper. "Arthas? Is something wrong?"

He grinned. "You up for an adventure?"

She tilted her head. "What sort of an adventure?"

"Trust me."

Jaina looked at him for a moment, then nodded. "All right."

She, like all of them, had gone to sleep mostly dressed and simply needed to pull on her boots and cloak. She rose, made a halfhearted attempt to comb her fingers through her blond hair, and nodded.

Jaina followed him as they ascended the same ridge they had explored earlier that day. The climb was more challenging at night, but the moonlight was quite bright and their feet did not slip.

"There's our destination," he said, pointing.

Jaina gulped. "The internment camp?"

"Have you ever seen one up close?"

"No, and I don't want to."

He frowned, disappointed. "Come on, Jaina. It's our one chance to get a good look at an orc. Aren't you curious?"

Her face was hard to read in the moonlight, her eyes dark pools of shadow. "I—they killed Derek. My older brother."

"One of them killed Varian's father, too. They've killed a lot of people, and that's why they're in these camps. It's the best place for them. A lot of people don't like the fact that my father is raising taxes to pay for the camps, but—come on and judge for yourself. I missed a chance to get a good look at Doomhammer when he was in the Undercity. I don't want to miss a chance to see one now."

She was silent, and at last he sighed. "All right, I'll take you back."

"No," she said, surprising him. "Let's go."

Quietly they made their descent. "All right," Arthas whispered. "When we were up here earlier, I made note of their patrols. It doesn't look like they're much different at night, except maybe even more infrequent. With the orcs not having much spirit left in them, I guess the guards think that the chances of escape aren't that likely." He smiled at her reassuringly. "Which works out well for us. Other than patrols, someone is always stationed in those two watchtowers. They're the ones we have to be most careful of, but hopefully they'll be looking for any disturbance to come from the front rather than behind, since the camp backs up against a sheer wall face. Now, let this fellow here complete his circuit, and we should have ample time to get close to that wall right there and take a good look."

They waited for the bored-looking guard to meander past, then a few more breaths after that. "Put your hood up," Arthas said. Both had fair hair, and it would be far too easy for the guards to spot. Jaina looked nervous but excited, and obeyed. Fortunately both she and Arthas wore cloaks of a dark shade. "Ready?" She nodded. "Good. Let's go!"

They slipped quickly and quietly down the rest of the way. Arthas held her back for a moment until the guard in the tower was looking in the other direction, then motioned to her. They ran forward, making sure their hoods were securely in place, and a few steps later they were pressing against the wall of the camp.

The camps were rough but efficient. They were made of wood, little more than logs fastened together, sharpened at the top and embedded deep into the ground. There were plenty of chinks in the "wall" that a curious boy and girl could look through.

It was hard to see at first, but there were several large shapes inside. Arthas turned his head for a better look. They were orcs all right. Some of them were on the ground, curled up and covered by blankets. Some walked here and there, almost aimlessly, like animals in cages, but lacking a caged beast's almost palpable yearning for freedom. Over there was what looked like a family unit—a male, a female, and a young one. The female, slighter and shorter than the male, held something small to her chest, and Arthas realized it was an infant.

"Oh," whispered Jaina beside him. "They look . . . so sad."

Arthas snorted, then remembered the need to be quiet. He quickly glanced up at the tower, but the guard had heard nothing. "Sad? Jaina, these brutes destroyed Stormwind. They wanted to render humankind extinct. They killed your brother, for Light's sake. Don't waste any pity on them."

"Still—somehow I didn't think they would have children," Jaina continued. "Do you see the one with the baby?"

"Well of course they have children, even rats have children," Arthas said. He was irritated, but then, maybe he should have expected a reaction like that from an eleven-year-old girl.

"They look harmless enough. Are you sure they belong here?" She turned her face to his, a white oval in the moonlight, seeking his opinion. "It's expensive to keep them here. Maybe they should be released."

"Jaina," he said, keeping his voice soft, "they're killers. Even if right now they're lethargic, who can say what would happen if they're released?"

She sighed softly in the darkness and didn't answer. Arthas shook his head. He'd seen enough—the guard would be back shortly. "Ready to go back?"

She nodded, stepping away and running quickly with him back toward the hill. Arthas glanced over his shoulder and saw the guard start to turn. He dove toward Jaina, grabbed her around the waist, and shoved her to the ground, hitting hard beside her. "Don't move," he said, "the guard is looking right at us!"

Despite the rough fall Jaina was smart enough to freeze at once. Carefully, keeping his face as shadowed as possible, Arthas turned his head to look at the guard. He couldn't see a face at this distance, but the man's posture bespoke boredom and weariness. After a long moment, during which Arthas heard his heart thundering in his ears, the guard turned to face the other direction.

"Sorry about that," Arthas apologized, helping Jaina to her feet. "You all right?"

"Yes," Jaina said. She grinned at him.

They were back in their respective sleeping areas a few moments later. Arthas looked up at the stars, completely satisfied.

It had been a good day.

Late that next morning, they arrived at Dalaran. Arthas had never been there before, though of course had heard a great deal about it. The magi were a private and mysterious lot—quite powerful, but they kept to themselves save when needed. Arthas remembered when Khadgar had accompanied Anduin Lothar and Prince—now King—Varian Wrynn to speak with Terenas, to warn them of the orcish threat. His presence had lent weight to Anduin's statements, and with good reason. Magi of the Kirin Tor didn't get involved in ordinary politics.

Nor did they do the ordinary political maneuvering such as inviting royalty to enjoy their hospitality. It was only because Jaina was coming to study that Arthas and his retinue were permitted admittance. Dalaran was beautiful, even more glorious than Capital City. It seemed almost impossibly clean and bright, as a city based so deeply on magic ought to be. There were several graceful towers reaching skyward, their bases white stone and their apexes violet encircled with gold. Many had radiant, hovering stones dancing around them. Others had windows of stained glass that caught the sunlight. Gardens bloomed, the fragrances from wild, fantastical flowers providing a scent so heady Arthas was almost dizzy. Or maybe it was the constant thrum of magic in the air that caused the sensation.

He felt very ordinary and dingy as they rode into the city, and almost wished they hadn't slept outside last night. If they had stayed at Ambermill, at least he'd have had a chance to have bathed. But then, he and Jaina wouldn't have gotten a chance to spy on the internment camp.

He glanced at his companion. Her blue eyes were wide with awe and excitement, her lips slightly parted. She turned to Arthas, those lips curving in a smile.

"Aren't I lucky to be studying here?"

"Sure," he said, smiling on her behalf. She was drinking this in like one who had been given water after a week in the desert, but he felt . . . unwanted. He clearly did not have the affinity for wielding magic as she did.

"I'm told that outsiders aren't usually welcome," she said. "I think that's a shame. It would be nice to see you again."

She blushed, and for a moment, Arthas forgot about the intimidation the city emanated, and heartily agreed that it would be nice to see Lady Jaina Proudmoore again, too.

Very nice indeed.

* * *

"Again, ye little gnome girl! I'll pull yer pigtails, ye— Ooof!"

The shield caught the taunting dwarf full in the helmed face, and he actually stumbled back a step or two. Arthas slashed with the sword, grinning beneath his own helm as it connected solidly. Then suddenly, he was sailing through the air to land hard on his back. His vision was filled with the image of a looming head with a long beard, and he was barely able to lift his blade in time to parry. With a grunt, he pulled his legs in to his chest and then extended them hard, catching Muradin in the gut. This time it was the dwarf who went hurtling backward. Arthas brought his legs down swiftly and leaped up in a single smooth motion, charging his teacher who was still on the ground, coming at him with blow after blow until Muradin spoke the words that Arthas honestly never thought he'd hear:

"I yield!"

It took everything Arthas had to halt the strike, pulling up and back so abruptly he lost his balance and stumbled. Muradin lay where he was, his chest rising and falling.

Fear squeezed Arthas's heart. "Muradin? Muradin!"

A hearty chuckle escaped from the thick, bronze beard. "Well done, lad, well done indeed!" He struggled to sit up and Arthas was there, reaching out a hand to help haul the dwarf to his feet. Muradin pumped the hand happily. "So, ye were payin' attention after all when I taught ye my special trick."

Relieved and pleased with the praise, Arthas grinned.

Some of what Muradin taught him would be repeated, honed, and reinforced in his paladin training. But other things—well, he didn't think Uther the Lightbringer would know about feet planted firmly in the belly, or the rather handy trick regarding the efficacy of a broken wine bottle. There was fighting and there was *fighting*, and Muradin Bronzebeard seemed determined that Arthas Menethil would understand all aspects of it.

Arthas was fourteen now, and had been training with Muradin several times a week, save for when the dwarf was away on diplomatic errands. At first, it had gone as both parties had expected—badly. Arthas left the first dozen or so sessions bruised, bloodied, and limping. He had stubbornly refused any offers of healing, insisting that the pain was part of the process. Muradin had approved, and he had shown it by pressing Arthas all the harder. Arthas never complained, not even when he wanted to, not even when Muradin scolded him or pressed the attack long after Arthas was too exhausted to even hold up a shield.

And for that stubborn refusal to whine or to quit, he was rewarded twofold: he learned and learned well, and he won the respect of Muradin Bronzebeard.

"Oh yes, sir, I was paying attention." Arthas chuckled.

"Good lad, good lad." Muradin reached up to clap him on the shoulder. "Now, off wi' ye. Ye've taken quite the beating today; ye deserve a bit o' rest."

His eyes twinkled as he spoke and Arthas nodded as if agreeing. Today, it was Muradin who had taken the beating. And he seemed as happy as Arthas at the fact.

The prince's heart suddenly swelled with affection toward the dwarf. Though a strict taskmaster, Muradin was someone of whom Arthas had grown terribly fond.

He whistled a little as he strode toward his quarters, but then a sudden outburst froze him in his tracks.

"No, Father! I will not!"

"Calia, I grow tired of this conversation. You have no say in this matter."

"Papa, please, no!"

Arthas edged a little closer to Calia's chambers. The door was ajar and he listened, slightly worried. Terenas doted on Calia. What in the world was he asking of her to make her beg with him and use the term of endearment that both she and Arthas had dropped as they grew toward adulthood?

Calia sobbed brokenly. Arthas could take it no longer. He opened the door. "I'm sorry, I couldn't help but overhear, but—what is wrong?"

Terenas had recently seemed to be acting strangely, and now he looked furious with his sixteen-year-old daughter. "It is no business of yours, Arthas," Terenas rumbled. "I have told Calia something I wish her to do. She will obey me."

Calia collapsed on the bed, sobbing. Arthas stared from his father to his sister in utter astonishment. Terenas muttered something and stormed out. Arthas glanced back at Calia, then followed his father.

"Father, please, what's going on?"

"Do not question me. Calia's duty is to obey her father." Terenas marched through a door and into a receiving room. Arthas recognized Lord Daval Prestor, a young noble whom Terenas seemed to hold in very high regard, and a pair of visiting Dalaran wizards he did not know.

"Run along back to your sister, Arthas, and try to calm her. I'll be with you as soon as I can, I promise."

With a final glance at the three visitors, Arthas nodded and went back to Calia's rooms. His older sister had not moved, although her sobs had quieted somewhat. At a total loss, Arthas simply sat beside her on the bed, feeling awkward.

Calia sat up on the bed, her face wet. "I'm sorry you h-had to see that, Arthas, but m-maybe it's for the best."

"What did Father want you to do?"

"He wishes me to marry against my will."

Arthas blinked. "Calie, you're only sixteen, you're not even *old* enough to get married."

She reached for a handkerchief and dabbed at her swollen eyes. "That's what I said. But Father said it didn't matter; we'd formalize the betrothal and on my birthday I'd marry Lord Prestor."

Arthas's sea-green eyes widened in comprehension. So that was why Prestor was here. . . .

"Well," he began awkwardly, "he's very well connected, and—I guess he's handsome. Everyone says so. At least he's not some old man."

"You don't understand, Arthas. I don't care how well connected or handsome or even kind he is. It's that I don't have any choice in the matter. I'm—I'm like your horse. I'm a thing, not a person. To be given away as Father sees fit—to seal a political bargain."

"You—you don't love Prestor?"

"Love him?" Her blue, bloodshot eyes narrowed in anger. "I barely know him! He's never taken the slightest . . . oh, what's the use? I know that this is common practice among royalty and nobility. That we are pawns. But I just never expected Father—"

Nor had Arthas. He'd honestly never given much thought to marriage for himself or his sister. He was much more interested in training with Muradin and riding Invincible. But Calia was right. It was common among the nobility to make good marriages to ensure their political status.

He'd just never thought his father would sell his daughter like—like a broodmare.

"Calie, I'm really sorry," he said, and meant it. "Is there someone else? Maybe you could convince Father that there's a better match—one that makes you happy as well."

Calia shook her head bitterly. "It's no use. You heard him. He didn't ask me, didn't suggest Lord Prestor—he ordered me." She looked at him pleadingly. "Arthas, when you are king, promise me—promise me you won't do that to your children."

Children? Arthas was in no way ready to think about that. There weren't even any—well, there *was,* but he hadn't thought about her in—

"And when you marry—Papa cannot order you as he orders me. Make sure you care for this girl and—and that she cares for you. Or is at least *asked* about whom she wants to share her life and her b-bed with."

She started to weep afresh, but Arthas was too shaken by the revelation that burst upon him. He was only fourteen now, but in four short years, he'd be of age to wed. He suddenly recalled snatches of conversation he'd heard here and there about the future of the Menethil line. His wife would be the mother of kings. He'd have to choose carefully, but also, as Calia had asked, kindly. His parents obviously cared greatly for each other. It was reflected in their smiles and gestures, despite many years of marriage. Arthas wanted that. He wanted a companion, a friend, a—

He frowned. But what if he couldn't have that? "I'm sorry, Calie, but maybe you're the lucky one. It might be worse to have the freedom to choose, and know that you couldn't have what you wanted."

"I would trade that for being a—a piece of meat in a heartbeat."

"We each have our duties, I guess," Arthas said quietly, somberly. "You to marry whomever Father wants, and me to marry well for the kingdom." He rose abruptly. "I'm sorry, Calie."

"Arthas—where are you going?"

He didn't answer, but practically raced through the palace to the stables and, without waiting for a groom, quickly saddled Invincible himself. Arthas knew it was only a temporary solution, but he was fourteen, and a temporary solution was still a solution.

He bent low over Invincible's back, the white mane whipping his face as the horse galloped, all sleekly coiled muscle and grace. Arthas's face stretched in a grin. He was never happier than when he rode like this, the two of them merging into one glorious whole. He had waited, his patience sorely tested, for so long to be able to ride the animal he had watched coming into the world, but it had been worth it. They were the perfect team. Invincible wanted nothing from him, asked nothing of him, only seemed to wish to be allowed to escape the confines of the stables as Arthas longed to escape the confines of his royalty. They did so together.

They were coming up on the jump Arthas loved now. To the east of Capital City and close to the Balnir farmstead was a small cluster of hills. Invincible surged, the earth devoured by his pounding hooves, pulling himself upward toward the precipice almost as fast as if they were on level ground. He wheeled and turned along the narrow pathways, sending stones scattering with his hooves, his heart and Arthas's both racing in excitement. Then Arthas guided the stallion to the left, over an embankment—a shortcut to the Balnir property. Invincible did not hesitate, had not hesitated even the first time that Arthas had asked him to leap. He gathered himself and launched forward, and for a glorious, heart-stopping moment, horse and rider were airborne. Then they landed securely on soft, springy grass, and were off again.

Invincible.

CHAPTER FOUR

"**A**s you can see, Your Highness," said Lieutenant General Aedelas Blackmoore, "the taxes have been put to good use. Every precaution has been taken in the operation of this facility. In fact, security is so tight we've been able to stage gladiatorial combat here."

"So I've heard," said Arthas, as he walked with the commander of the internment camps on a tour of the grounds. Durnholde, not an internment camp itself, but the nerve center of all of the others, was huge, and indeed had almost a festival air about it. It was a crisp but bright autumn day, and the breeze caused the blue and white banners that flew over the keep to snap energetically. The wind stirred Blackmoore's long raven hair and tugged at Arthas's cloak as they strolled along the ramparts.

"And so you shall also see," Blackmoore promised, giving his prince an ingratiating grin.

It had been Arthas's idea for a surprise inspection. Terenas had praised Arthas for his initiative and compassion. "It's only right, Father," Arthas had said, and by and large he meant it, although his primary reason for the suggestion was to satisfy his curiosity about the pet orc the lieutenant general kept. "We should make sure the money is going into the camps and not Blackmoore's pocket. We can ascertain if he is taking proper care of the gladiatorial participants—and also, make sure he is not walking the path of his father."

Blackmoore's father, General Aedelyn Blackmoore, had been a notorious traitor, tried and convicted of selling state secrets. While his crimes had taken place long ago, when his son had been but a child, the stain had dogged Aedelas throughout his military career. It was only his record of victory in battles, and particular ferocity in fighting the orcs, that had enabled the current Blackmoore to rise in the ranks. Still, Arthas could detect the smell of liquor on the man's breath, even at this hour of the morning. He suspected that particular piece of information would not be news to Terenas, but he'd make sure he told his father anyway.

Arthas looked down, feigning interest in watching the dozens of guards who stood at rigid attention. He wondered if they were that attentive when their future king wasn't watching them.

"I look forward to the bout today," he said. "Will I be able to watch your Thrall in action? I've heard quite a bit about him."

Blackmoore grinned, his neatly trimmed goatee parting to reveal white teeth. "He was not scheduled to fight today, but for you, Your Highness, I shall pair him up against the worthiest foes available."

Two hours later, the tour was complete, and Arthas shared a delicious meal with Blackmoore and a younger man named Lord Karramyn Langston, whom Blackmoore introduced as "my protégé." Arthas took an instinctive dislike to Langston, noting the man's soft hands and languid demeanor. At least Blackmoore had fought in battle for his title; this boy—Arthas thought of him as a boy, although in truth Langston was older than Arthas's seventeen years—had been handed everything on a platter.

Well, so have I, he thought, but he also knew what sacrifices a king would be expected to make. Langston looked like he'd never denied himself a thing in his life. Nor did he deny himself now, helping himself to the choicest cuts of meat, the most lavish pastries, and more than one glass of wine to wash it down with. Blackmoore, in contrast, ate sparingly, though he had more alcohol than Langston.

Arthas's dislike of the pair was completed when their serving girl entered and Blackmoore reached to touch her in a proprietary manner. The girl, golden-haired and simply clad, with a face that needed no artifice to be beautiful, smiled as if she enjoyed it, but Arthas caught a quick flash of unhappiness in her blue eyes.

"This is Taretha Foxton," Blackmoore said, one hand still caressing the girl's arm as she gathered the plates. "Daughter of my personal servant, Tammis, whom I'm sure you'll see later."

Arthas gave the girl his most winning smile. She reminded him a bit of Jaina—her hair brightened by the sun, her skin tanned. She returned the smile fleetingly, then demurely looked away as she gathered the plates, dropping a quick curtsey before leaving.

"You'll have one like that soon enough, lad," Blackmoore said, laughing. It took Arthas a second to grasp the meaning and then he blinked, startled. The two men laughed harder, and Blackmoore raised his goblet in a toast.

"To fair-haired girls," he said, in a purring voice. Arthas looked back at Taretha, thought of Jaina, and forced himself to raise his glass.

An hour later Arthas had forgotten all about Taretha Foxton and his indignation on her behalf. His voice was raw from screaming, his hands hurt from clapping, and he was having the time of his life.

At first, he'd felt a little uncomfortable. The first few combatants in the ring were simple beasts pitted against one another, fighting to the death for no reason other than the enjoyment of the onlookers. "How are they treated prior to this?" Arthas had asked. He was fond of animals; it unsettled him to see them used so.

Langston had opened his mouth, but Blackmoore shushed him with a quick gesture. He had smiled, leaning back in his chaise lounge and snagging a bunch of grapes. "Well, of course we want them at their fighting peak," he said. "So they are captured and treated quite well. And as you can see, the bouts go quickly. If an animal survives and is not able to continue fighting again, we put him down at once, mercifully."

Arthas hoped the man was not lying to him. A sick feeling in his gut told him Blackmoore probably was, but he ignored it. The feeling vanished when the fighting involved men against the beasts. As he watched, riveted, Blackmoore said, "The men are paid well. They in fact become minor celebrities."

Not the orc, though. And Arthas knew it, and approved. That's what he was waiting for—the chance to see Blackmoore's pet orc, found as an infant and raised to be a fighter in these rings, in combat.

He was not disappointed. Apparently, everything up until now had been a warm-up for the crowd. When the doors creaked open and a huge green shape strode forward, everyone stood, roaring. Somehow Arthas found himself among them.

Thrall was enormous, appearing even larger because he was obviously so much healthier and alert than the other specimens Arthas had seen in the camps. He wore little armor and no helm, and green skin stretched tightly over powerful muscle. Too, he stood straighter than others. The cheering was deafening, and Thrall walked a circle around the ring, lifting his fists, turning his ugly face up to be showered with rose petals usually reserved for holidays.

"I taught him to do that," Blackmoore said with pride. "It's an odd thing, really. The crowd cheers for him, yet they come hoping every time he'll get beaten."

"Has he ever lost a bout?"

"Never, Your Highness. Nor will he. Yet people keep hoping, and the money keeps flowing."

Arthas eyed him. "As long as the royal coffers see their proper percentage of your earnings, Lieutenant General, you'll be permitted to continue the games." He turned again to the orc, watching him as he completed his circuit. "He . . . is completely under control, isn't he?"

"Absolutely," Blackmoore said immediately. "He was raised by humans and taught to fear and respect us."

As if he had heard the comment, though he could not possibly have done so over the thundering cries of the crowd, Thrall turned to where Arthas, Blackmoore, and Langston sat watching. He thumped his chest in a salute and then bowed deeply.

"You see? Utterly my creature," Blackmoore purred. He rose and lifted a flag, waving it, and across the ring a solidly built red-haired man waved another flag. Thrall turned toward the door, gripping the massive battle axe that was his weapon in this bout.

The guards began to raise the door, and before it had even opened fully, a bear the size of Invincible surged forward. Its hackles had risen and it barreled straight for Thrall as if it had been launched from a cannon, its snarl audible even over the roar of the crowd.

Thrall held his ground, stepping aside at the absolute last minute and bringing the huge axe around as if it weighed nothing at all. It tore a great rent in the bear's side, and the animal roared in maddened pain, whirling and sending blood spattering. Again, the orc stood his ground, resting on the balls of his bare feet until he moved with a speed that belied his size. He met the bear head-on, shouting taunts in a guttural voice in perfect Common, and brought the axe crunching down. The bear's head was nearly severed from its neck, but it kept running for a few moments before toppling into a quivering heap.

Thrall threw back his head and cried out his victory. The crowd went mad. Arthas stared.

There wasn't a scratch on the orc, and as far as Arthas could tell, the brute wasn't even particularly winded.

"That's just the opener," Blackmoore said, smiling at Arthas's reaction. "Next will be three humans attacking him. He's also hampered by the fact that he's not to kill them, just defeat them. More a strategic battle than one of brute force, but I confess, there's something about watching him decapitate a bear in a single blow that always makes me proud."

Three human gladiators, all large, powerfully muscled men, entered the arena and saluted their opponent and the crowd. Arthas watched as Thrall sized them up and wondered just how smart it was of Blackmoore to make his pet orc so damn good at fighting. If Thrall ever escaped, he could teach those skills to other orcs.

It was possible, despite the increased security. After all, if Orgrim Doomhammer could escape from the Undercity, in the very heart of the palace, Thrall could escape from Durnholde.

The state visit lasted five days. During one of those days, late in the evening, Taretha Foxton came to visit the prince in his private quarters. He was puzzled that his servants did not answer the tentative knock on the door and was even more startled to see the pretty blond girl standing there carrying a tray of delicacies. Her eyes were downcast, but her dress was revealing enough that he didn't speak immediately.

She dropped a curtsey. "My lord Blackmoore sent

me with this offering of things to tempt you," she said. Color suffused her cheeks. Arthas was confused.

"I—tell your master thank you, although I am not hungry. And I'm wondering what he's done with my servants."

"They have been invited to a repast with the other servants," Taretha explained. She still didn't look up.

"I see. Well, that's kind of the lieutenant general; I'm sure the men appreciate it."

She didn't move.

"Is there anything else, Taretha?"

The pink in her cheeks deepened, and she lifted her eyes to him. They were calm, resigned. "My lord Blackmoore sent me with this offering of things to tempt you," she repeated. "Things you might enjoy."

Understanding burst upon him then. Understanding, and embarrassment, and irritation, and anger. He composed himself with an effort—it was hardly the girl's fault, indeed, she was the one being ill used.

"Taretha," he said, "I'll take the food, with thanks. I need nothing else."

"Your Highness, I'm afraid he will insist."

"Tell him I said it's fine."

"Sir, you don't understand. If I come back he—"

He glanced down at the hands holding the tray, at the long hair draped just so. Arthas stepped forward and lifted her trailing hair out of the way, frowning at the brownish-blue fading marks on her wrists and throat.

"I see," he said. "Come inside, then." Once she had entered, he closed the door and turned to her.

"Stay for as long as you feel comfortable, then go

back to him. In the meantime, I can't possibly eat all this." He gestured for her to sit and took a chair opposite her, snagging a small pastry and grinning.

Taretha blinked at him. It took a moment for her to understand what he was saying, and then cautious relief and gratitude spread over her face as she poured the wine. After a little while, she began to respond to his questions with more than a few polite words, and they spent the next few hours talking before they agreed it was time for her to return. As she picked up the tray, she turned to him.

"Your Highness—it pleases me so much to know that the man who will be our next king has such a kind heart. The lady you choose to make your queen will be a very lucky woman."

He smiled and closed the door behind her, leaning on it for a moment.

The lady he would choose to make his queen. He recalled his conversation with Calia; fortunately for his sister, Terenas had started to have some suspicions about Prestor—nothing that could be proven, but enough for second thoughts.

Arthas was almost of age—a year older than Calia had been when their father had nearly betrothed her to Prestor. He supposed he'd have to start thinking about finding a queen sooner or later.

Tomorrow he would be leaving, and not a minute too soon.

The winter chill was in the air. Autumn's last glorious days were gone, and the trees, once shades of gold and red and orange, were now bare skeletons against a gray sky. In a few more months, Arthas would reach his nineteenth year and be inducted into the Order of the Silver Hand, and he was more than ready. His training with Muradin had ended a few months ago, and he had now begun sparring with Uther. It was different, but similar. What Muradin had taught was attentiveness and a willingness to win the battle no matter what. The paladins had a more ritualistic way of looking at battle, and focused more on the attitude one brought into the fight than the actual mechanics of swordplay. Arthas found both methods valid, although he was beginning to wonder if he'd ever have the chance to use what he had learned in a true battle.

Normally, he'd be in prayer session now, but his father was off on a diplomatic visit to Stromgarde, and Uther had accompanied him. Which meant that now Arthas had afternoons free for a few days, and he was not about to waste them, even if the weather was less than perfect. He clung easily and familiarly to Invincible as they galloped over the glade, the animal's stride only slightly slowed by a few inches of snow on the ground. He could see his breath and that of the great white horse as Invincible tossed his head and snorted.

It was starting to snow again now, not the soft fat flakes that drifted lazily down but small, hard crystals that stung. Arthas frowned and pressed on. A little farther, then he would turn back, he told himself. He might even stop at the Balnir farm. It had been a while since he had been there; Jorum and Jarim would likely be interested to see the magnificent horse that the gawky little colt had grown into.

The impulse, having struck, now demanded to be obeyed, and Arthas turned Invincible with a subtle pressure from his left leg. The horse wheeled, obedient and completely in tune with his master's desires. The snow was picking up, tiny needles digging into his exposed skin, and Arthas pulled the cape up over his head for a little more protection. Invincible shook his head, his skin twitching as it did when he was being annoyed by insects in the summer. He galloped down the path, stretching his neck forward, enjoying the exertion every bit as much as Arthas.

They were coming up on the jump soon, and shortly after that, a warm stable for the steed and a hot mug of tea for his rider before they headed back to the palace. Arthas's face was starting to become numb with the cold, and his hands in their fine leather gloves weren't much better. He tightened his chilled hands over the reins, forcing his fingers to bend, and gathered himself as Invincible leaped—no, he reminded himself, *flew,* they flew over this jump like—

—except they didn't fly. At the last minute, Arthas felt the hideous sensation of Invincible's rear hooves slipping on the icy stone, and the horse flailed, neighing, his legs frantically trying to get a secure footing on thin air. Arthas's throat was suddenly raw, and he realized he was screaming as jagged stone, not smooth snow-encrusted grass, rushed up to meet them with lethal speed. He pulled hard on the reins, as if that could do something, as if anything could do something—

The sound cut through his stupor, and he blinked his way back to consciousness with the bone-chilling shriek of a beast in agony clawing at his brain. He couldn't move at first, though his body spasmed of its own accord, trying to move toward the awful cries. Finally he was able to sit up. Pain shot through him and he added his own gasp of agony to the hideous cacophony, and he realized he'd probably broken at least one rib, probably more.

The snow had picked up and was coming down hard and heavy now. He could barely see three feet in front of him. He shut out the pain, craning his neck, trying to find—

Invincible. His eye was drawn to movement and the widening pool of crimson that melted the snow, that steamed in the cold.

"No," Arthas whispered, and struggled to his feet. The world went black around the edges and he almost lost consciousness again, but through sheer will hung on. Slowly, he made his way to the panicked animal, struggling against the pain and the driving wind and snow that threatened to knock him over.

Invincible was churning up the bloodied snow with two powerful, unharmed rear legs and two shattered forelegs. Arthas felt his stomach heave at the sight of the limbs, once so long and straight and clean and powerful, hanging at odd angles as Invincible kept trying and failing to stand. Then the image was mercifully blurred by the snow and the rush of hot tears that spilled down his cheeks.

He slogged toward his horse, sobbing, dropping to

his knees beside the maddened animal and trying to do—what? This was no scratch, to be quickly bound so that Invincible could be led to a warm stable and hot mash. Arthas reached for the animal's head, wanting to touch him, to calm him somehow, but Invincible was manic with agony. And he kept *screaming*.

Help. There were priests and Sir Uther—maybe they could heal—

Pain greater than physical shot through the youth. The bishop had gone with his father to Stromgarde, as had Uther. There might be a priest in another village, but Arthas didn't know where, and with the storm—

He shrank back from the animal, covering his ears and closing his eyes, sobbing so that his whole body shook. With the storm, he could never find a healer before Invincible either died of his injuries or froze to death. Arthas wasn't even sure he could find the Balnir homestead, even though it could not be far. The world was white, everywhere save where the dying horse, who had trusted him enough to leap off an icy embankment, lay churning up a steaming crimson pool.

Arthas knew what he had to do, and he couldn't do it.

He would never know how long he sat there, weeping, trying to shut out the sight and sound of his beloved horse in agony, until finally Invincible's struggles slowed. He lay in the snow, his sides heaving, his eyes rolling in torment.

Arthas couldn't feel his face or limbs, but somehow he managed to move toward the beast. Every breath was agony, and he welcomed the pain. This was his fault. His fault. He took the great head in his lap, and for a brief, merciful moment he wasn't sitting in the snow with a wounded beast, but sitting in a stable while a broodmare gave birth. For that moment, everything was all just beginning, and not coming to this shocking, sickening, *avoidable* end.

His tears fell on the horse's broad cheek. Invincible trembled, his brown eyes wide with now-silent pain. Arthas removed his gloves and ran his hand along the pink-gray muzzle, feeling the warmth of Invincible's breath against his hands. Then, slowly, he eased the horse's head from his lap, got to his feet, and fumbled with his warmed hand for his sword. His feet sank in the red puddle of melted snow as he stood over the fallen animal.

"I'm sorry," he said. "I'm so sorry."

Invincible regarded him calmly, trustingly, as if he somehow understood what was about to happen, and the need for it. It was more than Arthas could bear, and for a moment tears again clouded his vision. He blinked them back hard.

Arthas lifted the sword and brought it straight down.

He did this right, at least; pierced Invincible's great heart with a single strong blow from arms that should have been too chilled to do so. He felt the sword pierce skin, flesh, scrape against bone, and impale itself into the earth below. Invincible arched once, then shuddered and lay still.

Jorum and Jarim found him there some time later, after the snow had tapered off, curled up tightly against the cooling corpse of a once-glorious animal brimming with life and energy. As the elder man bent to pick him up, Arthas cried out with pain.

"Sorry, lad," Jorum said, his voice almost unbearably kind. "For hurting you, and for the accident."

"Yes," Arthas said weakly, "the accident. He lost his footing . . ."

"And no wonder in this weather. That storm came on quickly. You're lucky you're alive. Come on—we'll get you inside and send someone to the palace."

As he shifted in the farmer's strong grip, Arthas said, "Bury him . . . here? So I can come visit?"

Balnir exchanged glances with his son, then nodded. "Aye, of course. He was a noble steed."

Arthas craned his neck to look at the body of the horse he had named Invincible. He would let them all think it was an accident, because he could not bear to tell anyone what he had done.

And he made a vow then and there that if anyone else ever needed protection—that if sacrifices had to be made for the welfare of others—he would do it.

Whatever it takes, he thought.

CHAPTER FIVE

Summer was in full blaze, and the merciless sun beat down on His Royal Highness Prince Arthas Menethil as he rode through the streets of Stormwind. He was in a foul mood, despite the fact that this was a day that he was supposed to have been looking forward to all his life. The sun glinted off the full plate armor he wore, and Arthas thought he'd bake to death before he reached the cathedral. Sitting atop his new charger only served to remind him that the horse, while powerful, well-trained, and well-bred, was not Invincible, gone for only a few months and bitterly missed. And he found that his mind had suddenly gone blank regarding what he was supposed to do once the ceremony began.

Beside him rode his father, who seemed completely unaware of his son's irritation. "This has been a day long in coming, my son," Terenas said, turning to smile at Arthas.

Despite the heat and the weight of the helm he wore, Arthas was glad of it; it concealed his face, and he wasn't sure he could fake a convincing smile right now. "Indeed it has, Father," he replied, keeping his voice calm.

It was one of the biggest celebrations Stormwind had ever seen. In addition to Terenas, many other kings, nobility, and famous personages were in attendance, riding like a parade through the city's white cobbled streets to the massive Cathedral of Light, damaged during the First War but now restored and even more glorious than before.

Arthas's boyhood friend Varian, king of Stormwind, was now married and a new father. He had opened the palace to all the visiting royalty and their retinues. Sitting with Varian last night, drinking mead and talking, had been the highlight of the trip for Arthas so far. The hurting, traumatized youth of a decade ago had grown into a confident, handsome, centered king. Somewhere along about early morning, after midnight and before dawn, they had gone to the armory, fetched wooden training swords, and gone at each other for a long time, laughing and recounting memories, their prowess only a little the worse for the alcohol they'd consumed. Varian, trained since early childhood, had always been good and now he was better. But so was Arthas, and he gave as good as he got.

But now it was all formality, incredibly hot armor, and a nagging sense that he didn't deserve the honor that was about to be bestowed upon him.

In a rare moment, Arthas had spoken of his feelings to Uther. The intimidating paladin, who, since Arthas was old enough to remember, had been the very image of rock-solid steadfastness to the Light, had startled the prince with his reply.

"Lad, no one feels ready. No one feels he deserves it. And you know why? Because no one *does*. It's grace, pure and simple. We are inherently unworthy, simply because we're human, and all human beings—aye, and elves, and dwarves, and all the other races—are flawed. But the Light loves us anyway. It loves us for what we sometimes can rise to in rare moments. It loves us for what we can do to help others. And it loves us because we can help it share its message by striving daily to be worthy, even though we understand that we can't ever truly become so."

He'd clapped a hand on Arthas's shoulder, giving him a rare, simple smile. "So stand there today, as I did, feeling that you can't possibly deserve it or ever be worthy, and know that you're in the same place every single paladin has ever stood."

It comforted Arthas a little.

He squared his shoulders, tilted the visor back, and smiled and waved to the crowd that was cheering so happily on this hot summer day. Rose petals were showered upon him, and from somewhere trumpets blared. They had reached the cathedral. Arthas dismounted and a groom led away his charger. Another servant stepped up to take the helm he tugged off. His blond hair was damp with sweat, and he quickly ran a gauntleted hand over it.

Arthas had never been to Stormwind before, and he was impressed by the combination of serenity and power the cathedral radiated. Slowly, he moved up the carpeted carved stairs, grateful for the sudden coolness of the building's stone interior. The fragrance of the incense was calming and familiar; it was the same as that which his family burned in their small chapel.

There was no giddy throng here now, just silent, respectful rows of prominent personages and clergy. Arthas recognized several faces: Genn Greymane, Thoras Trollbane, Admiral Daelin Proudmoore—

Arthas blinked, then his lips curved into a smile. Jaina! She had certainly grown up in the years since he had last seen her. Not quite a drop-dead beauty, but pretty, the liveliness and intelligence he'd responded to as a boy still radiating from her like a beacon. She caught Arthas's look and smiled a little in return, inclining her head in respect.

Arthas returned his attention to the altar he approached, but felt a little bit of the trepidation leave his heart. He hoped there would be a chance for him to talk to her after all the formalities were taken care of.

Archbishop Alonsus Faol awaited him at the altar. The archbishop reminded Arthas more of Greatfather Winter than of any of the rulers he had hitherto met. Short and stout, with a long flowing snow-white beard and bright eyes, even in the midst of solemn ceremony Faol radiated warmth and kindliness. Faol waited until Arthas approached him and knelt before him respectfully before opening a large book and speaking.

"In the Light, we gather to empower our brother. In its grace, he will be made anew. In its power, he shall educate the masses. In its strength, he shall combat the shadow. And in its wisdom, he shall lead his brethren to the eternal rewards of paradise."

On his left, several men—and a few women, Arthas

noticed—dressed in flowing white robes stood still and poised. Some held censers, which swayed almost hypnotically. Others bore large candles. One carried an embroidered blue stole. Arthas had been introduced to many of them earlier, but found that their names had gone right out of his head. That was unusual for him— he was genuinely interested in those who worked for him and served under him, and made an effort to get to know all their names.

Archbishop Faol asked the clerics to bestow their blessings upon Arthas. They did, the one who bore the blue stole coming forward to drape it about the prince's neck and anointing his brow with holy oil.

"By the grace of the Light, may your brethren be healed," the cleric said.

Faol turned to the men on Arthas's right. "Knights of the Silver Hand, if you deem this man worthy, place your blessings upon him."

In contrast to the first group, these men, standing at attention in heavy, gleaming plate armor, were all known to Arthas. They were the original paladins of the Silver Hand, and it was the first time they had assembled since their induction many years past. Uther, of course; Tirion Fordring, aging but still powerful and graceful, now governor of Hearthglen; the six-and-a-half-foot Saidan Dathrohan, and the pious, bushy-bearded Gavinrad. One was missing from their number—Turalyon, right hand to Anduin Lothar in the Second War, who was lost with the company that had ventured through the Dark Portal when Arthas was twelve.

Gavinrad stepped forth, holding an enormous,

heavy-looking hammer, its silver head etched with runes and its sturdy haft wrapped in blue leather. He placed the hammer in front of Arthas, then stepped back to stand with his brethren. It was Uther the Lightbringer himself, Arthas's mentor in the order, who next came forward. In his hands he carried a pair of ceremonial shoulder plates. Uther was the most controlled man Arthas had ever known, and yet his eyes were bright with unshed tears as he placed the armor on Arthas's broad shoulders. He spoke in a voice that was both powerful and trembling with emotion.

"By the strength of the Light, may your enemies be undone." His hand lingered a moment on Arthas's shoulder, then he, too, retreated.

Archbishop Faol smiled at the prince kindly. Arthas met the gaze evenly, no longer worried. He remembered everything now.

"Arise and be recognized," Faol bade him. Arthas did so.

"Do you, Arthas Menethil, vow to uphold the honor and codes of the Order of the Silver Hand?"

Arthas blinked, momentarily surprised at the lack of his title. *Of course,* he reasoned, *I'm being inducted as a man, not a prince.* "I do."

"Do you vow to walk in the grace of the Light and spread its wisdom to your fellow man?"

"I do."

"Do you vow to vanquish evil wherever it be found, and protect the innocent with your very life?"

"I d—by my blood and honor, I do." That was close, he'd almost messed up.

Faol gave him a quick wink of reassurance, then turned to address both the clerics and the paladins. "Brothers and sisters—you who have gathered here to bear witness—raise your hands and let the Light illuminate this man."

The clerics and paladins all lifted right hands, which were now suffused by a soft, golden glow. They pointed at Arthas, directing the radiance toward him. Arthas's eyes were wide with wonder, and he waited for the glorious glow to envelop him.

Nothing happened.

The moment stretched on.

Sweat broke out on Arthas's brow. What was going wrong? Why wasn't the Light wrapping itself around him in blessing and benediction?

And then the sunlight streaming in through windows in the ceiling slowly began to move toward the prince standing alone in shining armor, and Arthas exhaled in relief. This had to be what Uther had spoken of. The feeling of unworthiness that Uther assured him all paladins felt simply seemed to drag out the moment. The words Uther had spoken came back to him: *No one feels he deserves it . . . it is grace, pure and simple . . . but the Light loves us anyway.*

Now it shone down on him, in him, through him, and he was forced to shut his eyes against the almost blinding radiance. It warmed at first, then seared, and he winced slightly. He felt—scoured. Emptied, scrubbed clean, then filled again, and he felt the Light swell inside him and then fade away to a tolerable level. He blinked and reached for the hammer, the symbol of the order. As his hand closed about the haft, he looked up at Archbishop Faol, whose benign smile widened.

"Arise, Arthas Menethil, paladin defender of Lordaeron. Welcome to the Order of the Silver Hand."

Arthas couldn't help it. He grinned as he grasped the enormous hammer, so large that for a brief moment he thought he wouldn't be able to lift it, and swung it upward with a whoop. The Light, he realized, made the hammer seem to weigh less in his hands. At his exultant cry, the cathedral suddenly began to ring with the sound of answering cheers and applause. Arthas found himself roughly embraced by his new brothers and sisters, and then all remnants of formality were torn away as his father, Varian, and others crowded the altar area. Much laughter was had as Varian tried to clap him on the shoulder, only to have his hand sting when he struck the hard metal of the shoulder plates. And then somehow Arthas was turned around and stared into the blue-eyed, smiling face of Lady Jaina Proudmoore.

They were mere inches apart, jostled and pressed together by the throng that had somehow sprung up around the newest member of the Order of the Silver Hand, and Arthas wasn't about to let the unique opportunity slip away. Almost at once his left arm slipped around her trim waist and he pulled her to him. She looked startled, but not displeased, as he hugged her. She returned the hug, laughing against his chest for a moment, then pulling back, still smiling.

For a moment, the happy sounds of a celebrating crowd on a hot summer afternoon went away, and all Arthas could see was this sun-tanned, smiling girl.

Could he kiss her? *Should* he kiss her? He certainly wanted to. But even as he debated she disentangled herself and stepped back, and her fair-haired, girlish form was replaced by another fair-haired, girlish form. Calia laughed and hugged her brother tightly.

"We're all so proud of you, Arthas," she exclaimed. He grinned and returned the embrace, happy to hear his sister's approval, sorry that he'd not gone ahead and kissed the admiral's daughter. "You will make a wonderful paladin, I'm sure of it."

"Well done, my son," Terenas said. "I am a proud father today."

Arthas's eyes narrowed. Today? What was meant by that? Was his father not proud of him on other days? He was suddenly angry, and not certain why or with whom. The Light, delaying its approval; Jaina backing away from him right at the moment when he could have kissed her; Terenas and his comment.

He forced a smile and began to shoulder his way through the crowd. He'd had enough of this press of people, few of whom really knew him, none of whom understood.

Arthas was nineteen. At the same age, Varian had been king for a full year. He was of an age to do whatever he wanted to, and now had the blessing of the Silver Hand to guide him. He didn't want to simply linger at the palace of Lordaeron, or do boring state visits. He wanted to do something . . . fun. Something that his power, his position, his abilities would earn him.

And he knew exactly what he wanted that something to be.

PART TWO

THE BRIGHT LADY

INTERLUDE

It was exactly the sort of day Jaina Proudmoore didn't like—sullen, stormy, and bitterly cold. While the ocean breezes always made Theramore feel cool, even in the hot summer months, the chill of the wind and rain that now pummeled the city cut to the bone. The ocean churned unhappily, the sky above it gray and menacing. It showed no signs of letting up. Outside, training fields turned to mud, travelers sought the shelter of the inn, and Dr. VanHowzen would need to watch the injured in his care for signs of illness brought on by the sudden cold and wetness. Jaina's guards stood in the downpour without complaint. No doubt they were miserable. Jaina ordered one of her attendants to take the pot of tea she had just brewed for her and her chancellor down to the stalwart guards enduring their duty. She could wait for a second pot to be ready.

Thunder rumbled and there was a flash of lightning. Jaina, snug in her tower surrounded by the books and papers she so loved, shivered and drew her cloak about her more closely, then turned to one who was doubtless even more uncomfortable than she.

Magna Aegwynn, former Guardian of Tirisfal, mother to the great Magus Medivh, once the most powerful woman in the world, sat in a chair drawn close to the fire, sipping a cup of tea. Her gnarled hands closed about the cup, seeking its warmth. Her long hair, white as freshly fallen snow, was loose about her shoulders. She looked up as Jaina approached and sat in the chair across from her. Her green eyes, a deep, knowing emerald, missed nothing.

"You're thinking about him."

Jaina scowled and looked into the fire, trying to distract herself with the dancing flames. "I didn't know being a Guardian meant you could read minds."

"Minds? Pfft. It's your face and bearing I can read like a primer, child. That furrow in your brow crinkles just so when it's he who occupies your mind. Besides, you always get in this mood when the weather turns."

Jaina shivered. "Am I truly so easy to read?"

Aegwynn's sharp features softened and she patted Jaina's hand. "Well, I've got a thousand years of observation under my belt. I'm a bit better at reading people than most."

Jaina sighed. "It's true. When the weather is cold, I do think of him. About what happened. About whether I could have done anything."

Aegwynn sighed. "A thousand years and I don't think I've ever really been in love. Too much else to worry about. But if it's any consolation to you—he's been on my mind, too."

Jaina blinked, surprised and unsettled by the comment. "You've been thinking about Arthas?"

The former Guardian regarded her keenly. "The Lich King. He's not Arthas, not anymore."

"I don't need to be reminded of that," Jaina said, a touch too sharply. "Why do you—"

"Can't you feel it?"

Slowly, Jaina nodded. She had tried to chalk it up to the weather and the tensions that always ran high when it was so damp and unpleasant. But Aegwynn was suggesting that there was more to it than that, and Jaina Proudmoore, thirty years of age, ruler of Theramore Isle, knew the old woman was right. *Old woman.* A smile flickered on her lips as she thought about the words. She herself was well past her own youth, a youth in which Arthas Menethil had played so significant a role.

"Tell me of him," Aegwynn said, sitting back in her chair. At that moment, one of the servants came with a fresh pot of tea and cookies hot from the oven. Jaina accepted a cup gratefully.

"I've told you all I know."

"No," Aegwynn retorted. "You told me the facts of what happened. I want you to tell me about *him.* Arthas Menethil. Because whatever's going on right now up in Northrend—and yes, I think something *is* going on— it's about Arthas, not the Lich King. Not yet at any rate. Besides," and the old woman grinned, the wrinkles that lined her face overshadowed by the impish, girlish glint in her emerald eyes, "it's a cold and rainy day. And that's exactly the sort of day stories were made for."

CHAPTER SIX

Jaina Proudmoore hummed a little as she strode through the gardens of Dalaran. She'd been here for eight years now, and the city never lost its sense of wonder. Everything here emanated magic, and to her it was almost like a scent, a fragrance of everything in bloom, and she inhaled it with a smile.

Of course, some of that "fragrance" was that of actual flowers in bloom; the gardens of this place were as saturated with magic as everything else. She had never seen healthier, more colorful flowers, or eaten more delicious fruits and vegetables than here. And the knowledge! Jaina felt she had learned more in the last eight years than in her entire life—and most of that in the last two, since Archmage Antonidas had formally taken her as his apprentice. Few things contented her more than sitting curled up in the sun with a cold glass of sweet nectar and a pile of books. Of course, some of the rarer parchments needed to be protected from sunlight and spilled nectar, so the next best thing was sitting inside one of the many rooms, wearing gloves so her hands would not damage the fragile paper, carefully perusing something that was older almost than she could comprehend.

But for now, she just wanted to wander in the gardens, feeling the living earth beneath her feet, smelling the incredible scents, and, when hunger gnawed at her stomach, reaching up and plucking a ripe golden-bark apple warm from the sunlight and crunching it happily.

"In Quel'Thalas," came a smooth, cultured voice, "there are trees that tower over these in a glory of white bark and golden leaves, that all but sing in the evening breezes. I think you would enjoy seeing them someday."

Jaina turned to offer Prince Kael'thas Sunstrider, son to Anasterian, king of the quel'dorei elves, a smile and a deep curtsey. "Your Highness," she said. "I wasn't aware you'd returned. A pleasure. And yes, I'm certain I would."

Jaina was the daughter, if not of royalty, of nobility and of a ruler. Her father, Admiral Daelin Proudmoore, ruled the city-state of Kul Tiras, and Jaina had grown up accustomed to interaction with nobility. And yet, Prince Kael'thas unnerved her. She wasn't quite sure what it was. He was handsome, certainly, with that grace and beauty that all elves possessed. Tall, with hair like spun gold that fell halfway down his back, he always looked to her like a figure out of legend rather than a real, living person. Even though he was currently clad in the simpler violet and gold robes of a mage of Dalaran and not the lavish robes he would wear to official occasions, he never seemed to lose his stiffness. Perhaps that was it—there was a sort of . . . antiquated formality about him. Too, he was much older than she, though he looked about her age. He was sharply intelligent and an extremely talented and powerful mage, and some of the students whispered that he was one of the Six, the secret membership of the highest ranking magi of Dalaran. So she supposed she wasn't that much of a country bumpkin to find him intimidating.

He reached up and took an apple himself, biting into it. "There is a certain heartiness about food native to human lands that I have come to appreciate." He smiled conspiratorially. "Sometimes elven food, while certainly delicious and attractively presented, leaves one still hungry for something more substantial."

Jaina smiled. Prince Kael'thas always tried so hard to put her at ease. She only wished it worked better. "Few things are nicer than an apple and a slice of Dalaran sharp," she agreed. The silence stretched between then, awkward despite the casualness of the setting and the warmth of the sun. "So, you are back for a while?"

"Yes, my business in Silvermoon has concluded for the time being. So I should not need to depart again anytime soon." He looked at her as he took another bite of the apple, his handsome features schooled to be impassive. Still, Jaina knew he was waiting for her reaction.

"We are all pleased at your return, Your Highness."

He wagged a finger at her. "Ah, I've told you, I would prefer it if you would simply call me Kael."

"I'm sorry, Kael."

He looked at her and a hint of sorrow passed over his perfect features, gone so quickly that Jaina wondered if she had imagined it. "How do your studies progress?"

"Very well," she said, warming to the conversation now that it was back on scholastic ground. "Watch!" She pointed to a squirrel perched in a high branch, nibbling on an apple, and murmured a spell. At once it transformed into a sheep, a look of comical surprise on its face as the branch broke beneath its weight and it started to fall. Immediately Jaina extended a hand and the squirrel-sheep halted in midair. Gently she lowered it unharmed to the ground. It bleated at her, twitching its ears, and after a moment again resumed the shape of a very confused-looking squirrel. It sat on its haunches, chattered at her angrily, then with a flick of its fluffy tail leaped up into the tree again.

Kael'thas chuckled. "Well done! No more setting books on fire, I hope?"

Jaina turned scarlet, remembering the incident. When she'd first arrived, her talent with fire had needed some desperate honing. She'd accidentally incinerated a tome while working with Kael'thas—one he'd actually been holding at the time. He'd responded by insisting that for the next few months, she would need to practice all fire spells in the vicinity of the pools that encircled the prison area. "Er . . . no, that hasn't happened for a while."

"I'm pleased to hear it. Jaina . . ." He stepped forward, tossing away the half-eaten apple, smiling gently. "I wasn't making idle conversation when I invited you to come to Quel'Thalas. Dalaran is a marvelous city, and some of the finest magi in Azeroth live here. I know you're learning much. But I think you would enjoy visiting an entire land where magic is so much a part of the culture. Not just a part of the city, or confined to a handful of elite, educated magi. Magic is the birthright of every citizen. We are all embraced by the Sunwell. Surely you must have some curiosity about it yourself?"

She smiled at him. "I do indeed. And I would love to go there someday. But I think for the moment, my studies can be best advanced here." Her smile stretched into a grin. "Where people know what to do when I light books on fire."

He chuckled at that, but his sigh was sad. "Perhaps you are right. And now if you will excuse me—" He gave her a wry grin. "Archmage Antonidas demands a recounting of my time in Silvermoon. Nonetheless, this prince and mage looks deeply forward to more demonstrations of how your training has advanced . . . and more time spent with you."

Kael'thas placed a hand to his heart and bowed. Not knowing how to respond, Jaina settled for a curtsey, then watched him go, striding through the gardens like the sun, head high, every inch of him exuding confidence and coiled grace. Even the dirt seemed unwilling to cling to his boots and robe hem.

Jaina crunched a final bite of the apple, then she, too, tossed it away. The squirrel she'd polymorphed earlier scurried headfirst down the trunk, to claim a prize more reachable than the apple that still hung on the tree.

A pair of hands abruptly covered her eyes.

She started, but only in mild surprise—no one who posed a threat would be able to breach the powerful wards erected about the magical city.

"Guess who?" a male voice whispered, but still holding tones of mirth. Jaina, her eyes covered, considered, fighting back a smile.

"Hm. . . . your hands are calloused, so you're not a wizard," she said. "You smell like horses and leather. . . ." Her own small hands brushed feather-light over strong fingers, touching a large ring. She felt the shape of the stone, the design—the seal of Lordaeron.

"Arthas!" she exclaimed, surprise and delight warming her voice as she turned to face him. He uncovered her eyes at once, and grinned down at her. He was less physically perfect than Kael'thas; his hair, like the elven prince's, was blond, but simply yellow rather than looking like spun gold. He was tall and well-built, seeming solid rather than fluidly graceful to her. And despite the fact that he was of a rank equal to Kael'thas—although she wondered if privately Kael doubted that; the elves seemed to think themselves superior to all humans, regardless of rank—there was an ease about him that Jaina responded to immediately.

Decorum returned to her and she dropped a curtsey. "Your Highness, this is an unlooked-for surprise. What are you doing here, if I may ask?" A sudden thought sobered her. "All is well in Capital City, is it not?"

"Arthas, please. In Dalaran, the magi rule, and mere men must give deference." His sea-green eyes twinkled with good humor. "And we are comrades in mischief, after sneaking off to see the internment camps, aren't we?"

She relaxed and smiled. "I suppose we are."

"In answer to your question, everything is just fine. In fact, so little of real import is going on that my father agreed to my request to come here for a few months to study."

"Study? But—you are a member of the Order of the Silver Hand. You're not going to become a mage, are you?"

He laughed and drew her arm through his as they walked back toward the students' quarters. She easily fell in step with him.

"Hardly. Such intellectual dedication is beyond me, I fear. But it did occur to me that one of the best places in Azeroth to learn about history, the nature of magic, and other things a king needs to know about is right here in Dalaran. Fortunately, Father and your archmage agreed."

As he spoke, he covered Jaina's hand, resting on his arm, with his own. It was a friendly and courteous gesture, but Jaina felt a little spark go through her. She glanced up at him. "I'm impressed. The boy who sneaked me out in the middle of the night to go spying on orcs was not quite so interested in history and knowledge."

Arthas chuckled and bent his head conspiratorially down to hers. "Honestly? I'm still not. I mean, I am, but that's not the real reason I came here."

"All right, now I'm confused. Why *did* you come to Dalaran then?" They had reached her quarters and she stopped, turning to face him and releasing his arm.

He didn't answer at first, merely held her gaze with his and smiled knowingly. Then he took her hand and kissed it—a courtly gesture, one she had experienced many times from many noble gentlemen. His lips lingered just an instant longer than was strictly proper, and he didn't release her hand at once.

Her eyes widened. Was he implying . . . had he really contrived to come to Dalaran for a few months—no mean feat, Antonidas was notoriously leery of outsiders—simply . . . to see her? Before she could recover sufficiently to ask the question, he winked at her and bowed.

"I will see you tonight at dinner, my lady."

The dinner was a formal one. The return of Prince Kael'thas and the arrival of Prince Arthas on the same day had sent those who served the Kirin Tor into a flurry of activity. There was a large dining room that was reserved for special occasions, and it was here that the dinner was hosted.

A table large enough to seat over two dozen stretched from one end of the room to the other. Overhead, three chandeliers twinkled with brightly burning candles, echoed by the candles burning on the table. Sconces along the walls held torches, and to keep the ambiance gentle while still providing sufficient illumination, several globes hovered around the sides of the room, ready to be summoned where a little extra light might be needed. Servants rarely intruded, save to bring out and clear the courses; bottles of wine poured themselves with the flick of a finger. Flute, harp, and lute provided soothing background music, their graceful notes created by magic rather than human hands or breaths of air.

Archmage Antonidas presided in one of his rare appearances. He was a tall man, seeming all the taller because of his extremely thin build. His long beard now had much more gray than brown in it, and his head was completely bald, but his eyes were alert and piercing. Present also was Archmage Krasus, upright and alert, his hair catching the candle- and torchlight to gleam mostly silver, with red and black streaks. Many others were in attendance, all of high rank. Jaina, in fact, was far and away the lowest-ranking person present, and she was the archmage's apprentice.

Jaina came from a military background, and one of the things her father had instilled in her was a solid understanding of her strengths and weaknesses. "It is as much of a mistake to underestimate yourself as to overestimate yourself," Daelin had once told her. "False modesty is as bad as false pride. Know exactly what you are capable of at any moment, and act accordingly. Any other path is folly—and could be deadly in battle."

She knew she was deft in the magical arts. She was intelligent and focused, and had learned much in the short time she had already been here. Surely Antonidas would not take on an apprentice as a charity case. With no sense of the false pride her father had warned her so judiciously about, she understood she had the potential to become a powerful mage. She wanted to succeed on her own merit, not be advanced because an elven prince enjoyed her company. She fought to keep her face from betraying her irritation as she spooned up another mouthful of turtle bisque.

The conversation, not surprisingly as the internment

camps were located fairly close to Dalaran, focused on the orcs, although the mage city liked to think itself above such things.

Kael reached a long, elegant hand for another slice of bread and began buttering it. "Lethargic or no," he said, "they are dangerous."

"My father, King Terenas, agrees with your assessment, Prince Kael'thas," Arthas said, smiling charmingly at the elf. "That's why the camps exist. It is unfortunate that they cost so much to maintain, but surely, a little gold is a small price for the safety of the people of Azeroth."

"They are beasts, brutes," said Kael'thas, his normally tenor voice dropping in his disgust. "They and their dragons damaged Quel'Thalas badly. Only the Sunwell's energies prevented them from wreaking even more havoc than they did. You humans could solve the problem of protecting your people without taxing them so severely by simply executing the creatures."

Jaina recalled the one glimpse she had seen of the orcs. They had looked weary to her, broken and dejected. They'd had children with them.

"Have you been to the camps, Prince Kael'thas?" she said tartly, speaking before she could stop herself. "Have you actually seen what they have become?"

Color rose in Kael'thas's cheeks for a moment, but he kept his expression pleasant. "No, Lady Jaina, I have not. Nor do I see any need to. I see what they have done whenever I behold the burned trunks of the glorious trees of my homeland, and pay my respects to those slain in that attack. And surely you have not seen them, either. I cannot imagine that so refined a lady would wish to be given a tour of the camps."

Jaina very carefully did not look at Arthas as she replied, "While His Highness gives me a lovely compliment, I do not think that refinement has any bearing on one's desire to see justice. Indeed, I think it rather more likely that a *refined* individual would not wish to see sentient beings slaughtered like animals." She gave him a pleasant smile and continued eating her soup. Kael'thas gave her a searching look, confused by her reaction.

"The law is Lordaeron's, and King Terenas may do as he sees fit in his own realm," Antonidas broke in.

"Dalaran and every other Alliance kingdom also must pay for their upkeep," said a mage Jaina did not know. "Surely we have a voice in this, since we are paying for it?"

Antonidas waved a thin hand. "It is not the issue of who pays for the camps, or indeed whether the camps are even necessary. It is this strange lethargy of the orcs that intrigues me. I have researched what little we have on orcish history, and I do not believe it is confinement that renders them so listless. Nor do I believe it is an illness—at least, not one that we need worry about contracting."

Because Antonidas never indulged in idle chatter, everyone stopped their bickering and turned to listen to him. Jaina was surprised. This was the first she had heard from any of the magi regarding the orcish situation at all. She had no doubt that this was a deliberate decision on Antonidas's part to reveal this information at this time. With both Arthas and Kael'thas present, word would travel swiftly throughout Lordaeron and Quel'Thalas. Antonidas did little by accident.

"If it is not an illness, nor a direct result of their internment," Arthas said pleasantly, "then what do you think it is, Archmage?"

Antonidas turned toward the young prince. "It is my understanding that the orcs were not always so bloodthirsty. Khadgar told me what he had learned from Garona, who—"

"Garona was the half-breed who murdered King Llane," Arthas said, all trace of good humor gone. "With all due respect, I do not think we can trust anything such a creature says."

Antonidas lifted up a calming hand, as some of the others began to murmur agreement. "This information came before she turned traitor," he said. "And it has been verified through—other sources." He smiled a little, deliberately refusing to identify what "other sources" he had consulted. "They committed themselves to demonic influence. Their skin turned green, their eyes red. I believe they were saturated with this external darkness by the time of the first invasion. Now they have been cut off from that source of sustenance. I think we are seeing not an illness, but withdrawal. Demonic energy is a potent thing. To be denied it would have dire consequences."

Kael'thas waved a hand dismissively. "Even if such a theory is correct, why should we care about them? They were foolish enough to trust demons. They were thoughtless enough to permit themselves to become addicted to these corruptive energies. I, for one, do not think it is wise to 'help' them find a cure for this addiction, even if it could return them to a peaceful state. Right now, they are powerless and crushed. It is how I—and anyone in his right mind—prefer to see them, after what they have done to us."

"Ah, but if they can be returned to a peaceful state, then we will not have to keep them locked up in the camps, and the money can be distributed elsewhere," Antonidas said mildly, before the entire table could erupt in argument. "I'm sure King Terenas does not levy these fees simply to line his own pockets. How *does* your father fare, Prince Arthas? And your family? I regret that I was unable to attend your initiation ceremony, but I hear it was quite the event."

"Stormwind was most gracious to me," Arthas said, smiling warmly and digging into the second course of delicately broiled trout served with sautéed greens. "It was good to see King Varian again."

"His lovely queen has recently provided him with an heir, I understand."

"Indeed. And if the way little Anduin grips my finger is any indication of how he'll grip a sword one day, he'll make a fine warrior."

"While we all pray your coronation day is many years distant, I daresay that a royal wedding would be welcomed," Antonidas continued. "Have any young ladies caught your eye, or are you still Lordaeron's most eligible bachelor?"

Kael'thas turned his attention to his plate, but Jaina knew he was following the conversation keenly. She kept her own face carefully composed.

Arthas did not look in her direction as he laughed and

reached for the wine. "Ah, that would be telling, would it not? And where's the fun in that? There's plenty of time left for such things."

Mixed feelings washed over Jaina. She was a little disappointed, but also somewhat relieved. Perhaps it was best if she and Arthas remained only friends. After all, she had come here to learn how to be the most accomplished mage she could become, not flirt. A student of magic needed to be disciplined, to be logical, not emotional. She had duties, and needed to perform them with her full attention.

She needed to study.

"I need to study," Jaina protested a few days after the dinner, when Arthas approached her leading two horses.

"Come on, Jaina." Arthas grinned. "Even the most diligent student needs to take a break now and then. It's a beautiful day and you should be out enjoying it."

"I am," she said. It was true; she was in the gardens with her books, rather than cloistered in one of the reading rooms.

"A bit of exercise will help you think better." He extended a hand to her as she sat underneath the tree. She smiled despite herself.

"Arthas, you will be a magnificent king one day," she said teasingly, grasping his hand and allowing herself to be pulled to her feet. "No one can seem to deny you anything."

He laughed at that and held her horse while she mounted. She was wearing trousers today, light linen breeches, and was able to sit astride rather than side-saddle with long robes. He swung up easily on his own horse a moment later.

Jaina glanced at the horse he was riding—a bay mare, rather than the white stallion fate had snatched from him. "I don't think I ever said how sorry I was about Invincible," she said quietly. The mirth left his face, and it was like a shadow passing over the sun. Then the smile returned, slightly sobered.

"It's all right, but thanks. Now—I have picnic supplies and the day awaits. Let's go!"

It was a day Jaina would remember for the rest of her life, one of those perfect late summer days where the sunlight seemed thick and golden as honey. Arthas set a hard pace, but Jaina was an experienced rider and kept up easily. He took her far away from the city and along stretches of green, expansive meadows. The horses seemed to be enjoying themselves as much as their riders, their ears pricked forward and their nostrils flaring as they inhaled the rich scents.

The picnic was simple but delicious fare—bread, cheese, fruit, some light white wine. Arthas lay back, folding his arms behind his head, and dozed for a bit while Jaina kicked off her boots, digging her feet into the thick, soft grass as she sat with her back to a tree, and read for a while. The book was interesting—*A Treatise on the Nature of Teleportation*—but the languid heat of the day, the vigorous exercise, and the soft hum of cicadas served to lull her to sleep as well.

Jaina awoke some time later slightly chilled; the sun was starting to go down. She sat up, knuckling the sleep out of her eyes, to realize that Arthas was nowhere to be seen. Nor was his horse. Her own gelding, reins draped about a tree branch, grazed contentedly.

Frowning, she got to her feet. "Arthas?" There was no answer. Likely he had just decided to go for a quick exploration and would be back any moment. She strained to listen for the sound of hoofbeats, but there were none.

There were still orcs loose, wandering around. Or so the rumors went. And mountain cats and bears—less alien but no less dangerous. Mentally Jaina went over her spells in her mind. She was sure she'd be able to defend herself if she was attacked.

Well—fairly sure.

The attack was sudden and silent.

A thump against the back of her neck and cold wetness was the first and only clue she had. She gasped and whirled. Her attacker was a blur of motion, leaping to another hiding space with the speed of a stag, pausing only long enough to fire another missile at her. This one caught her in the mouth and she started to choke—with laughter. She pawed at the snow, gasping a little as some of it slid down her shirt.

"Arthas! You don't fight fair!"

Her answer was four snowballs rolled in her direction, and she scrambled to pick them up. He'd obviously climbed high enough to find the places in the mountains where winter had come early, and returned with snowballs as trophies. Where was he? There—a flash of his red tunic—

The fight continued for a while, until both had run out of ammunition. "Truce!" Arthas called, and when

Jaina agreed, laughing so hard she could barely get the word out, he leaped from his place of concealment among the rocks and ran to her. He hugged her, laughing as well, and she was pleased to see that he, too, had traces of snow in his hair.

"I knew it all those years ago," he said.

"Knew w-what?" Jaina had been pelted with so many snowballs that despite the fact that it was late summer, she was chilled. Arthas felt her shivering and tightened his arms around her. Jaina knew she should pull back; a friendly and spontaneous hug was one thing, but to linger in his embrace was something else. But she stayed where she was, letting her head rest against his chest, her ear pressed against his heart, hearing it thump rhythmically and rapidly. She closed her eyes as one hand came up to stroke her hair, removing bits of snow as he spoke.

"The day I first saw you, I thought that this would be a girl I could have fun with. Someone who wouldn't mind going for a swim on a hot summer day, or"—he stepped back a little, brushing a few bits of melting pieces of winter off her face and smiling—"or getting a snowball in the face. I didn't hurt you, did I?"

She smiled in return, suddenly warmed. "No. No you didn't." Their eyes met and Jaina felt heat coming to her cheeks. She moved to step back, but his arm encircled her as firmly as an iron band. He continued to touch her face, trailing strong, calloused fingers down the curve of her cheek.

"Jaina," he said quietly, and she shivered, but not from cold, not this time. It was not proper. She should move back. Instead she lifted her face and closed her eyes.

The kiss was gentle at first, soft and sweet, the first Jaina had ever known. As if of their own will, her arms crept up to drape around his neck and she pressed against him as the kiss deepened. She felt as though she was drowning, and he was the only solid thing in the world.

This was what—who—she wanted. This youth who was her friend despite his title, who saw and understood her scholarly character but also knew how to coax forth the playful and adventurous girl who didn't often have a chance to come out—who wasn't often glimpsed.

But he had seen all of who she was, not just the face she presented to the world.

"Arthas," she whispered as she clung to him. "Arthas . . ."

CHAPTER SEVEN

It was a good few months, in Dalaran. Arthas found, somewhat to his surprise, that he actually *was* learning things that would be useful for a king to know. There were also plenty of opportunities to enjoy the lingering summer and first cool hints of autumn, and he loved riding, even if he felt a pang in his chest every time he mounted a horse that was not Invincible.

And there was Jaina.

He'd not planned on kissing her initially. But when he found himself with her in his arms, her eyes bright with laughter and good humor, he'd done so. And she'd responded. Her schedule was more demanding and rigorous than his, and they had not seen each other nearly as much as they had wanted to. When they had, it was usually at public functions. And both had agreed without discussing it at all that it would not do to give the rumor mill any grist.

It lent an extra spice to the relationship. They stole moments when they could—a kiss in an alcove, a fleeting look at a formal dinner. Their first outing had been completely innocent at the outset; but now they avoided such things assiduously.

He memorized her schedule so as to "bump" into her. She found excuses to wander into the stables or in the courtyard that Arthas and his men used as practice areas to keep their battle skills sharp.

Arthas loved every risky, daring minute of it.

Now he waited in a little-used hallway, standing in front of a bookshelf, pretending to peruse the titles. Jaina would be coming in from her fire spell practice; out of habit, she told him with a slightly embarrassed grin, she still trained near the jail area and the many pools of water. She'd have to cross through this area to get to her room. His ears strained for the sound. There it was—the soft, swift pad of her slippered feet moving across the floor. He turned, taking a book down and pretending to look at it, watching for her out of the corner of her eye.

Jaina was clad, as usual, in traditional apprentice robes. Her hair looked like sunshine and her face was set in her typical expression of a concentrated furrow, one of deep thought, not displeasure. She hadn't even noticed him. Quickly he put the book away and darted out into the hallway before she could get too far, grasping her arm and tugging her into the shadows.

As ever, she was never startled by him, and met him halfway, clutching the books to her chest with one arm while the other went around his neck as they kissed.

"Hello, my lady," he murmured, kissing her neck, grinning against her skin.

"Hello, my prince," she murmured happily, sighing.

"Jaina," came a voice, "why are you—"

They sprang apart guiltily, staring at the intruder. Jaina gasped softly and color sprang to her face. "Kael . . ."

The elf's face was carefully composed, but anger burned in his eyes, and his jaw was set. "You dropped a book as you left," he said, lifting the tome. "I followed you to return it."

Jaina glanced up at Arthas, biting her lower lip. He was as startled as she, but he forced an easy smile. He kept his arm around Jaina as he turned to Kael'thas.

"That's very kind of you, Kael," he said. "Thanks."

For a moment, he thought Kael'thas would attack him. Anger and outrage fairly crackled around the mage. He was powerful, and Arthas knew that he wouldn't stand a chance. Even so, he kept his gaze even with the elven prince's, not backing down an inch. Kael'thas clenched his fists and remained where he was.

"Ashamed of her are you, Arthas?" Kael'thas hissed. "Is she only worth your time and attention if no one knows about her?"

Arthas's eyes narrowed. "I had thought to avoid the ravages of the rumor mill," he said quietly. "You know how those things work, Kael, don't you? Someone says something and next thing you know, it's believed to be true. I would protect her reputation by—"

"Protect?" Kael'thas barked the word. "If you cared about her, you would court her openly, proudly. Any man would." He looked at Jaina, and the anger was gone, replaced by a fleeting expression of pain. Then that, too, disappeared. Jaina looked down. "I will leave you two to your . . . tryst. And do not fear, I will say nothing."

With an angry hiss, he scornfully tossed the book toward Jaina. The tome, likely invaluable, landed with a thump at Jaina's feet, and she started at the sound. Then he was gone in a swirl of violet and gold robes. Jaina let out her breath and laid her head on Arthas's chest.

Arthas patted her back gently. "It's all right, he's gone now."

"I'm sorry. I guess I should have told you."

His chest contracted. "Told me what? Jaina—are you and he—"

"No!" she answered at once, gazing up at him. "No. But—I think he wanted to. I just—he's a good man, and a powerful mage. And a prince. But he's not . . ." Her voice trailed off.

"He's not what?" The words came out sharper than he had intended. Kael was so many things Arthas wasn't. Older, more sophisticated, experienced, powerful, and almost impossibly physically perfect. He felt jealousy growing inside him in a cold, hard knot. If Kael had reappeared at that moment, Arthas wasn't so sure he wouldn't take a swing at him.

Jaina smiled softly, the furrow in her brow uncreasing. "He's not you."

The icy knot inside him melted like winter retreating before the warmth of spring, and he pulled her to him and kissed her again.

Who cared what a stuffy elven prince thought anyway?

The year unfolded largely without incident. As summer gave way to a crisp fall and then winter, more complaints rose about the cost of tending to the orc camps, but both Terenas and Arthas expected such. Arthas continued to train with Uther. The older man was adamant that while training at arms was important, so was prayer and meditation. "Yes, we must be able to cut down our enemies," he said. "But we must also be able to heal our friends and ourselves."

Arthas thought about Invincible. His thoughts always drifted to the horse in winter, and Uther's comment only reminded him yet again of what he regarded as the one failure in his entire life. If only he had begun training earlier, the great white stallion would still be alive. He had never revealed to anyone exactly what had happened on that snowy day. They all believed it was an accident. And it was, Arthas told himself. He had not deliberately intended to harm Invincible. He loved the horse; he would sooner have harmed himself. And if he'd begun paladin training earlier, like Varian had done with sword fighting, he'd have been able to save Invincible. He swore that would not happen again. He would do whatever was necessary so that he would never be caught unawares and impotent, would never not be able to make it right.

The winter passed, as all winters must, and spring came to Tirisfal Glades again. And so did Jaina Proudmoore, arriving and looking to Arthas as beautiful, fresh, and welcome a sight as the new blossoms on the awakening trees. She had come to assist him in publicly celebrating Noblegarden, the major spring celebration in Lordaeron and Stormwind. Arthas found that staying up late the night before, sipping wine and filling eggs with candy and other treats, was not quite the boring task it would have been had Jaina not been there with him, her brow furrowed in the endearing fashion he had come to recognize as hers and hers alone, as she carefully and intently filled the eggs and set them aside.

While there was still no public announcement, Arthas and Jaina both knew their parents had spoken with one another, and there was a tacit agreement that the courtship would be permitted. So it was that more and more Arthas, beloved already by his people, was sent to represent Lordaeron at public functions rather than Uther or Terenas. With the passing of time, Uther had increasingly withdrawn into the spiritual aspect of the Light, and Terenas seemed more than content to not have to travel.

"It is exciting when you are young, to travel for days on horseback and sleep under the stars," he told Arthas. "When you are my age, though, horseback riding is best left for recreation, and the stars one can glimpse by looking out the window are quite close enough."

Arthas had grinned, diving with pleasure into the new responsibilities. Admiral Proudmoore and Archmage Antonidas had apparently come to the same conclusions. For more and more often, when messengers from Dalaran were sent to Capital City, Lady Jaina Proudmoore accompanied them.

"Come for the Midsummer Fire Festival," he said suddenly. She looked up at him, holding an egg carefully in one hand, brushing a lock of golden hair from her face with the other.

"I can't. Summer is a very intensive time for the students at Dalaran. Antonidas has already told me to expect to stay there the whole time." Regret was in her voice.

"Then I'll come visit you for Midsummer, and you can come for Hallow's End," Arthas said. She shook her head and laughed at him.

"You are persistent, Arthas Menethil. I will try."

"No, you'll come." He reached across the table, littered with carefully hollowed out, brightly painted eggs and small candies, and placed his hand over hers.

She smiled, still a little shy after all this time, her cheeks turning pink.

She would come.

There were several smaller festivals leading up to Hallow's End. One was somber, one was celebratory, and this one was a bit of both. It was believed to be a time when the barrier between the living and the dead was thin, and those who had passed on could be sensed by those still alive. Tradition had it that at the end of the harvest season, before the winds of winter began to blow, that a straw effigy would be erected right outside the palace. At sunset on the night of the ceremony, it would be lit on fire. It was an awesome sight—a giant flaming wicker man, burning bright against the encroaching night. Anyone who wished could approach the fiery effigy, toss a branch into the crackling flames, and in so doing metaphorically "burn away" anything he did not wish to carry into the quiet, deep reflection time provided by winter's enforced inactivity.

It was a peasant ritual, sprung up from time immemorial. Arthas suspected that few nowadays truly believed that tossing a branch into a fire would really solve their problems; even fewer believed that contact with the dead was possible. He certainly didn't. But it was a popular celebration, and it brought Jaina back to Lordaeron, and for those reasons, he was looking forward to it.

He had a little surprise for her in mind.

It was right after sunset. The crowds had begun gathering in late afternoon. Some had even brought picnics and made an event out of enjoying the last few days of late autumn among the hills of Tirisfal. There were guards stationed about, keeping an eye out for the mishaps that often happen when large numbers of people are gathered in one place, but Arthas really didn't expect any difficulties. When he came out of the palace, clad in a tunic, breeches, and cloak of rich autumnal hues, cheers erupted. He paused and waved at the onlookers, accepting their applause, then turned and extended his hand to Jaina.

She looked a little surprised, but smiled, and the cheers now lifted her name to the darkening sky as well as his. Arthas and Jaina walked down the path to the giant wicker man and stood before it. Arthas held up a hand for silence.

"My countrymen, I join you in celebration of this most revered of nights—the night when we remember those who are no longer with us, and cast aside the things that hold us back. We burn the effigy of the wicker man as a symbol of the year that is passing, much as the farmers burn the remains of the harvested fields. The ashes nourish the soil, and this rite nourishes our souls. It is good to see so many here tonight. I am pleased to be able to offer the distinct honor of lighting the wicker man to Lady Jaina Proudmoore."

Jaina's eyes went wide. Arthas turned to her, grinning wickedly.

"She is the daughter of war hero Admiral Daelin Proudmoore, and promises to be a powerful mage in her own right. As magi are masters of fire, I think it only right that she light our wicker man this evening. Do you agree?"

Those assembled roared with delight, as Arthas knew they would. Arthas bowed at Jaina, then leaned in and whispered, "Give them a show—they'll love it."

Jaina nodded imperceptibly, then turned to the crowd and waved. Their cheering increased. She tucked a lock of hair behind her ear, briefly revealing her nervousness, then composed her face. She closed her eyes and lifted her hands, murmuring an incantation.

Jaina was dressed in fire hues of red, yellow, and orange. As small balls of flame began to materialize in her hands, glowing faintly at first and then with increasing brightness, she looked to Arthas like fire itself for a moment. She held the fire in her hands with ease, comfort, and mastery, and he knew that the days when she had little control over her spells were long gone. She wasn't going to "become" a powerful mage; she obviously already was one, in fact if not in title.

And then she extended both hands. The balls of fire leaped like bullets fired from a gun, hurtling toward the enormous straw effigy. It erupted into flame at once, and the onlookers gasped, then broke into wild applause. Arthas grinned. The wicker man never caught on fire that quickly when an ordinary brand was touched to its base.

Jaina opened her eyes at the sound and waved, smiling delightedly. Arthas leaned close and whispered, "Spectacular, Jaina."

"You asked me to give them a show," she shot back, grinning at him.

"Indeed I did. But that was almost *too* good a show. They're going to demand that you light the wicker man every year now, I'm afraid."

She turned to look at him. "Would that be a problem?"

The light from the blazing fire danced over her, illuminating her lively features, catching the glint of a gold circlet adorning her head. Arthas caught his breath as he regarded her. She'd always been attractive to him, and he'd liked her from the moment they'd met. She'd been a friend, a confidant, an exciting flirtation. But now he couldn't help but see her, quite literally, in a whole new light.

It took a moment for him to find his voice. "No," he said softly. "No, it wouldn't be a problem at all."

They joined the throngs dancing by the fire that night, causing the guards no end of consternation as they went right down among the populace and shook hands and exchanged greetings. And then they gave the dutiful guards the slip, losing themselves in the crowd and stealing away unnoticed. Arthas led her through the back corridors to the private living quarters of the palace. Once they were almost caught by some servants taking a shortcut to the kitchens, and had to flatten themselves against the wall and stay perfectly still for several long moments.

Then they were in Arthas's rooms. He closed the door, leaned back up against it, and swept her into his arms, kissing her deeply. But it was she, shy, studious Jaina, who broke the kiss and moved toward the bed, leading him by the hand, the orange light from the still-blazing wicker man outside dancing on their skin.

He followed, almost as in a daze, a dream, as they stood beside the bed, their hands clasped so tightly Arthas feared her fingers would snap in his grip. "Jaina," he whispered.

"Arthas," she said, the word a whimper, and kissed him again, her hands reaching up to clasp his face between her hands. He was dizzy with wanting her, and felt suddenly bereft as she drew back. Her breath was soft and warm on his face as she whispered, "I . . . are we ready for this?"

He started to answer flippantly, but he knew what she was really asking. He could not imagine being more ready to bring this girl the rest of the way into his heart. He had turned down the lovely Taretha, and she had not been the first he had said no to. Jaina, he knew, was even less experienced than he in such matters.

"I am if you are," he whispered hoarsely, and as he bent to kiss her again, he saw the familiar furrow of worry cross her brow. *I will kiss it away,* he vowed, bringing her onto the bed with him. *I will make everything you could ever worry about go away forever.*

Later, when the wicker man had finally burned out and the only light on Jaina's sleeping form was the cool blue-white of moonlight, Arthas still lay awake, running his fingers along the curves of her body and alternately wondering where this would all lead and feeling content to simply be in the moment.

He had not tossed in a branch to the wicker man fire, because he had nothing he wished to be rid of. Nor did he now, he thought, bending forward to kiss her. Jaina awakened with a soft sigh, reaching for him.

"No one can seem to deny you anything," she murmured, repeating the words she had said to him the day of their first kiss, "least of all me."

He clutched her to him then, a sudden cold shivering over him, though he had no idea why. "Don't deny me, Jaina. Don't ever deny me. Please."

She looked up at him, eyes glittering in the cool moonlight. "I never would, Arthas. Never."

CHAPTER EIGHT

The palace had never been so cheerily decorated for the Feast of Winter Veil as it was this year. Muradin, ever a good ambassador of his people, had brought the dwarven tradition to Lordaeron upon his arrival. Over the years it had increased in popularity, and this year the people seemed to truly take it to heart.

The festive tone had been established a few weeks earlier, when Jaina had delighted them so with her theatrical display of igniting the wicker man. She had been granted permission to stay through the winter if she so chose, although Dalaran was not far to one who could teleport herself. Something had changed. It was both subtle and profound. Jaina Proudmoore was starting to be treated as more than the daughter of the ruler of Kul Tiras, more than a friend.

She was starting to be treated as a member of the royal family.

Arthas first realized it when his mother took both Jaina and Calia to be fitted for the formal dresses fashion required for the Winter Veil Eve ball. Other guests had spent Winter Veil here; Lianne had never before wanted to coordinate their outfits with her own and that of her daughter.

Too, Terenas now often requested that Jaina join him and Arthas when they sat to listen to the people's petitions. She sat on the king's left, Arthas on his right. In a position nearly equal to the king's own son.

Well, Arthas thought, he supposed that it was the logical conclusion. Wasn't it? He recalled his words to Calia years ago: *"We each have our duties, I guess. You to marry whomever Father wants, and me to marry well for the kingdom."*

Jaina would be good for the kingdom. Jaina, he thought, would be good for him, too.

So why did the thought make him feel so uneasy?

They had fresh snow for the night before Winter Veil. Arthas stood looking out of a large window at Lordamere Lake, frozen over now. The snow had begun falling at dawn, and had stopped about an hour ago. The sky was black velvet, the stars small icy diamonds against the soft darkness, and moonlight made everything look still, hushed, and magical.

A soft hand slipped into his. "Beautiful, isn't it?" Jaina said quietly. Arthas nodded, not looking at her. "Plenty of ammunition."

"What?"

"Ammunition," Jaina repeated. "For snowball fights."

He finally turned to her and his breath caught. He'd not been permitted to see the gowns she, Calia, and his mother would be wearing to the banquet and ball this evening, and he was stunned by her beauty. Jaina Proudmoore looked like a snow maiden. From shoes that looked to be made of ice, to a white gown tinged with the palest blue, to the circlet of silver that caught the warm glow of the torchlight, she was heartbreakingly lovely. But she was no ice queen, no statue; she was warm and soft and alive, her golden hair flowing about her shoulders, her cheeks pink beneath his admiring gaze, her blue eyes bright with happiness.

"You're like . . . a white candle," he said. "All white and gold." He reached for a lock of her hair, twirling it about his fingers.

She grinned. "Yes," she laughed, reaching to touch his own bright locks, "the children will almost certainly be blond."

He froze.

"Jaina—are you—"

She chuckled. "No. Not yet. But there's no reason to think we won't be able to have children."

Children. Again, the word that galvanized him in shock and peculiar distress. She was talking about the children *they* would have. His mind galloped into the future, a future with Jaina as his wife, their children in the palace, his parents gone, himself on the throne, the weight of the crown on his head. Part of him desperately wanted that. He loved having Jaina by his side, loved holding her in his arms at night, loved the taste and smell of her, loved her laughter, pure as a bell and sweet as the scent of roses.

He loved—

What if he ruined it?

Because suddenly he knew that until this moment, it had all been child's play. He'd thought of Jaina as a companion, just as she had been since his boyhood, except their games were now of a more adult nature. But something had suddenly shifted inside him. What if this was real? What if he really *was* in love with her, and she with him? What if he was a bad husband, a bad king—what if—

"I'm not ready," he blurted.

Her brow furrowed. "Well, we do not have to have little ones right away." She squeezed his hand in what was clearly intended to be a gesture of reassurance.

Arthas suddenly dropped her hand and took a step backward. Her frown deepened in confusion.

"Arthas? What's wrong?"

"Jaina—we're too young," he said, speaking rapidly, his voice rising slightly. "*I'm* too young. There's still—I can't—I'm not ready."

She paled. "You aren't—I thought—"

Guilt racked him. She'd asked him this, the night they became lovers. *Are you ready for this?* she had whispered. *I am if you are,* he had replied, and he'd meant it. . . . He really had thought he'd meant it. . . .

Arthas reached out and grabbed her hands, trying desperately to articulate the emotions racing through him. "I still have so much to learn. So much training to complete. And Father needs me. Uther's got so much he needs to teach and—Jaina, we've always been friends. You've always understood me so well. Can't you understand me now? Can't we still be friends?"

Her bloodless lips opened but no words came out at

first. Her hands were limp in his. Almost frantically he squeezed them.

Jaina, please. Please understand—even if I don't.

"Of course, Arthas." Her voice was a monotone. "We'll always be friends, you and I."

Everything, from her posture to her face to her voice, bespoke her pain and her shock. But Arthas clung instead to her words as a wave of relief, so profound it made his knees weak, swept over him. It was all going to be just fine. It might upset her now, a little, but surely she'd understand soon. They knew each other. She'd figure out that he was right, that it was too soon.

"I mean—this isn't forever," he said, feeling the need to explain. "Just for now. You've got studying to do—I'm sure I've been a distraction. Antonidas probably resents me."

She said nothing.

"This is for the best. Maybe one day it'll be different and we can try again. It's not that I don't—that you—"

He pulled her into his arms and hugged her. She was stiff as stone for a moment, then he felt the tension leave her and her arms went around him. They stood alone in the hall for a long time, Arthas resting his cheek against her bright gold hair, the hair that, no doubt, their children would indeed have been born with. Might still be born with.

"I don't want to close the door," he said quietly. "I just—"

"It's all right, Arthas. I understand."

He stepped back, his hands on her shoulders, peering into her eyes. "Do you?"

She laughed slightly. "Honestly? No. But it's all right. It will be eventually, anyway. I know that."

"Jaina, I just want to make sure this is right. For both of us."

I don't want to mess this up. I can't mess this up.

She nodded. She took a deep breath and steadied herself, giving him a smile . . . a real, if hurting, smile. "Come, Prince Arthas. You need to escort your friend to the ball."

Arthas somehow made it through the evening, and so did Jaina, although Terenas kept giving him strange glances. He didn't want to tell his father, not yet. It was a strained and unhappy night, and at one point during a pause in the dancing, Arthas looked out at the blanket of white snow and the moon-silvered lake, and wondered why everything bad seemed to happen in winter.

Lieutenant General Aedelas Blackmoore didn't look particularly happy to have this exclusive audience with King Terenas and Prince Arthas. In fact, he looked like he desperately would like to slink away unnoticed.

The years had not been kind to him, neither physically nor in the hand fate had dealt him. Arthas recalled a handsome, rather dashing military commander who, while doubtless overfond of his drink, at least seemed able to keep the ravages of it at bay. No longer. Blackmoore's hair was streaked with gray, he had put on weight, and his eyes were bloodshot. He was, fortunately, stone-cold sober. Had he showed up to this meeting intoxicated, Terenas, a firm believer in the need for moderation in all things, would have refused to see him.

Blackmoore was here today because he had messed up. Badly. Somehow the man's prized gladiator orc, Thrall, had escaped Durnholde in a fire. Blackmoore had tried to keep it quiet and conduct his search for the orc personally and on a small scale, but a secret as large as a massive green orc could not be contained forever. Once word had gotten out, rumors flew wildly, of course—it was a rival lord who had freed the orc, anxious to ensure winning in the rings; it was a jealous mistress, hoping to embarrass him; it was a clever band of orcs unaffected by the strange lethargy—no, no, it was Orgrim Doomhammer himself; it was dragons, infiltrating disguised as humans, who lit the place afire with only their breath.

Arthas had thought Thrall exciting to watch in combat, but he recalled that even then the question had crossed his mind whether it was wise to train and educate an orc. When information had come that Thrall was on the loose, Terenas had summoned Blackmoore immediately for an accounting.

"It was bad enough that you thought it a good idea to train an orc to fight in gladiatorial combat," Terenas began. "But to train him in military strategy, to teach him to read, to write . . . I must ask, Lieutenant General . . . what in the Light's name were you thinking?"

Arthas smothered a grin as Aedelas Blackmoore seemed to physically diminish right in front of his eyes.

"You assured me that the funds and materials went

directly into stepping up security, and that your pet orc was securely guarded." Terenas continued, "And yet somehow, he is out there instead of safely inside Durnholde. How is that possible?"

Blackmoore frowned and rallied somewhat. "It is certainly unfortunate that Thrall escaped. I'm sure you understand how I must feel."

It was a hit on Blackmoore's part; Terenas still smarted from the fact that Doomhammer had escaped from under his very nose. But it wasn't a particularly wise hit. Terenas frowned and continued.

"I hope this isn't part of some disturbing trend. The money is earned from the labor of the people, Lieutenant General. It goes toward keeping them safe. Do I need to send along a representative to ensure that the funds are properly distributed?"

"No! No, no, that won't be necessary. I will account for every penny."

"Yes," said Terenas with deceptive mildness, "you will."

When Blackmoore finally left, bowing obsequiously the whole way out, Terenas turned to his son.

"What are your thoughts on the situation? You saw Thrall in action."

Arthas nodded. "He wasn't at all like I had imagined orcs to be. I mean . . . he was huge. And fought fiercely. But it was obvious he was also intelligent. And trained."

Terenas stroked his beard, thinking. "There are pockets of renegade orcs out there. Some who might not have this lassitude that the ones we've imprisoned have demonstrated. If Thrall were to find them and teach them what he knows, it could be a very bad thing for us."

Arthas sat up straighter. This could be what he'd been looking for. "I've been training hard with Uther." And he had been. Unable to properly explain to others— and to himself—why he had ended the relationship with Jaina, he'd thrown himself into his training. He'd fought for hours a day until his body ached, attempting to sufficiently exhaust himself so that he could get her face out of his mind.

It had been what he wanted, hadn't it? She'd taken it well. So why was it he who lay awake at night, missing her warmth and presence with a pain that bordered on agony? He had even embraced hitherto despised hours spent in still, silent meditation in an effort to distract himself. Maybe if he focused on fighting, on learning how to accept and channel and direct the Light, he could get the hell *over* her. Over the girl he himself had broken up with.

"We could go looking for such orcs. Find them before Thrall does."

Terenas nodded. "Uther has informed me of your dedication, and he's been impressed with your progress." He reached a decision. "Very well then. Go tell Uther and start preparing. It's time for your first taste of real battle."

Arthas was hard put not to let out a whoop of excitement. He refrained, even in his delight picking up on the pained, worried look on his father's face. Maybe, just maybe, killing rebellious greenskins would erase the memory of Jaina's stricken expression when he'd ended their relationship.

"Thank you, sir. I'll do you proud."

Despite the regret in his father's blue-green eyes, so like Arthas's own, Terenas smiled. "That, my son, is the least of my worries."

CHAPTER NINE

Jaina raced through the gardens, late to her meeting with Archmage Antonidas. She'd done it again—lost track of time with her nose buried in a book. Her master was always chiding her about that, but she couldn't help it. Her slippered feet took her down between the rows of goldenbark apple trees, the fruit hanging heavy and ripe. She felt a brief brush of sorrow as she remembered a conversation held here only a few short years ago—when Arthas had appeared behind her, slipping his hands over her eyes, and whispering, "Guess who?"

Arthas. She missed him still. She supposed she always would. The breakup had been unexpected and hurtful, and the timing couldn't have been worse—she still cringed as she thought about having to continue through the formal Winter Veil ball as if nothing had gone wrong—but as the initial shock had faded she had grown to understand his reasoning. They were both young yet and, as he had pointed out at the time, they had responsibilities and training to complete. She'd promised him they'd always stay friends, and she had meant it, then and afterward. In order for her to keep that promise, she had had to heal. And so she had done.

Certainly much had happened in those few short years to keep her busy and focused elsewhere. Five years ago, a powerful wizard named Kel'Thuzad had drawn the ire of the Kirin Tor with his dabbling in unnatural necromantic magic. He had left, suddenly and mysteriously, after being severely reprimanded and told in no uncertain terms to cease his experiments immediately. The mystery had been one of many things that had helped distract her over the last three years.

Outside the gates of the magical city, things had happened too, though information was scattered, rumor-ridden, and chaotic. As best Jaina had been able to determine, the escaped orc Thrall, now calling himself the warchief of the new Horde, had begun attacking the internment camps and freeing the captive orcs. Later, Durnholde itself had been razed by this self-styled warchief, crumbling into ruins as Thrall called forth what Jaina had learned was the ancient shamanistic magic of his people. Blackmoore had fallen too, but by all accounts, he would not be mourned overlong. While troubled at what this new Horde might eventually mean for her people, Jaina could not find it in herself to mourn the loss of the camps. Not after what she had seen of them.

Voices reached her ears, one raised in anger. So unusual was that in this place that Jaina slid to an abrupt halt.

"As I told Terenas, your people are prisoners in their own lands. I repeat to you now—humanity is in peril. The tides of darkness have come again, and the whole world is poised upon the brink of war!" The voice was male, resonant and strong, and Jaina did not recognize it.

"Ah, now I know who you must be. You are the rambling prophet who was the subject of King Terenas's last letter. And I am no more interested in your babble than he is." The other speaker was Antonidas, as calm as the stranger was insistent. Jaina knew that she should discreetly withdraw before she was noticed, but the same curiosity that had driven the girl she had been to go along with Arthas to spy on the orc encampments now prompted her to cloak herself in invisibility and learn more. She moved closer as quietly as possible. She could see them both now; the first speaker, whom Antonidas had sarcastically referred to as a "prophet," clad in a cloak and hood decorated with black feathers, and her master on horseback. "I thought Terenas was quite plain in his opinion of your predictions."

"You must be wiser than the king! The end is near!"

"I told you before, I'm not interested in this nonsense." Clipped, calm, dismissive. Jaina knew that tone of voice.

The prophet was silent for a moment, then he sighed. "Then I've wasted my time here."

Before Jaina's startled gaze, the stranger's shape blurred. It compressed and shifted, and where an instant before a man in a cowled robe had stood, now there was only a large black bird. With a caw of frustration, it sprang skyward, flapping its wings, and was gone.

His eyes still on the interloper, now a vanishing dot in the blue sky, Antonidas said, "You can show yourself now, Jaina."

Heat washed over Jaina's face. She murmured a counterspell and edged forward. "I'm sorry for eavesdropping, Master, but—"

"It's your inquisitive nature that I've come to rely on, child," Antonidas said, chuckling a little. "That crazed fool's convinced that the world's about to end. That's taking the whole 'plague' thing a bit far, in my opinion."

"Plague?" Jaina started.

Antonidas sighed and dismounted, sending his steed off with an amiable slap to the rear. The horse pranced a little, then trotted obediently off to the stables, where a groom would attend to him. The archmage beckoned to his apprentice, who stepped forward and took the outstretched, gnarled hand. "You will recall I sent some messengers to Capital City a short time ago."

"I thought that was regarding the orc situtation." Antonidas murmured an incantation, and a few moments later they appeared in his private quarters. Jaina loved this place; loved the untidiness, the smell of parchment and leather and ink, and the old chairs into which one could curl and lose oneself in knowledge. He gestured for her to sit and with the crook of a finger had a pitcher pour nectar for them.

"Well, that was on the agenda, yes, but my representatives thought that a more dire threat was at our doorstep."

"More dire than the Horde re-forming?" Jaina extended her hand, and the crystal goblet, filled with golden liquid, floated into her palm.

"Orcs, potentially, could be reasoned with. Disease cannot. There are reports of a plague spreading in the northlands. Something I think the Kirin Tor should be paying close attention to."

Jaina peered at him, her brow furrowing as she sipped. Generally disease fell under the auspices of the priests, not magi. Unless—

"You think it's magical in nature somehow?"

He nodded his bald head. "It's a strong possibility. And that's why, Jaina Proudmoore, I am asking you to travel to these lands and investigate the matter."

Jaina nearly choked on her nectar. "Me?"

He smiled gently. "You. You have learned nearly everything I have to teach. It's time you utilized those skills outside of the safety of these towers." His eyes twinkled again. "And I have arranged for a special envoy to assist you."

Arthas lounged against a tree, turning his face up to the weak sunlight and closing his eyes. He knew he radiated calmness and confidence; he had to. His men were worrying enough for all of them. He couldn't let them see that he, too, was anxious. After all this time . . . how would they get along? Maybe it hadn't been so smart a decision after all. But all the reports had been glowing, and he knew she had the most level of heads. It would work out all right. It had to.

One of his captains, Falric, whom Arthas had known for years, stomped about, going a little way down one of the four paths at this crossroads, then returning to venture a short distance down another. His breath was visible in the chill, and his irritation was obviously growing by the minute. "Prince Arthas," he finally ventured, "we've been waiting here for hours. Are you sure this friend of yours is coming?"

Arthas's lips curved in a slight smile as he answered without opening his eyes. The men had not been told, for reasons of security. "I'm sure." He was. He thought about all the other times he had patiently waited for her. "Jaina usually runs a little late."

No sooner had the words left his lips than he heard a distant bellow and the barely decipherable words, "Me SMASH!"

Like a panther dozing in the sun only to waken instantly alert, Arthas sprang to attention, hammer in hand. He started down the road, to see a slender, feminine shape racing toward him as she crested the hill into his vision. Behind her loomed what he knew to be an elemental—a swirling blob of aqua-colored water, with a crude head and limbs.

And behind that . . . were two ogres.

"By the Light!" cried Falric, starting to race forward. Arthas would have beaten him to the girl except for the fact that right at that moment, he caught sight of Jaina Proudmoore's face.

She was grinning.

"Stay your blade, Captain," Arthas said, feeling his own lips curve into a grin. "She can take care of herself."

And so indeed the lady could—and efficiently. At that precise moment Jaina wheeled and began to summon

fire. Arthas realized that if he was going to feel sorry
for anyone in this conflict, it was the poor baffled ogres,
bellowing in pain as fire licked their pudgy, pale forms
and staring in shock at the tiny human female responsible for such astonishing agony. One of them had the
sense to run, but the other, seemingly unable to believe
it, kept coming. Jaina sent a blast of rumbling orange
flame at it again, and it cried out and collapsed, burning
to death quickly, the rank scent of charred flesh filling
Arthas's nostrils.

Jaina watched the second one flee, dusted her hands
off, and nodded. She hadn't even broken a sweat.

"Gentlemen, meet Miss Jaina Proudmoore," Arthas
drawled, walking up to his childhood friend and former lover. "Special agent to the Kirin Tor, and one of
the most talented sorceresses in the land. Looks like you
haven't lost your touch."

She turned to face him, smiling up at him. There was
no awkwardness in this moment, only happiness. She
was glad to see him, and he her, the pleasure swelling
inside him. "It's good to see you again."

So much in so few, almost formal words. But she
understood him. She had always understood him. Her
eyes were sparkling as she replied, "You, too. It's been a
while since a prince escorted me anywhere."

"Yes," he said, a slight hint of ruefulness coloring his
tone. "It has." Now it was awkward, and Jaina looked
down and he cleared his throat. "Well, I guess we should
get under way."

She nodded, dismissing the elemental with a wave of
her hand. "I don't need this fellow with such stalwart

soldiers," she said, gifting Falric and his men with one of her best smiles. "So, Your Highness, what do you know about this plague we're to investigate?"

"Not much," Arthas was forced to confess as they fell into step. "Father just now sent me to work with you. Uther's been fighting with me against the orcs most recently. But I'd guess that if the Dalaran wizards want to find out more about it, it's got something to do with magic."

She nodded, still smiling, although her brow was starting to furrow in that familiar fashion. Arthas felt an odd pang as he noticed it. "Quite right. Although exactly how, I'm not sure. That's why Master Antonidas sent me to observe and report back. We should check out the villages along the King's road. Talk to the inhabitants—see if they know anything useful. Hopefully they have not been infected and this is nothing more serious than a localized outbreak of some sort."

He, who knew her so well, could hear the doubt in her voice. He understood it. If Antonidas really believed it wasn't serious, he wouldn't have sent his prized apprentice to check it out—nor would King Terenas have sent his son.

He changed the topic. "I wonder if it had anything to do with the orcs." At her raised eyebrow, he continued. "I'm sure you've heard about the escapes from the internment camps."

She nodded. "Yes. I sometimes wonder if that little family we saw was among those who escaped."

He shifted uneasily. "Well, if they are, they might still be worshipping demons."

Her eyes widened. "What? I thought that was stamped out long ago—that the orcs were no longer using demonic energy."

Arthas shrugged. "Father sent Uther and me to help defend Strahnbrad. By the time I got there, orcs had already begun kidnapping villagers. We hunted them down at their encampment, but three men were . . . sacrificed."

Jaina was listening now as she always did, not just with her ears but with her whole body, concentrating on every word with the focus that he remembered. Light, but she was beautiful.

"The orcs said they were offering them up to their demons. Called it a paltry sacrifice—clearly they wanted more."

"And Antonidas seems to think this plague is magical in nature," Jaina murmured. "I wonder if there is a connection. It's disheartening to hear that they have reverted so. Perhaps it is only a single clan."

"Perhaps—or perhaps not." He recalled how Thrall had fought in the ring, recalled how even those ragtag orcs had put up a surprisingly good fight. "We can't afford to take risks. If we're attacked, my men have standing orders to kill them all." Briefly, he thought about the fury that raged in him when the orc leader had sent back his response to Uther's offer of surrender. The two men who had been sent in to parley had been killed, their horses returning riderless in a wordless, brutal message.

"Let's get in there and destroy the beasts!" he'd cried, the weapon he had been given at his initiation into the

Silver Hand glowing brightly. He would have charged in immediately had not Uther placed a restraining hand on his arm.

"Remember, Arthas," he had said, his voice calm, "we are paladins. Vengeance cannot be a part of what we must do. If we allow our passions to turn to blood-lust, then we will become as vile as the orcs."

The words penetrated the anger—somewhat. Arthas had clenched his teeth, watching as the frightened horses, their riders butchered, were led away. Uther's words were wisdom, but Arthas felt he had failed the men who'd been on those horses. Failed them, just as he'd failed Invincible, and now they were as dead as that great beast. He took a deep, steadying breath. "Yes, Uther."

His calmness had been rewarded—Uther had charged him with leading the attack. If only he'd been in time to save those three poor men.

A gentle hand on his arm called him back to the present, and without thinking, out of old habit, he covered Jaina's hand with his own. She started to pull away, then gave him a slightly strained smile.

"It's so very, very good to see you again," he said impulsively.

Her smile softened, became genuine, and she squeezed his arm. "You, too, Your Highness. By the way, thanks for holding your man back when we met." The smile became a full-fledged grin. "I told you once before, I'm not a fragile little figurine."

He chuckled. "Indeed not, my lady. You will fight alongside us in these battles."

She sighed. "I pray there is no fighting—only investigating. But I will do what I must. I always have."

Jaina withdrew her hand. Arthas hid his disappointment. "As we all do, my lady."

"Oh stop that. I'm Jaina."

"And I'm Arthas. Nice to meet you."

She shoved him then, and they laughed, and suddenly a barrier was gone between them. His heart warmed as he looked down at her, at his side once again. They were facing real danger together for the first time. He was conflicted. He wanted to keep her safe, but he also wanted to let her shine in her abilities. Had he done the right thing? Was it too late? He'd told her that he wasn't ready, and that had been true—he hadn't been ready for a lot of things then. But much had changed since that Winter Veil. And some things hadn't changed at all. All kinds of emotions tore at him, and he pushed them all away except one: simple pleasure in her presence.

They made camp that night before dusk, in a small clearing close to the road. There was no moonlight, only the stars, glittering in the ebony darkness above them. Jaina jokingly lit the fire, conjured some delicious breads and beverages, then declared, "I'm done." The men laughed and obligingly prepared the rest of the meal, skewering rabbits over spits and unpacking fruits. Wine was passed around, and the feeling was almost more of a group of comrades enjoying the evening than a battle-ready unit investigating a deadly plague.

Afterward, Jaina sat a little bit away from the group. Her eyes were on the skies, a smile playing on her lips. Arthas joined her and offered her more wine. She held out her goblet while he poured and then took a sip.

"This is a lovely vintage, Your H—Arthas," she said.

"One of the benefits of being a prince," he replied. He stretched out his long legs and lay down next to her, one arm behind his head as a pillow, the other arm holding the goblet steady on his chest as he looked up at the stars. "What do you think we're going to find?"

"I don't know. I was sent as an investigator. I do wonder if it doesn't have something to do with demons, though, given your encounter with the orcs."

He nodded in the darkness, then, realizing she couldn't see him, said, "I agree. I wonder if we shouldn't have brought a priest along with us now."

She turned to smile at him. "You're a paladin, Arthas. The Light works through you. Plus, you swing a weapon better than any priest I've seen."

He grinned at that. The moment hung between them, and just as he started to reach out a hand to her, she sighed and got to her feet, finishing the wine.

"It's late. I don't know about you, but I'm exhausted. I'll see you in the morning. Sleep well, Arthas."

But he couldn't sleep. He tossed and turned in his bedroll, staring up at the sky, the night sounds contriving to catch his attention even when he did start to drift off. He could take it no more. He'd always been impulsive, and he knew it, but dammit—

He threw back the blankets and sat up. The camp was still. They were in no danger here, so there was no one set to watch. Quietly, Arthas rose and went to the area where he knew Jaina was sleeping. He knelt down beside her and brushed her hair back from her face.

"Jaina," he whispered, "wake up."

As she had done that night so long ago, she again awoke in silence and unafraid, blinking up at him curiously.

He grinned. "You up for an adventure?"

She tilted her head, smiling, the memories obviously coming back to her as well. "What sort of an adventure?" she countered.

"Trust me."

"I always have, Arthas."

They spoke in whispers, their breath visible in the cold night air. She was propped up on one elbow now, and he imitated her, reaching with his other hand to touch her face. She did not pull back.

"Jaina . . . I think there was a reason we were brought together again."

There it was, the little furrow in her brow. "Of course. Your father sent you because—"

"No, no. More than that. We're working together as a team now. We—we work well that way."

She was very still. He continued to caress the smooth curve of her cheek.

"I—when this is all over—maybe we can . . . talk. You know."

"About what ended at Winter Veil?"

"No. Not about endings. About beginnings. Because things have felt very incomplete to me without you. You know me like no one else does, Jaina, and I've missed that."

She was silent for a long moment, then sighed softly and leaned her cheek into his hand. He shivered as she turned her head and kissed his palm.

"I have never been able to deny you, Arthas," she said, a hint of laughter in her voice. "And yes. It feels incomplete to me, too. I've missed you very much."

Relief washed over him and he leaned forward, wrapping her in his arms and kissing her passionately. They would get to the bottom of this mystery together, solve it, and come home heroes. Then they'd get married— maybe in the spring. He wanted to see her showered with rose petals. And later there'd be those fair-haired children Jaina had talked about.

They were not intimate, not here, surrounded as they were by Arthas's men, but he did join her under the blankets until the steely dawn called him reluctantly back to his own bed. Before he left, though, he caught her in his arms and held her tightly.

He did sleep a little then, secure in the knowledge that nothing—no plague, no demon, no mystery—could stand up to the joined efforts of Prince Arthas Menethil, paladin of the Light, and Lady Jaina Proudmoore, mage. They'd see it through together—whatever it took.

CHAPTER TEN

B y mid-morning the next day, they were starting to come across scattered farmsteads. "The village isn't too far distant," Arthas said, consulting the map. "None of these farms is mentioned here."

"Nay," said Falric firmly. There was a degree of familiarity in how he spoke to his prince due to how long the two had known each other. Arthas had come to rely on the man's forthrightness, and Falric had been first on the list of those he wanted to accompany him. Now Falric shook his graying head. "I grew up in this area, sir, and most of these farmers are the independent sort. They bring their produce and livestock in to the villages, sell it, and come home."

"Bad blood?"

"Not at all, Your Highness. It's just the way things are done."

"If that is the relationship," Jaina said, "then if someone fell ill, they might not summon outside aid. These people could be sick."

"Jaina raises a good point. Let's go see what we can

find out from these farmers," Arthas ordered, clucking to his mount. They approached slowly, giving the farmers time to notice and prepare for them. If they were isolationists and if the plague had indeed cut a swathe through here, the farmers would be wary of large parties sweeping down on them.

Arthas's eyes scanned the area as they approached the farmhouse. "Look," he said, pointing. "The gate's been smashed and the livestock is gone."

"That's not a good sign," Jaina muttered.

"Nor has anyone come out to greet us," Falric said. "Or even to challenge us."

Arthas and Jaina exchanged glances. Arthas signaled the group to halt.

"Greetings to you all!" he said in a strong voice. "I am Arthas, prince of Lordaeron, and my men and I mean you no harm. Please, come out and speak with us—we have questions concerning your safety."

Silence. The wind picked up, flattening the acres of grass that should have been grazing ground for cattle or sheep. The only sound was its soft sigh and the creaking of their own armor as they all shifted uneasily.

"No one's here," Arthas said.

"Or maybe they're too sick to come out," Jaina replied. "Arthas, we must at least go and see. They could need our help!"

Arthas glanced at his men. They looked none too keen on walking into a house that might be infested with plague victims, nor in truth was he. But Jaina was right. These were his people. He had vowed to help them. And so he would, wherever that promise led, whatever it took.

"Come on," he said, and swung down. Beside him Jaina did the same. "No, you stay here."

Her golden brows drew together in a frown. "I told you, I'm not a fragile little figurine, Arthas. I was sent to investigate the plague, and if there are indeed victims here, I need to see them for myself."

He sighed and nodded. "All right then."

He strode forward to the farmhouse. They were almost at the garden when the wind shifted.

The stench was horrific. Jaina covered her mouth and even Arthas struggled not to gag. It was the sickly sweet smell of the slaughterhouse—no, not even that fresh; it was the reek of carrion. One of his men turned and vomited. It was by sheer will that Arthas did not emulate him. The foul odor was coming from inside the house. It was by now obvious what had happened to the inhabitants.

Jaina turned to him, pale but resolute. "I have to examine—"

Horrible, liquid-sounding cries filled the air along with the stench of death as from inside the farmhouse and behind it *things* came at them with startling speed. Arthas's hammer suddenly began to glow with a light so bright he had to narrow his eyes against it. He whirled, lifting the hammer, and stared straight into the eye sockets of a walking nightmare.

It wore a rough shirt and overalls, and its weapon was a pitchfork. Once, it had been a farmer. But that had been back when it had been alive. It was obviously dead now, the gray-green flesh sloughing off its skeleton, its rotting fingers leaving smudged bits on the pitchfork handle. Black, congealed fluids oozed from pustules and its gurgling roar spat flecks of ichor on Arthas's unprotected face. So shocked was he by the apparition that he barely had time to swing the hammer before it jabbed him with the pitchfork. He got his blessed weapon up just in time, knocking the farming implement from the hands of the walking dead man and bringing the radiant hammer crashing into its torso. The thing went sprawling and did not rise.

But others came to take its place. Arthas heard the *fwhump* and telltale crackling of Jaina's firebolts and then suddenly another smell was added to the sickly miasma—the odor of burning flesh. All around him he heard the sound of weapons clashing, men screaming battle cries, the crackle of flame. One of the corpses stumbled distractedly into the house, its body and clothing ablaze. A few moments later, smoke began to billow from the open door.

That was it—

"Everyone get out, now!" Arthas cried. "Jaina! Burn the farmhouse! Burn it to the ground!"

Despite the horror and panic that was racing through his men—trained soldiers, all of them, but not trained for *this*—his orders were heard. The men turned and ran from the house. Arthas looked over at Jaina. Her mouth was set in a grim line, her eyes were fastened on the house, and fire crackled as comfortably in her small hands as if the flames were innocuous as flowers.

A huge fireball as big as a man exploded into the

house. It burst into flame and Arthas lifted his hand to shield his face from the blast. Several of the animated corpses had been trapped inside. For a moment Arthas stared at the conflagration, unable to tear his eyes from it, then he forced himself to turn his attention to slaughtering those that had not been caught in the pyre. It was the work of a few more moments, and then all the things were dead. Really dead this time.

For a long moment, there was silence except for the crackling sound of flames consuming the burning house. With a slow sigh, the building collapsed. Arthas was glad he could not see the corpses as they were turned to ash.

He caught his breath and turned to Jaina. "What . . ."

She swallowed hard. Her face was black with soot, save where streams of sweat had cleared a path. "They—they are called undead."

"Light preserve us," Falric muttered, his eyes bulging and his face pale. "I'd thought things like this were just stories to scare children."

"No, they're real enough all right. I just—I've never seen one. Never expected to. The, ah . . ." She took a deep breath and calmed herself, getting her voice under control. "The dead sometimes do linger on, if their deaths were traumatic. It's what gave rise to ghost stories."

Her demeanor was calming after the horror. Arthas noticed his men turning to listen to her, eager for some understanding of what the hell had just happened to them. He, too, was more grateful for her book learning than he could ever recall being before.

"The . . . the animation of corpses by powerful individual necromancers is not unheard of. We saw exam-
ples of this in both the First War, when the orcs were
able to animate skeletal remains, and in the Second,
with the appearance of what would come to be known
as death knights," Jaina went on, as if she were reciting
a passage rather than trying to explain a horror that the
mind could barely grasp. "But as I say—I've never seen
any of them before."

"Well, they're really dead now," one of the men said.
Arthas gave him an encouraging smile.

"We have your swords, the Light, and the Lady Jaina's
fire to thank for that," he told them.

"Arthas," Jaina said. "A moment?"

They walked away a little bit while the men began
to clean themselves up and recover from the unnerving
encounter. "I think I know what you're going to say,"
Arthas began. "You were sent here to see if this plague
was magical in nature. And it's starting to look like it is.
Necromantic magic."

Jaina nodded wordlessly. Arthas glanced over at his
men. "We haven't even hit the main villages yet. I have
a feeling we're going to see more of these . . . undead."

Jaina grimaced. "I have a feeling you're right."

As they departed the cluster of farmsteads, Jaina
drew her horse up and paused.

"What are you looking at?" Arthas stepped beside
her. Jaina pointed. He followed her gaze, to see a silo
standing alone on a hill. "The granary?"

She shook her head. "No . . . the land around it." She
dismounted, knelt, and touched the soil, scooping up a

handful of dry dirt and dead grass. She examined it, poking at a small insect, its six legs curled up in death, then sifted the dirt through her fingers as the slight wind took the powdery soil and bore it away in a little puff of dust. "It's as if the land around that granary is . . . dying."

Arthas glanced from her hand to the earth. She was completely right, he realized. Several yards behind him, the grass was green and healthy, the soil presumably still rich and fertile. But beneath his feet and in the area around the granary, it was as dead as if it were the middle of winter. No—that wasn't a good analogy—winter was when the land slept. There was still life in it, dormant, but ready to be awakened when spring came.

There was no life here.

He stared at the granary, sea-green eyes narrowing. "What could have caused this?"

"I'm not sure. It reminds me of what happened with the Dark Portal and the Blasted Lands. When the portal was opened, the demonic energies that sapped the life from Draenor spilled through into Azeroth. And the land around the portal—"

". . . died," Arthas finished. A thought struck him. "Jaina—could the grain *itself* be plagued? Carrying this—this demonic energy?"

Her eyes widened. "Let's hope not." She pointed at the crates the men were hauling out of the granary. "Those crates bear the regional seal of Andorhal, the distribution center for the northern boroughs. If this grain can spread the plague, there's no telling how many villages might be infected."

She almost whispered the words, looking wan and

sick. He stared at her hands, pale with the dust of the dead land. Fear suddenly shot through Arthas and he grabbed her hand. Closing his eyes, he murmured a prayer. Warm light filled him, spread from his hand to hers. Jaina glanced at him, confused, then down at her own hand clasped in his gloved one. Her eyes widened with horror at what she only now realized could have been a very narrow escape.

"Thank you," she whispered.

He gave her a shaky grin, then called out to his men, "Gloves! Every man here wears gloves in this area! No exceptions!"

His captain heard him and nodded, repeating the order. Most of the men were in full armor, and so were already wearing gauntlets. Arthas shook his head, dispelling the worry that still clung to him. He had sensed no sickness in Jaina at all.

Thank the Light.

He pressed her hand to his lips. Jaina, moved, blushed, and smiled softly. "That was foolish of me. I wasn't thinking."

"Lucky for you I was."

"A reversal of our roles," she said wryly, offering him a grin and kiss to take the sting out of the gibe.

Their mission was now clear—to find and destroy any infected granaries they could. Their task was aided the following day when Arthas's troops crossed paths with a pair of quel'dorei priests. They, too, had begun to sense the wrongness that was starting to creep through the land, and had come to offer what healing they could.

They offered more tangible help as well—they were able to direct Arthas toward a warehouse at the far end of the village they were approaching.

"There are some houses up ahead, sir," Falric said.

"Well, then," Arthas said, "let's—

A sudden *boom* took him completely by surprise and his horse reared, spooked. "What the—?" He looked in the direction from which the sounds had come. Small shapes, barely visible, but there was no mistaking the noise. "That's mortar fire. Come on!" He regained control of his horse, yanked its head around, and galloped toward the sound.

Several dwarves looked up as they approached, as surprised to see Arthas as he was to see them. He wheeled to a halt. "What the hell are you shooting at?"

"We're blasting those damned skeletons. This whole flaming village is crawling with them!"

A chill ran up Arthas's spine. He could see them now, the by-now-too-familiar figures of undead shuffling with their unmistakable gait closing the distance. "Fire!" cried the leader of the dwarves, and several skeletons were blown into bones that flew in several directions.

"Well, I could use your help," Arthas said. "We've got a warehouse to destroy at the end of town."

The dwarf turned to him, brown eyes wide. "A warehouse?" he echoed in disbelief. "We're being set upon by tha walkin' dead and ye're fretting about a *warehouse*?"

Arthas had no time for this. "What's in the warehouse is killing these people," he snapped, pointing at the remains of the skeletons. "And when they die . . ."

The dwarf's eyes widened. "Och, I ken ye now. Lads! Move up. We're tae be helping this bonny boy's troops!" He peered up at Arthas. "By the way, who exactly *are* ye, bonny boy?"

Even in the midst of the horror, the offhanded nature of the question made Arthas grin. "Prince Arthas Menethil. And you are?"

The dwarf gaped for just an instant, then quickly recovered. "Dargal, at yer service, Yer Highness."

Arthas did not waste further breath on pleasantries, instead attempting to calm his steed sufficiently to keep up with the now-moving unit. The horse was a charger, bred for battle, and while it had not given him a moment's trouble while he was fighting orcs, it clearly did not like the scent of the undead in its nostrils. He couldn't blame it, but its skittishness made him think of Invincible's great heart and utter lack of fear. He forced the thought away; it was a distraction. He needed to focus, not mourn a beast even more surely dead than the lumbering corpses that were being blown to bits.

Jaina and his men fell in behind him, catching those who weren't quite destroyed by mortar fire and those who stumbled in from the sides and behind him. Energy filled him, flowed through him, as he swung his hammer tirelessly. He was grateful for Dargal's timely arrival. There were so very many of these undead things, he was not sure his troops could handle them all.

The combined units of humans and dwarves made slow but inexorable progression toward the granary. The undead came more thickly as they approached, and by the time they saw silos looming in the distance, there were still more. He leaped from his unhappy mount and charged into their midst, gripping his hammer that glowed with the power of the Light. Now that the initial shock and horror had passed, Arthas found that slaughtering these monstrosities was even better than killing orcs. Maybe the orcs, as Jaina had said, were indeed people—were individuals. These things were nothing more than corpses, jerking around like marionettes, activated by some twisted necromantic puppeteer. They fell like puppets with the strings cut, too, and he smiled fiercely as two undead toppled from the same broad, sweeping blow of the mighty weapon.

These had been dead longer, it seemed; the stench around them was not so ripe, and the bodies were almost more mummified than decaying. Several of them, like those of the first wave, were nothing more than skeletons, bits of clothing or makeshift armor on their bony frames as they rattled toward Arthas and his men.

The acrid odor of burning flesh assaulted his nostrils and he grinned, grateful again for Jaina's presence, and he still fought on. He glanced about, panting. Thus far he had lost not a single man, and Jaina, though pale with exertion, was unharmed.

"Arthas!" Jaina's voice, strong and clear, pierced through the din. Arthas dispatched the carcass that was attempting to decapitate him with a scythe and, in the brief pause that afforded him, glanced at her. She was pointing up ahead, preparatory fire already glowing in her palms and limning her fingers. "Look!"

He turned his gaze to where she was pointing and his eyes narrowed. Up ahead was a cluster of humans—obviously living humans judging by their movements—clad in black. They were gesturing—casting, or pointing—clearly directing the movements of the waves of undead that were being hurled at them now.

"Over there! Target them!" Arthas cried.

The cannons were swung around and his men charged, hacking their way through the undead, their eyes fixed upon the living men in black robes. *We've got you now,* Arthas thought with savage delight.

But as soon as they came under fire directly, the men ceased their activities. The undead they had been controlling suddenly halted, still animated, but no longer directed. They were easy marks for the dwarven mortar fire and Arthas's men, who cut them down with single blows and pushed forward. The magi gathered together and a few of them began casting, their hands fluttering, and Arthas recognized the familiar image of whirling space that indicated they were attempting to create a portal.

"No! Don't let them escape!" he cried, slamming his hammer into the chest of a skeleton, bringing it back around in an arc to cave in the head of a shuffling zombie. From the Light only knew where, the wizards summoned more of the walking dead—skeletons, rotting corpses, and something that was huge and pale and had altogether too many limbs. Across its maggoty-white, glistening torso it sported stitches as wide as Arthas's hand, looking like a disturbed child's idea of a rag doll. It towered above the others, ghastly weapons clutched in its three hands, and fixed Arthas with a single working eye.

Jaina had somehow appeared by his side and cried, "By the Light—that creature looks like it was sewn together from different corpses!"

"Let's study it *after* we kill it, okay?" Arthas shot back, and charged. The abominable experiment approached, uttering guttural noises and swinging an axe as big as Arthas was tall. He leaped out of the way, rolling and springing lightly back up on his feet to charge the monstrosity from behind. Three of his men, two with polearms, did the same, and the hideous thing was quickly dispatched. Even as he battled fiercely, he watched the magi out of the corner of his eye as they turned and rushed through their portal. And then they were gone. The undead they had abandoned all stopped in their tracks, undirected corpses that were quickly destroyed.

"Dammit!" Arthas cried. A hand fell on his arm and he jerked it back, his features softening slightly as he saw it was Jaina. He wasn't in the mood for comforting or explanations, and he had to do something, anything, to compensate for the men in black robes vanishing on him. "Destroy that warehouse, now!"

"Aye, Yer Highness! Let's go lads!" The dwarves surged forward, as eager as he to seize some kind of victory. The cannons rolled over the dead men and the dead soil, until they were within range.

"Fire!" Dargal cried. As one, the cannons roared, and Arthas felt a hot surge of pleasure as the granary crumbled beneath the assault.

"Jaina! Burn what's left of it!" She was already lifting her hands before he started speaking; they did work well together, he thought. An enormous ball of crackling flame sprang from her hands, and the granary and its contents ignited immediately. They waited, watching it burn, so that the fire did not spread. With the land so desiccated, a fire could quickly get out of control.

Arthas ran a hand through his sweat-stiff blond hair. The heat coming off the burning granary was oppressive and he yearned for a breeze. He walked away a short distance and prodded the fallen pale thing with a plated boot. His foot sank into the soft flesh and he wrinkled his nose. Jaina followed him. Upon closer examination, it looked like she had been right—that the thing was indeed cobbled together out of other body parts.

Arthas suppressed a shudder. "The magi—dressed in black . . ."

"I—I'm afraid they were necromancers," Jaina said. "Just like we discussed earlier."

"What noo?" Dargal had come up behind them and was eyeing the fallen abomination with disgust on his face.

"Necromancers. Magi who have dabbled in dark magic—who can raise and control the dead. Obviously, they and whomever they serve are behind this plague." She lifted her serious blue eyes to Arthas. "Demonic energy may be involved, but I think it's clear that we started down the wrong path."

"Necromancers . . . creating a plague to get more raw material for their unholy army," Arthas murmured, glancing back toward the now-smoking ruins of the granary. "I want them. No—no, I want their leader." His gauntleted fists clenched. "I want that bastard who is deliberately slaughtering my people!" He thought about the crates they had seen earlier, and the seal they bore. He lifted his eyes and looked down the road. "And it's a good bet that we'll find him, and the answers we're looking for, in Andorhal."

CHAPTER ELEVEN

Arthas was pushing his men too hard and he knew it, but time was a precious resource and could not be squandered. He felt a tug of guilt when he saw Jaina chewing on some dried meat as they rode. The Light refreshed him when he worked with it; magi drew on different energies, and he knew that Jaina was exhausted after the superb effort she had put forth earlier. But there was no time for rest, not when thousands of lives depended upon their actions.

He'd been sent on a mission to find out what was going on and stop it. The mystery was starting to unravel, but he was beginning to doubt his ability to halt the plague. Nothing was as easy as it had looked at first. Still, Arthas would not give up. *Could* not give up. He had vowed to do whatever it took to stop this, to save his people, and so he would.

They saw and smelled the smoke rising in the sky before they reached the gates of Andorhal. Arthas hoped that if the town had burned, then maybe at least the grain had been destroyed as well, and then felt a twinge of guilt at the callousness of the thought. He buried it in action, kicking his mount hard and riding through the gates, expecting to be assaulted at any moment.

Around them buildings burned, black smoke stinging his eyes and making him cough. Through tear-filled eyes he peered around. There were no villagers, but neither were there any undead. What was—

"I believe you have come looking for me, children," came a smooth voice. The wind shifted, driving the smoke in a different direction, and Arthas could now see a black-robed figure standing only a short distance away. Arthas tensed. This, then, was the leader. The necromancer was smiling now, his face dimly glimpsed in the shadow of his hood, a smirk that Arthas burned to cut off his face. Beside him were two of his pet undead. "You've found me. I am Kel'Thuzad."

Jaina gasped in recognition at the name, and her hand flew to her mouth. Arthas spared her a quick glance, then returned his full attention to the speaker. He gripped his hammer tightly.

"I've come to deliver a warning," said the necromancer. "Leave well enough alone. Your curiosity will be the death of you."

"I thought this magic taint felt familiar!" It was Jaina, her voice shaking with outrage. "You were disgraced, Kel'Thuzad, precisely for your experiments along this line! We told you it would lead to disaster. And you have learned nothing!"

"Lady Jaina Proudmoore," Kel'Thuzad purred.

"Looks like Antonidas's little apprentice is all grown up. And quite the contrary my dear . . . as you can see, I have learned a great deal."

"I saw the rats you experimented with!" Jaina cried. "That was bad enough—but now you—"

"Have furthered my research and perfected it," Kel'Thuzad answered.

"Are you responsible for this plague, necromancer?" Arthas shouted. "Is this cult your doing?"

Kel'Thuzad turned to him, his eyes glittering in the shadow of his cowl. "I ordered the Cult of the Damned to distribute the plagued grain. But the sole credit is not mine."

Before Arthas could speak, Jaina had burst out, "What do you mean?"

"I serve the dreadlord Mal'Ganis. He commands the Scourge that will cleanse this land and establish a paradise of eternal darkness!"

A chill swept over Arthas despite the heat of the surrounding fires at the tone of the man's voice. He did not know what a "dreadlord" was, but the meaning of "Scourge" was clear. "And what exactly is this Scourge meant to cleanse?"

The thin-lipped mouth beneath the white mustache again curled in a cruel smile. "Why, the living, of course. His plan is already in motion. Seek him out at Stratholme if you need further proof."

Arthas had had enough of teasing hints and taunts. He growled, gripped the haft of his hammer, and charged forward. "For the Light!" he cried.

Kel'Thuzad had not moved. He stood his ground,

then, at the last minute, the air around him twisted and puckered, and he was gone. The two creatures who had stood silently at his sides now clamped their arms on Arthas, trying to wrestle him down to the earth, their fetid stench vying with the smell of smoke to choke him. He twisted free, landing a strong, clean blow to the head of one of them. Its skull shattered like a fragile piece of blown glass, brains spattering the earth as it collapsed. The second was as easily dealt with.

"The granary!" he cried, running to his horse and leaping atop it. "Come on!"

The others mounted up and they charged down the main path through the burning village. The granaries loomed up ahead of them. They were untouched by the fire that seemed to be racing through the rest of Andorhal.

Arthas drew his horse up sharply and leaped off it, running as fast as he could toward the buildings. He pulled open the door, hoping desperately to see crates piled high. Grief and rage swept through him as the only thing to meet his gaze were empty chambers— empty save for small, scattered bits of grain and the corpses of rats on the floor. He stared, sick, for a moment, then raced to the next one, and the next, yanking the doors open even though he knew exactly what he would find.

They were all empty. And had been for some time, if the layers of dust on the floor and the spiderwebs in the corners were any indication.

"The shipments have already been sent out," he said brokenly as Jaina stepped up beside him. "We're too late!" He slammed his gauntleted fist into the wooden door and Jaina jumped. "Dammit!"

"Arthas, we did the best we—"

He whirled on her furiously. "I'm going to find him. I'm going to find that undead-loving bastard and rip him limb from limb for this! Let *him* get someone to sew him back together."

He stormed out, shaking. He'd failed. He'd had the man right there and he'd failed. The grain had been sent out, and Light alone knew how many people would die because of that.

Because of *him*.

No. He was not going to let that happen. He would protect his people. He would die to protect them. Arthas clenched his fists.

"North," he said to the men who trailed behind him, unaccustomed to seeing their generally good-natured prince in the grip of such fury. "That's the next place he'll go. Let's exterminate him like the vermin he is."

He rode like a man possessed, galloping north, almost absently slaughtering the shambling wrecks of human beings who attempted to stop him. He was no longer moved by the horror of it all; his mind's eye was filled with the vision of the man manipulating it and the disgusting cult that perpetrated it. The dead would rest soon enough; Arthas had to ensure that no more would be made.

At one point there was a huge cluster of the undead. Rotting heads lifted as one, turning toward Arthas and his men, and they moved toward him. Arthas cried out, "For the Light!", kicked his steed, and charged in among them, swinging his hammer and crying out incoherently, venting his anger and frustration on these, the perfect targets. At one point, there was a lull, and he was able to look around.

Safe and secure away from the field of battle, overseeing everything while risking nothing, stood a tall figure in a fluttering black cloak. As if waiting for them.

Kel'Thuzad.

"There!" he cried. "He's there!"

Jaina and his men followed him, Jaina blasting clear passage with fireball after fireball, and his men hacking the undead that did not fall in the first round of attacks. Arthas felt righteous fury singing in his veins as he drew closer and closer to the necromancer. His hammer rose and fell, seemingly effortlessly, and he didn't even see those he struck down. His eyes were fixed on the man—if you could even call such a monster that—responsible for everything in the first place. Cut off the head, and the beast would die.

Then Arthas was there. A bellow of raw fury exploded from him and he swung, sweeping his brilliantly glowing hammer parallel to the ground, striking Kel'Thuzad at the knees and sending him flying. Others pressed in, swords slicing and hacking, the men venting their grief and outrage on the source, the cause, of the entire disaster.

For all his power and magic, it seemed as though Kel'Thuzad could indeed die like any other man. Both legs were shattered by Arthas's sweeping blow and lay at odd angles. His robes were wet with blood, shiny black against a matte black, and red trickled from his mouth.

He propped himself up on his arms and tried to speak, spitting out blood and teeth. He tried again.

"Naïve . . . fool," he managed, swallowing. "My death will make little difference in the long run . . . for now . . . the scourging of this land . . . begins."

His elbows buckled and, eyes closing, he fell.

The body began to rot immediately. Decomposition that should have taken days happened in mere seconds, the flesh paling, bloating, bursting open. The men gasped and started back, covering their noses and mouths. Some of them turned and vomited from the stench. Arthas stared, horrified and enraptured at the same time, unable to look away. Fluids gushed from the corpse, the flesh taking on a creamy consistency and turning black. The unnatural decomposition slowed and Arthas turned away, gasping for fresh air.

Jaina was deathly pale with dark circles around her wide, shocked eyes. Arthas went to her and turned her away from the disgusting image. "What happened to him?" he asked quietly.

Jaina swallowed, trying to calm herself. Again, she seemed to find strength in her detachment. "It is believed that, ah, if necromancers are not perfectly precise in their magical workings that, um . . . if they are killed they are subject to . . ." Her voice trailed off and suddenly she was a young woman, looking sickened and shocked. "That."

"Come on," Arthas said gently. "Let's get to Hearthglen. They need to be warned—if we're not too late already."

They left the body where it had fallen, not granting

it another glance. Arthas said a silent prayer to the Light that they were not too late. He did not know what he would do if he failed again.

Jaina was exhausted. She knew that Arthas wanted to make the best time possible, and she shared his concern. Lives were at stake. So when he asked her if she could go through the night without stopping, she nodded.

They had been riding hard for four hours when she found herself half off her mount. She was so bone-weary she'd fallen unconscious for a few seconds. Fear shot through her and she grabbed onto the horse's mane wildly, pulling herself back up into the saddle and yanking on the reins so the horse would stop.

She sat there, the reins clutched in her hands, trembling, for several minutes before Arthas realized she'd fallen behind. Dimly she heard him calling a halt. She looked up at him mutely as he cantered up to her.

"Jaina, what's wrong?"

"I . . . I'm sorry Arthas. I know you want to make good time and so do I, but—I was so tired I almost fell off. Could we stop, for just a little while?"

She saw the concern for her and frustration at the situation warring on his face, even in the dim light. "How long do you think you'll need?"

A couple of days, she wanted to say, but instead she said, "Just long enough to eat something and rest for a bit."

He nodded, reaching up to her and helping her off the horse. He bore her to the side of the road, where he set her down gently. Jaina fished in her pack for some cheese with hands that trembled. She expected him to head off and talk to the men, but instead he sat down beside her. Impatience radiated from him like heat from a fire.

She took a bite of cheese and looked up at him as she chewed, analyzing his profile in the starlight. One of the things she most loved about Arthas was how accessible, how human and emotional, he was to her. But now, while he was certainly in the grip of powerful emotions, he felt distant, as if he was a hundred miles away.

Impulsively she reached a hand to touch his face. He started at her touch, as if he had forgotten she was there, then smiled thinly at her. "Done?" he asked.

Jaina thought about the single bite she had eaten. "No," she said, "but . . . Arthas, I'm worried about you. I don't like what this is doing to you."

"Doing to *me*?" he snapped. "What about what it's doing to the villagers? They're dying and then getting turned into corpses, Jaina. I have to stop it, I *have* to!"

"Of course we do, and I'll do everything I can to help; you know that. But . . . I've never seen you hate anything like this."

He laughed, a short harsh bark. "You want me to love necromancers?"

She frowned. "Arthas, don't twist my words like that. You're a paladin. A servant of the Light. You're a healer as much as a warrior, but all I see in you is this desire to wipe out the enemy."

"You're starting to sound like Uther."

Jaina didn't reply. She was so weary, it was difficult to compose her thoughts. She took another bite of cheese, focusing on getting the badly needed nourishment into her body. For some reason it was hard for her to swallow.

"Jaina . . . I just want innocent people to stop dying. That's all. And . . . I admit, I'm upset that I can't seem to make that happen. But once this is over, you'll see. Everything will be fine again. I promise."

He smiled down at her, and for a moment she saw the old Arthas in his handsome face. She smiled back in what she hoped was a reassuring fashion.

"Are you done now?"

Two bites. Jaina put the rest of the cheese away. "Yes, I'm done. Let's keep going."

The sky was turning from black to the ashy gray of dawn when they first heard the gunfire. Arthas's heart sank. He spurred his horse as they wound their way north up the long road that cut through the deceptively pleasant hills. Just outside the gates of Hearthglen, they saw several men and dwarves armed with rifles—all trained on them. Wafted to him on the light breeze, mixed in with the smell of gunpowder, was the incongruously pleasant, slightly sweet scent of baking bread.

"Hold your fire!" Arthas cried as his troops galloped up. He drew rein so hard his mount reared in startlement. "I am Prince Arthas! What's going on? Why are you so armed?"

They lowered their rifles, clearly surprised to see their prince standing right in front of them. "Sir, you won't believe what's been going on."

"Try me," Arthas said.

Arthas was not surprised to hear the initial words—

that the dead had risen and were attacking. What did surprise him was the term "vast army." He glanced at Jaina. She looked utterly exhausted. The little break they had taken last night obviously hadn't been sufficient to restore her.

"Sir," cried one of the scouts, rushing in, "the army— it's heading this way!"

"Dammit," Arthas muttered. This small group of men and dwarves could handle a skirmish well enough, but not a whole damned army of the things. He made a decision. "Jaina, I'll stay here to protect the village. Go as quickly as you can and tell Lord Uther what's happened."

"But—"

"Go, Jaina! Every second counts!"

She nodded. Light bless her and that level head of hers. He spared her a smile of gratitude before she stepped through the portal she created and disappeared.

"Sir," said Falric, and something in the tone of his voice made Arthas turn. "You'd . . . better take a look at this."

Arthas followed the man's gaze and his heart sank. Empty crates . . . bearing the mark of Andorhal . . .

Hoping against hope that he was wrong, Arthas asked in a voice that shook slightly, "What did those crates contain?"

One of the Hearthglen men looked at him, puzzled. "Just a grain shipment from Andorhal. There's no need to worry, milord. It's already been distributed among the villagers. We've had plenty of bread."

That was the smell—not the typical smell of baking bread, but slightly off, slightly too sweet—and then Arthas understood. He staggered, just a little, as the enormity of the situation, the true scope of its horror, burst over him. The grain had been distributed . . . and suddenly there was a vast army of the undead. . . .

"Oh, no," he whispered. They stared at him and he tried again to speak, his voice still shaking. But this time, not with horror, but with fury.

The plague was never meant to simply kill his people. No, no, it was much darker, much more twisted than that. It was meant to turn them into—

Even as the thought formed, the man who had answered Arthas's question about the crate bent over double. Several others followed suit. A strange green glow limned their bodies, pulsing and growing stronger. They clutched their stomachs and fell to the earth, blood erupting from their mouths, saturating their shirts. One of them stretched out a hand to him, imploring for healing. Instead, Arthas, repulsed, recoiled in horror, staring as the man writhed in pain and died in a matter of seconds.

What had he done? The man had begged for healing, but Arthas had not even lifted a hand. But could this even *be* healed, Arthas wondered as he stared at the corpse. Could the Light even—

"Merciful Light!" Falric cried. "The bread—"

Arthas started at the shout, coming out of his guilty trance. Bread—the staff of life—wholesome and nourishing—had now become worse than lethal. Arthas opened his mouth to cry out, to warn his men, but his tongue was like clay in his mouth.

The plague embedded into the grain acted even before the shocked prince could find words.

The dead man's eyes opened. He lurched upright into a seated position.

And *that* was how Kel'Thuzad had created an undead army in so astonishingly short a time.

Insane laughter echoed in his ears—Kel'Thuzad, laughing maniacally, triumphant even in death. Arthas wondered if he was going mad from all he had been forced to bear witness to. The undead clambered to their feet, and their movement galvanized him to action and liberated his tongue.

"Defend yourselves!" Arthas cried, swinging his hammer before the man had a chance to rise. Others were swifter, though, getting to dead feet, turning the weapons that in life they would have used to protect Arthas upon him. The only advantage he had was that the undead were not graceful with their weapons, and most of the shots they fired went wide. Arthas's men, meanwhile, attacked with hard eyes and grim faces, bashing skulls, decapitating, smashing what had been allies just a few moments earlier into submission.

"Prince Arthas, the undead forces have arrived!"

Arthas whirled, his armor spattered with gore, and his eyes widened slightly.

So many. There were so many of them, skeletons who had been long dead, fresh corpses recently turned, more of the pale, maggoty abominations thundering down on them. He could sense the panic. They had fought handfuls, but not this—not an army of the walking dead.

Arthas thrust his hammer into the air. It flared to

glowing life. "Hold your ground!" he cried, his voice no longer weak and shaking or harsh and angry. "We are the chosen of the Light! *We shall not fall!*"

The Light bathing his determined features, he charged.

Jaina was more exhausted than she had admitted even to herself. Drained after the days of fighting with little or no rest, she collapsed after finishing the teleportation spell. She thought she had blacked out for a moment, because the next thing she knew her master was bending over her, lifting her off the floor.

"Jaina—child, what is it?"

"Uther," Jaina managed. "Arthas—Hearthglen—" She reached up and clutched Antonidas's robes. "Necromancers—Kel'Thuzad—raising the dead to fight—"

Antonidas's eyes widened. Jaina gulped and continued. "Arthas and his men are fighting in Hearthglen alone. He needs reinforcements immediately!"

"I think Uther is at the palace," Antonidas said. "I'll send several magi there right away to open portals for as many men as he needs to bring. You did well, my dear. I'm very proud of you. Now, you get some rest."

"No!" Jaina cried. She struggled to her feet, barely able to stand, forcing the exhaustion back by sheer will alone, holding out a shaking hand to keep Antonidas back. "I have to be with him. I'll be all right. Come on!"

Arthas had no idea how long he had been fighting. He swung his hammer almost ceaselessly, his arms shaking from the strain, his lungs burning. It was only the power of the Light, flowing through him with quiet strength and steadiness, that kept him and his men on their feet. The undead seemed to be weakened by its power, although that seemed to be their only weakness. Only a clean kill—Arthas fleetingly wondered if you could call it a "kill" if they were already dead—stopped them in their tracks.

They just kept coming. Wave after wave of them. His subjects—his *people*—turned into these *things*. He lifted his weary arms for another blow when over the din of battle came a voice Arthas knew:

"For Lordaeron! For the king!"

The men rallied at Uther the Lightbringer's impassioned shout, renewing their attacks. Uther had come with a solid core of knights, fresh and battle-hardened. They did not shirk from the undead—Jaina, who despite her bone-weariness had also portaled in with Uther and the knights, had apparently briefed them sufficiently so that precious seconds were not wasted in stunned reaction. The undead fell more quickly now, and each wave was met with fierce and impassioned attacks from hammer, sword, and flame.

Jaina sank down, her legs giving way beneath her, as the last of the walking dead burst into flames, stumbled about, and fell, dead in truth. She reached for a waterskin and drank deeply, shaking, and fished out some dried meat to gnaw on. The fight was over—for the moment. Arthas and Uther had both removed their helms. Sweat matted their hair. She chewed on the meat and watched as Uther looked out over the sea of undead corpses and nodded his satisfaction. Arthas was staring at something, his expression stricken. Jaina followed his gaze and frowned, not understanding. Corpses were everywhere—but Arthas was looking almost as if in a daze at the bloated, fly-riddled body of not one of his soldiers, or even a man, but of a horse.

Uther walked up to his student and clapped Arthas on the shoulder.

"I'm surprised that you kept things together as long as you did, lad." His voice was warm with pride and a smile was on his lips. "If I hadn't arrived just then—"

Arthas whirled. "Look, I did the best I could, Uther!" Both Uther and Jaina blinked at the harsh tone of voice. He was overreacting—Uther wasn't censuring him; he was *praising* him. "If I'd had a legion of knights riding at my back, I would've—"

Uther's eyes narrowed. "Now is not the time to be choking on pride! From what Jaina has told me, what we faced here was only the beginning."

Arthas's sea-green eyes darted to Jaina. He was still smarting from the perceived insult and for the first time since Jaina had met him, she found herself shrinking a little from that piercing gaze.

"Or did you not notice that the undead ranks are bolstered every time one of our warriors falls in battle?" Uther persisted.

"Then we should strike at their leader!" Arthas snapped. "Kel'Thuzad told me who it was and where to find him. It's—something called a dreadlord. His name is Mal'Ganis. And he's in Stratholme. *Stratholme,* Uther. The very place where you were made a paladin of the Light. Doesn't that mean anything to you?"

Uther sighed wearily. "Of course it does, but—"

"I'll go there and kill Mal'Ganis myself if I have to!" Arthas cried. Jaina stopped chewing and stared at him. She had never seen him like this.

"Easy, lad. Brave as you are, you can't hope to defeat a man who commands the dead all by yourself."

"Then feel free to tag along, Uther. I'm going, with or without you." Before either Uther or Jaina could protest further, he'd leaped into the saddle, yanked his steed's head around, and headed south.

Jaina got to her feet, stunned. He'd left without Uther—without his men . . . without *her.* Uther quietly stepped beside her. She shook her fair head.

"He feels personally responsible for all the deaths," she told the older paladin quietly. "He thinks he should have been able to stop this." She looked up at Uther. "Not even the magi of Dalaran—the ones who warned Kel'Thuzad in the first place—suspected what was going on. Arthas couldn't possibly have known."

"He's feeling the weight of the crown for the first time," Uther said quietly. "He's never had to before. This is all part of it, my lady—part of learning how to rule wisely and well. I watched Terenas struggle with the same thing, when he was a young man. Both good men, both wanting to do the right things for their people. To keep them safe and happy." His eyes were thoughtful as he watched Arthas fade into the distance. "But sometimes the only decision is which is the lesser evil.

Sometimes there's no way to fix everything. Arthas is learning that."

"I think I understand but—I can't let him just charge off by himself."

"No, no, once I get the men ready for a long march, we'll be on his trail. You should rest up too."

Jaina shook her head. "No. He shouldn't be alone."

"Lady Proudmoore, if I may," Uther said slowly. "It might be good to let him clear his head. Follow him if you must, but give him a little time to think."

His meaning was obvious. She didn't like it, but she agreed with him. Arthas was distraught. He was feeling angry and impotent and wasn't in a state to be reasoned with. And it was precisely for those reasons she couldn't let him be really alone.

"All right," she said. She mounted up and murmured the spell. She saw Uther grin as he suddenly realized he could no longer see her. "I'll follow him. Come as soon as your men are ready."

She would not follow him too closely. She was invisible, but not silent. Jaina squeezed her horse with her knees into a canter to pursue the bright, brooding prince of Lordaeron.

Arthas kicked the horse hard, angry that it was not going faster, angry that it was not Invincible, angry that he had not figured out what was going on in time to stop it. It was almost overwhelming. His father had had to deal with orcs—creatures from another world, flooding into their own, brutal and violent and bent on conquest. That seemed like child's play to Arthas now. How would his father and the Alliance have fared against this—a plague that not only killed people, but in a sick twist that only a deranged mind would find amusing animated their corpses to fight their own friends and families? Would Terenas have done any better? One moment Arthas thought he would have—that Terenas would have figured out the puzzle in time to stop it, to save the innocent—and the next he rationalized that no one could have done so. Terenas would have been as helpless as he in the face of this horror.

So deep in thought was he that he almost didn't see the man standing in the road, and it was with a sharp, startled yank that he pulled his mount to the side just in time.

Chagrined, worried, and furious at being made so, Arthas snapped, "Fool! What are you doing? I could have run you down!"

The man was unlike any Arthas had ever seen before, and yet he struck the youth as somewhat familiar. Tall, broad-shouldered, he wore a cloak that seemed to be made entirely out of shiny black feathers. His features were shadowed by the cowl, but his eyes were bright as they peered up at Arthas. A beard streaked with gray parted, revealing a white smile.

"You would not have harmed me, and I required your attention," he said, his voice deep and mild. "I spoke to your father, young one. He would not hear me. Now I come to you." He bowed, and Arthas frowned. It seemed to be—mocking. "We must talk."

Arthas snorted. Now he knew why this mysterious, dramatically clad stranger seemed so familiar. He was some kind of mystic—a self-styled prophet, Terenas had said; able to transform into a bird. He'd had the gall to come right into Terenas's own throne room, with some kind of doomsday blather.

"I have no time for this," Arthas growled, gathering up his horse's reins.

"Listen to me, boy." There was no mocking note in the stranger's voice now. His voice cracked like a whip and despite himself Arthas listened. "This land is lost! The shadow has already fallen, and nothing you do will deter it. If you truly wish to save your people, lead them across the sea . . . to the west."

Arthas almost laughed. His father had been right— this was a madman. "Flee? My place is here, and my only course is to defend my people! I will not abandon them to this hideous existence. I will find the one behind this and destroy him. You're a fool if you think otherwise."

"A fool, am I? I suppose I am, to think the son would be wiser than the father." The bright eyes looked troubled. "Your choice is already made. You will not be swayed by one who sees farther than you."

"I've only your word that you see farther. I know what I see, and what I have seen, and that is that my people need me here!"

The prophet smiled now, sadly. "It is not only with our eyes that we see, Prince Arthas. It is with our wisdom and our hearts. I will leave you one final prediction. Just remember, the harder you strive to slay your enemies, the faster you'll deliver your people into their hands."

Arthas opened his mouth for a furious retort, but

at that instant the stranger's shape shifted. The cloak seemed to close about him like a second skin. Wings, jet black and glossy, sprouted from his body even as he shrank to the size of an ordinary raven. With a final harsh caw that sounded frustrated to Arthas, the bird that had been a man leaped into the air, wheeled once, and flew off. He watched it go, vaguely troubled. The man had seemed . . . so certain. . . .

"I'm sorry for concealing myself, Arthas." Jaina's voice coming out of nowhere. Startled, Arthas whipped his head around, trying to find her. She materialized in front of him, looking contrite. "I just wanted to—"

"Don't say it!"

He saw her start in surprise, saw those blue eyes widen, and instantly regretted snapping at her. But she shouldn't have sneaked up on him like this, spied on him like this.

"He came to Antonidas, too," she said after a moment, doggedly continuing with what she had intended to say despite his reprimand. "I—I have to say that I sensed tremendous power about him, Arthas." She rode closer to him, peering up at him. "This plague of the undead—nothing like this has ever been seen before in the history of the world. It's not just another battle, or another war—it's something much bigger and darker than that. And maybe you can't use the same tactics to win. Maybe he's right. Maybe he can see things we can't—maybe he *does* know what will happen."

He turned away from her, grinding his teeth. "Maybe. Or maybe he's some ally of this Mal'Ganis. Or maybe he's just some crazy hermit. Nothing he can say

will make me abandon my homeland, Jaina. I don't care
if that madman has seen the future. Let's go."

They rode in silence for a moment. Then Jaina said
quietly, "Uther will be following. He just needed some
extra time to prepare the men."

Arthas stared straight ahead, still fuming. Jaina tried
again.

"Arthas, you shouldn't—"

"I am sick of people trying to tell me what I should
and shouldn't do!" The words burst from him, startling
himself as much as Jaina. "What's going on here is beyond horrible, Jaina. I can't even find words to describe
it. And I'm doing everything I possibly can. If you're not
going to support my decisions then maybe you don't
belong here." He eyed her, his expression softening.
"You look so tired, Jaina. Maybe . . . maybe you *should*
go back."

She shook her head, staring straight ahead, not meeting his gaze. "You need me here. I can help."

The anger bled away from him, and he reached for
her hand, closing fingers encased in metal over hers
gently. "I shouldn't have spoken to you like that and I'm
sorry. I'm glad you're here. I'm always glad of your company." He bent and kissed her hand. Color came to her
cheeks and she smiled at him, the furrow in her brow
uncreasing.

"Dear Arthas," she said softly. He squeezed her hand
and let it go.

They rode hard the rest of the day, not speaking
much, and halted to make camp as the sun was going
down. Both of them were too weary to hunt for any

fresh meat, so they simply took out some dried meat, apples, and bread. Arthas stared at the loaf in his hand. From the ovens of the palace, baked with grain grown locally—not from Andorhal. It was wholesome fare, nourishing and delicious, smelling yeasty and good and not sickly sweet. A simple, basic food, something that everyone, *anyone*, should be able to eat without fear.

His throat suddenly closed up and he placed the bread down, unable to eat a bite, and he put his head in his hands. For a moment he felt overwhelmed, as if a tidal wave of despair and helplessness washed over him. Then Jaina was there, kneeling beside him, resting her head on his shoulder while he struggled to compose himself. She said nothing; she did not need to, her simple, supportive presence was all he needed. Then with a deep sigh he turned to her and took her in his arms.

She responded, kissing him deeply, needing comfort and reassurance from him as much as he did from her. Arthas ran his hands through her silky golden hair and breathed her scent. And for a few brief hours that night, they permitted themselves to be lost in each other, pushing away thoughts of death and horror and plagued grain and prophets and choices, their world narrow and tender and comprised only of the two of them.

CHAPTER TWELVE

Still half asleep, Jaina awoke and reached out a hand for Arthas. He was not there. Blinking, she sat up. He was already awake and dressed, cooking some sort of hot cereal for them. He smiled when he saw her, but it didn't reach his eyes. Jaina tentatively returned the smile and reached for her robe, slipping it on and combing her hair with her fingers.

"There's something I learned," Arthas said without preamble. "Last night—I didn't want to mention it. But you need to know." His voice was flat and Jaina felt something inside her quail. At least he wasn't screaming, like he had been yesterday—but somehow this was worse. He ladled up a bowl of steaming grains and brought it over to her. She spooned it automatically into her mouth as he continued to speak.

"This plague—the undead—" He took a deep breath. "We knew that the grain was plagued. We knew that it killed people. But it's worse than that, Jaina. It doesn't just kill them."

The words seemed to catch in his throat. Jaina sat

there for a moment, as understanding dawned. She thought she'd throw up the grains she'd just eaten. Her breath seemed to come with difficulty.

"It . . . turns them, somehow. It makes them into the undead . . . doesn't it?" *Please tell me I'm wrong, Arthas.*

He didn't. Instead he nodded his golden head. "That's why there were so many of them so quickly. The grain reached Hearthglen a short time ago—long enough to be milled into flour and baked into bread."

Jaina stared at him. The implications of this—she couldn't even wrap her mind around them.

"That's why I rushed off yesterday. I knew I couldn't take Mal'Ganis by myself, but—Jaina, I just couldn't sit around and—and mend armor and make camp, you know?" She nodded dumbly. She did understand, now. "And that prophet—I don't care how powerful you think he is. I can't just leave and let all of Lordaeron turn into this—this—Mal'Ganis, whatever, whomever he is, has got to be stopped. We've got to find every last crate of this plagued grain and destroy it."

The telling of this shocking information seemed to agitate Arthas again, and he got to his feet, pacing. "Where the hell is Uther?" he said. "He had all night to ride here."

Jaina placed aside the half-eaten cereal, got to her feet, and finished dressing. Her mind was working a thousand miles a minute, trying to comprehend the situation fully and dispassionately, trying to think of some way to combat it. Wordlessly they broke camp and headed for Stratholme.

The ashy grayness of dawn only darkened as the

clouds closed off the sun. Rain began to fall, chilly and stinging. Both Arthas and Jaina flipped the hoods of their cloaks up, but that did little to keep Jaina dry, and she was shivering by the time they reached the gates of the great city. Almost as they drew rein, Jaina heard sounds behind her and turned to see Uther and his men coming up the dirt road that was now almost pure mud. By this point, Arthas had worked himself up again, and he turned to Uther with a bitter grin.

"Glad you could make it, Uther," he snapped.

Uther was a patient man, but he lost his temper now. Arthas and Jaina were not the only ones under strain. "Watch your tone with me, boy! You may be the prince, but I'm still your superior as a paladin!"

"As if I could forget," Arthas retorted. He moved quickly to the top of a rise, so he could look over the walls and into the city. He didn't know what he was looking for. Signs of life, of normalcy, perhaps. Signs that they'd gotten here in time. Anything to give him hope that he could still somehow do something. "Listen, Uther, there's something about the plague you should know. The grain—"

The wind shifted as he spoke, and the scent that reached his nostrils was not an unpleasant one. Nonetheless, Arthas felt as though he'd been punched in the gut. The smell, the strange, unique scent of bread baked with the tainted grain, unmistakable on the air damp with rain.

Light, no. Already milled, already baked, already—

The blood drained from Arthas's face. His eyes widened, staring starkly in horrified comprehension.

"We're too late. We're too damned late! The grain—these people—" He tried again. "These people have all been infected."

"Arthas—" Jaina began in a low voice.

"They may look fine now, but it's just a matter of time before they turn into the undead!"

"What?" cried Uther. "Lad, have you gone insane?"

"No," Jaina said. "He's right. If they've eaten the grain, they're infected—and if they're infected . . . they'll turn." She was thinking furiously. There had to be something they could do. Antonidas once told her, if a thing is magical in origin, then magic can combat it. If they just had a little time to think, if they could calm down and react from logic and not emotion, perhaps a cure could—

"This entire city must be purged."

Arthas's statement was blunt and brutal. Jaina blinked. Surely he hadn't meant that.

"How can you even consider that?" Uther cried, marching up to his former student. "There's got to be some other way. This isn't a blighted apple crop, this is a city full of human beings!"

"Damn it, Uther! We have to do it!" Arthas shoved his face within an inch of Uther's, and for a dreadful moment Jaina was convinced they'd draw weapons on each other.

"Arthas, no! We can't do that!" The words left her lips before she could stop them. He whirled on her, his sea-colored eyes now stormy with anger and hurt and despair. She realized immediately that he truly thought this was the only option—the only way to save other, uncorrupted lives was to sacrifice these cursed ones, these that could no longer be salvaged. His face softened slightly as she rushed on, trying to get the words out before he could interrupt her. "Listen to me. We don't know how many people are infected. Some of them might not have eaten any of the grain at all—others might not have eaten a lethal dose. We don't even know what a lethal dose *is* yet. We know so little—we can't just slaughter them like animals out of our own fear!"

It was the wrong thing to say, and she watched as Arthas's face closed up. "I'm trying to protect the innocent, Jaina. That's what I swore to do."

"They *are* innocent—they're victims! They didn't ask for this! Arthas, there are children in there. We don't know if it affects them. There's too much unknown for such a—a drastic solution."

"What of those who *are* infected?" he asked with a sudden, frightening quiet. "They'll kill those children, Jaina. They'll try to kill us . . . and spread out from here and keep killing. They're going to die regardless, and when they rise, they'll do things that in life they would never, ever have wanted to do. What would you choose, Jaina?"

She hadn't expected that. She looked from Arthas to Uther, then back again. "I—I don't know."

"Yes, you do." He was right, and despairingly, she knew it. "Wouldn't you rather die now than die from this plague? Die a clean death as a thinking, living human being rather than be raised as an undead to attack everyone, everything you loved in life?"

Her face crumpled. "I . . . that would be my personal

choice, yes. But we can't make that choice for them. Don't you see?"

He shook his head. "No. I don't see. We need to purge this city before any of them have a chance to escape and spread the contagion. Before any of them turn. It's a kindness and it's the only solution to stop this plague right here, right now, dead in its tracks. And that is exactly what I intend to do."

Tears of anguish burned in Jaina's eyes.

"Arthas—give me a little time. Just a day or two. I can teleport back to Antonidas and we can call an emergency meeting. Maybe we can figure out some way to—"

"We don't *have* a day or two!" The words exploded from Arthas. "Jaina, this affects people within hours. Maybe minutes. I—I saw it at Hearthglen. There's no time for deliberation or discussion. We have to act. Now. Or it will be too late." He turned to Uther, dismissing Jaina.

"As your future king, I *order* you to purge this city!"

"You're not my king yet, *boy*! Nor would I obey that command even if you were!"

The silence that fell crackled with tension.

Arthas . . . beloved, best friend . . . please don't do this.

"Then I must consider this an act of treason." Arthas's voice was cold, clipped. If he had struck her across the face, Jaina could not have been more shocked.

"Treason?" Uther spluttered. "Have you lost your mind, Arthas?"

"Have I? Lord Uther, by my right of succession and the sovereignty of my crown, I hereby relieve you of your command and suspend your paladins from service."

"Arthas!" Jaina yelped, her tongue freed in her shock. "You can't just—"

He whirled on her furiously and spat, "It's done!"

She stared at him. He turned to look at his men, who had stood by silent and wary as the argument had progressed. "Those of you who have the will to save this land, follow me! The rest of you . . . get out of my sight!"

Jaina felt sick and dizzy. He was really going to do this. He was going to march into Stratholme and cut down every living man, woman, and child within its walls. She swayed and clutched the reins of her horse. It lowered its head and whickered at her, blowing warm breath from its soft muzzle across her cheek. She was fiercely envious of its ignorance.

She wondered if Uther would attack his former pupil. But he was bound by an oath to serve his prince, even if he had been relieved of command. She saw the tendons on his neck stand out like cords, could almost hear him gritting his teeth. But he did not attack his liege.

Loyalty, however, did not still his tongue. "You've just crossed a terrible threshold, Arthas."

Arthas looked at him a moment longer, then shrugged. He turned to Jaina, his eyes searching hers, and for a moment—just a moment—he looked like himself, earnest, young, a little scared.

"Jaina?"

The single word was so much more. It was both question and plea. Even as she stared at him, frozen like the bird before the snake, he reached out a gauntleted hand to her. She stared at it for a moment, thinking of all the times that hand had clasped hers warmly, had caressed

her, had been laid on the wounded and glowed with healing light.

She could not take that hand.

"I'm sorry, Arthas. I can't watch you do this."

There was no mask on his face now, no merciful coldness to shutter his pain away from her. Shocked disbelief radiated from him. She couldn't bear to look at him anymore. Gulping, her eyes filled with tears, Jaina turned away to find Uther regarding her with compassion and approval. He held out his hand to help her mount and she was grateful for his steadiness and composure. Jaina was shaking, badly, and clung to her horse as Uther mounted and, holding her horse's reins, led them both away from the greatest horror they had yet encountered in this whole dreadful ordeal.

"Jaina?" Arthas's voice followed her.

She closed her eyes, tears slipping from beneath closed lids. "I'm sorry," she whispered again. "I'm so sorry."

"Jaina? . . . *Jaina!*"

She had turned her back on him.

He couldn't believe it. For a long moment he simply stared, dumbfounded, at her retreating figure. How could she abandon him like this? She knew him. She knew him better than anyone else in the world had known him, better maybe than he knew himself. She had always understood him. His mind suddenly went back to the night they had become lovers, bathed first in the orange glow of the wicker man's fire, and later the cool blue of moonlight. He'd held her to him, pleading.

Don't deny me, Jaina. Don't ever deny me. Please.

I never would, Arthas. Never.

Oh yes, powerful words, whispered in a powerful moment, but now, now when it really counted, she had done exactly that—denied him and betrayed him. Dammit, she'd even agreed that if it were her, she'd want to be killed outright before the plague came and twisted her into a violation of everything good and true and natural. She'd left him, alone. If she'd stabbed him in the gut, he didn't think he could hurt worse.

The thought came, brief and bright and sharp: Was she right?

No. No, she couldn't be. Because if she was right, then he was about to become a mass murderer, and he knew that wasn't who he was. He knew it.

He shook off the dazed horror, licking lips suddenly gone dry, and took a deep breath. Some of the men had departed with Uther. A lot of them. Too many, truth be told. Could he even take this city with this few?

"Sir, if I may," Falric said, "I'm . . . well . . . I would rather be hacked into a thousand pieces than turn into one of them undead."

There were murmurs of agreement and Arthas's heart lifted. He grasped his hammer. "There is no pleasure in what we do here," he said, "only grim necessity. Only the need to halt the plague, here and now, with the fewest casualties possible. Those within these walls are already dead. We know it, even if they do not, and we must kill them quickly and cleanly before the plague does it for us." He looked at each of them in turn, these men who had not shirked their duty. "They must be slain, and their homes destroyed, lest the dwellings become shelter for those whom we are too late to save." The men nodded their understanding, gripping their own weapons. "This is not a great and glorious battle. It is going to be ugly and painful, and I regret its necessity with my whole heart. But it is with my whole heart that I know we must do this."

He lifted his hammer. "For the Light!" he cried, and in answer his men roared and lifted their weapons. He turned to the gate, took a deep breath, and charged in.

The ones that had risen were easy. They were the enemy; human no longer, but vile caricatures of what they had once been in life, and smashing their skulls or slicing their heads off was no more of a hardship than putting down a rabid beast. The others—

They looked up at the armed men, at their prince, in first confusion and then in terror. At first, most of them didn't even reach for weapons; they knew the tabards, knew that the men who had come to kill them were supposed to be protecting them. They simply could not grasp why they were dying. Pain clenched Arthas's heart at the first one he struck down—a youth, barely out of puberty, who gazed up at him with incomprehension in his brown eyes and got out the words, "My lord, why are—" before Arthas cried out, as much in anguish at what he was being forced to do as anything else, and caved the boy's chest in with a hammer that he absently realized was no longer radiant with the Light. Perhaps the Light, too, grieved the dire necessity of its actions. A sob ripped through him and he bit it back, willed it back, and turned to the boy's mother.

He thought it would get easier. It didn't. It just got worse. Arthas refused to yield. The men looked to him for an example; if he wavered, they would too, and then Mal'Ganis would triumph. So he kept his helm on so they would not see his face, and himself lit the torches that burned down the buildings full of screaming people locked inside, and refused to let the horrible sights and sounds slow him.

It was a relief when some of the citizens of Stratholme began to fight back. Then the self-defense instinct kicked in. They still did not have a chance against professional soldiers and a trained paladin. But it mitigated that horrible sensation of—well, as Jaina had said, slaughtering them like farm animals.

"I've been waiting for you, young prince."

The voice was deep and shivered in his mind as well as his ears, resonant and . . . there was no other word for it . . . evil. A dreadlord, Kel'Thuzad had said. A dark name for a dark being.

"I am Mal'Ganis."

Something like joy shot through Arthas. He was vindicated. Mal'Ganis *was* here, he *was* behind the plague, and even as Arthas's men, who also heard the voice, turned and sought the source, the doors of a house where villagers had been hiding was flung open and walking corpses hastened out, their bodies limned by a green, sickly glow.

"As you can see, your people are now mine. I will now turn this city household by household, until the flame of life has been snuffed out . . . forever." Mal'Ganis laughed. The sound was unsettling, deep and raw and dark.

"I won't allow it, Mal'Ganis!" Arthas cried. His heart swelled with the rightness of what he was doing. "Better that these people die by my hand than serve as your slaves in death!"

More laughter, and then the disturbing presence was gone as swiftly as it had come, and Arthas was busy battling for his very life as a throng of undead, three deep, charged him.

How long it took to slaughter every living—and dead—person in the city, Arthas would never be able to tell. But at last it was done. He was exhausted, shaking, nauseated by the smell of blood, smoke, and the sick, sweet scent of poisoned bread, hanging in the air even though the bakery itself was a burning building. Blood and ichor covered his once-bright armor. But he was not done. He waited for what he knew would come, and sure enough, a mere moment later, his enemy arrived, descending from the air to land on the roof of one of the few buildings still intact.

Arthas staggered. The creature was enormous. His skin was blue-gray, like animated stone. Horns curved forward and up from his bald skull, and two mighty wings like those of bats stretched out behind him like living shadows. His legs, encased in metal adorned with spikes and decorated with disturbing images of bones and skulls, curved backward and ended in hooves, and the very light of his glowing green eyes revealed sharp teeth bared in an arrogant sneer.

He stared up at the creature, rapt with horror, disbelief warring with the evidence before his eyes. He had heard tales; had seen pictures in old books, both

in the library at home and in the Dalaran archives. But
beholding this monstrous thing, towering over him,
the sky behind him crimson and black with fire and
smoke—

A dreadlord was a demon. A thing out of myth. It
couldn't be real—and yet it was here, standing before
him in all its dreadful glory.

Dreadlord.

Fear threatened to overwhelm Arthas, and he knew
if he let it it would cripple him. He would die at the hand
of this monster—die without even a fight. And so with
sheer will, he drowned out the mindless terror with
another, better emotion. Hatred. Righteous fury. He
thought of those who had fallen beneath his hammer,
the living and the dead, the ravening ghouls and the terrified women and children who didn't understand that
he was trying to save their souls. Their faces bolstered
him; they could not—would not—have died for nothing. Somehow Arthas found the courage to meet the
demon stare for stare, clutching his hammer.

"We're going to finish this right now, Mal'Ganis,"
he shouted. His voice was strong and firm. "Just you
and me."

The dreadlord threw back his head and laughed.
"Brave words," he rumbled. "Unfortunately for you, it
won't end here." Mal'Ganis grinned, black lips pulling
back from sharp, pointed teeth. "Your journey has just
begun, young prince."

He swept an arm out, indicating Arthas's men, long,
sharp claws glittering in the light of the flames that
still burned and consumed the great city. "Gather your

forces and meet me in the arctic land of Northrend. It is there that your true destiny will unfold."

"My true destiny?" Arthas's voice cracked with anger and confusion. "What do you—" The words died in his throat as the air around Mal'Ganis began to shimmer and whirl in a familiar pattern.

"No!" Arthas shrieked. He surged forward, blindly, recklessly, and would have been cut down in a heartbeat had not the teleportation spell been completed. Arthas cried out incoherently, swinging his faintly glowing hammer at empty air. "I'll hunt you down to the ends of the earth if I have to! Do you hear me? *To the ends of the earth!*"

Manic, raging, screaming, he swung his hammer wildly at nothing until sheer exhaustion alone forced him to lower it. He propped it up and leaned on it, sweating, shaking with raw sobs of frustration and anger.

To the ends of the earth.

CHAPTER THIRTEEN

Three days later, Lady Jaina Proudmoore walked the streets of what had once been a proud city, the glory of northern Lordacron. Now, it was the stuff of nightmares.

The stench was almost unbearable. She lifted a handkerchief, liberally scented with peacebloom essence, to her face in a partially successful attempt to filter out the worst of it. Fires that ought to have consumed themselves, or have abated at least slightly from lack of fuel, continued to rage at their full height, telling Jaina that some dark magic was afoot. Combined with the acrid smell of smoke that stung her eyes and throat was the reek of putrefaction.

They lay as they had fallen, most of them unarmed. Tears welled in Jaina's eyes and slipped down her cheeks as she moved as if in a trance, carefully stepping over the bloated bodies. A soft whimper of pain escaped as she saw that Arthas and his men, in their misguided mercy, had not even spared the children.

Would these bodies, lying still and stiff in death,

have risen to attack her if Arthas had not slain them? Perhaps. Many of them, certainly; the grain *had* indeed been distributed and consumed. But every single one? She would never know, nor would he.

"Jaina—I ask you again, come with me." His voice was intense, but it was clear his mind was a thousand leagues away. *"He escaped me. I saved the city's inhabitants from becoming his slaves, but—at the last minute he got away. He's in Northrend. Come with me."*

Jaina closed her eyes. She did not want to remember that conversation of a day and a half ago. She did not want to remember how he had looked, cold and angry and distant, fixated on killing this dreadlord—Light, a demon—at the expense of everything else.

She stumbled across a body and her eyes snapped open again to the horror that the man she had loved— still did love, despite everything, how she could still love him after this she did not know, but Light save her, she did—

"Arthas—it's a trap. He's a demon lord. If he was powerful enough to elude you in St-Stratholme, he will certainly defeat you in his own territory, where he is strongest. Don't go . . . please . . ."

She had wanted to throw herself into his arms, physically keep him there beside her. He couldn't go to Northrend. He would be going to his death. And although he had dealt out so much to others, Jaina found she could not wish for his.

"So much death," she murmured. "I can't believe Arthas could've done this." And yet she knew he had. A whole city . . .

"Jaina? Jaina Proudmoore!"

Jaina started violently, snapped out of her sickened trance by the sound of the familiar voice. Uther. A strange feeling of relief swept over her as she turned in the direction of the hail. Uther had always intimidated her slightly; he was so large and powerful and . . . well . . . so deeply entrenched in the Light. She recalled with an incongruously guilty flush how, when she and Arthas were younger, they used to make fun of Uther's piety, which to them verged on the pompous and sanctimonious, behind the knight's back. He was a fairly easy target. But three excruciating days ago, she and Uther had both stood against Arthas.

"You swore you would never deny me, Jaina," Arthas accused, his voice sharp as an icy knife blade. *"But when I most needed your support, your understanding, you turned against me."*

"I—you—Arthas, we didn't know enough to—"

"And now, you refuse to aid me. I'm going to Northrend, Jaina. I would have you with me. To help me stop this evil. Won't you come?"

Jaina winced. Uther noticed, but said nothing. Clad in full plate armor despite the overwhelming heat of the unnaturally blazing fires, he strode swiftly toward her. His stature and presence was now a picture of strength and solidity rather than intimidation to her. He did not embrace her, but did grasp her arms reassuringly.

"I thought I might find you here. Where has he gone, girl? Where has Arthas taken the fleet?"

Jaina's eyes widened. "The fleet?"

Uther grunted an affirmation. "He's commandeered

the entire Lordaeron fleet and taken off with them. Sent only the briefest message to his own father. We don't know why they obeyed without direct orders from their commanders."

Jaina gave him a small, sad smile. "Because he's their prince. He's Arthas. They love him. They didn't know about . . . this."

A flicker of pain crossed Uther's rugged features and he nodded. "Aye," he said softly. "He's always been good to the men who serve him. They can tell that he genuinely cares about them, and they'll serve him with their lives."

Regret laced the words. They were true, insofar as they went, and once Arthas had deserved such undying devotion.

"And now you refuse to aid me. . . ."

Uther shook her gently, bringing her back to the present. "Do you know where he might have taken them, child?"

Jaina took a deep breath. "He came to me before he left. I pleaded with him not to go. I told him it sounded like a trap—"

"Where?" Uther was relentless.

"Northrend. He's gone to Northrend to hunt Mal'Ganis—the demon lord who is responsible for the plague. He couldn't defeat him . . . here."

"A demon lord? Damn that boy!" The outburst startled Jaina. "I've got to inform Terenas."

"I tried to stop him," Jaina repeated. "Then . . . and when he . . ." She gestured helplessly at the almost inconceivable number of dead that kept them silent company.

She wondered for the thousandth time if she could have stopped it—if she had found the right words, touched Arthas the right way, if he would have been swayed. "But I failed."

I failed you, Arthas. I failed these people—I failed myself.

Uther's heavy, gauntleted hand dropped on her slim shoulder. "Don't be too hard on yourself, girl."

She laughed humorlessly. "Is it that obvious?"

"Anyone with a heart would wonder the same. I know I do." She glanced up at him, startled at the admission.

"You do?" Jaina asked.

He nodded, his eyes bloodshot from exhaustion, and there was a pain in those depths that struck her to the core. "I could not fight him. He is still my prince. But I wonder . . . could I have stood in his path? Said something else, done something else?" Uther sighed and shook his head. "Perhaps. Perhaps not. But that moment is in the past and my choices cannot be undone. You and I must both look to the future now. Jaina Proudmoore, you had nothing to do with this . . . slaughter. Thank you for telling me where he has gone."

She lowered her head. "I feel like I've betrayed him again."

"Jaina, you may have saved him—and all the men who are going with him in ignorance of what he's become."

Startled at his choice of words, she looked up sharply. "What he's become? He's still Arthas, Uther!"

Uther's eyes looked haunted. "Aye, he is. But he made a dreadful choice—and one with repercussions we've yet to see played out. I don't know that he can come back from this." Uther turned and eyed the dead. "We know the dead can be raised to unlife. That demons truly exist. Now I wonder if there are such things as ghosts, too. If there are, our prince will be ten thick in them." He bowed to her. "Come away from this place, lady."

She shook her head. "No, not yet. I'm not ready."

He searched her eyes, then nodded. "As you will. Light be with you, Lady Jaina Proudmoore."

"And you, Uther the Lightbringer." She gave him the best smile she could muster and watched as he strode off. Arthas would no doubt see this as yet another betrayal, but if it saved his life—then she could live with that.

The smell was starting to become more than even her stubborn will would permit her to handle. She paused for a last look. Part of her wondered why she had come here; the other part knew. She had come to brand these images into her brain, to understand the depth of what had happened. She must never, ever forget. Whether or not Arthas was past reaching, she didn't know, but what happened here would need to never become a footnote in the history books.

A raven wheeled down slowly. She wanted to rush forward and shoo it away, to try to protect the poor, battered corpses, but it was only doing what its nature told it to do. It did not have a conscience to tell it that what it was doing was offensive to human sensibilities. She looked at the raven for a moment, and then her eyes widened.

It began to shift, change, grow, and in an instant, where a carrion bird had once perched stood a man. She gasped in recognition—this same prophet she had seen twice before.

"You!"

He inclined his head, and gave her an odd smile that told her without words, *I recognize you, too.* This was the third time she had seen him—once when he was speaking with Antonidas, and once with Arthas. She had been invisible on both occasions—and clearly, her invisibility spell had not fooled him for a moment, either time.

"The dead in this land might lie still for the time being, but don't be fooled. Your prince will find only death in the cold north."

His blunt words made her flinch slightly. "Arthas is only doing what he believes is right." The words were true, and she knew it. Whatever his failings were, he had been utterly sincere in his belief that the purging of Stratholme was the only option.

The prophet's gaze softened. "Commendable as that may be," he said, "his passions will be his undoing. It falls to you now, young sorceress."

"What? Me?"

"Antonidas has dismissed me. Terenas and Arthas as well. Both rulers of men and masters of magic have turned their faces from true understanding. But I think you may not."

The aura of power around him was palpable. Jaina could almost see it, swirling about him, heady and strong. He stepped closer to her and placed his hand on her shoulder. She gazed up into his eyes, confused.

"You must lead your people west to the ancient lands of Kalimdor. Only there can you combat the shadow and save this world from the flame."

Staring into those eyes, Jaina knew he was right.

There was no control, no compelling—just a knowing, deep and certain and down to her bones.

"I—" Swallowing hard, she took one last look at the horrors wrought by the man she loved and still did love, and nodded.

"I will do as you say."

And leave my Arthas to the destiny he has chosen. There is no other way.

"It will take time, to gather them all. To make them believe me."

"I do not know that you have that much time left. So much of it has already been squandered."

Jaina lifted her chin. "I cannot go without trying. If you know so much about me, then surely you must know that."

The raven prophet seemed to relax marginally and smiled at her, squeezing her shoulder. "Do what you feel you must, but do not tarry overlong. The hourglass empties swiftly, and delay could be deadly."

She nodded, too overcome to speak. So many to talk to—Antonidas's chief among them. If he would listen to anyone, she thought, it would be her. She would bear witness for these dead—for the folly of not retreating to Kalimdor while the living yet walked here.

The prophet's form dwindled and shifted, becoming once again that of the large black bird, and he flew off with a rustle of wings. And somehow as it brushed her face, the wind from those black wings did not smell of carrion, or smoke, or death. It smelled clean and fresh.

It smelled of hope.

CHAPTER FOURTEEN

Northrend was the name of the land, Daggercap Bay the site where the Lordaeron fleet made harbor. The water, deep and choppy with an unforgiving wind, was a cold blue-gray. Sheer cliffs were dotted with tenacious pine trees soaring upward, providing a natural defense of the small, flat area where Arthas and his men would make camp. A waterfall tumbled down, crashing in a billow of spray from a great height. It was all in all more pleasant a place than he had expected, at least for the moment; certainly not the obvious home for a demon lord.

Arthas leaped from the boat and slogged onto the shore, his eyes darting about, absorbing everything. The wind, keening like a lost child, stirred his long blond hair, caressing it with cold fingers. Beside him, one of the captains of the ships he had commandeered without consulting his father shivered and clapped his hands together, trying to warm them.

"This is a Light-forsaken land, isn't it? You can barely even see the sun! This howling wind cuts to the bone and you're not even shaking."

Vaguely surprised, Arthas realized that the man was right. He felt the cold—felt it knifing into him—but he did not tremble.

"Milord, are you all right?"

"Captain, are all my forces accounted for?" Arthas didn't bother to answer the question. It was a foolish one. Of course he wasn't all right. He had been forced to slaughter the populace of an entire city in order to stop a worse atrocity. Jaina and Uther had both turned their backs on him. And a demon lord was awaiting his arrival.

"Nearly. There are only a few ships that—"

"Very well. Our first priority is to set up a base camp with proper defenses. There's no telling what's waiting for us out there in the shadows." There, that would shut the man up and give him something to do. Arthas lent his assistance, working as hard as the men he commanded to erect basic shelter. He missed Jaina's handiness with flames as they lit fires against the encroaching darkness and cold. Hell, he missed Jaina. But he would learn not to. She failed him when he most needed her, and he would not hold such people in his heart any longer. It needed to be strong, not soft; determined, not aching. There was no place in it for weakness, if he would defeat Mal'Ganis. There was no place in it for warmth.

The night passed without incident. Arthas stayed awake in his tent until the small hours of the morning, perusing what incomplete maps he had been able to find. When at last he fell asleep, he dreamed, and it was both joyous and nightmarish. He was again a youth, with everything in the world to look forward to, riding the glorious white horse he so loved. Again, they were one, perfectly paired, and nothing would stop them. And even as he dreamed, Arthas felt the horror descend upon him as he urged Invincible to make the fatal jump. The anguish, not in the slightest abated by the fact that this was a mere dream and he knew it as such, ripped through him yet again. And again, he drew his sword, and stabbed his devoted friend through his heart.

But this time . . . this time he realized that he was holding a completely different sword than the simple, basic weapon he had held at that dreadful moment. This time the sword was huge, two handed, beautifully fashioned. Runes glowed along its length. Cool blue mist wafted from it, cold as the snow in which Invincible lay. And when he withdrew the sword, Arthas did not find himself staring at a slain beast. Instead Invincible whickered and leaped to his feet, completely healed, somehow stronger than before. He seemed to glow now, his coat radiant rather than merely white, and Arthas bolted upright from where he had fallen asleep over the maps, tears in his eyes and a sob of joy on his lips. Surely, this was an omen.

The morning dawned frigid and gray, and he was up before first light, eager to begin combing the land for signs of the dreadlord. He was here; Arthas knew it.

But that first day, they found nothing more than a few pockets of undead. As the days passed, with more and more territory charted, Arthas's spirits started to sink.

Intellectually, he realized that Northrend was a vast continent, barely explored. Mal'Ganis was a dreadlord, yes, and the clusters of undead they had found thus far would likely be a good indicator of his presence. But not the only one. He could be anywhere—or nowhere. This whole revelation that he would be in Northrend could have been nothing more than an elaborate trick to get Arthas out of his way, so that the demon could move somewhere else entirely and—

No. That way lay madness. The dreadlord was arrogant, certain he would eventually best the human prince. Arthas had to believe he was here. Had to. Of course, that could also mean that Jaina had been right. That Mal'Ganis was indeed here, and had laid a trap for him. None of these thoughts was pleasant, and the more Arthas chewed on them, the more agitated he became.

It was well into the second week of searching before Arthas found anything to offer him hope. They had marched off in a different direction, after the initial pair of scouts returned bearing news of large clusters of undead. They found the reported undead—lying in pieces on the frozen earth. Before Arthas could even form a thought, he and his men had come under fire.

"Take cover!" Arthas cried, and they dove for whatever they could find—trees, rocks, even snowbanks. Almost as soon as it had started, the attack ceased and a shout rang out.

"Bloody hell! Ye're not undead! Ye're all alive!"

It was a voice that Arthas recognized and had never thought to encounter in this desolate land. Only one person he knew could swear so enthusiastically, and for a moment, he forgot why he was here, what he was searching for, and felt only delight and fond remembrance of a time long past.

"Muradin?" Arthas cried in shock and pleasure. "Muradin Bronzebeard, is that you?"

The stout dwarf stepped out from behind the row of weapons, peering cautiously. The scowl on his face was replaced by an enormous grin. "Arthas, lad! I never imagined that ye'd be th' one tae come tae our rescue!"

He strode forward, his face even more hidden by the bushy beard Arthas remembered from his youth, if such a thing was possible, his eyes more lined but now twinkling with pleasure. He spread his arms, marched up to Arthas, and embraced the prince about the waist. Arthas laughed—Light, it had been so long since he had laughed—and hugged his old friend and trainer back. As they drew apart, the meaning of Muradin's words registered on Arthas.

"Rescue? Muradin, I didn't even know you were here. I came to—" He snapped his mouth closed on the words. He didn't know how Muradin would react yet, and so simply smiled at the dwarf. "That can all wait," he said instead. "Come, my old friend. We've got a base camp set up not too far from here. Looks like you and your men could use a hot meal."

"If ye have ale as well, that'd be a yes from me," Muradin grinned.

There was a celebratory air as Arthas, Muradin, his second in command Baelgun, and the other dwarves marched into camp that even managed to take a slight edge off the never-ending cold of the place. Arthas knew that dwarves were used to cold climates and were a solid, strong people, but he noted the looks of relief and gratitude that flitted across the bearded faces as they

were handed bowls of steaming hot stew. It was difficult, but Arthas bit his tongue against the questions that
wanted to come pouring out of him until Muradin and
his men were taken care of. He then beckoned Muradin
to join him a ways away from the center of the camp,
near where his own personal tent was set up.

"So," he said, as his former trainer began shovel-
ing hot food down with the regularity and seemingly
unstoppable quality of a well-built gnomish machine,
"what were you doing up here anyway?"

Muradin swallowed his bite of food and reached for
some ale to wash it down with. "Well, lad, this isn't nec-
essarily something tae be sharin' wi' everyone."

Arthas nodded his understanding. Only a few of the
members of the fleet he'd commandeered knew the
whole story of why they were in Northrend. "I appreciate your trusting me, Muradin."

The dwarf clapped him on the shoulder. "Ye've
grown up right bonny, ye have, lad. If ye can find yer
way tae this forsaken land, ye've a right tae know what
me and me men are doing here. I'm looking fer a legend." His eyes twinkled as he gulped some ale, wiped
his mouth, and continued. "My people have always been
interested in rare items, ye ken tha'."

"Indeed." Arthas recalled hearing something
about Muradin helping to form something called the
Explorer's League. It was based in Ironforge, and its
members traveled the world to gather knowledge and
search for archeological treasures. "So you're on League
business here?"

"Aye, indeed. I've been here many times before.

Oddly compelling land, this one. Doesn't give up its secrets easily . . . an' that makes it intriguin'." He fished
in his pack and came out with a leather-bound journal
that looked like it had seen better days and shoved it at
Arthas with a grunt. The prince took it and began to
thumb through the pages. There were hundreds of
sketches of creatures, landmarks, and ruins. "There's
more here than meets the eye at first glance."

Looking at the images, Arthas was forced to agree.
"Most of the time, it's just research," Muradin continued. "Learnin'."

Arthas closed the book and gave it back to Muradin.
"When you saw us you were surprised—not that we
might be undead, but that we weren't. How long have
you been here—and what is it you've learned?"

Muradin scraped the last bit of stew from his bowl,
wiped it clean with a hunk of bread, and ate that as well.
He sighed a little. "Ah, I do miss th' pastries yer palace baker used tae make." He fished for his pipe. "An'
in answer tae yer question, long enough to know that
something is amiss here. There's some . . . force growin'.
It's bad and it's getting badder. I talked to yer father; I
think this power is nae happy with just sitting here in
Northrend."

Arthas fought back a double rush of both worry and
excitement, trying to appear composed. "You think it
might pose a danger to my people?"

Muradin leaned back and lit the pipe. The smell of
his preferred tobacco, its familiarity comforting in this
alien land, teased Arthas's nostrils. "Aye, I do. I think it's
part o' the creation o' these pesky undead."

Arthas decided it was time to share what he knew. He spoke quickly but calmly, telling Muradin about the plagued grain. About Kel'Thuzad, and the Cult of the Damned, and his own first horrifying encounter with the transformed farmers. About learning that Mal'Ganis, a dreadlord in the flesh, was the one behind the plague, and about the demon's taunting invitation to come here to Northrend.

He mentioned Stratholme obliquely. "The plague had reached even there," he said. "I made sure that Mal'Ganis had no more corpses to use for his own sick purposes." That was enough; it was all true, and he was not certain that Muradin would understand the awful necessity of what Arthas had been forced to do. Jaina and Uther certainly hadn't, and they'd actually seen what Arthas had been up against.

Muradin grunted. "Bad business, that. Perhaps this certain artifact I'm lookin' fer can be of use to you in fighting this dreadlord. As far as rare an' magical things go, this one's a beaut. Information about it has only recently begun to surface, but ever since we learned about it—well, we've been looking long and hard. Have a few special magical items tae try an' track it down, but no luck yet." He lifted his eyes from Arthas and looked beyond the prince, toward the wilderness that loomed. For a moment, the twinkle in his eyes abated, replaced by a somberness that the more youthful Arthas had never seen there.

Arthas waited, burning with curiosity, but not wanting to appear the impatient child Muradin no doubt remembered him as being.

Muradin refocused, regarding Arthas intently. "We're searching for a runeblade called Frostmourne."

Frostmourne. Arthas felt a slight shiver in his soul at the word. An ominous name, for a weapon of legend. Runeblades were not unheard of, but they were extremely rare and terribly powerful weapons. He glanced over at his hammer, sitting propped up against a tree where he'd placed it after returning from his discovery of Muradin. It was a beautiful weapon, and he had cherished it, although recently the Light seemed to shine from it sluggishly, sometimes not at all.

But a runeblade—

A sudden certainty seized him, as if fate were whispering in his ear. Northrend was a vast place. Surely it was not coincidence that he had encountered Muradin. If he had Frostmourne—surely he could slay Mal'Ganis. End this plague. Save his people. The dwarf and he had come together for a reason. It was destiny at work.

Muradin was speaking and Arthas jerked his attention back to him. "We came here tae recover Frostmourne, but the closer we come tae doin' so, the more undead we encounter. And I'm too old tae think that mere coincidence."

Arthas smiled softly. So Muradin, too, did not believe in coincidence. The certainty inside his gut grew. "You think Mal'Ganis doesn't want us to find it," Arthas murmured.

"I wouldna think that he'd be happy tae see ye charging at him wi' that kind o' weapon in yer fist, that's true enough."

"It sounds like we can help each other, then," Arthas

said. "We'll help you and your League find Frostmourne, and you can help us against Mal'Ganis."

"A sound plan," Muradin agreed, the smoke writhing up about him in fragrant blue-black plumes. "Arthas, me lad . . . any more o' that ale available?"

The days passed. Muradin and Arthas compared notes. They had a double quest now—Mal'Ganis and the runeblade. Eventually they decided that the wisest course of action would be to press inward and send the fleet northward, to establish a new camp there. They found themselves fighting not only undead, but famished and vicious packs of wolves, strange beings that seemed to be part wolverine and part human, and a race of trolls that seemed as at home here in the frigid north as their cousins did in the steamy jungles of Stranglethorn. Muradin was not as surprised as the human prince to find such beings; apparently small clusters of similar so-called "ice trolls" lurked near the dwarven capital of Ironforge.

Arthas learned from Muradin that the undead had bases here; strange, ziggurat-like structures, pulsing with dark magic, that had belonged to an older and presumably extinct race, since the former residents didn't seem to object. So not only did the walking corpses themselves need to be destroyed, their refuges needed to be as well. Yet each day seemed to bring Arthas no nearer to his goal. There were plenty of traces of Mal'Ganis's evil, but none of the dreadlord himself.

Nor was Muradin's quest for the enticing Frostmourne more successful. The clues, arcane and mundane both, were narrowing the search area, but thus far, the runeblade remained only a legend for all the reality it held for them.

The day when things changed, Arthas was in a foul temper. He was returning to their makeshift traveling camp, hungry and tired and cold, after yet another fruitless foray. So lost in his irritation was he that it was several seconds before comprehension dawned.

The guards were not at their posts. "What the—" He turned to look at Muradin, who immediately gripped his axe. There were no bodies, of course; if the undead had attacked while he was away, the corpses would have been raised in the cruelest example of conscription the world had ever known. But there should have been blood, signs of a struggle . . . but there was none.

They advanced cautiously, quietly. The camp was deserted—packed up, even, save for a handful of men. They looked up as Arthas entered and saluted him. In answer to his unvoiced question, one captain, Luc Valonforth, said, "Apologies, milord. Your father had our troops recalled at Lord Uther's request. The expedition is cancelled."

A muscle twitched near Arthas's eye. "My father—recalled my troops. Because Lord Uther told him to?"

The captain looked nervous and glanced sideways at Muradin, then replied, "Aye, sir. We wanted to wait for you but the emissary was quite insistent. All the men headed northwest to meet up with the fleet. Our scout informed us that the roads, such as they are, are being held by the undead, so they're busy clearing a path through the woods. I'm sure you'll be able to catch up with them quickly, sir."

"Of course," Arthas said, and forced a smile. Inwardly he was seething. "Excuse me a moment." He dropped a hand on Muradin's shoulder and steered the dwarf off to an area where they could speak quietly.

"Eh, I'm sorry, lad. It's frustrating tae have tae pick up an—"

"No."

Muradin blinked. "Come again?"

"I'm not going back. Muradin, if my warriors abandon me, I'll never defeat Mal'Ganis! That plague won't ever *stop*!" Despite himself, his voice rose at the last word and a few curious glances were thrown his way.

"Lad, it's yer father. The king. Ye can't countermand an order. That's treason."

Arthas snorted. *Perhaps it is my father who is turning traitor to his own people,* he thought, but did not say.

"I stripped Uther of his rank. I dissolved the order. He's got no right to do this. Father has been deceived."

"Well, then, ye'll have tae' take it up wi' him when ye get back. Make him see reason, if it's all as ye say it is. But ye canna disobey."

Arthas shot the dwarf a harsh glance. *If it's all as I say it is?* What, was the damned dwarf implying that Arthas was lying to him? "You're right about one thing. My men are loyal to what they understand as the chain of command. They'd never refuse to go home if they had direct orders." He rubbed his chin thoughtfully, and smiled as the idea took shape. "That's it! We'll simply deny them the way to get home. They won't be disobeying—they'll simply be *unable* to obey."

Muradin's bushy brows drew together in a frown. "What are ye saying?"

For answer, Arthas gave him a wolfish grin and told him his plan.

Muradin seemed shocked. "Isn't that a bit much, lad?" Muradin's tone told him that he thought it was indeed a bit much, perhaps a whole hell of a lot more than a "bit." Arthas ignored him. Muradin hadn't seen what he had seen; hadn't been forced to do what he had done. He would understand, soon enough. When they finally faced Mal'Ganis. Arthas knew that he would defeat the dreadlord. He had to. He would end the plague, end the threat to his people. Then the destruction of the vessels would be nothing more than an inconvenience—comparatively minor when measured against the survival of the citizens of Lordaeron.

"I know it sounds drastic, but it has to be this way. It has to."

A few hours later, Arthas stood on the Forgotten Shore and watched his entire fleet burn.

The answer had been simple. The men could not take the ships home—could not abandon him—if there were no ships to take. And so Arthas had burned them all.

He had cut through the woods, hiring mercenaries first to help them slaughter the undead and then to douse the wooden vessels liberally with oil and set them aflame. In this land of constant cold and feeble light, the heat coming off the fiery vessels was disconcertingly welcome. Arthas lifted his hand to shield his eyes from the brightness.

Beside him, Muradin sighed and shook his head. He and the other dwarves, who muttered under their breaths as they watched the conflagration, were still not certain this was the right path. Arthas folded his arms, his back cold, his face and front almost scorched with the heat, solemnly watching the flaming skeleton of one of the ships crack apart with a *whumph*.

"Damn Uther for making me do this!" he murmured.

He would show the paladin—the *former* paladin. He would show Uther, and Jaina, and his father. He had not shirked his duty, no matter how awful or brutal it was. He would return triumphant, having done what needed to be done—things that the softer-hearted had cringed from doing. And because of him, because of his willingness to shoulder the burden of responsibility, his people would survive.

So loud was the sound of flames licking at the oil-drenched wood that for a moment, it drowned out the despairing cries of the men as they emerged and beheld the sight.

"Prince Arthas! Our ships!"

"What happened? How are we getting home?"

The idea had been simmering in the back of his mind for several hours now. Arthas knew his men would be aghast at discovering that they were stranded here. They had agreed to follow him, true, but Muradin had been right. They would have seen orders from his father as superseding any order he could give them. And Mal'Ganis would have won. But they would not understand how very badly they needed to stop the threat here, now—

His eyes fell on the mercenaries he had hired.

No one would miss them.

They could be bought and sold. If someone had paid them to kill him, they would have done so as readily as helping him. So many had died—good people, noble people, innocents. Their senseless deaths cried out to be avenged. And if Arthas's men were not with him with all their hearts, he would not triumph.

Arthas could not bear it.

"Quickly, my warriors!" he cried, lifting his hammer. It did not glow with the Light; he was starting to cease expecting it to. He pointed at the mercenaries just now dragging the small boats filled with supplies ashore from the burning ships. "These murderous creatures have burned our ships and robbed you of your way home! Slay them all in the name of Lordaeron!"

And he led the charge.

CHAPTER FIFTEEN

Arthas recognized the sound of Muradin's short but heavy stride even before the dwarf yanked the tent flap back and glared at him. They stared at each other for a long moment, then Muradin jerked his head toward the outside and let the flap fall. For a moment, Arthas was hurtled back in time to when he was a child accidentally flinging a training sword across the room. He frowned and rose, following Muradin to an area far away from the men.

The dwarf didn't mince words. "Ye lied tae yer men and betrayed the mercenaries who fought for ye!" Muradin snapped, shoving his face up to Arthas's as best he could from his much shorter height. "That's nae the lad I trained. That's nae the man who was inducted into th' order of the Silver Hand. That's nae King Terenas's boy."

"I am no one's *boy*," Arthas spat, shoving Muradin away. "I did what I deemed necessary."

He half expected Muradin to strike him, but instead the anger seemed to bleed away from his old trainer.

"What's happening tae ye, Arthas?" Muradin said quietly, his voice holding a world of pain and confusion. "Is vengeance all that's important to ye?"

"Spare me, Muradin," Arthas growled. "You weren't there to see what Mal'Ganis did to my homeland. What he did to innocent men, women, and children!"

"I've heard what ye did," Muradin said quietly. "Some o' yer men have been a wee bit free wi' their tongues when ale has loosened them. I know what I think—but I also know that I canna judge ye. Ye're right, I wasn't there. Thank the Light, I didn't have tae make that kind o' decision. But even so—something's happening. Ye—"

Mortar fire and cries of alarm interrupted him. In a heartbeat, Muradin and Arthas had their weapons out and had turned back to the encampment. The men were still scrambling for weapons. Falric was barking orders to the humans, while Baelgun was organizing the dwarves. There came the sound of engagement from outside the encampment, and Arthas could see the press of undead closing in. His hands clenched on his hammer. This had all the earmarks of a coordinated attack, rather than a random encounter.

"The Dark Lord said you would come," came a voice that was by now familiar to Arthas. Elation filled him. Mal'Ganis was here! It had not been a wild-goose chase after all. "This is where your journey ends, boy. Trapped and freezing at the roof of the world, with only death to sing the tale of your doom."

Muradin scratched his beard, his sharp eyes darting about. From outside the perimeter of the camp came the sounds of battle. "This looks bad," he admitted with characteristic dwarven understatement. "We're completely surrounded."

Arthas stared, agonized. "We could have done it," he whispered. "With Frostmourne . . . we could have done it."

Muradin glanced away. "There . . . well lad, I have been having me doubts. About th' sword. And, tae speak truly, about ye as well."

It took a second for Arthas to realize what Muradin was saying. "You—are you telling me you've figured out how to find it?"

At Muradin's nod, Arthas seized him by the arm. "Whatever your doubts, Muradin, you can't possibly have them now. Not with Mal'Ganis right here. If you know where it is, then take me to it. Help me claim Frostmourne! You said it yourself—you didn't think that Mal'Ganis would like to see me with Frostmourne in my fist. Mal'Ganis has more troops than we do. Without Frostmourne, we'll fall, you know we will!"

Muradin gave him an agonized look, then closed his eyes.

"I have a bad feeling about this, lad. It's why I've nae pressed on before—something about this artifact, how the information has come—it doesnae feel right. But I promised I'd see this through. Ye go gather a few men and I'll find ye that runeblade."

Arthas clapped his old friend on the shoulder. This was it. *I'll get that damned runeblade, and I'll shove it through your black heart, dreadlord. I'll make you pay.*

"Close that gap over there!" Falric was shouting. "Davan, fire!" The boom of mortar fire echoed through the camp as Arthas raced toward his second in command.

"Captain Falric!"

Falric turned to him. "Sir . . . we're utterly surrounded. We can hold out for a while, but eventually they're going to wear us down. Who—what—we lose in numbers, they'll gain."

"I know, Captain. Muradin and I are going to go find Frostmourne." Falric's eyes widened slightly in both shock and hope. Arthas had shared the knowledge of the sword—and its supposed vast power—with a few of his most trusted men. "Once we have it, victory will be certain. Can you buy us the time?"

"Aye, Your Highness." Falric grinned, but he still looked worried even as he said, "We'll hold these undead bastards off."

A few moments later, Muradin, armed with a map and a strange glowing object, joined Arthas and a handful of men. His mouth was etched in a frown and his eyes were unhappy, but his body was straight. Falric gave the signal, and began to create a distraction. Most of the undead suddenly turned and concentrated their efforts on him, leaving the back area of the camp open.

"Let's go," Arthas said grimly.

Muradin barked out directions as he alternately peered at his map and at the glowing object that seemed to pulse erratically. They moved as quickly as possible through the deep snow where he indicated, stopping only occasionally for the briefests of breaks to reassess. The sky darkened as clouds gathered. Snow began to fall, slowing them further.

Arthas began to move automatically. The snow made it impossible to see more than a few feet ahead. He no longer noticed or cared in which direction he went, simply moving his legs as he followed Muradin's lead. Time seemed to have no meaning. He could have been moving for minutes or days.

His mind was consumed with thoughts of Frostmourne. Their salvation. Arthas knew it would be. But could they reach it before his men at the camp fell to the undead and their demonic master? Falric had said they could hold—for a time. How much longer? To finally know that Mal'Ganis was here—at his own base camp—and to not be able to attack was—

"There," Muradin said, almost reverently, pointing. "It's inside there."

Arthas halted, blinking eyes that were narrowed to slits against the driving snow, their lashes crusted with ice. They stood before the mouth of a cavern, stark and ominous-seeming in the snow-swirled darkness of the gray day. There was some kind of illumination inside, a soft, blue-green radiance he could just barely glimpse. Bone-weary, frozen as he was, excitement shot through him. He forced his numbed mouth to form words.

"Frostmourne . . . and the end of Mal'Ganis. The end of the plague. Come on!"

A second wind seemed to take him and he hastened forward, forcing his legs to obey.

"Lad!" Muradin's voice brought him up sharply. "So precious a treasure won't be just left sitting around for anyone tae find. We must proceed wi' a bit o' caution."

Arthas chafed, but Muradin had more experience in these matters. So he nodded, gripped his hammer firmly, and entered warily. The immediate relief from the wind and driving snow heartened him, and they moved deeper into the heart of the cavern. The illumination he had glimpsed from outside proved to be coming from softly glowing turquoise crystals and veins of ore embedded in the rock walls, floors, and ceilings themselves. He had heard of such luminescent crystals and was now grateful for the light they provided. His men would be able to concentrate on holding their weapons, not torches. Once, his hammer would have glowed with enough radiance to guide them. He frowned at the thought, then pushed it down. It did not matter where light to see by came from, only that it was present.

It was then that they heard the voices. Muradin had been right—they were expected.

The voices were deep, hollow, and cold-sounding, and their words were dire as they floated to Arthas's ears. "Turn back, mortals. Death and darkness are all that await you in this forsaken vault. You shall not pass."

Muradin halted. "Lad," he said, his voice soft, though in this place it seemed to echo endlessly, "perhaps we should listen."

"Listen to what?" Arthas cried. "A pathetic last effort to turn me from my path to save my people? It's going to take more than ominous words to do that."

Gripping his hammer he hastened forward, rounded

a corner—and stopped in his tracks, trying to take in everything at once.

They had found the owners of the icy voices. For a moment, Arthas was reminded of Jaina's obedient water elemental, who had helped her fight off the ogres on that long-ago day before everything had taken such grim and horrific turns. The beings hovered over the cold stone floor of the cavern, made of ice and unnatural essence instead of water, wearing armor that looked as if it had grown of and from them. They had helms, but no faces; gauntlets, weapons and shields, but no arms.

Alarming though they were, Arthas gave these fearsome elemental spirits no more than a passing glance as his eye was drawn to the reason they had come here.

Frostmourne.

It was caught in a hovering, jagged chunk of ice, the runes that ran the length of its blade glowing a cool blue. Below it was a dais of some sort, standing on a large gently raised mound that was covered in a dusting of snow. A soft light, coming from somewhere high above where the cavern was open to daylight, shone down on the runeblade. The icy prison hid some details of the sword's shape and form, exaggerated others. It was revealed and concealed at the same time, and all the more tempting, like a new lover imperfectly glimpsed through a gauzy curtain. Arthas knew the blade—it was the selfsame sword he had seen in his dream when he first arrived. The sword that had not killed Invincible, but that had brought him back healed and healthy. He'd thought it a good omen then, but now he knew it was a true sign. This was what he had come to find. This sword would change everything. Arthas stared raptly at it, his hands almost physically aching to grasp it, his fingers to wrap themselves around the hilt, his arms to feel the weapon swinging smoothly in the blow that would end Mal'Ganis, end the torment he had visited upon the people of Lordaeron, end this lust for revenge. Drawn, he stepped forward.

The uncanny elemental spirit drew its icy sword.

"Turn away, before it is too late," it intoned.

"Still trying to protect the sword, are you?" Arthas snarled, angry and embarrassed at his reaction.

"No." The being's voice rumbled the word. "Trying to protect you from *it*."

For a second, Arthas stared in surprise. Then he shook his head, eyes narrowing in determination. This was nothing more than a trick. He could never turn away from Frostmourne—turn away from saving his people. He would not fall for the lie. He charged and his men followed. The entities converged on them, attacking with their unnatural weapons, but Arthas focused his attention on the leader, the one assigned to guard Frostmourne. All his pent-up hope, worry, fear, and frustration, he unleashed on the strange protector. His men did likewise, turning to attack the other elemental guardians of the sword. His hammer rose and fell, rose and fell, shattering the icy armor as cries of anger were ripped from his throat. How dare this thing stand between him and Frostmourne? How dare it—

With a final agonized sound, like that of the rattle coming from a dying man's throat, the spirit flung up what passed for hands and disappeared.

Arthas stood staring, panting, the breath coming from his chilled lips in white puffs. Then he turned to the hard-won prize. All misgivings disappeared as he again laid eyes on the sword.

"Behold, Muradin," he breathed, aware that his voice was shaking, "our salvation, Frostmourne."

"Hold, lad." Muradin's blunt words, almost an order, were like cold water doused on Arthas. He blinked, startled out of his trancelike rapture, and turned to look at the dwarf.

"What? Why?" he demanded.

Muradin was staring, eyes narrowed, at the hovering sword and the dais below it. "Something's not right here." He pointed a stubby finger at the runeblade. "This has been too easy. And look at it, sitting here wi' light coming from who knows where, like a flower waiting tae be plucked."

"Too easy?" Arthas shot him a disbelieving glance. "It's taken you long enough to find it. And we had to fight these things to get to it."

"Bah," snorted Muradin. "Everything I ken about artifacts is telling me that there's something as fishy here as the Booty Bay docks." He sighed, his brow still furrowed. "Wait . . . there's an inscription on the dais. Let me see if I can read this. It might tell us something."

Both of them advanced, Muradin to kneel and peer at the writing, Arthas to draw closer to the beckoning sword. Arthas gave the inscription that so intrigued Muradin a cursory glance. It was not written in any language he knew, but the dwarf seemed to be able to read it, judging by how his eyes flickered across the letters.

Arthas lifted a hand and stroked the ice that separated them—smooth, slick, deathly cold—ice, yes, but there was something unusual about it. It wasn't simply frozen water. He didn't know how he could tell, but he could. There was something very powerful, almost unearthly, about it.

Frostmourne...

"Aye, I thought I recognized this. It's written in Kalimag—the elemental language," Muradin continued. He frowned as he read. "It's . . . a warning."

"Warning? Warning of what?" Perhaps shattering the ice would damage the sword somehow, Arthas thought. The unnatural ice block itself, though, seemed to have been—almost cut from another, larger piece of ice. Muradin translated slowly. Arthas listened with half an ear, his eyes on the sword.

"Whosoever takes up this blade shall wield power eternal. Just as th' blade rends flesh, so must power scar th' spirit." The dwarf leaped to his feet, looking more agitated than Arthas had ever seen him. "Och, I should've known. Th' blade is cursed! Let's get the hell out of here!"

Arthas's heart gave a strange wrench at Muradin's exclamation. Leave? Leave this sword behind, hovering in its frozen prison, untouched, unused, with such vast power to offer him? "Power eternal," the inscription had promised, along with the threat of scarring the spirit.

"My spirit is already scarred," Arthas said. And so it was. It had been scarred by the needless death of a beloved steed, by the horror of watching the dead rise, by the betrayal of one he loved—yes, he had loved Jaina Proudmoore, he could say it now in this moment when his soul seemed to lie naked in front of the sword's judgment. It had been scarred by being forced to slaughter hundreds, by the need to lie to his men and forever silence those who would question and disobey him. It had been scarred by so very much. Surely the marks left by the power to right a horrible wrong could not be greater than these.

"Arthas, lad," Muradin said, his rough voice pleading. "Ye've enough tae deal wi' without bringing a curse on yer head."

"A curse?" Arthas laughed bitterly. "I would gladly bear any curse to save my homeland."

Out of the corner of his eye, he saw Muradin shiver. "Arthas, ye ken I'm a solid one, no given tae flights o' fancy. But I tell ye, this is bad business, lad. Leave it be. Let it stay here, lost and forgotten. Mal'Ganis is here, well, that's fine. Let him freeze his demonic arse here in the wilderness. Forget this business and let's lead your men home."

An image of the men suddenly filled Arthas's mind. He saw them, and beside them he saw the hundreds that had already fallen to this horrible plague. Fallen only to rise, unthinking rotting hunks of flesh. What of them? What of their souls, their suffering, their sacrifice? Another image appeared—a huge piece of ice, the same ice that now encased Frostmourne. He saw now where this chunk of ice had come from. It was part of something larger, stronger—and it, with the runeblade inside it, had been somehow sent to him to avenge those who had fallen. A voice whispered in his mind: *The dead demand vengeance.*

What was a handful of living men compared to the torment of those who had fallen in so horrible a fashion?

"Damn the men!"

The words seemed to explode from someplace deep in his gut. "I have a duty to the dead. Nothing shall prevent me from having my revenge, old friend." Now he tore his gaze away from the sword long enough to meet Muradin's worried gaze, and his face softened slightly. "Not even you."

"Arthas—I taught ye tae fight. I wanted tae help ye be a good warrior as well as a good king. But part o' being a good warrior is picking which battles tae fight—and which weapons tae fight wi'." He stabbed a stubby forefinger at Frostmourne. "And *that's* a weapon ye'll nae want to be putting in your arsenal."

Arthas put both hands up against the ice that was the sword's sheath and brought his face to within an inch of the smooth surface. As if from somewhere far away, he heard Muradin still speaking.

"Listen tae me, lad. We'll find another way tae save yer people. Let's leave now, go back and find that way."

Muradin was wrong. He simply didn't understand. Arthas had to do this. If he walked away now, he would have failed, again, and he couldn't let that happen. He had been thwarted at every turn.

Not this time.

He believed in the Light, because he could see it and had used it, and he believed in ghosts and the walking dead, because he had fought them. But until this moment, he had scoffed at the idea of unseen powers, of spirits of places or things. But now, his heart racing in anticipation and with a yearning, a craving that seemed to gnaw at his very soul, the words came from his lips as if of their own accord, laced with his dreadful wanting.

"Now, I call out to the spirits of this place," he said, his breath frosting in the cold, still air. Just beyond his reach, Frostmourne hung, suspended, awaiting him. "Whatever you be, good or ill or neither or both. I can feel you here. I know you are listening. I'm ready. I understand. And I tell you now—I will give anything, or pay any price, if only you will help me save my people."

For a long, terrible moment, nothing happened. His breath frosted, faded, frosted again, and cold sweat dotted his brow. He had offered everything he had—had he been refused? Had he failed yet again?

And then with a low groan that made his breath catch, a sudden crack ran up the smooth surface of the ice. It raced its way upward, zigzagging and spreading, until Arthas could barely glimpse the sword it held within its heart. Then he was stumbling backward, clutching his ears at the sudden loud cracking noise that filled the chamber.

The icy casket encasing the sword exploded. Shards flew across the chamber, swords themselves, sharp and jagged. They shattered against the unyielding stone floor and walls, but even as Arthas dropped to his knees, his arms flying up automatically to cover his head, he heard a cry suddenly cut off.

"Muradin!"

The impact of the ice shard had knocked the dwarf back several feet. Now he lay sprawled on the cold stone floor, a spear of ice impaling his midsection, the blood sluggishly flowing around it. His eyes were closed and he was limp. Arthas scrambled to his feet and hastened over to his old friend and trainer, tugging off his gauntlet. He slipped an arm around the limp form, placing his hand on the wound, staring at it, willing the Light to come and limn his hands with healing energy. Guilt racked him.

So this was the dreadful price. Not his own life, but that of a friend. Someone who had cared for him, taught him, supported him. He bowed his head, tears stinging his eyes, and prayed.

It's my folly. My price. Please—

And then, like a familiar caress from a loved friend, he felt it. The Light raced through him, comforting and warm, and he bit back a sob as he saw the glow again begin to embrace his hand. He had fallen so far, but it wasn't too late. The Light had not abandoned him. All he needed to do was drink it in, open his heart to it. Muradin would not die. He could heal him, and together they—

Something stirred at the back of his neck. No, no, not the back of his neck . . . the back of his mind. He looked up quickly—

And stared in wonder.

It had flung itself free to embed itself in front of him, its blue-white runes enveloping it in a cold and glorious light. His own Light faded from his hands as he rose to his feet, almost hypnotized. Frostmourne was waiting for him, a lover needing the touch of the desired one to waken to full glory.

The whispering in the back of his mind continued. *This* was the path. It was foolish to trust in the Light. It had failed him, repeatedly. It had not been there to save Invincible, had not been enough to stop the inexorable march of this plague that was on its way to wiping out the population of his kingdom. The power, the strength of Frostmourne—*that* was the only thing that could stand against the might of a dreadlord.

Muradin was a casualty of this awful war. But hopefully, his sacrifice would be the last. Arthas got to his feet and took unsteady steps toward the radiant weapon, his hand, still wet with the blood of his friend, outstretched and trembling. It closed on the shaft and his fingers curled around it, fitting it perfectly, as if the one was made for the other.

Cold shot through him, shivering up his arms, spreading over his body and into his heart. It was painful for a moment and he knew a hint of alarm, and then suddenly it was all right. It was all all right; Frostmourne was his and he was its, and its voice was speaking, whispering, caressing inside his mind as if it had always been there.

With a cry of joy, he lifted the weapon, gazing at it in wonder and fierce pride. He would make things right— he, Arthas Menethil, and the glorious Frostmourne that was now as much a part of him as his mind or his heart or his breath, and he listened intently to the secrets it revealed.

CHAPTER SIXTEEN

Arthas and his men ran toward the encampment to discover that the battle had not abated in his absence. The numbers of his men had dwindled, but there were no corpses. He did not expect to see any—those who fell rose as adversaries, under the command of the dreadlord.

Falric, his armor spattered with gore, cried out to him. "Prince Arthas! We've done what we could and—Where is Muradin? We can't hold out any longer!"

"Muradin is dead," Arthas said. The cold but comforting essence of the sword seemed to abate a little, and pain swelled in his heart. Muradin had paid the price—but it was worth it, if it would fell Mal'Ganis. The dwarf would have agreed, had he known everything, understood as Arthas understood. Muradin's men looked stricken even as they continued to fire round after round into the waves of undead that continued to pound against them. "His death was not in vain. Take heart, Captain. The enemy will not stand long against the might of Frostmourne!"

As they watched, disbelief washing over their faces, Arthas charged into the fray.

He had thought he fought well with his blessed hammer, now lying discarded and forgotten in the icy vault where Frostmourne had once been imprisoned, but it was nothing to the damage he dealt now. Frostmourne felt more like an extension of himself rather than a weapon. He quickly found a rhythm and began to slice the undead down as if they were so many stalks of grain falling before the harvesting scythe. How balanced and perfect a weapon it was in his hands. One arcing blow severed the head from the shoulders of a ghoul. He swept Frostmourne around, scattering the bones of a skeleton. Another rhythmic stroke downed a third foe. They fell all around him, the rotting bodies beginning to pile up, as he cut a path through them. At one point, looking for his next enemy, he caught sight of Falric staring at him. There was awe on the familiar face, but also shock and— horror? Only at the carnage he was wreaking, surely. Frostmourne was all but singing in his hands.

The wind picked up and the snow began to fall, thick and fast. Frostmourne seemed to approve, for the increased snowfall did not seem to hamper Arthas in the slightest. Again and again the blade found its mark, and more and more undead things fell. At last, the minions had been dealt with. It was time for their master.

"Mal'Ganis, you coward!" Arthas cried, even his voice sounding different in his own ears now, as it carried easily over the howling wind. "Come show yourself! You taunted me into coming here, now stand and face me!"

And then the demon lord was there, bigger than Arthas remembered, smirking down at the prince. He straightened to his full imposing height, his wings beating the air, his tail lashing. The undead warriors at his command stilled as he casually flicked a finger.

Arthas was prepared for the dreadlord's frightening appearance this time. It did not rattle him. Staring at his enemy, he wordlessly lifted Frostmourne, and the runes etched along its length gleamed. Mal'Ganis recognized the weapon and a hint of a frown curved his blue lips.

"So, you've taken up Frostmourne at the expense of your comrades' lives, just as the Dark Lord said you would. You're stronger than I thought."

The words were heard, but there were other words, whispering silkily in his brain. Arthas listened, and then grinned fiercely.

"You waste your breath, Mal'Ganis. I heed only the voice of Frostmourne now."

The dreadlord threw back his horned head and laughed. "You hear the voice of the Dark Lord," Mal'Ganis retorted. He pointed a sharp, black-nailed finger at the mighty runeblade. "He whispers to you through the blade you wield!"

Arthas felt the blood drain from his face. The dreadlord's master . . . *spoke* to him through Frostmourne? But . . . how could that be? Was this the final trick? Had he been gulled and delivered directly into Mal'Ganis's taloned hands?

"What does he say, young human?" The smirk came again, the expression of one who knows something another does not. The dreadlord was gloating, reveling in this twist. "What does the Dark Lord of the Dead tell you now?"

The whispers came again, but this time it was Arthas who smirked, a mirror image of the same expression the dreadlord bore. Now it was he who knew something Mal'Ganis did not.

Arthas whirled Frostmourne over his head, the enormous blade light and graceful in his hands, and then he eased into an attack position. "He tells me that the time for my vengeance has come."

The green, glowing eyes widened. "What? He can't possibly mean to—"

Arthas charged.

The mighty runeblade lifted, descended. The dreadlord was taken by surprise, but only for an instant, and managed to get his staff up in time to deflect the blow. He leaped aside, great bat wings creating a quick gust of wind that blew Arthas's golden hair about wildly but did not affect his balance or speed. He came in again and again, coldly in control but swift and deadly as a viper, the blade glowing with eagerness. A brief thought crossed his mind: *Frostmourne hungers.*

And a part of him responded with a frisson of fear: *Hungers for what?*

It did not matter. He, Arthas, hungered for revenge, and he was going to have it. Every time Mal'Ganis tried to cast a spell, Frostmourne was there, knocking him aside, slicing his flesh, harrying him until the moment came when the deathblow would be dealt. He felt

Frostmourne's anticipation, its craving, and he cried out as he swung the runeblade in a shimmering blue arc to neatly carve a deadly furrow across Mal'Ganis's midsection.

Dark blood spurted in an arc, pattering on the snow, as the dreadlord fell. There was astonishment on his face; even at the end, he had not believed he could be defeated.

For a moment Arthas stood, the wind and snow writhing about him, the glow of the runes on Frostmourne's blade, partially obscured by dark demonic blood, illuminating the glorious scene.

"It is finished," he said softly.

This part of your journey, yes, young prince, Frostmourne whispered—or was it truly the Dark Lord Mal'Ganis had spoken of? He did not know or care. Carefully he bent and wiped the blade clean in the snow. *But there is more. So much more. So much power that could be yours. So much knowledge and control.*

Arthas remembered Muradin's reading of the inscription. His hand went to his heart without his immediately realizing it. The blade was part of him now, and he was part of it.

The snowstorm was becoming worse. He realized with dawning surprise that he was not at all cold. He straightened, holding Frostmourne, and looked about him. The demon lay stiffening at his feet. The voice—Frostmourne's, or the mysterious Dark Lord's—was right.

There was more. So much more.

And the winter would teach it.

Arthas Menethil clutched the runeblade, gazed out into the snowstorm, and ran to embrace it all.

Arthas knew he would remember the bells all his life. They were rung only on occasions of great state import—a royal wedding, the birth of an heir, the funeral of a king, all the things that marked passages in the life of a kingdom. But today, they were being rung in celebration. He, Arthas Menethil, had returned home.

He had sent word ahead of his triumph. Of discovering who had been behind the plague. Of searching him out. Of slaying him, and of this day, his glorious return to his place of birth. As he strode along the road toward Capital City, on foot, he was greeted with cheers and applause, the grateful outpouring of thanks of a nation saved from disaster by their beloved prince. He accepted this as his due, but his mind was on seeing his father after so long.

"I would speak with you in private, Father, and tell you of the things I have learned and seen," he had written into his letter, delivered a few days earlier by a swift courier. "You have, I am certain, spoken with Jaina and Uther. I can imagine what they have said—tried to turn you against me. I assure you I have only done what I believe to be the greatest good for the citizens of Lordaeron. In the end, I have destroyed the one who began this plague upon our people, and I return home victorious, eager to begin a new era for our kingdom."

Those who marched behind him were as silent as he, their faces as cowled. The crowd did not seem to require their response to wildly celebrate their return.

The mighty drawbridge was lowered and Arthas strode across it. The cheering throngs were here, too, no longer comprised of commoners, but of diplomats, lesser nobility, visiting dignitaries from the elves, dwarves, and gnomes. They stood not just in the courtyard but also above it in viewing boxes. Rose petals, pink and white and red, rained down upon the land's returning hero.

Arthas remembered that once, he had thought to see Jaina standing before him on their wedding day, the petals falling upon a face lit with a smile, turned up to kiss him.

Jaina . . .

Moved by the image, he caught one of the red petals in a gloved hand. He thumbed it thoughtfully, and then frowned as a stain appeared. It grew before his eyes, desiccating and destroying the petal, until it was more brown than red in his palm. With a quick, dismissive gesture, he tossed the dead thing away and continued.

He pushed open the huge doors to the throne room he knew so well, strode forward, glanced at Terenas briefly, and threw his father a smile that was mostly hidden by the cowl. Arthas knelt in obeisance, Frostmourne held before him, its tip touching the seal carved into the stone floor.

"Ah, my son. Glad I am to see you safely home," Terenas said, rising somewhat unsteadily.

Terenas looked unwell, Arthas thought. The incidents of the last several months had aged the monarch. His hair was grayer now, his eyes tired.

But it was all going to be all right now.

You no longer need to sacrifice for your people. You no lon-

ger need to bear the weight of your crown. I've taken care of everything.

Arthas rose, his armor clattering with the movement. He lifted a hand and drew back the hood from his face, watching for his father's reaction. Terenas's eyes widened as he took in the change that had come over his only son.

Arthas's hair, once golden as the wheat that had given sustenance to his people, was now bone-white. He knew his face was pale as well, as if the blood had been drained from it.

It is time, Frostmourne whispered in his mind. Arthas moved toward his father, who had halted on the dais, staring, uncertain. There were several guards positioned about the room, but they would be no match against him, Frostmourne, and the two who had accompanied him. Arthas strode boldly up the carpeted steps and seized his father by the arm.

Arthas drew back his blade. Frostmourne's runes brightened in anticipation. And then a whisper, not from the runeblade, but a memory—

—the voice of a dark-haired prince, seemingly from another lifetime ago—

"He was assassinated. A trusted friend . . . she killed him. Stabbed him right in the heart . . ."

Arthas shook his head and the voice was silenced.

"What is this? What are you doing, my son?"

"Succeeding you . . . Father."

And Frostmourne's hunger was sated—for the moment.

* * *

Arthas turned them loose then—his new, unquestioning, obedient subjects. Dispatching the guards who charged him upon the death of his father was a simple matter, and he stormed with cold purpose back out into the courtyard.

It was madness.

What had once been revelry had now become frenzy. What had once been celebration had now become a frantic flight for life. Few escaped. Most of those who had waited for hours in line to welcome their prince back now lay dead, blood congealing from hideous wounds, limbs ripped off, bodies broken. Ambassadors now lay with commoners, men and women with children, all hideously equal in death.

Arthas did not care what their eventual fate was—carrion for the crows, or new subjects to follow his rule. He would leave that to his captains, Falric and Marwyn, as bone-white as he and twice as merciless. Arthas marched through the way he had come, focused and intent upon one single thing.

Once clear of the courtyard and the corpses, animated or still, he broke into a run. No horse would bear him now; the beasts grew frantic at the smell of him and those who followed him. But he had found that he did not tire; not when Frostmourne, or the Lich King who spoke to him through the runeblade, was whispering to him. And so he ran swiftly, his legs carrying him to a place he had not been in years.

Voices swirled in his head, memories, snippets of conversations:

"You know you were not supposed to ride him yet."

"You missed your lessons. Again . . ."

Invincible's horrible screams of agony, echoing in his mind. The Light, pausing for that awful moment, as if deciding whether or not he was worthy of its grace. Jaina's face as he ended their relationship.

"Listen to me, boy. . . . The shadow has already fallen, and nothing you do will deter it. . . . The harder you strive to slay your enemies, the faster you'll deliver your people into their hands. . . ."

". . . This isn't a blighted apple crop; this is a city full of human beings! . . ."

". . . We know so little—we can't just slaughter them like animals out of our own fear!"

"Ye lied tae yer men and betrayed the mercenaries who fought for ye! . . . That's nae King Terenas's boy."

But they were the ones who could not see, could not grasp. Jaina—Uther—Terenas—Muradin. All of them, at some point, by word or look, had told him he had been wrong.

He slowed his pace as he came to the farmstead. His subjects had been here before him, and now there were only corpses lying, stiffening in the earth. Arthas steeled himself against the pain that recognition brought with it even now; they had been the lucky ones, to simply die. A man, a woman, a youth his own age.

And the snapdragons . . . blooming like mad this year, it would seem. Arthas stepped close and extended a hand to touch one of the beautiful, tall, lavender-blue flowers, then hesitated, remembering the rose petal.

He had not come here for flowers.

He turned and strode to a grave, nearly seven years

old now. Grass had overtaken it, but the marker was still readable. He did not need to read it to know what lay here.

For a moment he stood, more moved by the death of the one in this grave than by that of his own father, by his own hand.

The power is yours, came the whispers. *Do as you will.*

Arthas extended one hand, Frostmourne firmly gripped in the other. Dark light began to swirl around the outstretched hand, increasing in speed. It moved from his fingers like a serpent, undulating and writhing of its own accord, and then it speared down into the earth.

Arthas felt it connect with the skeleton below. Joy flooded him, and tears stung his eyes. He lifted his hand, pulling the no-longer-dead thing from its seven-year slumber in the cool dark earth.

"Arise!" he commanded, the word bursting from his throat.

The grave erupted, showering bits of earth. Bony legs pawed, hooves seeking purchase on the shifting soil, and a skull thrust upward, breaking the surface. Arthas watched breathlessly, a smile on his too-pale face.

I saw you being born, he thought, remembering a membrane enshrouding a wriggling, wet, new little life. *I helped you come into this world, and I helped you leave it . . . and now by my hand, you are reborn.*

The skeletal steed struggled through the earth and finally emerged, planting its forelegs firmly and hoisting itself up. Red fire burned in its empty eye sockets. It tossed its head, pranced and somehow whinnied, though its soft tissue had long since rotted away.

Trembling, Arthas extended a hand to the undead creature, who whickered and nuzzled his hand with its bony muzzle. Seven years ago, he had ridden this horse to its death. Seven years ago, he had wept tears that had frozen on his face as he lifted his sword and stabbed the beloved beast straight through its gallant heart.

He had carried the guilt of that act alone all this time. But now he realized—it was all part of his destiny. If he had not slain his steed, he could not now bring it back. Alive, the horse would have feared him. Undead as it was, with fire for eyes, its bones held together by the necromantic magic that Arthas now could wield thanks to the gift of the mysterious Lich King, horse and rider could at last be reunited, as they had always been meant to be. It hadn't been a mistake, seven years ago; he hadn't been wrong. Not then, not now.

Not ever.

And this was proof.

Throughout the land that he now ruled, his father's blood still slick and crimson on Frostmourne, death was coming. The change.

"This kingdom shall fall," he promised his beloved steed as he threw his cloak over its bony back and mounted. "And from the ashes shall arise a new order that will shake the very foundation of the world!"

The horse whickered.

Invincible.

PART THREE

THE DARK LADY

INTERLUDE

Sylvanas Windrunner, former ranger-general of Quel'Thalas, banshee, and Dark Lady of the Forsaken, strode from the royal quarters with the same quick, lithe stride she had had in life. She preferred her corporeal form for ordinary, everyday activities. Her leather boots made no sound on the stone floor of the Undercity, but all heads turned to watch their lady. She was unique and unmistakable.

Once, her hair had been golden, her eyes blue, her skin the color of a fresh peach. Once, she had been alive. Now her hair, often covered by a blue-black cowl, was black as midnight with white streaks and her formerly peach-hued skin a faint, pearly blue-gray. She'd chosen to don the armor she had worn in life, well-tooled leather that revealed most of her slender but muscular torso. Her ears twitched at the murmurings; she did not often venture forth from her chambers. She was ruler of this city, and the world came to her.

Beside her hurried Master Apothecary Faranell, head of the Royal Apothecary Society, who was talking ani-

matedly and simpering. "I am most grateful you agreed
to come, my lady," he said, trying to bow and walk and
speak at the same time. "You did say you wished to be
informed when the experiments were successful, and
you wanted to see them yourself once we—"

"I am well aware of my own orders, Doctor," Sylvanas
snapped as they began to descend a winding corridor
into the bowels of the Undercity.

"Of course, of course. Here we are." They emerged
into a room that to one with weaker sensibilities would
seem like a house of horrors. On a large table, a stooped
undead was busily sewing together pieces of different
corpses, humming a little under his breath. Sylvanas
smiled slightly.

"It is good to see someone who enjoys his work so,"
she replied a trifle archly. The apprentice started slightly,
and then bowed deeply.

There was a low buzz of some kind of energy crackling. Other alchemists bustled about, mixing potions,
weighing ingredients, jotting notes. The smell was a
combination of putrefaction, chemicals, and, incongruously, the clean sweet smell of certain herbs. Sylvanas
was startled by her reaction. The scent of the herbs made
her oddly . . . homesick. Fortunately, the softer emotion
did not last long. Such emotions never did.

"Show me," she demanded. Faranell bowed and ush-
ered her through the main area, past pieces of bodies
hanging on hooks, into a side room.

The faint sound of sobbing reached her ears. As she
entered, Sylvanas saw several cages on the floor or
swinging slowly from chains, all of them filled with test

subjects. Some were human. Some were Forsaken. All were dull-eyed with fear that had pierced so deep and had gone on so long that they were almost numb.

They would not be so for much longer.

"As you can imagine, my lady," Faranell was saying, "it is difficult to transport Scourge as test subjects. Of course for experimental purposes, Forsaken are identical to Scourge. But I am delighted to report that our tests in the field have been well documented and quite successful."

Excitement began to stir in Sylvanas, and she graced the apothecary with a rare and still beautiful smile. "That pleases me greatly," she said. The undead doctor fairly quivered in delight. He beckoned to his assistant Keever, a Forsaken whose brain had obviously been damaged by his first death and who muttered to himself in the third person as he removed two test subjects. One was a human woman, who was apparently not so lost in fear and despair as not to start weeping silently when Keever dragged her from her cage. The Forsaken male, however, was utterly impassive and stood quietly. Sylvanas eyed him.

"Criminal?"

"Of course, my lady." She wondered if it were true. But in the end, it didn't matter. He would serve the Forsaken, even so. The human girl was on her knees. Keever stooped down, yanked her head up by her hair, and when she opened her mouth to cry out in pain, he poured a cup of something down her throat and covered her mouth, forcing her to swallow.

Sylvanas watched while she struggled. Beside her,

the Forsaken male accepted the cup that Faranell offered without protest, draining it dry.

It happened quickly. The human girl soon stopped struggling, her body tensing, and then going into paroxysms. Keever let her go, watching almost curiously as blood began to stream from her mouth, nose, eyes, and ears. Sylvanas turned her gaze to the Forsaken. He still regarded her steadily, silently. She began to frown.

"Perhaps this is not as effective as your—"

The Forsaken shuddered. He struggled to stand erect for a moment longer, but his rapidly weakening body betrayed him and he stumbled, falling hard. Everyone stepped back. Sylvanas watched raptly, her lips parted in excitement.

"The same strain?" she asked Faranell. The human female whimpered once and then was still, her eyes open. The alchemist nodded happily.

"Indeed it is," he said. "As you can imagine, we are quite—"

The undead spasmed, his skin breaking open in spots and weeping black ichor, and then he, too, was still.

"—pleased with the results."

"Indeed," Sylvanas said. She was hard put to conceal her own elation; "pleased" was a pale word indeed. "A plague that kills both humans and Scourge. And, obviously, affects my own people as well, as they, too, are undead."

She gave him a look from glowing silver eyes. "We must take care that this never falls into the wrong hands. The results could be . . . devastating."

He gulped. "Indeed, my lady, indeed they could."

She forced a neutral expression as she returned to the royal quarters. Her mind was racing with a thousand things, but foremost among them, burning as brightly and wildly as the wicker man she lit every Hallow's End, was a single thought:

At last, Arthas, you will pay for what you have done. The humans who spawned such as you shall be slaughtered. Your Scourge shall be stopped in their tracks. You will no longer be able to hide behind your armies of mindless undead puppets. And we will grace you with the same mercy and compassion you showed us.

Despite her great control, she found herself smiling.

CHAPTER SEVENTEEN

It was, Arthas mused as he rode upon the back of the skeletal, faithful Invincible toward Andorhal, a truly great irony that he who had slain the necromancer Kel'Thuzad was now charged with resurrecting him.

Frostmourne whispered to him, although he did not need the voice of the sword—the voice of the Lich King, as he desired to be known—to reassure him. There was no going back. Nor did he wish to.

After the fall of Capital City, Arthas had retreated into a dark version of a paladin's pilgrimage. He had ridden the length and breadth of his land, bringing his new subjects to town after town and unleashing them upon the populace. He thought the Scourge, which Kel'Thuzad had called them, a fitting name. The instrument of self-flagellation of the same name, sometimes used by some of the more fringe elements of the priesthood, was meant to cleanse impurities. His Scourge would cleanse the land of the living. He stood straddling the worlds; he was alive after a fashion, but the Lich King's soft whispers were calling him *death knight,* and the leeching of color from his hair and skin and eyes seemed to indicate that it was more than a title. He did not know; he did not care. He was the Lich King's favored, and the Scourge was his to command, and in a strange, twisted way, he found that he cared for them.

Arthas now served the Lich King through one of his sergeants, a dreadlord, almost identical in form to Mal'Ganis. This, too, was irony; this, too, did not distress him.

"Like Mal'Ganis, I am a dreadlord. But I am not your enemy," Tichondrius had reassured him. The lips twisted in a smile that was more of a sneer. "In truth, I've come to congratulate you. By killing your own father and delivering this land to the Scourge, you have passed your first test. The Lich King is pleased with your . . . enthusiasm."

Arthas felt buffeted by twin emotions—pain and exultation.

"Yes," he said, keeping his voice steady in front of the demon, "I've damned everyone and everything I've ever loved in his name, and I still feel no remorse. No pity. No shame."

And in his heart of hearts, there came another whisper, but not from Frostmourne: *Liar.*

He forced the sentiment down. That voice would be silenced, somehow. He could not afford to permit the softness to grow. It was like gangrene; it would eat him, if he let it.

Tichondrius seemed not to notice. He pointed to Frostmourne. "The runeblade you carry was forged by my kind, long ago. The Lich King has empowered it to steal souls. Yours was the first one it claimed."

Emotions warred within Arthas. He stared at the blade. Tichondrius's word choice had not escaped him. *Stolen.* Had the Lich King asked for his soul in exchange for saving his people, Arthas would have given it. But the Lich King had asked no such thing; he had simply taken it. And now it was there, locked inside the glowing weapon, so close to Arthas that the prince—the king—could almost, but not quite, touch it. And had Arthas even gotten what he had set out to get? Had his people been saved?

Did it matter?

Tichondrius watched him closely. "Then I'll make do without one," Arthas said lightly. "What is the Lich King's will?"

It had been, it turned out, to rally what was left of the Cult of the Damned in order to have aid for a greater undertaking—the recovery of Kel'Thuzad's remains.

They lay, he had been told, in Andorhal, where Arthas himself had left them, a puddle of reeking, decaying flesh. Andorhal, where the shipments of plagued grain had come from. He recalled his fury as he had attacked the necromancer, but felt it no longer. A smile curved his pale lips. Irony.

The buildings that had once been a conflagration were now charred timbers. No one save the undead should be here now . . . and yet . . . Arthas frowned, drawing rein. Invincible halted, as obedient in death as he had been in life. Arthas could glimpse figures moving about. What little light there was on this dim day glinted off—

"Armor," he said. There were armored men stationed about the perimeter of the cemetery and one near a small tomb. He squinted, and then his eyes widened. Not just living beings, not just warriors, but paladins. And he knew why they were here. Kel'Thuzad, it seemed, drew the interest of many.

But he had dissolved the order. There shouldn't *be* any paladins, let alone gathered here. Frostmourne whispered; it was hungry. Arthas drew the mighty runeblade, lifted it so the little army of acolytes who accompanied him could see and be inspired by it, and charged. Invincible sprang forward, and Arthas saw the shock on the faces of the cemetery's guardians as he bore down on them. They fought valiantly, but in the end, it was futile; and they knew it, he could see it in their eyes.

He had just tugged Frostmourne free, feeling the sword's joy in taking another soul, when a voice cried, "Arthas!"

It was a voice Arthas had heard before, but he couldn't quite place it. He turned toward the speaker.

The man was tall and imposing. He had removed his helm, and it was the thick beard that jogged Arthas's memory. "Gavinrad," he said, surprised. "It has been a long time."

"Not long enough. Where is the hammer we gifted you with?" Gavinrad said, almost spitting the words. "The weapon of a paladin. A weapon of honor."

Arthas remembered. It had been this man who had placed the hammer at his feet. How clean, how pure, how simple it had all seemed then.

"I have a better weapon now," Arthas said. He lifted Frostmourne. It seemed to pulse eagerly in his hand. A whim struck him, and he obeyed it. "Stand aside, brother," he said, an odd gentleness tingeing his voice. "I've come to collect some old bones. For the sake of that day, and for the order to which we both belonged, you will not come to harm if you let me pass."

Gavinrad's bushy brows drew together and he spat in Arthas's direction. "I can't believe that we ever called you brother! Why Uther ever vouched for you is beyond me. Your betrayal has broken Uther's heart, boy. He would have given his life for yours in a second, and this is how you repay his loyalty? I knew it was a mistake to accept a spoiled prince into our order! You've made a mockery of the Silver Hand!"

Fury rose in Arthas, so swift and so intense he almost choked on it. How dare he! Arthas was a death knight, the hand of the Lich King. Life, death, and unlife—all fell within his purview. And Gavinrad spat upon his offer of safety. Arthas gritted his teeth.

"No, my *brother*," he growled softly. "When I slay your body and raise it as my servant, and make you dance to my tune, *that,* Gavinrad, will be a mockery of the Silver Hand."

Grinning, he beckoned tauntingly. The undead and the cultists who had accompanied him waited silently. Gavinrad did not rush in, but gathered himself, praying to the Light that would not save him. Arthas let him complete his prayer, let his weapon glow, as Arthas's own hammer had once done. With Frostmourne gripped tightly in his hand and the Lich King's powers surging through his dead-not-dead body, he knew that Gavinrad did not stand a chance.

Nor did he. The paladin fought with everything he had, but it was not enough. Arthas toyed with him a little, easing the sting that Gavinrad's words had caused, but soon tired of the game and dispatched his erstwhile brother in arms with a single mighty sword blow. He felt Frostmourne take in and obliterate yet another soul, and shivered slightly as Gavinrad's lifeless body fell to the earth. Despite what he had promised his now-vanquished foe, Arthas let him stay dead.

With a curt gesture he ordered his servants to begin retrieving the corpse. He had left Kel'Thuzad to rot where he had fallen, but someone, doubtless the necromancer's devout followers, had cared enough to put the body in a small crypt. The acolytes of the Cult of the Damned now rushed forward, finding the tomb and with effort pushing aside the lid. Inside was a coffin, which was quickly lifted out. Arthas nudged it with his foot, grinning a little.

"Come along now, necromancer," he said teasingly as the casket was borne into the back of a vehicle referred to as a "meat wagon." "The powers that you once served have need of you again."

"Told you my death would mean little."

Arthas started. He had become somewhat accustomed to hearing voices; the Lich King, through Frostmourne, whispered to him almost constantly now. But this was something different. He recognized the voice; he had heard it before, but arrogant and taunting, not confidential and conspiratorial.

Kel'Thuzad.

"What the . . . am I hearing ghosts now?"

Not only hearing them. *Seeing* them. Or one specific ghost, at least. Kel'Thuzad's shape slowly formed before his eyes, translucent and hovering, the eyes dark holes. But it was unmistakably him, and the spectral lips curved in a knowing smile.

"I was right about you, Prince Arthas."

"It took you long enough." The bass, angry rumble of Tichondrius seemed to come out of nowhere, and the specter—if it had indeed actually been there—disappeared. Arthas was shaken. Had he imagined it? Was he starting to lose his sanity along with his soul?

Tichondrius had not noticed anything and continued, removing the casket and peering disgustedly inside at the nearly-liquefied corpse of Kel'Thuzad. Arthas found the stench more tolerable than he had expected, though it was still horrific. It seemed like a lifetime ago he had struck at the necromancer with his hammer and watched the too-rapid decomposition of the newly dead man. "These remains are badly decomposed. They will never survive the trip to Quel'Thalas."

Arthas seized on the distraction. "Quel'Thalas?" The golden land of the elves . . .

"Yes. Only the energies of the high elves' Sunwell can bring Kel'Thuzad back to life." The dreadlord's frown deepened. "And with each moment, he decays further. You must steal a very special urn from the paladin's keeping. They are bearing it here now. Place the necromancer's remains within it, and he will be well protected for the journey."

The dreadlord was smirking. There was more to this than at first was apparent. Arthas opened his mouth to inquire; then closed it. Tichondrius would not tell him anyway. He shrugged, mounted Invincible, and rode where he was told.

Behind him, he heard the demon's dark laughter.

Tichondrius had been right. Moving slowly along the road, on foot, was a small funeral procession. A military funeral, or one for an important dignitary; Arthas recognized the trappings of such things. Several men in armor marched single file; one man in the center carried something in powerful arms. The faint sun glinted on his armor and upon the item he bore—the urn of which Tichondrius had spoken. And suddenly Arthas understood why Tichondrius had been amused.

The paladin's carriage was distinctive, his armor unique, and Arthas gripped Frostmourne with hands that had suddenly become slightly unsteady. He forced the myriad, confusing, unsettling sensations down, and ordered his men to approach.

The funeral party was not large, though it was filled with fighters of distinction, and it was an easy matter to completely surround them. They drew their weapons, but did not attack, turning instead for instructions to the man who bore the urn. Uther—for it could be no one else—seemed completely in control as he regarded his former student. His face was impassive, but more lined than Arthas remembered. His eyes, however, burned with righteous fury.

"The dog returns to his vomit," Uther said, the

words cracking like a whip. "I'd prayed you'd stay away."

Arthas twitched slightly. His voice was rough as he replied, "I'm a bad copper—I just keep turning up. I see you still call yourself a paladin, even though I dissolved your order."

Uther actually laughed, though it was bitter laughter. "As if you could dissolve it yourself. I answer to the Light, boy. So did you, once."

The Light. He still remembered it. His heart lurched in his chest and for a moment, just a moment, he lowered the sword. Then the whispers came, reminding him of the power he now bore, emphasizing that walking the path of the Light had not gotten him what he craved. Arthas gripped Frostmourne firmly once more.

"I did many things, once," he retorted. "No longer."

"Your father ruled this land for fifty years, and you've ground it to dust in a matter of days. But undoing and destruction is easy, isn't it?"

"Very dramatic, Uther. Pleasant as this is, I've no time to reminisce. I've come for the urn. Give it to me, and I'll make sure you die quickly." No sparing this one. Not even if he begged. Especially not if he begged. There was too much history between them. Too much—feeling.

Now Uther showed emotion other than anger. He stared at Arthas, aghast. "This urn holds your father's *ashes*, Arthas! What, were you hoping to piss on them one last time before you left his kingdom to rot?"

A sudden jolt went through Arthas.

Father—

"I didn't know what it held," he murmured, as much

to himself as to Uther. So this was the second reason the dreadlord had smirked as he had given Arthas his instructions. He, at least, had known what the urn contained. Test after test. Could Arthas fight his mentor . . . could he blaspheme his father's ashes. Arthas was growing sick of it. He harnessed that anger as he spoke, dismounting and drawing Frostmourne.

"Nor does it matter. I'll take what I came for one way or another."

Frostmourne was almost humming now, in his mind and in his hand, eager for the battle. Arthas settled into attack position. Uther regarded him for a moment, then slowly lifted his own glowing weapon.

"I didn't want to believe it," he said, his voice gruff, and Arthas realized with horror that tears stood in Uther's eyes. "When you were younger and selfish, I called it a child's failing. When you pushed on stubbornly, I dismissed it as a youth's need to move out from under his father's shadow. And Stratholme—aye, Light forgive me, even that—I prayed you would find your own path to see the error of your judgment. I could not stand against my liege's son."

Arthas forced a smile as the two began to circle each other. "But now you do."

"It was my last promise to your father. To my friend. I would see his remains treated with reverence, even after his own son brutally slaughtered him, unaware and unarmed."

"You'll die for that promise."

"Possibly." It didn't seem to bother Uther much. "I'd rather die honoring that promise than live at your mercy. I'm glad he's dead. I'm glad he doesn't have to see what you've become."

The remark . . . hurt. Arthas hadn't expected it to. He paused, emotions warring within him, and Uther, ever the better in their bouts, used that brief hesitation to charge forward. "For the Light!" he cried, pulling the hammer back and swinging it at Arthas with all his strength. The gleaming weapon arced at Arthas so swiftly he could hear the sound of its movement.

He leaped aside, barely in time, and felt the air brush his face as the weapon rushed past. Uther's expression was calm and focused . . . and deadly. It was his duty as he saw it to slay the betraying son, and stop the spread of evil.

Just as Arthas knew it was his duty to slay the man who had once mentored him. He needed to kill his past . . . all of his past. Or else it would forever reach out with the deceptively sweet hope of compassion and forgiveness. With an incoherent cry, Arthas brought Frostmourne down.

Uther's hammer blocked it. The two men strained, their faces within inches of each other, the muscles in their arms shaking with effort, until with a grunt Uther shoved Arthas backward. The younger man stumbled. Uther pressed the attack. His face was calm, but his eyes were fierce and resolute, and he seemed to fight as if his victory was inevitable. The utter confidence shook Arthas. His own blows were powerful, but erratic. He'd never been able to best Uther before—

"It ends here, boy!" Uther cried, his voice ringing. Suddenly to Arthas's horror the paladin was limned in a glowing, brilliant light. Not just his hammer, but his entire body, as if he himself was the true weapon of the Light that would strike Arthas down. "For the Light's justice!"

The hammer descended. All the air in Arthas's body was knocked out of him with a rush as the blow landed straight and true across his midsection. Only his armor saved him, and even that crumpled beneath the glowing hammer wielded by the holy, radiant paladin. Arthas went sprawling, Frostmourne flying from his grip, agony shooting through him as he struggled to breathe, struggled to rise. The Light—he had turned his back on it, had betrayed it. And now it was exacting retribution through Uther the Lightbringer, its greatest champion, infusing his old teacher with the purity of its brilliance and purpose.

The glow enveloping Uther increased, and Arthas grimaced in agony as the Light seared his eyes as well as his soul. He'd been wrong to forsake it, horribly wrong, and now its mercy and love had been transformed into this radiant, implacable being. He stared upward into the white light that was Uther's eyes, tears filling his own as he awaited the killing blow.

Had he grasped the sword without realizing it, or had it leaped into his hands of its own volition? In the swirling mental chaos that was that moment, Arthas could not tell. All he knew was that suddenly, his hands were closing on Frostmourne's hilt, and its voice was in his mind.

Every Light has its shadow—every day has its night—and even the brightest candle can be snuffed out.

And so can the brightest life.

He let out a gulping inhalation, sucking breath into his lungs, and for just a second, Arthas saw the Light enveloping Uther dim. Then Uther lifted the hammer again, ready to deal the killing blow.

But Arthas was not there.

If Uther was a bear, enormous and powerful, Arthas was a tiger, strong and coiled and swift. The hammer, strong and Light-blessed though it and its wielder might be, was not a fast weapon, nor was Uther's style of fighting. Frostmourne, however, though it was an enormous two-handed runeblade, seemed to almost be able to fight on its own.

He moved forward again, no hesitancy this time, and began to fight in earnest. He gave no quarter as he attacked Uther the Lightbringer; offered no moment's breathing space for the paladin to draw back the weapon to deliver a crushing blow. Uther's eyes widened with shock, then narrowed in determination. But the Light that had once surged so brightly from his powerful frame was diminishing with each passing second.

Diminishing before the power granted to him by the Lich King.

Again and again Frostmourne landed—here on the hammer's glowing head, here on the shaft, here on Uther's shoulder, in that narrow space between gorget and shoulder pauldrons, biting deep—

Uther grunted and staggered back. Blood poured from the wound. Frostmourne craved more, and Arthas wanted to give it more.

Snarling like a beast, his white hair flying, he pressed the attack. The hammer, great and glowing, fell from

Uther's nerveless fingers as Frostmourne nearly severed the arm. A blow dented Uther's breastplate; a second in the same spot cleaved it and tore at the flesh beneath. Uther's tabard, the blue and gold of the Alliance he had once fought for, fluttered to the snow-covered earth in pieces as Uther the Lightbringer fell heavily to his knees. He looked up. His breathing came with difficulty. Blood trickled from his mouth, seeping into his beard, but there was no hint of surrender on his face.

"I dearly hope that there's a special place in hell waiting for you, Arthas." He coughed, the blood bubbling up.

"We may never know, Uther," Arthas said coldly, lifting Frostmourne for the final blow. The sword nearly sang in anticipation. "I intend to live forever."

He brought the runeblade straight down, through Uther's throat, silencing the defiant words, piercing the great heart. Uther died almost immediately. Arthas tugged the blade free and stepped back, shaking. Surely, it was only from the release of tension and exultation.

He knelt and picked up the urn. He held it for a long moment, then slowly broke the seal and tipped the jar over, pouring out its contents. The ashes of King Terenas fell like gray rain, like plagued flour, drifting down onto the snow. Abruptly, the wind shifted. The gray powder that was all that was left of a king suddenly took flight, as if animated, whirling to shower the death knight. Startled, Arthas took a step backward. His hands automatically came up to shield his face, and he dropped the urn, which landed with a dull thunk on the ground. He shut his eyes and turned away, but not quickly enough,

and began to cough violently, the ashes acrid and choking. Abruptly, panic seized him. His gauntleted hands
came up to swipe at his face, trying to wipe off the fine
powder that clogged his throat and nose and stung his
eyes. He spat, and for a moment his stomach roiled.

Arthas took a deep breath and forced calm upon himself. A moment later, he rose, composed once again. If
he felt anything at all, he had locked it so deep he did
not know it. Stone-faced, he returned to the wagon that
bore the reeking, nearly liquid remains of Kel'Thuzad
and shoved it at one of the Scourge.

"Put the necromancer in here," he ordered.

He mounted Invincible.

Quel'Thalas was not far.

CHAPTER EIGHTEEN

During the six days it took to reach the high elven lands, Arthas spoke with the shade of Kel'Thuzad and gathered many, many more to his side.

From Andorhal eastward he went, the meat wagons grinding along in his wake, past the little hamlets of Felstone Field, Dalson's Orchard, and Gahrron's Quickening, across the Thondroril River into the eastern part of Lordaeron. Risen plague victims were everywhere, and a simple mental command brought them to heel like faithful hounds. Care of them was easy—they fed on the dead. It was very . . . tidy.

These Arthas was expecting to come to his side; the plague victims, the abominations sewn together of many parts, the ghosts of the fallen. But a new ally joined him—one that startled, appalled, and then delighted him.

His army was halfway to Quel'Thalas when he first saw them. Far in the distance, it first appeared as if the earth itself was moving. No, that wasn't right. These were beasts, of a sort. Cattle or sheep, that had broken out of their pens when their owners turned into the walking dead? Bears or wolves, foraging and feasting on corpses? And then Arthas gasped and grasped Frostmourne tightly, his eyes wide with shock and disbelief.

They did not move like four-legged creatures. They scuttled, scurried, moving over the hills and grasses like—

"Spiders," he murmured.

Now they poured down the slopes, purple and black and dangerous-looking, multiple legs scurrying quickly to bear them to Arthas. They were coming for him—they—

"These are the new warriors the Lich King sends to his favored one," came Kel'Thuzad's voice. The ghost apparently could be heard and seen only by Arthas, and he had been doing a great deal of talking in the last few days. He had recently focused on sowing the seeds of suspicion in the death knight's mind. Not of himself—of Tichondrius and the other demons. "The dreadlords cannot be trusted," he had said. "They are the Lich King's jailers. I will tell you all . . . when I walk this world again."

They had had enough time; Arthas wondered if Kel'Thuzad was dangling the information in front of him like bait, to ensure that Arthas completed the task.

Now Arthas asked, "He sent these . . . to me? What are they?"

"They once were nerubians," Kel'Thuzad said. "Descendants of an ancient and proud race called the aqir. In life, they were fiercely intelligent, their will dedicated to wiping out any who were not like themselves."

Arthas eyed the arachnid creatures with a shiver of disgust. "Lovely. And now?"

"Now, these are those who fell battling the one we serve. He has raised them and their lord, Anub'arak, into undeath, and now they come to aid you, Prince Arthas. To serve his glory and yours."

"Undead spiders," Arthas mused. They were huge, hideous, deadly. They came chittering and scuttling, merging into step with the corpses, specters, and abominations. "To fight the elves of Quel'Thalas."

This Lich King, whomever he was, had a flair for the dramatic.

Arthas's coming, of course, was witnessed. The elves bred notoriously fine scouts. Chances were by the time Arthas himself noticed them, word had already gone ahead. It didn't matter. The force he had assembled had grown to a truly impressive size, and he had no doubt, despite Kel'Thuzad's fretful warnings, that he would be able to gain entry into the wondrous, eternal land, move through it swiftly, and reach the Sunwell.

They had captured a prisoner, a young priest who in an act of defiance had inadvertently revealed some important information. Arthas would use the information wisely and well. Too, there was another, one who, unlike the priest, would willingly betray his people and their land for the power that Arthas and the Lich King had promised him.

It surprised the death knight how readily this elven mage had turned. Surprised, and unsettled him. Arthas had once been loved by his people, as his father before him had been. He had enjoyed basking in the warm approval from those who served under him. He had taken time to learn their names, to listen to stories of their families. He had wanted them to love him. And they had, following him loyally, as Captain Falric had done.

But Arthas had to assume that the elven leaders, too, loved their people. Assumed, as Arthas assumed, that they would stay loyal. And yet this mage had betrayed his people for nothing more than the mere promise of power, the simple, glittering allure of it.

Mortals could be corrupted. Mortals could be swayed, or bought.

He looked over his current army and smiled. Yes . . . this was better. There was no question of loyalty when those he led could do nothing but obey.

"It is true," the scout gasped. "All of it."

Sylvanas Windrunner, Ranger-General of Silvermoon, knew this elf well. Kelmarin's information was always accurate and detailed. She listened, wanting to disbelieve, knowing she did not dare.

They had all heard the rumors, of course. That some sort of plague had begun to creep across the human lands. But the quel'dorei had thought themselves safe here in their homeland. It had withstood attacks from dragons, orcs, and trolls over the centuries. Surely, what was occurring in the human lands would not touch them.

Except it had.

"You are sure it is Arthas Menethil? The prince?"

Kelmarin nodded, still catching his breath. "Aye, my lady. I heard him called so by those who served him. I do not think the rumors painting him as the slayer of his father and the instigator of the troubles in Lordaeron are exaggerations, from what I have seen."

Sylvanas listened, her blue eyes widening, as the scout spun a tale that sounded too fantastical to be believed. Risen corpses, both fresh and desiccated. Enormous, mindless patchwork creations of various body parts; strange beasts who could fly and looked like stone creations come to life; giant spiderlike beings that reminded her of tales of the thought-vanished aqir. And the smell— Kelmarin, who was not given to exaggeration, spoke in halting tones about the reek that preceded the army. The forests, the first bastion of defense of the land, were falling beneath the strange engines of war he had brought with him. Sylvanas thought back to the red dragons, which had set the woods aflame not so very long ago. Silvermoon had endured, of course, but the woodlands had suffered terribly. As they were suffering now. . . .

"My lady," Kelmarin finished, lifting his head and giving her a stricken gaze. "If he breaks through—I do not think we have the numbers to defeat him."

The bitter statement gave her the anger she needed. "We are quel'dorei," she snapped, straightening. "Our land is impregnable. He will not enter. Do not fear. He must first know *how* to break the enchantments that protect Quel'Thalas. Then he must be able to do so. Better and wiser foes than he have tried to take our realm ere now. Have faith, my friend. In the Sunwell's strength . . . and in the strength and will of our people."

As Kelmarin was led off to where he could drink and eat and recover before returning to his post, Sylvanas turned to her rangers. "I would see this human prince for myself. Summon the first battle units. If Kelmarin is correct . . . we should prepare for a preemptive strike."

Sylvanas lay atop the great gate that, along with the jagged ring of mountains, helped protect her land. She wore full but comfortable leather armor, and her bow was slung across her back. She and Sheldaris and Vor'athil, the other two scouts who had gone on ahead and had waited for her to come with the bulk of the rangers, stared, aghast. As Kelmarin had warned, they had smelled the reek of the decaying army long before they had seen them.

Prince Arthas rode atop a skeletal horse with fiery eyes, a huge sword that she recognized at once as a runeblade strapped to his back. Humans in dark clothing scurried to obey his commands. So did the dead. Sylvanas choked back bile as her gaze roved over the collection of various rotting corpses, and she was silently thankful that the wind had shifted and was now blowing the stench away from her.

She signaled her plan, long fingers moving quickly, and the scouts nodded. They slipped back, silent as shadows, and Sylvanas turned her eyes toward Arthas. He did not seem to have noticed anything. He looked human, still, though pale, and his hair was white instead of golden, as she recalled it had been described to her. How then, could he stand this? Being surrounded by the dead—the horrible stench, the grotesque images . . .

She shuddered and instructed herself to focus. The undead who obeyed him simply stood, awaiting orders. The humans—necromancers, Sylvanas thought, a wave of loathing rushing through her—were too busy creating new monstrosities to post lookouts. They could not conceive of defeat.

Their arrogance would be their undoing.

She waited, watching, until her archers were in position. Forewarned by Kelmarin, she had summoned fully two thirds of her rangers. She believed firmly that Arthas could not breach the magical elfgates that protected Quel'Thalas. There was too much he could not possibly know about them to do so. Still . . . she had also not believed things that her eyes now told her was truth. Better to wipe out the threat here and now.

She glanced at Sheldaris and Vor'athil. They caught her gaze and nodded. They were ready. Sylvanas yearned to simply strike, to take the enemy unawares, but honor forbade it. There would be no tales sung of how Ranger-General Sylvanas Windrunner defended her homeland by underhanded means.

"For Quel'Thalas," she whispered underneath her breath, and then stood.

"You are not welcome here!" she cried, her voice clear and musical and strong. Arthas turned his skeletal steed—Sylvanas spared a moment to pity the poor beast—and faced her, peering at her intently. The necromancers fell silent, turning to their lord, awaiting instructions.

"I am Sylvanas Windrunner, Ranger-General of Silvermoon. I advise you to turn back now."

Arthas's lips—gray, she noticed, gray in a white face, although she knew somehow he yet lived—curled back in a smile. He was amused.

"It is you who should turn back, Sylvanas," he said, deliberately omitting her title. His voice would have been a pleasant baritone had it not been underscored by . . . something. Something that made even her fierce heart stop for a moment as she heard it. She forced herself not to shiver. "Death itself has come to your land."

Her blue eyes narrowed. "Do your worst," she challenged. "The elfgate to the inner kingdom is protected by our most powerful enchantments. You shall not pass."

She nocked her bow—the signal for the attack. An instant later, the air was filled with the sudden hum of dozens of arrows in flight. Sylvanas had taken aim for the human—or once-human—prince, and her aim was as true as ever. The arrow sang as it sped toward Arthas's unprotected head. But an instant before it struck, she saw a flash of blue-white.

Sylvanas stared. More swiftly than she could fathom, Arthas had brought up his sword, the runes in it emitting that cold blue-white glow, and sliced the arrow in two. He grinned at her and winked.

"To battle, my troops—slay them all, that they may serve me and my lord!" Arthas cried. His voice echoed with that strange thrum of power. She growled deep in her throat and took aim again. But he was in motion now, the dead horse bearing him with unnatural swiftness, and she realized that his horrific troops were on the offensive now.

She thought of a swarm of insects as they converged,

perfect in their mindless unity, upon her rangers. The archers had their instructions—cut down the living first, and then dispatch the dead with arrows set aflame. The first volley of arrows dropped nearly every single one of the cultists. The second saw dozens of blazing arrows embedded in the walking corpses. But even as they stumbled about, some of them almost tinder-dry, others moist and rotting, the sheer number of them began to turn the tide.

They somehow managed to scramble up the nearly vertical walls of earth and stone where her rangers were positioned. Some of them, mercifully, were too decayed to get far, their rotting limbs ripping from their bodies and causing them to fall. But the fall did not halt them. They pressed onward, upward, toward her rangers who now had to wield swords instead of arrows. They were trained warriors, of course, and could fight in close quarters. Fight against foes who could be slowed by the loss of blood, or limbs. But against these—

Dead hands, more like claws than fingers, reached out to Sheldaris. Grim faced, the red-haired ranger fought fiercely, her lips moving in cries of defiance that Sylvanas could not hear. But they were closing in on her, ringing her, and Sylvanas felt a deep pain as she watched Sheldaris fall beneath them.

She drew and fired, drew and fired, almost quicker than thought, focusing on her duty. Out of the corner of her eye she saw one of the grotesque winged creatures, its skin gray and appearing as hard as stone, swoop down within ten feet of her. Its batlike face snarled in glee as it reached down and, as easily as she might pluck ripe fruit from a tree, snatched Vor'athil and bore him aloft. Its fingers dug deeply into the scout's shoulders, and blood spattered on Sylvanas as the thing swooped upward with its prize.

Vor'athil struggled in the creature's grasp, his fingers finding and freeing a dagger. Sylvanas turned her aim from the groaning undead below her to the monstrosity above. She fired, right at the creature's neck.

The arrow glanced off harmlessly. The creature tossed its head and snarled, tiring of toying with Vor'athil. It lifted one hand and raked its claws across the scout's throat, then dropped him carelessly and circled back for more.

Grieving silently, Sylvanas watched her friend fall lifeless to the earth, his body striking the pile of dead cultists her rangers had slain moments earlier.

And then she gasped.

The cultists were moving.

Arrows protruding from their bodies, sometimes over a dozen brightly fletched missiles in a single corpse, and yet they stirred.

"No," she whispered, sickened. Her horrified gaze went to Arthas.

The prince was looking straight at her, grinning that damnable grin. One powerful, gauntleted hand grasped the runeblade. The other was lifted in a beckoning gesture, and as she watched, yet another slain human stirred and shambled to its feet, pulling out the arrow from its eye as if it were plucking a burr from its clothing. Her attack had cost Arthas nothing. Any who fell would be raised by his dark magic. He saw the realization and the anger in her eyes, and the grin turned into a laugh.

"I did try to tell you," he cried, his voice rising above the din of battle. "And still you provide me with new recruits. . . ."

He gestured again, and another body twitched as it was hauled upward and forced to stand on its feet. A body that had been slender but muscular, with long black hair swept back in a ponytail, with tanned skin and pointed ears. Blood still ran in red rivulets from the four scores in its throat, and the head bobbed erratically, as if the neck had been too badly damaged to support it much longer. Dead eyes that had once been blue as summer skies sought out Sylvanas. And then, slowly at first, it began to move toward her.

Vor'athil.

At that moment she felt the gate beneath her shudder, ever so slightly. So distracted had she been by the slaughter and reanimation of things that ought to stay dead that she had not noticed his siege engines maneuvering into position. The ogre-sized things that appeared to be comprised of various different corpses were battering away at the gate as well. So were the enormous, spider-like creatures.

Then something hit the wall with a soft, plopping sound. Wetness spattered Sylvanas. For a fraction of a second, her mind refused to accept what she had just witnessed, and then clarity broke upon her.

Arthas was not only raising the corpses of the fallen elves. He was hurling their bodies—or pieces of them— back at Sylvanas as ammunition.

Sylvanas swallowed hard, then issued the order that a few moments ago she never would have dreamed she would utter.

"Shindu fallah na! Fall back to the second gate! Fall back!"

Those who were left—*ai*, piteous few there were still, at least still alive and fighting under her command—obeyed at once, gathering up the wounded and slinging them over their shoulders, their faces pale and sweat-streaked and reflecting the same forcibly contained terror that raced through her. They fled. There was no other word for it. This was no orderly, synchronized, martial retreat, but an all-out flight. Sylvanas ran with the rest of them, bearing the wounded as best she could, and her mind was racing.

Behind her she heard the once-inconceivable sound of the gate cracking and the roar of the undead as they howled their triumph. Her own heart seemed to crack in agony.

He had done it—but how? How?

His voice, strong, resonant, with that undercurrent of something dark and terrible, rose over the noise. "The elfgate has fallen! Onward, my warriors! Onward to victory!"

Somehow, to Sylvanas, the worst, most awful thing about that gleeful, gloating cry was the . . . *affection* . . . that laced through it.

She seized the sleeve of a young man racing beside her. "Tel'kor," Sylvanas cried. "Make for the Sunwell Plateau. Tell them what we have seen here. Tell them—to be prepared."

Tel'kor was young enough to let disappointment flicker over his handsome features at the thought of not standing to fight, but he nodded his golden head in comprehension. Sylvanas hesitated.

"My lady?"

"Tell them—we may have been betrayed."

Tel'kor blanched at that, but nodded. Like an arrow shot from a bow, he raced away. He was a good archer, but Sylvanas did not suffer any illusion that one more bow would make a difference in the battle that was to come. But if the magi who controlled and directed the Sunwell's energies knew what they faced—that might.

They were racing northward now, and as her troops crossed a bridge she suddenly stopped in mid-run, whirled on her heel, and looked back.

Sylvanas gasped. That Arthas and his dark army were coming, she expected to see. That would have been a horrific enough sight; the undead, the abominations, the flying batlike things, the grotesque spidery beings—hundreds, bearing down with implacable determination. What she did not expect to see was what they left in their wake.

Like a trail left by a slug, like a furrow left by a plow, the land where the undead feet had trod was blackened and barren. Worse; Sylvanas remembered the burned woods the orcs had left behind, knew that nature would eventually reclaim it. This—it was a horrible dark line of death, as if the unnatural energies that were used to propel the corpses forward were killing the very earth upon which they shambled. Poison, they were poison; it was dark magic of the foulest kind.

And it had to be stopped.

She had paused only an instant, although to her it felt as though she had been frozen in place for a lifetime. "Hold!" she cried, her voice clear and strong and purposeful. "We will make our stand here."

They were puzzled only briefly, then they understood. Quickly she spoke instructions, and they leaped to obey. Many of them paused, shocked, as they caught their first stunned glimpse of the grievous wound to the land that had so horrified their ranger-general, but they recovered quickly. Time enough to worry about healing the brutalized earth later. For now, they had to stop that dreadful scar from spreading.

The stench preceded the army, but Sylvanas and her rangers now had a grim familiarity with it. It did not unnerve them as it had before. She stood on the bridge, her head held high, her black hood slipping a little to show bright golden hair. The army of the dead slowed and halted, confused by the sight. The ugly wagons, catapults, and trebuchets rumbled to a halt. Arthas's skeletal horse reared, and he reached down and stroked the bony neck as if it were a living beast. Sylvanas felt a shiver of nausea at the wrongness of the tableau as the thing responded to its master's touch.

"Goodness," Arthas said, humor lacing the word with something akin to warmth. "This can't be one of the oh-so-imposing elfgates I've heard so much about."

Sylvanas forced herself to grin back. "No, not quite. But you'll still find it a challenge."

"It is but a simple bridge, my lady. But then again, the

elves are very fond of putting paper manes on cats and calling them lions."

She eyed his army for a moment, her anger penetrating her forced smugness. "You've won through this gate, butcher, but you won't get through the second. The inner gate to Silvermoon can only be opened with a special key, and it shall never be yours!"

She nodded to her companions, and they raced across the bridge to join their fellows on the other side.

Arthas's humor faded and his pale eyes flashed. His gauntleted hand tightened on the runeblade. Its markings thrummed. "You waste your time, woman. You cannot outrun the inevitable. Though I admit it is amusing to watch you scurry."

Now Sylvanas did laugh, an angry, satisfied sound that rolled up from some place deep in her soul. "You think I'm running from you? Apparently you've never fought elves before."

Some things, she mused, were deliciously simple. Sylvanas lifted her hand, threw the extremely non-magical, quite practical incendiary device, then turned to run as the bridge exploded. The trees welcomed them, arching above them in hues of gold and silver, hiding them from their enemy. Before the sounds faded from earshot, she heard something that made her grin fiercely.

"The ranger woman is starting to vex me greatly."

Yes. Vex you. Harry you like a sparrow does the hawk. The Elrendar bisects Eversong Woods, and you will find no crossing for your monstrous engines of war anytime soon. She knew it was a delay, nothing more. But if the army was delayed long enough, perhaps she could get a message through.

Worry fluttered at her mind. Arthas had seemed supremely confident that he would be able to defeat the magic that powered the elfgates. He had already shown some knowledge in that he had been able to destroy the first gate. Of course, the first gate was not as magically defended as the second. And, from what she had seen, arrogance seemed to be his normal state, but—was it possible? The nagging uncertainty that had prompted her to add a final warning to Tel'kor's message to the magi stirred within her again.

Did Arthas know about the key?

CHAPTER NINETEEN

The traitor, a wizard by the name of Dar'Khan Drathir, should have made it easy. And to some extent he had, of course. Arthas would otherwise never have known about the Key of the Three Moons—a magical item that had been split into three separate mooncrystals stashed in heavily-guarded, hidden locations throughout Quel'Thalas. Each temple was constructed on an intersection of ley lines, similar to the Sunwell itself, the traitorous elf had told him, gleeful to be betraying his people so. The ley lines were like blood vessels of the earth, carrying magic instead of scarlet fluid. Thus interconnected, the crystals created a field of energy known as Ban'dinoriel—the Gatekeeper. All he needed to do was find these sites at An'telas, An'daroth, and An'owyn, slay the guards, and find the mooncrystals.

But the excessively pretty, surprisingly tough elves presented a challenge. Arthas sat astride Invincible, idly fingering Frostmourne, and reflected on how it was that so fragile-seeming a race could stand up to his army. For army now it truly was—many hundreds of soldiers, all already dead and so more difficult to permanently dispatch.

The ranger-general's clever little trick of blowing up the bridge had indeed cost Arthas precious time. The river ran through Quel'Thalas until it bumped up against several foothills to the east—foothills that posed the same challenge to the mobility of his engines of war that the water did.

It had taken a while, but eventually they had crossed the river. As he pondered the solution, something had twinged at the back of his mind, a tingling sensation he couldn't quite figure out. Annoyed, he dismissed the strange sensation and instructed several of his unfailingly loyal soldiers to create their own bridge—a bridge made of rotting flesh. Dozens of them waded into the river and simply lay there, forming layer upon layer of corpses, until there were enough of them that the meat wagons, catapults, and trebuchets could make their lurching way across. Some of the undead, of course, were no longer of use, their bodies too broken or torn to hold cohesion. These Arthas almost gently released from his control, granting them true death. Besides, their bodies would foul the purity of the river. It was an additional weapon.

He, of course, could and did cross easily. Invincible plunged without hesitation into the water, and Arthas was abruptly reminded of the horse's fatal jump in the middle of winter, slipping on the icy rocks as he leaped, utterly obedient to the will of his master then as now. The memory crashed on him unexpectedly, and for a moment he couldn't breathe as pain and guilt washed over him.

It was gone as quickly as it had come. Everything was better now. He was no longer an emotionally shattered child, racked by guilt and shame, sobbing in the snow as he lifted his sword to pierce the heart of a loyal friend. No, nor was Invincible a mere living creature, to be harmed by such a thing. They were both more powerful now. Stronger. Invincible would exist forever, serving his master, as he had always done. He would not know thirst, or pain, or hunger, or exhaustion. And he, Arthas, would take what he wished when he wished it. There was no more silent disapproval from his father, no more scolding from the too-pious Uther. No more dubious glances from Jaina, her brow furrowed in that dearly familiar expression of—

Jaina . . .

Arthas shook his head sharply. Jaina had had her chance to join with him. She had refused. Denied him, although she had sworn she would never do so. He owed her nothing. Only the Lich King commanded him now. The mental shift calmed him, and Arthas smiled and patted the jutting vertebrae of the undead beast, who tossed his bony head in response. Surely, it was the beautiful and willful ranger-general who had unsettled him and made him question, even momentarily, the wisdom of his path. She, too, had had her chance. Arthas had come for a purpose, and that purpose had not been to obliterate Quel'Thalas and its populace. Had they not resisted him, he would have let them be. Her sharp tongue and defiant behavior had brought her people's doom upon them, not he.

The water seeped in through the joins of his armor

and the breeches, shirt, and gambeson he wore beneath the metal plate grew wet and cold. Arthas did not feel it. A moment later Invincible surged forward, clambering out onto the opposite bank. The last of the meat wagons rumbled onto the bank as well, and what corpses were sufficiently intact slogged onto land. The rest lay where they had fallen, the once crystal-clear water flowing over and around them.

"Onward," the death knight said.

The rangers had retreated to Fairbreeze Village. Once the shock had passed, the citizens did everything they could, from tending the wounded to offering what weapons and skills they had. Sylvanas ordered those who could not fight to head to Silvermoon as quickly as possible.

"Take nothing," she said as a woman nodded and hurried to ascend the ramp to an upper area.

"But our rooms upstairs have—"

Sylvanas whirled, her eyes flaring. "Do you not yet understand? *The dead are marching upon us!* They do not tire, they do not slow, and they take our fallen and add them to their ranks! We have delayed them, little more. Take your family and *go!*"

The woman seemed taken aback by the ranger-general's response, but obeyed, wasting only a few moments rounding up her family before hastening down the road to the capital.

Arthas would not be stopped for long. Sylvanas cast a sweeping, appraising glance over the wounded. None of them could stay here. They, too, would need to be evacuated to Silvermoon. As for those who were still hale, few though they were, she would need to ask yet more from them. Perhaps everything they had. They, like she, had sworn to defend their people. Now was the day of reckoning.

There was a spire close by, between the Elrendar and Silvermoon. Somehow, she felt certain Arthas would find a way to cross and continue his march. Continue to wound the land with the purplish-black scar. The spire would be a good place to mount a defense. The ramps were narrow, preventing the crush of undead that had been so disastrous previously, and there were several stories to the building, all open to the air. She and her archers could do a great deal of damage before they were—

Sylvanas Windrunner, Ranger-General of Silvermoon, took a calming breath, dashed water on her heated face, drank a deep draft of the soothing liquid, and rose to prepare the uninjured and walking wounded for what would no doubt be their final battle.

They were almost too late.

Even as the rangers marched on the spire that would be their bastion, the air, once so sweet and fresh, was tainted with the sickly odor of putrefaction. Overhead, mounted archers hovered on their dragonhawks. The great creatures, golden and scarlet, stretched their serpentine heads against the reins unhappily. They, too, scented death, and it disturbed them. Never had the beautiful beasts been pressed into such a ghastly service. One of the riders signaled Sylvanas, and she signaled back.

"The undead have been sighted," she told her troops calmly. They nodded. "Positions. Hurry."

Like a well-oiled gnomish machine, they obeyed. The dragonhawk riders surged south, toward the approaching enemy. A unit of archers and hand-to-hand fighters hurried forward as well, the first line of defense. Her finest archers raced up the curving ramps of the spire. The rest spread out at the base of the structure.

They did not have long to wait.

If she had harbored any faint hope that somehow the numbers of the enemy might have suffered from the delay, it was dashed like fine crystal falling to a stone floor. She could glimpse the hideous vanguard now: rotting undead, followed by skeletons and the huge abominations whose three arms each carried massive weapons. Above them flew the stonelike creatures wheeling like buzzards.

They are breaking through. . . .

How strange the mind was, Sylvanas thought with a trace of macabre humor. Now, as the hour of her death doubtless approached, an ancient song played in her head; one she and her siblings had loved to sing, when the world was right and they were all together, Alleria, Vereesa, and their youngest brother, Lirath, at twilight when soft lavender shadows spread their gentle cloaks and the sweet scent of the ocean and flowers wafted across the land.

Anar'alah, anar'alah belore, quel'dorei, shindu fallah na. . . . By the light, by the light of the sun, high elves, our enemies are breaking through. . . .

Without her realizing it at first, her hand fluttered upward to close on the necklace she wore about her slender throat. It had been a gift, from her oldest sister, Alleria; delivered not by Alleria herself, but in her stead by one of her lieutenants, Verana. Alleria was gone, vanished through the Dark Portal in an attempt to stop the Horde from visiting their atrocities again on Azeroth and on other worlds as well.

She had never returned. She had melted down a necklace given to her by their parents, and made individual necklaces out of the three stones for each of the Windrunner sisters. Sylvanas's was a sapphire. She knew the inscription by heart: *To Sylvanas. Love always, Alleria.*

She waited, grasping the necklace, feeling the connection with her dead sister it always provided, then slowly forced her hand away. Sylvanas took a deep breath and shouted, "Attack! For Quel'Thalas!"

There would be no stopping them. In truth, she did not expect to stop them. From the expressions on the grim, bloodied faces around her, Sylvanas realized her rangers knew this as well as she. Sweat dewed her face. Her muscles screamed with exhaustion, and still Sylvanas Windrunner fought. She fired, nocking and releasing and nocking again so swiftly that her hands were almost a blur. When the swarm of corpses and monsters came too close for arrows, she flung her bow away and seized her short sword and dagger. She whirled and turned and stabbed, crying out incoherently as she battled.

Another one fell, its head toppling from its shoulders to be trampled, bursting open like a melon beneath the feet of one of its own. Two more monstrosities surged forward to take its place. Still Sylvanas fought like one of the savage lynxes of Eversong Woods, channeling her pain and outrage into violence. She would take as many with her as she could before she fell.

They are breaking through. . . .

They pressed in, close, the reek of decay almost overwhelming her. Too many of them now. Sylvanas did not slow. She would fight until they had utterly destroyed her, until—

The press of corpses suddenly was gone. They stepped back and stood still. Gasping for breath, Sylvanas looked down the hill.

He was there, waiting on his undead steed. The wind played with his long white hair as he regarded her intently. She straightened, wiping blood and sweat from her face. A paladin, he had been once. Her sister had loved one such as him. Suddenly Sylvanas was fiercely glad that Alleria was dead, could not see this, could not see what a former champion of the Light was doing to everything the Windrunners loved and cherished.

Arthas lifted the glowing runeblade in a formal gesture. "I salute your bravery, elf, but the chase is over." Oddly, he sounded like he meant the compliment.

Sylvanas swallowed; her mouth was dry as bone. She tightened her grip on her weapons. "Then I'll make my stand here, butcher. Anar'alah belore."

His gray lips twitched. "As you will, Ranger-General."

He did not even bother to dismount. Instead the skeletal steed whinnied and galloped straight toward her. Arthas gripped the reins with his left hand, his right drawing back the massive sword. Sylvanas sobbed, once. No cry of fear or regret came from those lips. Only a short, harsh sob of impotent anger, of hatred, of righteous fury that she was not able to stop them, not even when she had given all she could, not even with her life's blood.

Alleria, sister, I come.

She met the deadly blade head-on, striking it with her own weapons, which shattered upon impact. And then the runeblade had pierced her. Cold, so cold it was, slicing through her as if it was made of ice itself.

Arthas leaned in to her, his gaze locked with hers. Sylvanas coughed, fine droplets of blood spattering his bone-pale face. Was it her imagination, or was there a hint of regret on his still-fine features?

He tugged back his weapon and she fell, blood gushing out of her. Sylvanas shivered on the cold stone floor, the movement causing agony to rip through her. One hand fluttered, foolishly, to the gaping wound in her abdomen, as if her hands could close on it and stop the flood.

"Finish it," she whispered. "I deserve . . . a clean death."

His voice floated to her from somewhere as her eyes closed. "After all you've put me through, woman, the last thing I'll give you is the peace of death."

Fear spiked in her for a heartbeat, then faded as everything else was beginning to. He would raise her, as one of those grotesque shambling things?

"No," she murmured, her voice sounding as if it came from a long way off. "You wouldn't . . . dare. . . ."

And then it went away. It all went away. The coldness,

the stench, the searing pain. It was soft and warm and dark and calm and comforting, and Sylvanas permitted herself to sink into the welcoming darkness. At last she could rest, could lay down the arms she had borne for so long in service to her people.

And then—

Agony shot through her, agony such as she had never known, and Sylvanas suddenly knew that no physical pain she had ever endured could hold a pale candle to this torment. This was an agony of the spirit, of her soul leaving her lifeless form and being trapped. Of a . . . ripping, tearing, yanking back from that warm sanctuary of silence and stillness. The violence of the act added to the exquisite torment, and Sylvanas felt a scream welling up, forcing its way from deep inside, past lips that somehow she knew were no longer physical, a deep keening wail of a suffering that was not hers alone, that froze blood and stopped hearts.

The blackness faded from her vision, but colors did not return. She did not need reds or blues or yellows to see him, though, her tormentor; he was white and gray and black even in a world with color. The runeblade that had taken her life, had taken and consumed her soul, glittered and gleamed, and Arthas's free hand was lifted in a beckoning gesture as he ripped her from the soothing embrace of death.

"Banshee," he told her. "Thus I have made you. You can give voice to your pain, Sylvanas. I will give you that much. It is more than the others get. And in so doing, you shall cause pain to others. So now you, troublesome ranger, shall serve."

Terrified beyond reason, Sylvanas hovered over her bloodied, broken corpse, gazing into her own staring eyes, then back at Arthas.

"No," she said, her voice hollow and eerie, yet still recognizably hers. "I will never serve you, butcher."

He gestured. It was the merest thing, a twitch of a gauntleted finger. Her back arched in agony and another scream was torn from her, and she realized with a racking, raging sense of grief that she was utterly powerless before him. She was his tool, as the rotting corpses and the pale, reeking abominations were his tools.

"Your rangers serve as well," he said. "They are now in my army." He hesitated, and there was genuine regret in his voice when he said, "It did not have to be this way. Know that your fate, theirs, and that of your people, rests upon your choices. But I must press on to the Sunwell. And you will assist me."

The hate grew inside Sylvanas like a living thing in her incorporeal body. She floated beside him, his shiny new toy, her body gathered up and flung on one of the meat wagons to who knew what sick end Arthas could devise. As if there was a thread that bound her to him, she never was more than a few feet away from the death knight.

And she was beginning to hear the whispers.

At first, Sylvanas wondered if she was insane in this new, abhorrent incarnation. But it soon became apparent that even the refuge of the mad was denied her. The voice in her mind was unintelligible at first, and in her wretched state she did not wish to hear. But soon she understood to whom it belonged.

Arthas kept giving her sidelong glances as he continued his inexorable march to Silvermoon and beyond, watching her closely. At one point, as this army of which she was a captive part surged forward, destroying the land as it passed, she heard it very clearly.

For my glory, you will serve, Sylvanas. For the dead, you will toil. For obedience, you will hunger. Arthas is the first and most beloved of my death knights; he will command you forever, and you will find it joyous.

Arthas saw her shiver, and he smiled.

If she had thought she despised him when she first beheld him outside the gates of Quel'Thalas, when the wondrous land within was still clean and pure and had not known the killing touch; if she had thought she hated him as his minions slew her people and raised them to become lifeless puppets, and when he impaled her in a single, savage blow with the monstrous runeblade—it was as nothing to what she felt now. A candle to a sun, a whisper to a banshee's scream.

Never, she told the voice in her head. *He directs my actions, but Arthas cannot break my will.*

The only answer was hollow, cold laughter.

On they pushed, past Fairbreeze Village and the East Sanctum. At the gates of Silvermoon itself they halted. Arthas's voice should not have carried as it did, but Sylvanas knew that it was heard in every corner of the city as he stood in front of the gates.

"Citizens of Silvermoon! I have given you ample

opportunities to surrender, but you have stubbornly refused. Know that today, your entire race and your ancient heritage will end! Death itself has come to claim the high home of the elves!"

She, Ranger-General Sylvanas Windrunner, was paraded in front of her people as an example of what would happen to them if they did not surrender. They did not, and she loved them fiercely for it even as she was pressed into service by her dark master.

And so it fell, the shining, beautiful city of magic, its glories shattered and reduced to rubble as the army of undead—the Scourge, she heard Arthas call them, twisted affection in his voice—pressed on. As he had before, Arthas raised the fallen to serve, and if Sylvanas had still possessed a heart, it would have broken at the sight of so many friends and loved ones shambling beside her, mindlessly obedient. On through the city they marched, cleaving it in twain with the vile purple-black scar, its citizens lurching to their feet with wounds that had smashed skulls, or trailing viscera behind them as they shambled forward.

She had hoped the channel between Silvermoon and Quel'Danas would prove an impassable barrier, and for a moment that hope seemed realized. Arthas drew rein, staring at the blue water glinting in the sun, and frowned. For a moment he sat atop his unnatural steed, his white brows knitted together. "You cannot fill this channel with corpses, Arthas," Sylvanas had gloated. "Not even the whole city would be enough. You are stopped here, and your failure is sweet." And then the being who had once been human, who had once by all accounts been a good man, turned and grinned at her blistering words of defiance, sending her into a paroxysm of agony and wrenching another soul-splitting scream from her incorporeal lips.

He had found a solution.

He cast Frostmourne toward the shore, watching it almost rapturously as it flipped end over end to land with its tip impaled in the sand.

"Frostmourne speaks. . . ."

Sylvanas heard it, too, the voice of the Lich King emanating from the unholy weapon as before her shocked gaze the water lapping at its rune-inscribed blade began to turn to ice. Ice that his weapons, and his warriors, could cross.

He took her life, he took her beloved Quel'Thalas and Silvermoon, then he took her king before the final violation.

They had resisted, on Quel'Danas, resisted with all they had in them. When Anasterian appeared before Arthas, his fiery magics wreaked havoc on the death knight's icy bridge, but Arthas recovered. He frowned, his eyes flashing, drew Frostmourne, and bore down upon the elven king.

Even as she hoped desperately that Anasterian would defeat Arthas, Sylvanas knew he would not. Three millennia rested upon those shoulders; the white hue of hair that fell almost to his feet was due to age, not dark magics. He had been a powerful fighter once, and was still a powerful mage, but to her new, spectral sight, there was a frailty about him she had not seen when she breathed. Still, he stood, his ancient weapon,

Felo'melorn, "Flamestrike," in one hand, a staff with a powerful, glittering crystal in the other.

Arthas struck, but Anasterian was no longer standing in front of the charging steed. Somehow, faster than Sylvanas could see, he was kneeling, swinging Felo'melorn in a clean horizontal strike across the horse's forelegs, severing both of them. The horse shrieked and fell, its rider with it.

"Invincible!" Arthas cried, seeming stricken as the undead horse rolled and tried to get to its feet while missing its two forelegs. It seemed an odd battle cry to Sylvanas, considering Anasterian had just gained an advantage. But the face Arthas turned toward the elven king was full of naked rage and pain. He looked almost human now; a human male seeing something he loved in torment. He scrambled to his feet, glancing back distractedly at the horse, and for a wild moment Sylvanas thought maybe, just maybe—

The ancient elven weapon was no match for the runeblade, as Sylvanas knew it would not, could not be. It snapped as the blades clashed, the severed piece whirling away crazily as Anasterian fell, his soul ripped from him and consumed by the glowing Frostmourne, as had been so many others.

He sprawled on the ice, limp, blood pooling beneath him, white hair spread out like a shroud, while Arthas rushed to the undead horse and mended its severed legs, patting the bones while it pranced and nuzzled at him. And Sylvanas, although she knew it would harm those she still loved, could not carry the weight of the pain and anguish and sheer burning hatred of Arthas and all he had done. Her head fell back, her arms spreading as her mouth opened, and a cry, beautiful and terrible at once, was torn from an insubstantial throat.

She had cried out before, as he had tortured her. But that was only her own pain, her own despair. This was so much more. Torment, agony, yes, but more than that, a hatred so profound as to be almost pure. She heard other cries of pain mingling with hers, saw elves dropping to their knees clutching ears that began to bleed. Their voices and their spells were stopped, changed from words of magic to incoherent cries of raw grief and startled pain. Some of them fell, their armor shattering and breaking off of them in jagged shards; their very bones breaking beneath their flesh.

Even Arthas stared at her for a moment, his white brows drawn together in an appraising gesture. She wanted to stop. She wanted to silence herself, muffle this cry of destruction that only served he whom she hated so passionately. At last it wore down beneath her pain, and Sylvanas, banshee, fell sickly silent.

"What a fine weapon you are indeed," Arthas murmured. "And mayhap you will be a double-edged sword. I will be watching you."

The horrible army pressed on. Arthas reached the plateau. He reached it, and slew those who guarded the Sunwell, and forced her to participate in the slaughter. And then he visited the ultimate horror upon her people, marching up to the glorious pool of radiance that had sustained the quel'dorei for millennia. Beside it, waiting for him, stood a figure Sylvanas recognized— Dar'Khan Drathir.

So it had been he who had betrayed Quel'Thalas. He who, even more than Arthas, had the blood of thousands upon his well-manicured hands. Fury raged through her. She watched the glow she knew to be golden play upon Arthas's features, softening them and lending them an artificial warmth. Then he upended the contents of an exquisitely crafted urn into the waters, and the radiance changed. It began to pulse and swirl, and inside the swirling center of the damaged magical glow—

—a shadow—

Even after all she had witnessed this dark day, even after what she had become, Sylvanas was stunned at what emerged from the befouled Sunwell, rising and lifting its arms to the skies. A skeleton, horned and grinning, its eye sockets burning with fire. Chains snaked around it and purple vestments fluttered with its movements.

"I am reborn, as promised! The Lich King has granted me eternal life!"

It had all been for this? To raise this single entity? All the slaughter, the torment, the terror; the unspeakably precious and vital Sunwell corrupted, a way of life that had lasted for thousands of years shattered—for this?

She stared sickly at the cackling lich, and the only thing that gave her even a hint of surcease from the agony was watching Dar'Khan, who had attempted to betray his master as he had betrayed his people, dying, as she had done, from Frostmourne's keen edge.

CHAPTER TWENTY

The cold wind tousled Arthas's white hair, caressed his face, and he smiled. It was good, to be again in the colder part of this world. The elven land, with its eternal early summer, heavy with the scents of blossoms and growth, had made him uneasy. It reminded him too much of the gardens of Dalaran, where he had spent so much time with Jaina; of the snapdragons of the Balnir farm. Better the wind, to scour him clean, and the coldness, to quell those memories. They no longer served him, but weakened him, and there was no room for weakness in the heart of Arthas Menethil.

He was, as ever, atop his loyal horse, Invincible. He had had a bad moment in Quel'Thalas, when that bastard king Anasterian had cowardly attacked an innocent steed rather than its rider, severing its legs in the same way that in life had caused Invincible's death. The incident had catapulted Arthas back in time to those horrible moments, shaking him to the core and, in the case of the battle with Anasterian, unleashing an icy rage that in the end had served him well. Before and behind him, his army marched through the snowy pass, untiring, unaffected by the cold. Somewhere in among their ghastly number floated a banshee. Arthas would let Sylvanas be, for the moment. He was more interested in Kel'Thuzad, who glided beside him almost serenely, if such a word could ever be applied to a lich. He was the one who had directed the Scourge to this remote, frozen place, and Arthas had until now not questioned. But the trek was getting boring, and he was curious. The prince felt a smile curve his lips.

"So," he quipped, "you're not upset about me killing you that one time?"

"Don't be foolish," the undead necromancer replied. "The Lich King told me how our encounter would end."

That surprised Arthas. "The Lich King knew that I would kill you?" He frowned, glancing down at the blade that stretched across his lap. It was silent now, dormant. No whispers came from it, nor did the runes pulse with power.

"Of course," Kel'Thuzad responded, a hint of superiority in his sepulchral voice. "He chose you to be his champion long before the Scourge even began."

Arthas's unease deepened. No one had asked him, or even *told* him, about his destiny. But would he have embraced it, had he known? No, he decided. He did not like being manipulated, but he knew that he had had to be tempered if he was to be a formidable weapon. He had to go step by step to his fate, otherwise he would have rejected it. He would then still be with Jaina and Uther and his father would—

"If he's so all-knowing, then how can the dreadlords control him like they do?"

"They are agents of the one who created our master: the fiery lords of the Burning Legion."

The words sent a shiver through Arthas. Burning Legion. Two words only, but the power they promised was heady, somehow. In his lap, Frostmourne flickered.

"It is a vast demonic army that has consumed countless worlds beyond our own." Kel'Thuzad's voice was almost hypnotic, and Arthas shut his eyes for a moment. Behind the closed lids, scenes played out in his mind as the lich spoke. He saw a red sky arcing over a red world. Over a ridge poured a wave of creatures. They ran like hounds, but no natural beasts were they—they had fearsome jaws crammed with teeth, and strange tentacles sprouting from their shoulders. Stones crashed to the earth, leaving trails of green fire, to come to life as animated rock that marched on their foes.

"Now, it comes to set this world to the flame. Our master was created to pave the way for its arrival. The dreadlords were sent to make sure he succeeded."

The scene in Arthas's mind shifted. He was looking at an ornate carved gateway. He knew it to be the Dark Portal, although he had never seen it with his own eyes. It radiated green fire, and a host of demons were clustered around it. Arthas shook his head and the vision evaporated.

"So the plague in Lordaeron, the citadels in Northrend, the slaughtering of the elves . . . it was all just to prepare for some huge demonic invasion?"

"Yes. In time, you will find that our entire history has been shaped by the coming conflict."

Arthas pondered this. Frostmourne was definitely awakening, and he removed the gauntlet from his right hand to caress it. Cold, bone cold it was, so cold that even his death knight's hand, which had been tempered for such a task, ached as he touched it. He felt the whispers again, and smiled.

"There is more, lich, is there not?" he asked, turning to regard Kel'Thuzad. "You have said that the dreadlords imprison our master. Tell me now."

Not possessing flesh any longer, Kel'Thuzad had no facial expressions with which to betray his emotions. But Arthas knew by the slight hunching of the undead's form that he was uncomfortable. Nonetheless, he spoke.

"The first phase of the Lich King's plan was to engineer the Scourge, which would eradicate any group that might resist the Legion's arrival."

Arthas nodded. "Like the forces of Lordaeron . . . and the high elves." He felt a vague knot in the pit of his stomach, but dismissed it.

"Exactly. The second phase is to actually summon the demon lord who will spark the invasion." The lich lifted a bony finger and pointed in the direction in which they traveled. "There is a nearby encampment of orcs who maintain a functional demon gate. I must use the gate to commune with the demon lord and receive his instructions."

Arthas sat quietly atop Invincible for a moment. His mind went back to when he had fought orcs alongside Uther the Lightbringer at Strahnbrad. He recalled the orcs had performed human sacrifices to their demon lords. He and Uther had both been disgusted and appalled. Arthas himself had been so infuriated that Uther had had to lecture him on not fighting with rage in his heart. "If we allow our passions to turn to bloodlust, then we will become as vile as the orcs," Uther had chided.

Well, Uther was dead, and while Arthas was still killing orcs, he was now working with demons. A muscle twitched near his eye.

"What are we waiting for?" he snapped, and urged Invincible into a gallop.

The orcs fought bravely, but in the end, it was futile, as all attempts to halt the Scourge would be futile. Arthas galloped forward, Invincible leaping nimbly over fallen orc bodies. He regarded the gate for a long moment. Three stone slabs, strangely elegant for so brutal a race. Erected nearby, though, were huge animal bones that glowed a dull red hue. In the confines outlined by the slabs of stone, green energy swirled sluggishly. A passage to another world. Jaina would be intrigued—but too horrified to pursue her curiosity. That was what made her weak.

It . . . was what made her Jaina. . . .

"The brutes have been slain," Arthas spat. "The demon gate is yours, lich."

The skeletal form shivered with delight, floating forward and lifting his arms imploringly. Steps led up to the archway; Arthas noticed that the lich did not ascend any of them. He stood at the bottom, out of respect—or out of a more pragmatic desire to avoid harm. Arthas hung back, watching intently from atop Invincible.

"I call upon thee, Archimonde! Your humble servant seeks an audience!"

The green mist continued to swirl. Then, Arthas realized he could make out a shape—features—that were both like and unlike the dreadlords he was more familiar with.

The being had what Arthas guessed to be blue-gray skin, though with the green light tingeing him, it was difficult to be certain. There was no question, however, that the demon's body was powerful, with a mighty barrel chest, large, strong arms, and a lower body that seemed to be shaped like that of a goat—Archimonde's legs curved back, ending in a pair of cloven hooves instead of feet. A tail twitched, perhaps belying Archimonde's calm, in-control demeanor. Arms, shoulders, and legs were encased in golden, gleaming armor adorned with shapes of skulls and spikes. Twin tentacles, long and thin, dangled from his chin. But the most arresting feature of his elongated face was his eyes, which glowed a sickly green color that was brighter and more compelling than the green mist that whirled about him. Even though Archimonde was not yet here, not yet physically in this world, Arthas was not unmoved by the demon's presence.

"You called my name, puny lich, and I have come," said the demon, his voice resonant and seeming to vibrate along Arthas's very bones. "You are Kel'Thuzad, are you not?"

Kel'Thuzad bowed his horned head. He was all but

groveling, Arthas noted. "Yes, great one. I am the summoner. I beg of you, tell me how I may expedite your passage into this world. I exist only to serve."

"There is a special tome you must find," the demon lord intoned. His gaze flickered to Arthas, examined him for a moment, then dismissed him. Arthas found himself growing annoyed. "The only remaining spellbook of Medivh, the Last Guardian. Only his lost incantations are powerful enough to bring me into your world. Seek out the mortal city of Dalaran. It is there that the tome is kept. At twilight, three days from now, you will begin the summoning."

The image disappeared. Arthas stared at where it had been for a long moment.

Dalaran. The greatest concentration of magic, other than Quel'Thalas, in Azeroth.

Dalaran. Where Jaina Proudmoore had trained. Where Jaina still would probably be. A flicker of pain blinked through him for an instant.

"Dalaran is defended by the most powerful magi in Azeroth," he said slowly to Kel'Thuzad. "There is no way to hide our approach. They will be prepared for us."

"As Quel'Thalas was?" Kel'Thuzad laughed, a hollow sound. "Think how easily this army crushed them. They will do the same there. Besides, remember—I was a member of the Kirin Tor, and close to Archmage Antonidas. Dalaran was my home, when I was nothing more than mortal flesh. I know its secrets, its protective spells, ways to slip inside they never thought to properly guard. It is sweet, to be able to visit terror upon those who would have seen me abandon my path and my destiny. Do not fear, death knight. We cannot fail. No one, no thing, can stop the Scourge."

Out of the corner of his eye, Arthas caught movement. He turned and beheld the floating spirit that had once been Sylvanas Windrunner. She had obviously been listening to the entire conversation and seen his reaction to his new orders.

"This talk of Dalaran moves you," she said archly.

"Silence, ghost," he muttered, despite himself remembering the first time he had entered the gates of Dalaran as escort to Jaina. The innocence of that time was almost impossible for him to conceive of anymore.

"Someone there you care for, perhaps? Pleasant memories?"

The damned banshee would not let up. He surrendered to his anger, lifted a hand, and she writhed in pain for a moment before he released her.

"You will say no more of this," he warned. "Let us be about our task."

Sylvanas was silent. But on her pale, ghostly face was a savage smirk of satisfaction.

"I can help." Jaina's voice was calm, calmer than she actually expected it to sound. She stood with her master, Antonidas, in his familiar, loved, wonderfully disorganized study, gazing at him intently. "I've learned so much."

The archmage stood gazing out the window, his hands clasped loosely behind his back, as if he were doing nothing more serious than looking down at students at practice.

"No," he said quietly. "You have other duties." He

turned to regard her then, and her heart sank at the expression on his face. "Duties I . . . and Terenas, Light rest his soul . . . both shirked. Because of his refusal to listen to that strange prophet, he ended up murdered by his son, and his kingdom lies in ruins, inhabited only by the dead."

Even now, Jaina cringed at the statement. Arthas . . .

It was still so hard to believe. She had loved him so much . . . loved him still. Her constant prayer, silent and known only to her, was that he was under some sort of influence he could not resist. Because if he had done all this of his own will—

"I, too, was asked, and I, too, had the arrogance to assume I knew best. And so, my dear, here we are. We all must live—or die—with our decisions." Antonidas smiled sadly. Her eyes stung with tears she blinked back and refused to shed.

"Let me stay. I can—"

"Keep safe those you have promised to take care of, Jaina Proudmoore," Antonidas said, a hint of sternness creeping into his voice and mien. "One more or one less here . . . will make no difference. Others look to you now."

"Antonidas . . ." Her voice broke on the word. She rushed toward him, flinging her arms around him. She had never dared embrace him before; he had always intimidated her far too much. But now, he looked . . . old. Old, and frail, and worst of all, resigned.

"Child," he said affectionately, patting her back, then chuckled. "No, you are a child no longer. You are a woman and a leader. Still . . . you had best go."

From outside a voice rang out, strong and clear and familiar. Jaina felt as though she had been struck. She gasped in sickened recognition, pulling back from her mentor's embrace.

"Wizards of the Kirin Tor! I am Arthas, first of the Lich King's death knights! I demand that you open your gates and surrender to the might of the Scourge!"

Death knight? Jaina turned her shocked gaze to Antonidas, who gave her a sad smile. "I would have spared you the knowing . . . at least for now."

She reeled with the knowledge. Arthas . . . *here* . . .

The archmage strode to the balcony. A slight flutter of age-gnarled hands, and his own voice was as magnified as Arthas's had been.

"Greetings, Prince Arthas," Antonidas called down. "How fares your noble father?"

"Lord Antonidas," Arthas replied. Where was he? Right outside? Would she see him if she stepped beside Antonidas on the balcony? "There's no need to be snide." Jaina turned her head away and wiped at her eyes. She struggled to speak, but the words seemed to stick in her throat.

"We've prepared for your coming, Arthas," Antonidas continued calmly. "My brethren and I have erected auras that will destroy any undead that pass through them."

"Your petty magics will not stop me, Antonidas. Perhaps you've heard what happened in Quel'Thalas? They thought themselves invulnerable as well."

Quel'Thalas.

Jaina thought she might be sick. She had been here in

Dalaran when word had come, from a handful of survivors who had managed to escape, about what had happened to Quel'Thalas. So too had been the quel'dorei prince. She had never seen Kael'thas so—so angry, so shattered, so raw. She had gone to him, words of compassion and comfort on her lips, but he whirled and gazed at her with such a look of fury that she instinctively drew back.

"Say nothing," Kael had snarled. His fists clenched; she could see, to her shock, that he was barely restraining himself from physically harming her. "Foolish girl. *This* is the monster you would take to your bed?"

Jaina blinked, stunned at the crudeness of the words coming from one so cultured. "I—"

But he was not interested in hearing anything she had to say. "Arthas is a butcher! He has slaughtered thousands of innocent people! There is so much blood on his hands that a whole ocean could never wash them clean. And you *loved* him? Chose him over *me*?"

His voice, normally so mellifluous and controlled, cracked on the last word. Jaina felt quick tears come to her eyes as she suddenly understood. He was attacking her because he could not attack his real enemy. He felt helpless, impotent, and was striking out at the nearest target—at her, Jaina Proudmoore, whose love he had wanted and failed to win.

"Oh . . . Kael'thas," she said softly, "he has done . . . terrible things," she began. "What your people have suffered—"

"You know nothing of suffering!" he cried. "You are a child, with a child's mind and a child's heart. A heart that you would give to that—that—he slaughtered them, Jaina. And then he raised their *corpses*!"

Jaina stared at him mutely, his words having no sting now that she knew the reason for them. "He murdered my father, Jaina, just as he murdered his own. I—I should have been there."

"To die with him? With the rest of your people? What good would throwing your life away do for—"

No sooner had the words left her lips than she realized that it was the wrong thing to say. Kael'thas tensed and cut her off sharply.

"I could have stopped him. I should have." He straightened, and coldness suddenly chased away the fire in him. He bowed low, exaggeratedly. "I will be departing Dalaran as soon as possible. There is nothing for me here." Jaina winced at the emptiness, the resignation in his voice. "I was a fool of the greatest order to ever think any of you humans could aid me. I will leave this place of doddering old magi and ambitious young ones. None of you can help. My people need me to lead now that my father—"

He fell silent and swallowed hard. "I must go to them. To what pathetically few remain. To those who have endured, rebirthed by the blood of those who now serve your *beloved*."

He had stalked off then, fury etched in every line of his tall, elegant body, and Jaina had felt her own heart ache with his pain.

And now, he was here; Arthas was here, at the head of the army of the undead, a death knight himself. Antonidas's voice startled her out of her reverie and she blinked, trying to return to the present moment.

"Pull your troops back, or we will be forced to unleash our full powers against you! Make your choice, death knight." Antonidas stepped back from the balcony and turned to regard Jaina. "Jaina," he said in his normal voice, "we will be erecting teleportation-blocking barriers momentarily. You must go before you are trapped here."

"Maybe I can reason with him . . . maybe I can . . ." She fell silent, hearing the unrealistic wanting in her own voice. She hadn't even been able to stop him from murdering innocents in Stratholme, or going to Northrend when she was certain it was a trap. He'd not listened to her then. If Arthas was indeed under some dark influence, how could she dissuade him now?

She took a deep breath and stepped back, and Antonidas nodded softly. There was so much she wanted to say to this man, her mentor, her guide. But all she could do was give him a shaky smile, now, as he fought what they both knew would likely be his last battle. She found she couldn't even say good-bye to him.

"I'll take care of our people," she said thickly, cast the teleportation spell, and disappeared.

The first part of the battle was over, and Arthas had gotten what he had come for. Arthas had obtained the requested spellbook of Medivh. It was large and curiously heavy for its size, bound in red leather with gold binding. Across its front was an exquisitely tooled black raven, its wings outspread. The book still had Antonidas's blood on it. He wondered if that would make it more potent.

Invincible shifted beneath him, stamping a hoof and shaking his neck as if he still had flesh that could be irritated by flies. They were on a hilltop overlooking Dalaran, whose towers still caught the light and gleamed in hues of gold and white and purple while its streets ran with blood. Many of the magi who had fought him hours before stood beside him now. Most of them were too badly damaged to be of use other than as fodder to throw at attackers, but some . . . some could still be used, the skills they had in life harnessed to serve the Lich King in death.

Kel'Thuzad was like a child on Winter Veil morning. He was perusing the pages of Medivh's spellbook, thoroughly engrossed with this new toy. It irritated Arthas.

"The circle of power has been prepared per your instructions, lich. Are you ready to begin the summoning?"

"Nearly," the undead thing replied. Skeletal fingers turned a page of the book. "There is much to absorb. Medivh's knowledge of demons alone is staggering. I suspect that he was far more powerful than anyone ever realized."

A blackish-green swirl had begun manifesting as Kel'Thuzad spoke, and Tichondrius appeared as he finished. Arthas's irritation deepened as the dreadlord spoke with his usual arrogance. "Not powerful enough to escape death, that is for certain. Suffice to say, the work he began, we will finish . . . today. Let the summoning commence!"

And that quickly, he was gone. Kel'Thuzad floated into the circle. The space was marked out by four small obelisks. In their center, a glowing circle with arcane markings had been etched. Kel'Thuzad bore the book with him, and once he fluttered into position, the lines of the circle flared to glowing purple life. At the same moment, there was a spitting, crackling sound and eight pillars of flame sprang up about him. Kel'Thuzad turned to gaze back at Arthas with glowing eyes.

"Those who yet live within Dalaran will be able to sense the power of this spell," Kel'Thuzad warned. "I must not be interrupted or we will fail."

"I'll keep your bones safe, lich," Arthas assured him.

As Kel'Thuzad had promised, it had been comparatively easy to enter Dalaran, slay those who had erected specific spells against them, and take what they had come for. Arthas had even been able to kill Archmage Antonidas, the man he had once thought so very powerful.

If Jaina had been there, he felt certain that she would have confronted him. Appealed to what they had once had, as she had done before. She would have had no better luck now than she had then, except—

He was glad he did not have to fight her.

Arthas's attention suddenly snapped back to the present. The gates were opening, and Arthas's gray lips curved in a grin. Previously, the Scourge had had the element of surprise on their side. Yes, many powerful magi lived in Dalaran at all times. But there was no trained militia, nor were all the magi of the Kirin Tor in Dalaran. But they had had several hours, and they had not been idle.

They had teleported in an army.

Good. A solid fight was just what he needed to drive distracting thoughts of Jaina Proudmoore and the youth he had once been to the back of his mind.

He lifted Frostmourne, feeling it tingle in his hand, hearing the soft voice of the Lich King caress his thoughts.

"Frostmourne hungers," he told his troops, pointing the sword at the armor-clad defenders of the great mage city. "Let us sate its appetite."

The Scourge army roared, Sylvanas's anguished wail rising above the cacophony, causing Arthas to grin even more. Even in death, even though she obeyed his commands, she defied him, and he relished forcing her to attack those she would have preferred to defend. Invincible gathered himself beneath his rider and surged forward at a full gallop, whinnying.

Some of his ghastly troops stayed behind to defend Kel'Thuzad, but most of them accompanied their leader. Arthas recognized the livery of many of those whom the Kirin Tor had teleported in to defend the city. Friends they had once been, but that was all in the past, as irrelevant to him as yesterday's weather. It was getting easier now, to feel nothing but satisfaction as Frostmourne, glowing and all but singing as it feasted upon souls, rose and fell, cutting through plate as easily as flesh.

After the first wave of soldiers fell, raised to serve in the Scourge or abandoned where they had fallen as of no use, a second one came. This one had magi with them, clad in the purple robes of Dalaran with an embroidered symbol of the great Eye upon them. But Arthas, too, had additional aid.

The demons, it would seem, wished to protect their own.

Giant stones screamed down from the sky, their tails streaks of fel green fire. The earth shook where they struck, and from the craters caused by their impact climbed what looked like stone golems, held together and directed by the sickly green energy.

Arthas glanced over his shoulder. Kel'Thuzad hovered, his arms spread, his horned head thrown back. Energy crackled and coursed from him, and a green orb began to form. Then, abruptly, the lich lowered his arms and stepped out of the circle.

"Come forth, Lord Archimonde!" Kel'Thuzad cried. "Enter this world and let us bask in your power!"

The green orb pulsed, expanding, growing taller and glowing yet more brightly. Suddenly a pillar of fire shot skyward, and several answering lightning bolts crackled down outside the circle. And then, where there had been nothing, a figure stood—tall, powerful, graceful in its own dark and dangerous way. Arthas returned his attention to the battlefield. A retreat sounded—clearly the magi, at least, had seen what was transpiring, and their troops wheeled their mounts and galloped back toward the safety—temporary though Arthas suspected it to be—of Dalaran. Even as they fled, a deep, resonant voice cut through the sound of battle.

"Tremble, mortals, and despair! Doom has come to this world!"

Arthas held up his hand, and with that simplest of gestures the swarm of Scourge halted and retreated as well. As he galloped back to Kel'Thuzad, eyeing the giant demon lord all the while, Tichondrius teleported in. As usual, *after* all the danger had passed.

The dreadlord made a deep obeisance. Arthas drew rein some distance away, preferring to observe.

"Lord Archimonde, all the preparations have been made."

"Very well, Tichondrius," replied Archimonde, giving the lesser demon a dismissive nod. "Since the Lich King is of no further use to me, you dreadlords will now command the Scourge."

Arthas was suddenly very grateful for all those hours spent in disciplined meditation. It was only that that kept his shock and fury from showing. Even so, Invincible felt the change in him and pranced nervously. He yanked on the reins and the undead beast stilled. The Lich King was of no further use? Why? Who exactly was he, and what had happened to him? What would happen to Arthas?

"Soon, I will order the invasion to begin. But first, I will make an example of these paltry wizards . . . by crushing their city into the ashes of history."

He strode off, his body erect and proud and commanding, his hooves landing firmly with each step, his armor gleaming in the rose and gold and lavender of the encroaching twilight. Beside him, still making obeisance, strode Tichondrius. Arthas waited until they were some distance away before he finally whirled on Kel'Thuzad and burst out, "This has got to be a joke! What happens to us now?"

"Be patient, young death knight. The Lich King foresaw this as well. You may yet have a part to play in his grand design."

May? Arthas whirled on the necromancer, his nostrils flaring, but he tamped back his anger. If anyone—either of the demons or the Lich King himself—thought for one moment that Arthas was a tool to simply be used and then discarded, he would soon show them the error of their thinking. He had done too much—lost too much, cut out too much of himself for this to be cast aside.

It couldn't all be for nothing.

It would *not* all be for nothing.

The earth rumbled. Invincible shifted uneasily, lifting his hooves as if to minimize contact with the earth. Arthas glanced up quickly at the mage city. The towers were lovely at this time of day, proud and glorious and glittering in the deepening twilight hues. But as he watched, he heard a deep cracking noise. The apex of the tallest, most beautiful tower in the city suddenly fell, slowly and inexorably, tumbling downward as if the length of the tower had been clenched by a giant, unseen hand.

The rest of the city fell quickly, shattering and crumbling, the sound of destruction loud and thrumming in Arthas's ears. He winced at the volume, but did not tear his eyes away.

He had instigated the fall of Silvermoon. Had directed his Scourge against it. But this—there was casualness about it, an ease . . . Silvermoon had been a hard-won prize. Archimonde appeared to be able to shatter the greatest of human cities without even being present.

Arthas thought about Archimonde and Tichondrius. He scratched his chin thoughtfully.

In his lap, Frostmourne glowed.

CHAPTER TWENTY-ONE

Kel'Thuzad, Arthas mused as he waited atop the verdant hill for the one he had been assured would come, was a useful lich to have around.

He was utterly loyal to the Lich King, even to the point of convincingly playing the lapdog to Archimonde and Tichondrius while in their presence, if that was what was required to secretly serve. Arthas had opted for silence; he did not trust himself to lie as convincingly as Kel'Thuzad. The two demons had deemed them nonessential. They would soon see how wrong they were. Carelessly they had left the Book of Medivh in the lich's bony hands. In that mind, too, were spells and magic so powerful that Arthas knew he would never be able to fully grasp their scope.

"The third part of the plan," Kel'Thuzad had said once the demons were gone, as idly as if he were conversing about the weather, "was the true heart of the Legion's plot."

Arthas remembered what Kel'Thuzad had told him earlier. First had been the creation of the Scourge, then the summoning of Archimonde. He listened now with intense interest as Kel'Thuzad continued. "The Legion is after nothing less than the taking of all magic and the devouring of all life upon this world. And to that end, they plan to consume the concentrated, powerful energies contained within the elves' Well of Eternity. In order to accomplish this, they must destroy the single thing that contains within it the truest, purest essence of life energy on Azeroth. The Well of Eternity lies across the ocean, on the continent of Kalimdor. And the thing that would thwart the Legion is called Nordrassil . . . the World Tree. It grants the kaldorei immortality, and they are bound to it."

"Kaldorei?" Arthas was confused. "I know of quel'dorei. Are they another race of elves?"

"The original race," Kel'Thuzad corrected. He waved a hand dismissively. "But those details are of no consequence. What matters is that we must stop the Legion from achieving this goal. And there is one among the kaldorei who would aid us."

And so it was that using his magics, Kel'Thuzad had teleported Arthas to this distant continent and this hill that afforded an expansive view. The forests here were lush, healthy, but Arthas could already see what the Legion had wrought in the distance. Where the land, trees, beasts were not dead, they had been corrupted. Devour all life, indeed.

A figure crested another hill below him, and Arthas smiled to himself. This was the one whose arrival he had been awaiting.

They were certainly different, these "night elves."

This one's skin was pale lavender, etched with swirling tattoos and scars cut into the skin in ritualistic patterns. A black cloth was tied around his eyes, but he appeared to have no difficulty in navigating the terrain. He carried a weapon that resembled nothing Arthas had ever seen. Instead of a traditional sword, which would be grasped by a hilt with a blade extending from it, this weapon had two jagged blades that glowed the sick green hue of something tainted with demonic energies.

So, this one had trafficked with demons before.

Arthas waited a while, observing. The night elf—Illidan Stormrage, Kel'Thuzad had said his name was—raged to himself. Apparently the list of wrongs piled against him was a lengthy one, and he ached for vengeance and power as much as Kel'Thuzad had said he would.

Arthas smiled.

"I am free after ten thousand years, yet still my own brother thinks I am a villain!" Illidan ranted. "I'll show him my true power. I'll show him the demons have no hold over me!"

"Are you certain of that, demon hunter?" Arthas said, his voice carrying. The night elf whirled, brandishing his weapon. "Are you certain your will is your own?"

The elf might have been blind in the traditional sense, but Arthas felt seen regardless. Illidan sniffed and growled. "You reek of death, human. You'll regret approaching me."

Arthas grinned. He was itching for a good one-on-one fight. "Come, then," he invited. "You'll find that we're evenly matched." Invincible reared and galloped down the hill, as eager for action as his master was. Illidan growled and ran to meet him.

It was almost like a dance, Arthas mused as the two warriors faced each other. Illidan was strong and graceful, his skills demonically enhanced. But Arthas, too, was no mere soldier, nor was Frostmourne an ordinary blade. The fight was fierce and swift; Arthas had been right. They were indeed evenly matched. After too short a time, both combatants fell back, breathing heavily.

"We could go on fighting like this forever," Illidan said. "What is it you truly want?"

Arthas lowered Frostmourne. "From your muttering earlier, I hear that you and your allies are beset by the undead. The dreadlord who commands this undead army is called Tichondrius. He controls a powerful warlock artifact called the Skull of Gul'dan. It is responsible for corrupting these forests."

Illidan cocked his head. "And you wish for me to steal it? Why?"

Arthas's white brows lifted. This one was indeed quick. He deserved a semi-truthful answer, Arthas decided. "Let's just say that I have no love for Tichondrius, and the lord I serve would . . . benefit from the Legion's downfall."

"Why should I believe anything you say, little human?"

Arthas shrugged. "A fair question. Let me answer. My master sees all, demon hunter. He knows that you've sought power your whole life. Now it lies within your grasp!" His gauntleted hand clenched into a fist in front of Illidan's blindfolded face and, as he expected, the night elf's head turned toward the gesture. "Seize it, and your enemies will be undone."

Illidan lifted his head slowly and turned his face to Arthas. He was unsettling, this blind man who could so obviously see. The elf stepped back, nodding thoughtfully. Without another word Arthas turned Invincible's head around and galloped off.

Kel'Thuzad would summon him back shortly. All had gone according to the Lich King's plan. He only hoped that Illidan had been as fully obedient as he had seemed. If not . . . there could be complications.

She was nothing of the living. Nor did she have the power to resist the commands of the one who had brought her screaming into this new existence.

But Sylvanas Windrunner had will. Somehow, Arthas had not broken that. He had done so with others; why was she, seemingly, the only one who had not caved utterly to him? Was it her own strength, or was it because he enjoyed tormenting her? The banshee that she was now would likely never know. But if her will was her own because Arthas found it amusing, she would have the last laugh.

So she had vowed to herself, and Sylvanas always kept her promises.

Time had passed in the world of the living since Arthas Menethil and the Scourge had swept through her beloved homeland. And much had occurred.

Her so-called "master" had objected to being used as a pawn. Together with that arrogant, floating sack of bones, Kel'Thuzad—the one responsible for corrupting the glorious Sunwell—Arthas had conspired against both the dreadlord Tichondrius and the demon lord Archimonde, whom Kel'Thuzad himself had helped usher into Azeroth. Sylvanas had paid keen attention; anything Arthas had to reveal about the way he thought and the way he battled was useful to her.

He had not attempted to slay Tichondrius himself, as he had Mal'Ganis. Oh no, the wily once-human prince had tricked another into doing his dirty work for him. Illidan, the luckless being had been named. Arthas had been able to smell Illidan's hunger for power and used that against him, goading him into stealing the Skull of Gul'dan, a legendary orcish warlock. To do so, Illidan would have to kill Tichondrius. Arthas would be rid of the demon lord, and Illidan would be rewarded with an artifact to sate his lust for power. Presumably all had gone according to plan. Arthas—and therefore Sylvanas—had heard nothing of Illidan since.

As for Archimonde . . . so mighty that he had been able to destroy Dalaran, the great mage city, with a single spell, he had fallen to the power of the life he had come here to consume. Sylvanas now hated the living with the same passion the Legion had had, and thus it was with mixed feelings that she learned of his fall. The night elves had sacrificed their immortality to defeat him. The pure, focused power of nature had destroyed the demon from inside, and then the World Tree had surrendered its vast power in a cataclysm that sent out a massive shock wave. And when Archimonde had fallen, his skeleton all that was left, so too had the

Legion's attempt to gain a foothold in this world been defeated.

Sylvanas returned her attention from her reverie to the present, as the name of the late unlamented demon lord caught her ear.

"It's been months since we last heard from Lord Archimonde," their leader, Detheroc, said. He stamped his hoof impatiently. "I grow tired of watching over these rotting undead! What are we still doing here?"

They were in what had once been the gardens of the palace, where Arthas had strode so long and so short a time ago to murder his own father and unleash doom on his own people. The gardens, too, were rotting as well as their populace.

"We were charged with overseeing this land, Detheroc," chided the one named Balnazzar. "It is our duty to remain here and ensure that the Scourge is ready for action."

"True," rumbled the third, Varimathras. "Although we should have received some kind of orders by now."

Sylvanas could hardly believe what she had just heard. She turned to Kel'Thuzad. She despised him as much as she despised the death knight he appeared to serve so willingly, but she hid her dislike well. "The Legion was defeated months ago," she said quietly. "How could they not know?"

"Impossible to say," the lich replied. "But the longer they remain in command, the more they run the Scourge into the ground. If something is not—"

He was interrupted by a sound Sylvanas had never expected to hear in this place—the distinctive sound of a gate being battered and broken. Both undead turned at the noise, and the demons growled angrily, instantly alert, black webbed wings flexing.

Sylvanas's glowing, spectral eyes widened slightly as none other than Arthas himself emerged through the gate. His familiar undead steed all but pranced beneath him. He wore no helm, letting his white hair fall freely about his pale face, and he wore that self-satisfied smirk that Sylvanas so despised. Her insubstantial hands attempted to clench into fists, but such was his control over her that all her fingers could manage was a brief twitch.

Arthas's voice was resonant and cheerful. "Greetings, dreadlords," he said. They stared at him, visibly bridling at his insolence. "I should thank you for looking after my kingdom during my absence. However, I won't be requiring your services any longer."

For a second, they simply gaped at him. Finally, Balnazzar recovered enough to retort, "This land is ours. The Scourge belongs to the Legion!"

Ah, thought Sylvanas, *here it comes*.

Arthas's smirk widened. His voice was positively gleeful. "Not anymore, demon. Your masters have been defeated. The Legion is undone. Your deaths will complete the circle."

Still grinning, he lifted Frostmourne. The runes along its blade danced and glowed. He tightened the reins and the skeletal horse bore down on the cluster of three demons.

"This isn't over, human!" Detheroc cried defiantly. The dreadlords were faster than Arthas's skeletal horse—Frostmourne sang only of frustration as it sliced through empty air. The demons had created a portal and vanished to safety. Arthas scowled, but his good humor returned quickly. Sylvanas realized it was because he had them on the run and their deaths would likely be only a matter of time.

He looked up and caught Sylvanas's eye, beckoning her to him. She was forced to obey. Kel'Thuzad needed no coercion, floating happily to his master's side like an obedient cur.

"We knew you would return to us, Prince Arthas!" the lich enthused.

Arthas barely spared his loyal servant a glance. His gaze was fixed on Sylvanas. "My heart is moved," he said sarcastically. "Did you, too, know I would return, little banshee?"

"I did," Sylvanas said coldly. It was true; he had to, or else she would never have her chance for revenge. He twitched a finger, demanding more from her, and she gasped as pain shuddered through her. "Prince Arthas," she added.

"Ah, but you will now address me as king. This is, after all, my land. I was born to rule and I shall. Once the—"

He broke off, inhaling sharply. His eyes widened and then his face contorted in pain. He hunched over the bony neck of his horse, his gauntleted hands clenching hard on the reins. A sharp cry of agony was wrenched from him.

Sylvanas watched, experiencing the most pleasure she had known since that dreadful day when Quel'Thalas had fallen. She drank in his pain like nectar. She had no idea why he was suffering so, but she savored every second of it.

Grunting, he lifted his head. His eyes stared at something she couldn't see, and he extended an imploring hand toward it. "The pain . . . is unbearable," Arthas growled through gritted teeth. "What is happening to me?" He appeared to listen, as if an unheard voice was replying.

"King Arthas!" Kel'Thuzad cried. "Do you need assistance?"

Arthas didn't reply at once. He gasped for breath, then slowly sat up, visibly composing himself. "No . . . no, the pain has passed but . . . my powers . . . are *diminished*." His voice was full of puzzlement. Had Sylvanas still possessed a beating heart, it would have leaped at the words. "Something is terribly wrong here. I—"

The pain took him again. His body spasmed, his head falling back as his mouth opened in a soundless cry of pain, the veins on his neck standing out like cords. Kel'Thuzad fluttered around his adored master like a fussy nursemaid. Sylvanas simply watched coldly until the spasm had passed. Slowly, carefully, he slid off Invincible. His booted feet hit the flagstones, slipped out from under him and he fell, hard. The lich reached out a skeletal hand to help the prince—no, self-styled king— to his feet.

"My old quarters," gasped Arthas. "I need rest—and then I have a long journey to prepare for."

Sylvanas watched him go, staggering weakly in the direction of the rooms he had grown up in. She let her lips curve into a smile. . . .

. . . and the spectral fingers on her hands twitched for a moment, then curled up into angry fists.

It was oddly peaceful in Silverpine. Soft mists swirled gently near the moist, pine-needle-covered earth. Sylvanas knew that if she had possessed physical feet, she would have felt it soft and springy beneath them; would have inhaled a rich evergreen scent from the moist air. But she felt nothing, smelled nothing. She floated, insubstantial, toward the meeting site. And such was her eagerness for the meeting that at this moment she did not regret her lack of senses.

Arthas had enjoyed turning beautiful, proud, strong-willed quel'dorei women into banshees, after his "success" with her. He had given them to she who had been their ranger-general in life, to control and command, tossing her a bone like she was a faithful hound. He would shortly see how faithful a pet she was. After overhearing the dreadlords' conversation earlier, she had sent one of her banshees after them to speak with them and gather information.

The demons had accepted her emissary with pleasure, and had asked for her mistress to join them tonight to discuss something of "mutual benefit regarding the Banshee Queen's current status."

In the depths of the forest, she could see a faint green glow, and floated toward it. Sure enough, they awaited her as they had said they would—three great demons turning to her, their wings flapping and betraying their agitation.

Balnazzar spoke first. "Lady Sylvanas, we are pleased that you came."

"How could I not?" she responded. "For some reason I no longer hear the Lich King's voice in my head. My will is my own once again." It was indeed; and it was purely by that will that she kept the elation from her voice. She did not wish them to know more than she chose. "You dreadlords seem to know why."

They exchanged glances, their faces curving into smiles. "We've discovered that the Lich King is losing his power," Varimathras said, hellish glee in his voice. "As it wanes, so too does his ability to command undead such as you."

That was good news indeed, if it were actually true. But it was not specific enough for Sylvanas. "And what of King Arthas?" she pressed, unable to keep a sneer out of her voice as she used the death knight's title. "What about his powers?"

Balnazzar waved a black-clawed hand dismissively. "He will cease to annoy us, like a summerfly whose time has come and gone. Though his runeblade, Frostmourne, carries powerful enchantments, Arthas's own powers will fade in time. It is inevitable."

Sylvanas was not so certain. She, too, had once underestimated Arthas, and along with the cold hatred in her heart, she also bore guilt for her part in his blood-soaked victory. "You seek to overthrow him, and want my help to do it," she said bluntly.

Detheroc, the one who appeared to be in charge, had stood quietly by while his brothers spoke to Sylvanas. They had been angry and impassioned, but his expression had remained neutral. Now, at last he spoke, in cold tones of utter loathing.

"The Legion may be defeated, but we are the nathrezim. We'll not let some upstart human get the best of us." He paused, looking at them each in turn. "Arthas must fall!"

The glowing green gaze settled upon Sylvanas. "As you have been watching us, little ghost, so have we been observing as well. It is obvious that the lich, Kel'Thuzad, is far too loyal to betray his master. There appears to be . . . affection between the two." His gray lips curved in a dangerous smile. "But you, on the other hand . . ."

"Hate him." She did not think she could hide that truth even if she wanted to, so fiercely did it burn inside her. "We are united in that much, dreadlord. I have my own reasons for seeking vengeance. Arthas murdered my people and turned me into this . . . monstrosity." She paused for a moment, the loathing—of both Arthas and what he had done to her—so intense it took away her ability to speak. They waited, patiently, smugly.

They thought they could use her. They would be wrong.

"I may take part in your bloody coup, but I will do so in my own way." She wanted them as allies, but they needed to know that she would be no toy. "I will not exchange one master for another. If you wish my aid, then you must accept that."

Detheroc smiled. "We will slay the death knight together, then."

Sylvanas nodded, and a slow smile crept across her ghostly face.

Your days have numbers, King Arthas Menethil. And I . . . I am the hourglass.

CHAPTER TWENTY-TWO

rthas rubbed his temple, going over and over the visions he had seen. Always before, communication from the Lich King had come only from Frostmourne. But the instant the crippling pain had struck him, Arthas had actually *seen* the being he served for the first time.

The Lich King was alone, in the middle of a vast cavern, as imprisoned in the unnatural ice as Frostmourne had been. But this had been no sleek covering of his form. The encasing ice had been fractured, as if someone had broken off a piece and left the jagged remains behind. Obscured by the ice as he was, the Lich King was imperfectly glimpsed, but his voice sliced in the death knight's mind as he cried out in torment:

"Danger draws near the Frozen Throne! Power is fading. . . . Time is running out. . . . You must return to Northrend immediately!" And then, piercing Arthas like a lance in the gut: *"Obey!"*

Each time it happened, Arthas felt dazed and sick. The power that had pumped through him like adrenaline when he was merely human was receding, taking with it more than it had originally given. He was weak and vulnerable . . . something he had never once imagined he would be when he first grasped Frostmourne and turned away from everything he thought he believed in. His face was greasy with sweat as he laboriously mounted Invincible and rode to meet Kel'Thuzad.

The lich was waiting for him, hovering, his fluttering robes and general demeanor somehow radiating concern.

"So the seizures have been getting worse?" he asked.

Arthas hesitated. Should he take the lich into his confidence? Would Kel'Thuzad attempt to wrest power from him? No, he decided. The former necromancer had never led him astray. Always, his loyalty was to the Lich King and Arthas himself.

The king nodded. He felt like his head would come off with the gesture. "Yes. With my powers drained, I can barely command my own warriors. The Lich King warned me that if I didn't reach Northrend soon, all could be lost. We must depart quickly."

If it was possible for blazing, empty eye sockets to exude worry, then Kel'Thuzad's did so now. "Of course, Your Majesty. You have not and will not be forsaken. We will depart as soon as you believe you are—"

"There's been a change of plans, King Arthas. You're not going anywhere."

It was evidence of his weakening powers that he had not even sensed them. Arthas stared, utterly taken by surprise as the three dreadlords surrounded him.

"Assassins!" cried Kel'Thuzad. "It's a trap! Defend your king from those—"

But the sound of a gate slamming shut drowned out the lich's call to action. Arthas drew Frostmourne. For the first time since he had touched, had bonded with the sword, it felt heavy and almost lifeless in his hands. The runes along its blade barely gleamed at all, and it felt more like a lump of metal than the well-balanced, beautiful weapon it had always been.

The undead rushed at him, and for a wild moment Arthas was catapulted back in time to his first encounter with the walking dead. He was again standing outside the little farmhouse, assaulted by the stench of decay and almost numbed with horror as things that should have been dead attacked him. He had long since moved past any horror or repugnance at their existence; indeed, he had come to think of them with affection. They were his subjects; he had cleansed them of life, to serve the great glory of the Lich King. It was not that they moved, or fought; it was that they fought *him*. They were utterly under the control of dreadlords. Grimly, using all the strength he yet possessed, he fought them back, a strange, sickening sensation filling him. He had never expected they would turn on him.

Over the sounds of the conflict, Balnazzar's voice reached Arthas, the tone gloating. "You should never have returned, human. Weakened as you are, we have assumed control over the majority of your warriors. It seems your reign was short-lived, *King* Arthas."

Arthas gritted his teeth and from somewhere deep

inside him dredged up more energy, more will to fight. He would *not* die here.

But there were so many of them—so many that he had once nearly effortlessly directed and commanded, now turning implacably against him. He knew they were mindless, that they would obey whoever was the strongest. And yet somehow . . . it hurt. He'd *made* them. . . .

He was growing increasingly weak, and at one point was even unable to block a blow directly to his midsection. The dull sword clanged against his armor, and he suffered no major wound, but that the ghoul had gotten past his defenses alarmed him.

"There are too many of them, my king!" Kel'Thuzad's sepulchral voice said, the tenor of loyalty in it bringing unexpected tears to Arthas's eyes. "Flee—escape from the city! I'll find my way out and meet you in the wilderness. It is your only chance, my liege!"

He knew the lich was right. With a cry, Arthas clumsily dismounted. A wave of his hand and Invincible became insubstantial, a ghost horse instead of a skeletal one, and disappeared. Arthas would summon him again when he was safely away. He charged, gripping the enfeebled Frostmourne in both hands and swinging, no longer trying to kill or even wound his opponents— they were indeed too many—but simply to clear a path.

The gates were closed, but this palace was where he had grown to manhood, and he knew it intimately. Knew every gate, wall, and hidden passageway, and instead of heading for the gates, which he would be unable to raise by himself, he went deeper into the palace.

The undead followed. Arthas raced through the back corridors that had once been the private quarters of the royal family, which he had once traversed with Jaina's hand clasped tightly in his. He stumbled and his mind reeled.

How had he come to this moment—fleeing through an empty palace from his own creations, his subjects, whom he had vowed to protect? But no—he'd slain them. Betrayed his subjects for the power the Lich King offered. The power that was now bleeding from him as if from a wound that could not be closed.

Father . . . Jaina . . .

He closed his mind against the memories. Distractions would not serve him. Only speed and cunning would.

The narrow passageways limited the number of undead able to follow, and he was able to close and bolt the doors against them, delaying them. Finally he reached his quarters and the secret exit built into the wall. He, his parents, and Calia each had one . . . known only to them, Uther, and the bishop. All were gone now, save he, and Arthas pushed aside the hanging tapestry to reveal the small door hidden behind it, closing and bolting it behind him.

He ran, stumbling in his weakness, down the tight, twining staircase that would lead to his freedom. The door was both physically and magically disguised to look exactly like the main walls of the palace from the outside. Arthas, gasping, fumbled with the bolt and half fell out into the dim light of Tirisfal Glades. The sound of battle reached his ears and he looked up, catching his breath. He blinked, confused. The undead . . . were fighting one another.

Of course—some of them were still under his command. Were still his subjects—

His tools. His weapons. Not his subjects.

He watched for a moment, leaning against the cold stone. An abomination under the control of his enemy lopped off a long-eared head and sent it flying. A shiver of disgust went through him at the sight of both sets of undead. Decomposing, maggot-ridden, shambling things. No matter who controlled them, they were foul. A glimmer caught his eye; a forlorn little ghost, hovering timidly, who had once been an adolescent girl. Once been alive. He'd killed her, too, directly or indirectly. His *subject*. She seemed still connected to that world of the living. Seemed to remember what being human had once meant. He could use that; use her. He extended his hand to this floating, spectral thing he had made out of his lust for power.

"I have need of your abilities, little shade," he said, pitching his voice to sound as kindly as possible. "Will you help me?"

Her face lit up and she floated to his side. "I live only to serve you, King Arthas," she said, her voice still sweet despite its hollow echo. He forced himself to return her smile. It was easier, when they were simply rotting flesh. But this had its advantages, too.

Through sheer will, he summoned more and more of them, exerting himself so hard his breath came in gasps. They came. They would serve whoever was strongest. With a roar, Arthas descended upon those who would dare stand in the way of the destiny he had bought so dearly. But even as more came to his side, so did more come to attack him. Weak, so weak he was, with only these lumps of meat to protect him. He was shaking and gasping, heaving Frostmourne about with arms that grew increasingly weary. The earth trembled and Arthas whirled to behold no fewer than three abominations lumbering toward him.

Grimly, he lifted Frostmourne. He, Arthas Menethil, King of Lordaeron, would not go down without a fight.

Suddenly there was a flurry of motion, accompanied by anguished cries. Like the ghosts of birds, the blurs dipped and dove, harrying the monstrosities who paused in their pursuit of Arthas to bat and roar at the spectral figures, who suddenly seemed to dive right inside the creatures.

The slimy, white, maggoty things froze, and then abruptly turned their attention to the shambling ghouls that were attacking Arthas. A grin spread across the death knight's pale face. The banshees. He had thought Sylvanas too lost in her hatred to come to his aid, or worse, like so many of his warriors, turned to become a pawn of his enemies. But it would seem that the former ranger-general's irritation with him was spent.

With the aid of the banshee-possessed abominations, the tide quickly turned, and a few moments later Arthas stood, weaving with a sudden weakness over a pile of corpses that were truly dead. The abominations turned on one another and hacked themselves to grisly bits. Arthas wondered if even their creators could have sewn back what was left of them. As they fell to the earth, the spirits that had possessed them darted free.

"You have my thanks, my ladies. I am glad to see that you and your mistress remain among my allies."

They hovered, their voices soft and haunting. "Indeed, great king. She sent us to find you. We've come to escort you across the river. Once we cross it we'll take refuge in the wilderness."

The wilderness—the same phrase Kel'Thuzad had used. Arthas relaxed even further. Clearly, his right and left hand were in agreement. He lifted a hand and concentrated. "Invincible, to me!" he called. A moment later a small patch of mist appeared, swirling and taking on the shape of a skeletal horse. A heartbeat later, Invincible was there in reality. Arthas was pleased to notice that the act took little effort; Invincible loved him. This was the one thing he had done completely right. The one dead thing that would never, ever turn against him, any more than the great animal would have done in its life. Carefully, he mounted, doing his best to hide his weakness from the banshees and the other undead.

"Lead me to your mistress and Kel'Thuzad, and I shall follow," he said.

They did, floating away from the palace and deep into the heart of Tirisfal Glades. Arthas noticed with a sudden unease that the path they were taking led uncomfortably near the Balnir farm. Fortunately, the banshees veered off, heading into a hillier area and through there to a wide-open field.

"This is the place, sisters. We'll rest here, great king."

There was no sign of Sylvanas, nor of Kel'Thuzad. Arthas drew rein on Invincible, looking around. He felt a sudden prickling of apprehension. "Why here?" he demanded. "Where is your mistress?"

The pain descended again and he cried out, clutching his chest. Invincible pranced beneath him, anxious, and Arthas clung on for dear life. The gray-green glade went away, replaced by the blues and whites of the oddly broken Frozen Throne. The Lich King's voice stabbed in his head and Arthas bit back a whimper.

"You have been deceived! Come to my side at once! *Obey!*"

"What is . . . happening here?" Arthas managed through gritted teeth. He blinked, forcing his vision to clear, and lifted his head, grunting with the effort.

She stepped out from behind the trees, carrying a bow. For a wild second, he thought he was back in Quel'Thalas, facing the living elf. But her hair was no longer golden, but black as midnight with streaks of white. Her skin was pale with a bluish tinge to it, and her eyes glowed silver. It was Sylvanas, and yet it was not. For this Sylvanas was neither alive, nor incorporeal. Somehow, she had gotten her body back from where he had ordered it left—safely locked in an iron coffin to be used as additional torment against her. But she had turned the tables on him.

As he struggled to make sense of what was happening through the pain, Sylvanas lifted her sleek black bow, drew, and took aim. Her lips curved in a smile.

"You walked right into this one, Arthas."

She released the arrow.

It impaled his left shoulder, piercing through his armor as if it were as flimsy as parchment, adding a fresh type of agony. He was confused for an instant—Sylvanas was a master archer. She couldn't possibly miss a fatal shot at this distance. Why the shoulder? His right hand went up automatically, but he found he couldn't even curl his fingers around the shaft. They were becoming numb—as were his feet, his legs . . .

He flung himself onto Invincible's neck, draping and doing what he could to cling to his mount with limbs that were rapidly becoming useless. He could barely turn his head to stare at her and rasp out the words, "Traitor! What have you done to me?"

She was smiling. She was happy. Slowly, languorously, she strode toward him. She was wearing the same outfit she had when he had killed her, revealing a great deal of her pale blue-white skin. Oddly, though, her body bore no scars from the innumerable wounds she had received on that day.

"It's a special poisoned arrow I made just for you," she said as she approached him. She shifted the bow to her back and drew a dagger, fingering it. "The paralysis you're experiencing now is but a fraction of the agony you've caused me."

Arthas swallowed. His mouth was dry as sand. "Finish me, then."

She threw back her head and laughed, hollow and ghostly. "A quick death . . . like the one you gave me?" Her mirth faded as quickly as it had come, and her eyes flashed red. She continued her approach until she was only an arm's length away. Invincible pranced uncertainly at her proximity, and Arthas's heart lurched as he almost slipped off.

"Oh no. You have taught me well, Arthas Menethil. You taught me about the folly of showing mercy to my enemies, and the delight of exacting torment from them. And so, my tutor, I'll show you how well I learned those lessons. You're going to suffer as I did. Thanks to my arrow, you can't even run."

Arthas's eyes seemed to be the only thing that could move, and he watched helplessly as she lifted the dagger. "Give my regards to hell, you son of a bitch."

No. Not this way—not paralyzed and helpless . . . Jaina . . .

Sylvanas suddenly staggered back, the pale hand that clutched the dagger twisting and opening. The look on her face was utter astonishment. A heartbeat later, the little shade that had come to Arthas's aid earlier materialized, smiling happily at the thought that she had helped to save her king. Happy to serve.

"Back, you mindless ones! You shall not fall today, my king!"

Kel'Thuzad! He had come as he had promised, finding Arthas all the way out here where the traitorous banshee had lured him. And he had not come alone. Well over a dozen undead were with him, and they now launched themselves at Sylvanas and her banshees. Hope rose inside him, but he was still paralyzed, still unable to move. He watched as the fight raged around him, and in a few moments it was obvious that Sylvanas would need to retreat.

She shot him a look, and again her eyes flashed red. "This isn't over, Arthas! I'll *never* stop hunting you."

Arthas was looking directly at her as she seemed to melt into the shadows. The last parts of her to vanish were her crimson eyes. With their mistress gone, the other banshees under Sylvanas's command disappeared as well. Kel'Thuzad hastened to Arthas's side.

"Did she harm you, my liege?"

Arthas could only stare at him, the paralysis so far gone he could not even move his lips. Bony hands folded with surprising delicacy around the arrow and tugged. Arthas bit back a cry of pain as the arrow came free. His red blood was mixed with a gooey black substance, which Kel'Thuzad examined carefully.

"The effects of her arrow will wear off in time. It seems the poison was meant only to immobilize you."

Of course, Arthas thought; otherwise she would not have needed the dagger. Relief shuddered through him, leaving him even more exhausted. He had come very close—too close—to his death. If not for the loyalty of the lich, the elf would have had him. He tried again to speak and managed, "I—you saved me."

Kel'Thuzad inclined his horned head. "I am grateful I could be of assistance, my king. But you must hasten from this place, to Northrend. All the preparations for your journey have been made. What is it you would have of me?"

Kel'Thuzad had been right. Even now, Arthas was beginning to feel some semblance of life returning to his limbs, though not enough that he could move under his own power.

"I need to find the Lich King as soon as possible. Much longer and . . . I don't know what the future holds, or if

I'll even return, but I want you to watch over this land. See to it that my legacy endures."

He trusted the lich, not out of affection or loyalty, but simply as a cold, hard fact. Kel'Thuzad was an undead thing, bound to the master they both served. Arthas's eyes flitted to the little ghost, hovering, smiling, a few feet away, and to the slack-faced, rotting corpses who would walk off a cliff if he told them to.

Just dead meat and sundered spirits. Not subjects. And they never had been. No matter what the little shade's smile said.

"You honor me, my liege. I shall do as you ask, King Arthas. I shall."

She had a body now, what her own had once been, though changed, as she had been changed. Sylvanas walked with the same easy stride she had had in life, wore the same armor. But it was not the same. She was forever, irrevocably altered.

"You seem troubled, mistress."

Sylvanas started from her reverie and turned to the banshee, one of the many who floated beside her. She could float with them, but she preferred the heaviness, the solidity, of the corporeal form she had stolen back for herself.

"Aren't you, sister?" she answered curtly. "Only days ago we were the Lich King's slaves. We existed only to slaughter in his name. And now we are . . . free."

"I don't understand, mistress." The banshee's voice was hollow and confused. "Our wills are our own now. Is that not what you fought for? I thought you'd be overjoyed."

Sylvanas laughed, aware that it was perilously close to hysteria. "What joy is there in this curse? We are still undead, sister—still monstrosities." She extended a hand, examined the blue-gray flesh, noticed the cold that clung to her like a second skin. "What are we if not slaves to this torment?"

He had taken so much. Even if she extended his death over a period of days . . . weeks . . . she would never be able to make Arthas suffer sufficiently. His death would not bring back the dead, cleanse the Sunwell, nor restore her to her living, peach-and-gold self. But it would feel . . . very good.

He had eluded her at their confrontation several days past. His lackey, the lich, had come at precisely the wrong moment. Arthas had gone far beyond her grasp now, trying to heal himself. She had learned that he'd left Kel'Thuzad in control of these plagued lands. But that was all right. She was dead. She had all the time in the world to plot an exquisite revenge.

A movement caught her eye and she got gracefully to her feet, drawing the bow and nocking it in one single, swift movement. The swirling portal opened and Varimathras stood there, grinning patronizingly down at her.

"Greetings, Lady Sylvanas." The demon actually bowed. Sylvanas raised an eyebrow. She did not for a minute think he meant it. "My brothers and I appreciate the role you played in overthrowing Arthas."

The role she played. Like this was some sort of theatrical game.

"Overthrow? I suppose one could call it that. He has scurried away, that much is sure."

The mighty being shrugged, his wings spreading slightly with the gesture. "Either way, he no longer troubles us. I've come to offer you a formal invitation to join our new order."

A "new order." Not very new at all, she mused; same subjugation, different master. She could not have been less interested.

"Varimathras," she said coldly. She did not bow in return. "My only interest was in seeing Arthas dead. Since I failed in my first attempt at this goal, I now wish to concentrate my efforts on succeeding the next time. I have no time for your petty politics or power mongering."

The demon bridled. "Careful, milady. It would be unwise to incur our wrath. We are the future of these . . . Plaguelands. You can either join us and rule, or be cast aside."

"You? The future? Kel'Thuzad did not go with his precious Arthas. He was left here for a reason. But perhaps a lich reborn by the very essence of the mighty Sunwell is nothing to beings as powerful as you." Her voice dripped scorn, and the dreadlord frowned terribly.

"I've lived as a slave long enough, dreadlord." Funny, how one used the word "lived," even though one was dead. Old habits died hard, it would seem. "I have fought tooth and nail to become more than what that bastard made me. I have my own will now, and I choose my own path. The Legion is defeated. You are the last pathetic remnants. You are a dying breed. I won't relinquish my freedom by shackling myself to you fools."

"So be it," Varimathras hissed. He was furious. "Our reply will come soon."

He teleported out, his face twisted in a scowl.

Her needling had gotten to him, and he fairly quivered with outrage. She noted this dispassionately. He was easy to anger; he was the one they had sent to her, thinking her no great threat.

She would need more than a handful of banshees to fight Arthas. She would need an army, a city of the dead . . . she would need Lordaeron. The Forsaken, she would call these lost souls who, like her, did not breathe but who yet had their own will. And even more immediately, she would need more than her spectral sisters to fight the three demonic brothers. Or maybe there would be only two she needed to fight.

Sylvanas Windrunner thought again of Varimathras, how easy he was to manipulate.

Perhaps this one could be useful. . . .

Yes. She and the Forsaken would find their own path in this world . . . and would slaughter anyone who stood in their way.

CHAPTER TWENTY-THREE

Northrend. There was an odd sense of coming home. As the shore came into view, Arthas remembered the first time he had arrived here, his heart full of pain at Jaina and Uther's betrayal, aching at the necessity of what he had been forced to do at Stratholme. So much had happened that it felt like a lifetime ago. He had come then with vengeance in his heart, to kill the demon lord responsible for turning his people into the walking dead. Now, he ruled those walking dead and was allies with Kel'Thuzad.

Strange, the twists and turns of fate.

He did not feel the cold, as he had then. Nor did the men who had followed him so loyally; death dulled sensations for such things. Only the human necromancers bundled up against the icy wind that sighed and moaned and the snow that began to drift lazily downward as they made anchor and debarked.

Arthas moved stiffly from the rowboat onto the shore. He might not feel the cold of this place, but his powers, and his physical self, were weak. As soon as his feet touched the earth, Arthas felt him—the Lich King. Not in his mind, not speaking to him through Frostmourne, although the runeblade's feeble glow strengthened slightly. No, Arthas sensed him *here,* his master, as he had not before. And there was a prickling sensation of increased threat.

He turned back to the rest of those who were following him ashore—ghouls, specters, shades, abominations, necromancers. "We must make haste," he cried. "Something out there is threatening the Lich King. We must reach Icecrown quickly."

"My lord!" one of the necromancers cried, and pointed. Arthas whirled, drawing Frostmourne.

Through the veil of the falling snow he could see golden-red shapes hovering in the air. They drew closer, and his eyes narrowed in surprise and anger as he recognized the creatures and realized who their masters must be.

Dragonhawks. He was astonished. He had all but exterminated the high elves. How could it be that any of them survived sufficiently to regroup, let alone determine where he had gone and confront him here? A slow smile spread across his handsome features, and he felt the sneaking sensation of admiration.

The dragonhawks came closer. He lifted Frostmourne in salute.

"I have to admit," he shouted, "I am surprised to see quel'dorei here. I would have thought the cold too unpleasant for so delicate a people."

"Prince Arthas!" The voice came from one of the riders, its beast hovering above Arthas. His voice rang clear and bright and strong. "You still do not see quel'dorei here. We are the *sin'dorei*—the blood elves! We have sworn to avenge the ghosts of Quel'Thalas. This dead land . . . will be cleansed! The disgusting things you have created will rest properly at last. And you, butcher, will finally receive your just punishment."

He was amused for a moment. Their numbers were not insignificant. Arthas realized that he was most likely looking at the last few of an all but extinct race. And they'd come just for him? Then his smugness faded into irritation. Despite his wearied state, anger filled his voice as he cried, "Northrend belongs to the Scourge, elf, and you will soon join them! You made a terrible mistake by coming here!"

More dragonhawks appeared, along with rangers on foot. Arrows flew through the skies, seemingly as numerous as snowflakes, peppering the undead as they charged. Most of them, however, did not fall; the sting of arrows, as long as it did not pierce a vital spot, troubled them not at all.

Not bothering to even mount Invincible, Arthas charged in. Frostmourne hungered; it seemed to gather energy and strength, as did Arthas himself, with each of the bright, shining souls it consumed. In the midst of the clamor of battle, he heard a voice that was deep and cold as Northrend itself call out from a hill above them.

"Onward for the Scourge! Slay them in Ner'zhul's name!"

Despite all he had seen, despite all he had done, Arthas felt a deep chill sweep over him at the sound of that bone-cold voice. He risked a quick glance upward and his eyes widened at what he beheld.

Nerubians! Of course—this was their homeland. His heart lifted as they poured forth. He could make out their shapes through the snow, the familiar, unsettling, scuttling speed with which the spidery beings descended on their prey. Arthas had to give these so-called sin'dorei credit—they fought valiantly—but they were hopelessly outnumbered, and soon Arthas was standing in a sea of red- and gold-clad bodies. He raised his hand, and one by one, the dead elves twitched and lurched to their feet, staring at him glassy-eyed.

"More soldiers for the one we serve," Arthas said. He looked again, and his eyes fell upon the nerubians' leader.

He was larger than those he commanded, towering over them as he moved easily down the snowy landscape toward Arthas. He moved among them like the king he was, with deliberateness and precision. Arthas tried to find something familiar in something so incredibly alien to him; to the human's eyes, Anub'arak looked like a cross between a beetle and the other, more spidery-appearing nerubians he commanded. Arthas found that he had taken an unintentional step backward and forced himself to stay where he was as the creature approached.

It kept coming until it was right in front of him, then loomed over him, gazing down with multiple eyes, a thing of utter horror. His ally.

Arthas found his voice and forced it to be calm. "Thanks for the assistance, mighty one."

The creature inclined its head, mandibles clacking gently as it spoke in that deep, sepulchral tone that still made Arthas uneasy. "The Lich King sent me to aid you, death knight. I am Anub'arak, ancient king of Azjol-Nerub. Where is the other?" It reared up on its hind legs, looking about.

"Other?"

"Kel'Thuzad," Anub'arak rumbled again in that hissing, sighing, reverberating voice. He lowered himself down and fixed Arthas with his multiple-eyed gaze. "I know him. I greeted him when he first came to serve the Lich King, as I greet you now."

Arthas wondered briefly if Kel'Thuzad had felt as unsettled as he upon first encountering this undead, insectoid king of an ancient race. Surely he had been, he told himself. Surely anyone would be.

"Your people were a welcome addition to our ranks the first time we attacked these elves," he said, glancing again at the fallen sin'dorei. He was very glad Anub'arak's "people" were on his side. "And I welcome your aid again now. But we have little time for pleasantries. Since the Lich King sent you, you must be aware that he is in danger. We must reach Icecrown immediately."

"It is so," rumbled Anub'arak. He bobbed his fearsome head and shifted, extending two of his forelegs. "I will gather the rest of my people, and we will march together to protect our lord."

The massive creature moved off imperiously, summoning his obedient subjects who scurried to him eagerly. Arthas suppressed a shudder and nudged one of the bodies of the fallen elves. It had been ripped limb from limb, too badly damaged to be of use. "These elves are pathetic. It's no wonder we destroyed their homeland so easily."

"Pity I wasn't there to stop you. It's been a long time, Arthas."

The voice was musical, smooth, cultured . . . and laced with hatred. Arthas turned, recognizing it, startled and pleased to find its owner here. The twists and turns of fate indeed.

"Prince Kael'thas," he said, grinning. The elf stood a few yards away, the shimmer of his teleportation spell still fading. Seemingly ageless, he looked exactly the same as Arthas remembered. No, not exactly. The blue eyes gleamed with suppressed anger. Not the hot rage he had seen upon the visage the last time they had encountered each other, but a cold, deep-seated fury. He no longer wore the purple and blue robes of the Kirin Tor, but the traditional crimson hues of his people.

"Arthas Menethil." The elf did not use a title. He obviously meant it as a slight, but it bothered Arthas not at all. He knew well enough what he was, and soon, this too-pretty princeling would know it also. "I would spit at the thought of your name in my mouth, but you aren't even worth that."

"Ah, Kael," Arthas said, grinning. "Even your insults are unnecessarily complicated. Glad to see you haven't changed—as ineffectual as ever. That raises a question. Why weren't you at Quel'Thalas anyway? Content to let other people die for you while you sat snug and secure in your Violet Citadel? I don't think you'll be doing that anymore."

Kael'thas gritted his teeth, his eyes narrowing. "That much I will give you. I should have been there. I was instead trying to help the humans fight the Scourge—the Scourge you unleashed on your own people. You may not care for your subjects—but I care for mine. I have lost far, far too much in dealing with humans. I stand only for the elves now. For the sin'dorei—the children of the blood. You will pay, Arthas. You will pay dearly for what you have done!"

"You know, I'm almost enjoying this banter. It's been a long time, hasn't it? I haven't seen you since . . ." He let the sentence trail away, watching as a muscle twitched near the elf prince's eye. Yes, Kael'thas remembered. Remembered stumbling across Jaina and Arthas locked in a deep kiss. The memory briefly unsettled Arthas as well, and the pleasure he took in inflicting the torment upon Kael'thas soured ever so slightly. "I must say though, I'm rather disappointed in these elves you lead. I'd hoped for a better fight. Maybe I killed all the ones with spirit in Quel'Thalas."

Kael didn't rise to the bait. "What you faced here was merely a scouting force. Don't worry, Arthas, you'll have a good challenge shortly. I assure you that defeating Lord Illidan's army will be far more difficult." The prince's full lips twisted in amusement as Arthas started at the name.

"Illidan? He's behind this invasion?" Dammit. It would have been better if he had killed Tichondrius himself, rather than involving the kaldorei. He'd known Illidan was power hungry. He just hadn't realized that the night elf would evolve into so great a threat.

"He is. Our forces are vast, Arthas." The silky, rich voice was laced now with delight. The bastard was really enjoying this. "Even now, they march upon Icecrown Glacier. You'll never make it in time to save your precious Lich King. Consider this payment for Quel'Thalas . . . and other insults."

"Other insults?" Arthas grinned. "Perhaps you'd like the details of these other insults. Shall I tell you what it was like to hold her in my arms, to taste her, to hear her call out my—"

The pain was worse than it had ever been before.

Arthas crumpled to his knees. His vision went red. Again he saw the Lich King—Ner'zhul, he recalled Anub'arak had named him—trapped in the icy prison.

"Make haste!" the Lich King cried. "My enemies draw near! Our time is almost spent!"

"Are you well, death knight?"

Arthas blinked and found himself staring up into the face, if it could be called that, of Anub'arak. A long arachnid leg was extended toward him, offering him assistance. He hesitated, but was too weak to rise unaided. Steeling himself, he gripped it and rose. It was like a stick in his hand, dried and almost—mummified to the touch. He let go as soon as he could stand by himself.

"My powers are weakening, but I'll be all right." He took a steadying breath and glanced around. "Where is Kael'thas?"

"Gone." The voice was cold as stone and laced with displeasure. "He used his magic to teleport away before we could rend him to pieces."

The cowardly mage trick of teleportation again. If

only Arthas's necromancers were capable of such, the Lich King would not be in the danger he was in. Arthas recalled the other corpses and knew that such would indeed have been Kael'thas's fate. "I hate to say it," he said, "but the damned elf was right." He turned to his intimidating ally. "Anub'arak—I had another vision—the Lich King is in immediate peril. They're closing in on him—Illidan and Kael'thas. We'll never reach the glacier in time!"

I've failed....

Anub'arak did not seem at all perturbed. "Overland, perhaps not," agreed the mammoth creature. "It is a long and arduous voyage. But . . . there is another route we might take, death knight. The ancient, shattered kingdom of Azjol-Nerub lies deep below us. It was where I once ruled for many years. I know its corridors and hidden places well. Though it has fallen on dark times, it could provide us a direct shortcut to the glacier."

Arthas looked up. As the raven flew, it was not that long a journey. But across the ice and the mountains that reared up before them . . .

"You're certain we can reach the glacier through these tunnels?" he asked.

"Nothing is certain, death knight." For a moment, it sounded like the nerubian was smirking. "The ruins will be perilous. But it's worth the risk."

Fallen on dark times. A curious phrase for an ancient, dead, spider-lord to use. Arthas wondered what that meant.

He supposed he was about to find out.

Anub'arak and his subjects set a brisk pace, heading

due north. Arthas and his Scourge followers fell into step, and soon the ocean was left behind. The sun moved quickly across the dim sky, low on the horizon. The long night was coming. As they marched, Arthas sent some of his warriors to gather what tree limbs and sticks they could; they would burn through many a torch passing through this dangerous subterranean kingdom.

After several hours of excruciatingly slow progress—the undead could not truly feel the cold, but the wind and snow slowed them—Arthas knew that despite Anub'arak's nearly wry words, one thing actually *was* certain. He never would have made it in time to save the Lich King—and thus himself—by heading overland. In the end, it was self-preservation that drove him so hard. The Lich King had found him, had made him into what he now was. Had granted him great power. Arthas knew and appreciated it, but his debt to the Lich King was nothing of loyalty. If this great being was slain, there was no doubt but that Arthas would be the next to die—and, as he had told Uther, he intended to live forever.

At last, they reached the gates. So covered with ice and snow were they that Arthas did not immediately recognize them as such, but Anub'arak halted, reared up, and spread wide two of his eight legs, indicating what lay ahead of them.

Curved stone, looking like sickles—or insect legs, Arthas thought—jutted upward, their tips bending toward one another to form a sort of symbolic tunnel. Ahead, he could make out the gates themselves. A giant spider was etched upon them. Arthas's lip curled in disgust, but then he thought of the statues dotting Stormwind. Was this really so different? The entrance "tunnel" and the gates led into the heart of what seemed to be an iceberg. For a moment, just a moment, Arthas glanced at the silent, enormous figure of Anub'arak, thought about spiders and flies, and wondered if he was doing the right thing.

"Behold the entrance to a once-powerful and ancient place," Anub'arak said. "I was lord here, and my word was obeyed without question. I was mighty and powerful, and I bowed to no one. But things change. I serve the Lich King now, and my place is defending him."

Arthas thought briefly of his outrage at the plague, of his burning need for vengeance . . . of the look in his father's eyes as Frostmourne drank his soul.

"Things do change," he said quietly. "But there's no time to reminisce." He turned to his strange new ally and smiled coldly. "Let us descend."

CHAPTER TWENTY-FOUR

Arthas did not know how long they spent beneath the frozen surface of Northrend, in the ancient and deadly nerubian kingdom. He only knew two things as he trudged out into the light, blinking like a bat forced out into the sun. One was that he hoped he was in time to defend the Lich King. The other was that he was grateful, bone-deep, to be *out* of that place.

It had been clear that the nerubian kingdom had once been beautiful. Arthas was not sure what he had expected, but it had not been the haunting, vivid colors of blue and purple, nor the intricate geometric shapes that denoted different rooms and corridors. These still retained their beauty, but were like a preserved rose; something that while still lovely, was nonetheless dead. A strange smell wafted through the place as they walked. Arthas could not place it, nor even categorize it. It was acrid and stale at once, but not unpleasant, not to one used to the company of the decaying dead.

It was likely in the end a shorter route, as Anub'arak

had promised, but every step had been bought with blood. Soon after they had entered, they had come under attack.

They scuttled out from the darkness, a dozen or more spider-beings chittering angrily as they descended. Anub'arak and his soldiers met them head-on. Arthas had hesitated for a fraction of a second, then joined in, ordering his troops to do the same. The vast caverns were filled with the shrieking and chittering of the nerubians, the guttural groans of the undead, and the agonized cries of the living necromancers as the nerubians attacked with gobbets of poison. Thick, sticky webbing trapped several of the fiercer corpses, holding them helpless until snapping mandibles lopped off heads or stiletto-sharp legs impaled and eviscerated them.

Anub'arak was a nightmare incarnate. He uttered a dreadful, hollow sound in his guttural native language, and fell upon his former subjects with devastating consequences. His legs, each working separately, grabbed and impaled his hapless victims. Vicious pincers sheared off limbs. And the whole time, the stale air was filled with cries that made Arthas, inured to such things as he was, shiver and swallow hard.

The skirmish was violent and costly, but the nerubians eventually retreated to the shadows that had birthed them. Several of their number were left behind, eight legs squirming violently before the hapless arachnids curled up on themselves and died.

"What the hell was that all about?" Arthas had asked, panting and whirling on Anub'arak. "These nerubians are your kin. Why are they hostile to us?"

"Many of us who fell during the War of the Spider were brought back to serve the Lich King," Anub'arak had replied. "These warriors, however," and he waved a foreleg at one of the bodies, "never died. Foolishly, they still fight to liberate Nerub from the Scourge."

Arthas glanced down at the dead nerubian. "Foolishly indeed," he murmured, and lifted a hand. "In death, they only serve that which they struggled against in life."

And so it was that when he finally emerged into the dim light of the overhead world, gulping in the cold, clean air, his army had swollen with new recruits, freshly dead and utterly his to command.

Arthas drew Invincible to a halt. He was trembling, badly, and wanted to simply sit and breathe fresh air for a few moments. The air quickly soured with the rotting stench of his own army. Anub'arak passed him, pausing to gaze at him implacably for a moment.

"No time to rest, death knight. The Lich King has need of us. We must serve."

Arthas shot the crypt lord a quick glance. Something in the tone of the being's voice spoke of the vaguest stirring of—was it resentment? Did Anub'arak serve only because he had to? Would he turn on the Lich King if he was able to do so—and more to the point, would he turn on Arthas?

The Lich King's powers were weakening—and so were Arthas's powers right along with him. If they got weak enough . . .

The death knight watched the retreating figure of the crypt lord, took a deep breath, and followed.

* * *

How long the trek through thick snow and scouring winds was, Arthas didn't know. At one point he nearly lost consciousness while riding, so weak was he. He came to with a start, terrified at the lapse, forcing himself to hang on. He could not falter, not now.

They crested a hill, and Arthas at last saw the glacier in the middle of the valley—and the army that awaited him. His spirits lifted at the sight of so many assembled to fight for him and the Lich King. Anub'arak had left many of his warriors behind, and they were there, stoic and ready. Farther down, though, closer to the glacier, he saw other figures milling about. He was too far away to distinguish them, but he knew whom they must be. His gaze traveled upward, and his breath caught.

The Lich King was there, deep inside the glacier. Trapped in his prison, Arthas had seen him so in the visions. He listened with half an ear as one of the nerubians hastened up to Anub'arak and Arthas to brief them on the situation.

"You've arrived just in time. Illidan's forces have taken up positions at the base of the glacier and—"

Arthas cried out as the worst pain he had yet tasted buffeted him. Again, his world turned the color of blood as agony racked his body. So close to the Lich King now, the torment he shared with that great entity was magnified a hundredfold.

"Arthas, my champion. You have come at last."

"Master," Arthas whispered, his eyes squeezed shut and his fingers pressed into his temples. "Yes, I have come. I am here."

"There is a fracture in my prison, the Frozen Throne,

and my energies are seeping from it," the Lich King continued. "That is why your powers have diminished."

"But how?" Had someone attacked him? Arthas saw no immediate foes in his vision, surely he was not too late—

"The runeblade, Frostmourne, was once locked inside the throne as well. I thrust it from the ice so that it would find its way to you . . . and then lead you to me."

"And so it has," Arthas breathed. The Lich King was immobilized, trapped inside the ice. It must have been through sheer will that he had been able to force the great sword through the ice and send it to Arthas. Now he recalled the ice that had held Frostmourne—how it had looked jagged, as if it had been broken off of a larger piece. Such vast power . . . and all bent toward bringing Arthas to this place. Step by step, Arthas had been led here. Directed. Controlled . . .

"You must make haste, my champion. My creator, the demon lord Kil'jaeden, sent his agents here to destroy me. If they should reach the Frozen Throne before you, all will be lost. The Scourge will be undone. Now hurry! I will grant you all the power I can spare."

Coldness suddenly began to seep through Arthas, numbing the angry, raw pain, calming his thoughts. The energy was so vast, so heady . . . it was more powerful even than what Arthas had known before. This, then, was why he had come. To drink deep of this icy draft, to take the cold strength of the Lich King into himself. He opened his eyes, and his vision was clear. Frostmourne's runes blazed to new life, a chill mist seeping up from it. Grinning fiercely, Arthas gripped the blade and lifted it high. When he spoke, his voice was clear and resonant and carried in the crisp, frigid air.

"I saw another vision of the Lich King. He has restored my powers! I know now what I must do." He pointed with Frostmourne at the doll-sized figures in the distance. "Illidan has mocked the Scourge long enough. He is attempting to gain entry to the Lich King's throne chamber. He will fail. It's time we put the fear of death back in him. Time to end the game . . . once and for all."

With a fierce challenging cry, he swung Frostmourne over his head. It sang out, hungry for more souls. "For the Lich King!" Arthas cried, and charged down to meet his enemies.

He felt like a god as he swung Frostmourne with almost careless ease. Each soul it took only strengthened him. Let the arrows of the blood elves shower upon them like the snow. They fell like wheat before the scythe. At one point, Arthas glanced over the battlefield. Where was the one he had to slay? He saw no sign of Illidan yet. Was it possible he had already gained entrance into the—

"Arthas! Arthas, turn and fight me, damn you!"

The voice was clear and pure and full of hatred, and Arthas turned.

The elven prince was but a few yards away, his red and gold bright as blood against the unforgiving whiteness of the snow upon which they fought. He was tall and proud, his staff planted in the snow before him, his eyes fixed on Arthas. Magic crackled around him.

"You will go no farther, butcher."

A muscle twitched near Arthas's eye. So Sylvanas

had called him, too. He made a slight *tsk*ing sound, and grinned at the elf who had once seemed so very powerful and learned to a young human prince. His mind went back to the moment when Kael had surprised Arthas and Jaina in a kiss. The boy that Arthas had been then had known himself outmatched by the older, much more powerful mage.

Arthas was no longer a boy.

"After you disappeared in so cowardly a fashion at our last confrontation, I admit, I'm surprised to see you show your face again, Kael. Don't be upset that I stole Jaina from you. You should let that go and move on. After all, there's so much left in this world for you to enjoy. Oh wait . . . no, there isn't."

"Damn you to hell, Arthas Menethil," Kael'thas snarled, trembling with outrage. "You've taken everything I ever cared for. Vengeance is all I have left."

He wasted no more time in venting his anger, but instead lifted the staff. The crystal affixed to its tip glowed brightly, and a ball of fire crackled in his free hand. A heartbeat later it had soared toward Arthas. Shards of ice rained down upon the death knight. Kael'thas was a master mage, and much faster than anyone Arthas had ever encountered. He barely got Frostmourne up in time to deflect the surging fiery globe. The frost shards, however, were ease itself. He swung the great runeblade over his head, and it called to its blade the shards of ice like iron shavings to a magnet. Grinning, Arthas whirled the sword over his head, directing the pieces of ice back to their sender. He'd been taken by surprise by Kael'thas's speed, but he would not make that mistake again.

"You might want to think twice about attacking me with ice, Kael," he said, laughing. He needed to goad the mage into acting rashly. Control was key to the manipulation of magic, and if Kael lost his temper, he would undoubtedly lose the fight.

Kael narrowed his eyes. "Thanks for the advice," he growled. Arthas tightened up on the reins, preparing to ride down his adversary, but at that instant the snow beneath him glowed bright orange for a moment and then became water. Invincible suddenly dropped two feet and his hooves slipped on the slick ground. Arthas leaped off and sent the beast cantering away, gripping Frostmourne with renewed determination in his right hand. He extended his left. A dark ball of swirling green energy formed in his flattened palm and sped toward Kael like an arrow shot from a bow. The mage moved to counter, but the attack was too swift. His face went a shade paler and he stumbled back, his hand going to his heart. Arthas grinned as some of the mage's life energy flooded him.

"I took your woman," he said, continuing to try to anger the mage, although he knew, and probably Kael knew, that Jaina had never belonged to the elf. "I held her in my arms at night. She tasted sweet when I kissed her, Kael. She—"

"Loathes you now," Kael'thas replied. "You sicken and disgust her, Arthas. Anything she felt for you has since turned to hatred."

Arthas's chest contracted oddly. He realized he had not thought about how Jaina regarded him now. He had always done his best to thrust all thoughts of her away when they drifted into his mind. Was it true? Did Jaina really—

An enormous crackling ball of fire exploded against his chest, and Arthas cried out as he was forced backward by the blow. Flame licked at him for precious seconds before he recovered his wits sufficiently to counter the spell. The armor had largely protected him, although its heat against his skin was agonizing, but he was aghast that he had been so taken by surprise. A second ball of fire came, but this time he was ready, meeting the fiery blast with his own deadly ice.

"I destroyed your homeland . . . fouled your precious Sunwell. And I killed your father. Frostmourne sucked the soul right out of him, Kael. It's gone forever."

"You're good at killing noble elderly men," sneered Kael'thas. The jab was unexpectedly painful. "At least you faced *my* father on the battlefield. What of your own, Arthas Menethil? How brave of you to cut down a defenseless parent opening his arms to embrace his—"

Arthas charged, closing the distance between them in a few strides, and brought Frostmourne down. Kael'thas parried with his staff. For a second, the stave held, then it broke beneath Frostmourne's onslaught. But the delay had bought Kael sufficient time to unsheathe a glittering, gleaming weapon, a runeblade that seemed to glow red in contrast to Frostmourne's cold, icy blue. The blades clashed. Both men pressed down, straining with effort, each one's blade holding off the other as the seconds ticked by. Kael'thas grinned as their eyes met.

"You recognize this blade, do you not?"

Arthas did. He knew the sword's name and its

lineage—Flamestrike, Felo'melorn, once wielded by Kael'thas's ancestor, Dath'Remar Sunstrider, the founder of the dynasty. The sword was almost unspeakably old. It had seen the War of the Ancients, the birth of the Highborne. Arthas returned the smirk. Flamestrike would have another significant event to bear witness to; it would now see the end of the last Sunstrider.

"Oh, I do. I saw it snap in two beneath Frostmourne, an instant before I slew your father."

Arthas was physically stronger, and the energy of the Lich King surged through him. With a ragged grunt, he shoved Kael'thas backward, thinking to knock him off balance. The mage recovered quickly and almost danced into another position, brandishing Felo'melorn, his eyes never leaving Arthas.

"And so I found it, and I had it reforged."

"Broken swords are weak where they are mended, elf." Arthas began to circle, watching for the instant when Kael would be vulnerable.

Kael'thas laughed. "Human swords, perhaps. Not elven. Not when they are reforged with magic, and hatred, and a burning need for revenge. No, Arthas. Felo'melorn is stronger than ever—as am I. As are the sin'dorei. We are the stronger for having been broken— stronger and filled with purpose. And that purpose is to see you *fall*!"

The attack came suddenly. One moment Kael was standing, ranting, and the next Arthas was fighting for his very life. Frostmourne clanged against Flamestrike, and damned if the elf wasn't right—the blade held. Arthas darted back, feinted, and then brought Frostmourne across in a mighty sweep. Kael lunged out of its path and whirled to counterattack with a violence and intensity that surprised Arthas. He was forced back, one step, then two, and then suddenly he slipped and fell. Snarling, Kael lunged in, thinking to deal the deathblow. But Arthas remembered training with Muradin, long ago, and the dwarf's favorite trick suddenly filled his mind. He pulled his legs in tightly and kicked Kael'thas with all his strength. The mage let out a grunt and was hurtled backward into the snow. Gasping, the death knight flipped to his feet, hefted Frostmourne with both hands and plunged it down.

Somehow Flamestrike was there. The blades again strained against each other. Kael'thas's eyes burned with hatred.

But Arthas was the stronger in armed combat; stronger, with the stronger sword, despite Kael's gloating about how Felo'melorn was reforged. Slowly, inexorably, as Arthas knew must happen, Frostmourne descended toward Kael'thas's bare throat.

". . . she hates you," Kael whispered.

Arthas cried out, fury blurring his vision for a moment, and shoved down with all his strength.

Into the snow and frozen earth.

Kael'thas was gone.

"Coward!" Arthas cried, although he knew the prince would not hear him. The bastard had again teleported away at the last second. Fury raged in him, threatening to cloud his judgment, and he pushed it aside. He'd been foolish to let Kael'thas rile him so.

Curse you, Jaina. Even now, you haunt me.

"Invincible, to me!" he cried, and realized his voice was shaking. Kael'thas was not dead, but he was out of the way, and that was all that mattered. He wheeled the head of his skeletal horse around, and charged again toward the fray and the throne chamber of his master.

He moved through the milling crowd of enemies as if they were so many insects. As they fell, he reanimated them and sent them against their fellows. The tide of the undead was unstoppable and implacable. The snow around the base of the spire was churned up and drenched with blood. Arthas looked about him, at the last few knots of fighting going on. Blood elves—but no sign of their master.

Where was Illidan?

A flurry of quick motion caught his eye and he turned. He growled beneath his breath. Another dreadlord. This one's back was toward him, black wings outstretched, cloven hooves melting into the snow.

Arthas lifted Frostmourne. "I've defeated your kind before, dreadlord," he snarled. "Turn and face me, if you dare, or flee into the Nether like the coward you demons are."

The figure turned, slowly. Massive horns crowned its head. Its lips curved back in a smile. And over its eyes was a ragged black blindfold. Two green, glowing spots appeared where eyes should have been.

"Hello, Arthas."

Deep and sinister, the voice had changed, but not as much as the kaldorei's body. It was still the same pale lavender hue, etched with the same tattoos and scarifications. But the legs, the wings, the horns . . . Arthas immediately understood what must have happened. So that was why Illidan had become so powerful.

"You look different, Illidan. I guess the Skull of Gul'dan didn't agree with you."

Illidan threw back his horned head. Dark, rich laughter rumbled from him. "On the contrary, I have never felt better. In a way, I suppose I should thank you for my present state, Arthas."

"Show your appreciation by stepping out of the way, then." Arthas's voice was suddenly cold, and there was no trace of humor in it. "The Frozen Throne is mine, demon. Step aside. Leave this world and never return. If you do, I'll be waiting."

"We both have our masters, boy. Mine demands the destruction of the Frozen Throne. It would seem we are at odds," Illidan replied, and lifted the weapon Arthas had fought once before. His powerful hands with their sharp black nails closed on the weapon's center and he whirled it with grace and a deceptive casualness. Arthas knew a ripple of uncertainty at the display. He had just finished a fight with Kael'thas, and while he would have been the victor had not the elf, coward that he was, teleported out at the last instant, he had been taxed by the battle. There was no hint of weariness in Illidan's bearing.

Illidan's smile grew as he noticed his enemy's discomfiture. He allowed himself a moment more of uncannily masterful handling of the unusual, demonic weapon, then struck a position, settling in, preparing for combat. "It must be done!"

"Your troops are either in pieces or part of my army."

Arthas drew Frostmourne. Its runes glowed brightly, and mist curled up from its hilt. Behind the blindfold, Illidan's eyes—much brighter and more intensely green than he remembered—narrowed at the sight of the runeblade. If the demonically-changed kaldorei had a powerful weapon, so too did Arthas. "You'll end up one or the other."

"Doubtful," Illidan sneered. "I am stronger than you know, and *my* master created yours! Come, pawn. I'll dispatch the servant before I dispatch your pathetic—"

Arthas charged. Frostmourne glowed and hummed in his hands, as eager for Illidan's death as he was. The elf did not seem at all startled by the sudden rush, and with the utmost ease lifted his double-bladed weapon to parry. Frostmourne had broken ancient and powerful swords before, but this time, it simply clanged and grated against the glowing green metal.

Illidan gave him a smirk as he held his ground. Arthas again felt unease flicker through him. Illidan was indeed changed by absorbing the power of the Skull of Gul'dan; for one thing, he was physically much stronger than he had been. Illidan chuckled, a deep and ugly sound, then shoved forcefully. It was Arthas who was forced to fall back, dropping to one knee to defend himself as the demon bore down on him.

"It is sweet to turn the tables thus," Illidan growled. "I might just kill you quickly, death knight, if you give me a good fight."

Arthas didn't waste breath on insults. He gritted his teeth and concentrated on battling back the blows that were being rained upon him. The weapon was a swirl of glowing green. He could feel the power of demonic energy radiating from it, just as he knew that Illidan could sense Frostmourne's grim darkness.

Suddenly Illidan was not there and Arthas lurched forward, his momentum taking him off balance. He heard a flapping sound and whirled to see Illidan overhead, his great, leathery wings creating a strong wind as he hovered out of reach.

They eyed each other, Arthas catching his breath. He could see Illidan was not unaffected by the battle either. Sweat gleamed on the massive, lavender-hued torso. Arthas settled himself, Frostmourne at the ready for when Illidan would swoop in for a renewed assault.

Then Illidan did something utterly unexpected. He laughed, shifted the weapon in his hands—and in a flurry of motion seemingly snapped it in two. Each powerful hand now held a single blade.

"Behold the Twin Blades of Azzinoth," Illidan gloated. He flew up higher, whirling the blades in his left and right hands, and Arthas realized that he favored neither one. "Two magnificent warglaives. They can be wielded as a single devastating weapon . . . or, as you see, as two. It was the favored weapon of a doomguard—a powerful demon captain whom I slew. Ten thousand years ago. How long have you fought with your pretty blade, human? How well do you know it?"

The words were intended to unsettle the death knight. Instead, they invigorated him. Illidan might have had this admittedly powerful weapon for longer—but Frostmourne was bound to Arthas, and he to it. It was not a sword as much as an extension of himself. He had known it when he first had the vision of it, when he had just arrived in Northrend. He had been certain of the connection when he laid eyes upon it, waiting for him. And now he felt it surge in his hand, confirming their unity.

The demon blades gleamed. Illidan dropped down on Arthas like a stone. Arthas cried out and countered, more certain of this blow than of any he had dealt with the runeblade before, swinging Frostmourne up underneath the descending demon. And as he knew must happen, he felt the sword bite deep into flesh. He pulled, drawing the gash across Illidan's torso, and felt a deep satisfaction as the former kaldorei screamed in agony.

And yet the bastard would not fall. Illidan's wings beat erratically, still somehow keeping him aloft, and then before Arthas's shocked gaze his body seemed to shift and darken . . . almost as if it was made of writhing black, purple, and green smoke.

"This is what you have given me," Illidan cried. His voice, bass to begin with, had somehow grown even deeper. Arthas felt it shiver along his bones. The demon's eyes glowed fiercely in the swirling darkness that was his face. "This gift—this power. And it will destroy you!"

A scream was torn from Arthas's throat, and he fell again to his knees. Blazing green fire chased itself along his armor, seared his flesh, even dulled Frostmourne's blue glow for a moment. Over the raw cry of his own torment he heard Illidan laughing. Again the fel fire cascaded over him and Arthas fell forward, gasping. But as the fire faded and he saw Illidan swooping in for the kill, he felt the ancient runeblade he still managed to grasp urge him to rally.

Frostmourne was his, and he its, and so united, they were invincible.

Just as Illidan lifted his blades for the kill, Arthas raised Frostmourne, thrusting upward with all his strength. He felt the blade connect, pierce flesh, strike deep.

Illidan fell hard to the ground. Blood gushed from his bare torso, melting the snow around it with a slow hissing sound. His chest rose and fell in gasps. His vaunted twin blades were of no use now. One had been knocked from his grasp, the other lay in a hand that could not even curl around its hilt. Arthas got to his feet, his body still tingling with the remnants of the fel fire Illidan had hurled at him. He stared at him for a long moment, branding the sight into his mind. He thought about dealing the killing blow, but decided to let the merciless cold of the place do it for him. A greater need burned in him now, and he turned, lifting his eyes to the spire that towered above him.

He swallowed hard and simply stood for a moment, knowing, without knowing how he knew it, that something was about to fundamentally change. Then he took a deep breath and entered the cavern.

Arthas moved almost as if in a daze, down the lengths of twining tunnels that led ever deeper into the bowels of the earth. His feet seemed guided, and while there was no noise, certainly no one to challenge his right to be here, he felt, rather than heard, a deep thrum of power. He continued to descend, feeling that call of power drawing him ever closer to his destiny.

Up ahead was a cold, blue-white light. Arthas moved toward it, almost breaking into a run, and the tunnel opened up into what Arthas could only think of as a throne chamber. For just ahead was a structure that made Arthas's breath catch in his throat.

The Lich King's prison sat atop of this twining tower, this spire of blue-green, shimmering ice-that-was-not-ice that rose up as if to pierce the very roof of the cavern. A narrow walkway wound, serpentine, about the spire, leading him upward. Still filled with the energy granted to him by the Lich King, Arthas did not tire, but unwelcome memories seemed to dart at him like flies as he ascended, putting one booted foot in front of the other. Words, phrases, images came back to him.

"Remember, Arthas. We are paladins. Vengeance cannot be a part of what we must do. If we allow our passions to turn to bloodlust, then we will become as vile as the orcs."

Jaina . . . oh, Jaina . . . *"No one can seem to deny you anything, least of all me."*

"Don't deny me, Jaina. Don't ever deny me. Please."

"I never would, Arthas. Never."

He kept going, relentlessly moving upward.

"We know so little—we can't just slaughter them like animals out of our own fear!"

"This is bad business, lad. Leave it be. Let it stay here, lost and forgotten. . . . We'll find another way tae save yer people. Let's leave now, go back, and find that way."

One foot followed the other. Upward, ever upward. An image of black wings brushed his memory.

"*I will leave you one final prediction. Just remember, the harder you strive to slay your enemies, the faster you'll deliver your people into their hands.*"

Even as these memories tugged at him, clutched at his heart, there was one image, one voice, that was stronger and more compelling than all the others, whispering, encouraging him: "Closer you draw, my champion. My moment of freedom comes . . . and with it, your ascension to true power."

Upward he climbed, his gaze ever on the peak. On the huge chunk of deep blue ice that imprisoned the one who had first set Arthas's feet on this path. Closer it drew, until Arthas came to a halt a few feet away. For a long moment, he regarded the figure trapped within, imperfectly glimpsed. Mist rolled off the huge chunk of ice, further obscuring the image.

Frostmourne glowed in his hand. From deep inside, Arthas saw the barest hint of an answering flare of two points of glowing blue light.

"RETURN THE BLADE," came the deep, rasping voice in Arthas's mind, almost unbearably loud. "COMPLETE THE CIRCLE. RELEASE ME FROM THIS PRISON!"

Arthas took a step forward, then another, lifting Frostmourne as he moved until he was running. This was the moment it had all been leading to, and without his realizing it, a roar built in his throat and tore free as he swung the blade down with all of his strength.

A massive cracking resounded through the chamber as Frostmourne slammed down. The ice shattered, huge chunks flying in every direction. Arthas lifted his arms to shield himself, but the shards flew past him harmlessly. Pieces fell from the imprisoned body, and the Lich King cried out, lifting his armored arms to the sky. More groaning, cracking sounds came from the cavern and from the being himself, so loud that Arthas winced and covered his ears. It was as if the very world was tearing itself apart. Suddenly the armored figure that was the Lich King seemed to shatter as his prison did, falling apart before Arthas's stunned gaze.

There was nothing—no one—inside.

Only the armor, icy black, clattering to lie in pieces. The helm, empty of its owner's head, slid to a halt to lie at Arthas's feet. He stared down at it for a long moment, a deep shiver passing through him.

All this time . . . he had been chasing a ghost. Had the Lich King ever really been here? If not—who had thrust Frostmourne from the ice? Who had demanded to be freed? Was he, Arthas Menethil, supposed to have been the one encased in the Frozen Throne all along?

Had this ghost he'd been chasing . . . been himself?

Questions that would likely never have answers. But one thing was clear to him. As Frostmourne had been for him, so was the armor. Gauntleted fingers closed over the spiked helm and he lifted it slowly, reverently, and then, closing his eyes, he lowered it onto his white head.

He was suddenly galvanized, his body tensing as he felt the essence of the Lich King enter him. It pierced his heart, stopped his breath, shivered along his veins, icy, powerful, crashing through him like a tidal wave. His eyes were closed, but he saw, he saw so much—all that Ner'zhul, the orc shaman, had known, all he had seen, had done. For a moment, Arthas feared he would be overwhelmed by it all, that in the end, the Lich King had tricked him into coming here so that he could place his essence in a fresh new body. He braced himself for a battle for control, with his body as the prize.

But there was no struggle. Only a blending, a melding. All around him, the cavern continued to collapse. Arthas was only barely aware of it. His eyes darted rapidly back and forth beneath his closed lids.

His lips moved. He spoke.

They . . . spoke.

"Now . . . we are one."

EPILOGUE: THE LICH KING

The blue and white world blurred in Arthas's dream vision. The cold, pure colors shifted, changed to the warm hues of wood and fire- and torchlight. He had done as he said he would; he had remembered his life, all that had gone before, had again walked the path that had taken him to the seat of the Frozen Throne and this deep, deep dreaming state.

But the dream was not over, it would seem. He again sat at the head of the long, beautifully carved table that took up most of this illusionary Great Hall.

And the two who had such an interest in his dream were still there, watching him.

The orc on his left, elderly but still powerful, searched his face, and then began to smile, the gesture stretching the image of the white skull painted on his face. And on his right, the boy—the emaciated, sickly boy—looked even worse than Arthas remembered him looking when he had entered the dream of remembrance.

The boy licked cracked, pale lips and drew breath as

if to speak, but it was the orc whose words shattered the stillness first.

"There is so much more," he promised.

Images crowded Arthas's mind, interweaving and lying atop one another into glimpses of the future and past entangled. An army of humans on horseback, carrying the flag of Stormwind . . . fighting alongside, not against, a Horde raiding party mounted atop snarling wolves. They were allies, attacking the Scourge together. The scene shifted, changed. Now the humans and orcs were attacking one another—and the undead, some crying out orders and fighting with minds that were clearly their own—were standing shoulder to shoulder with the orcs, strange-looking bull-men, and trolls.

Quel'Thalas—undamaged? No, no, there was the scar he and his army had left—but the city was being rebuilt. . . .

Faster now the images poured into his mind, dizzying, chaotic, disordered. It was impossible to tell the past from the future now. Another image, that of skeletal dragons raining destruction down on a city Arthas had never seen before—a hot, dry place crowded with orcs. And—yes, yes it was Stormwind itself that was now coming under attack from the undead dragons—

Nerubians—no, no, not nerubians, not Anub'arak's people, but kin to them, yes. A desert race, these were. Their servants were mammoth creatures with the heads of dogs, golems made of obsidian, who strode across the shining yellow stands.

A symbol appeared, one Arthas knew—the *L* of

Lordaeron, impaled by a sword, but depicted in red, not blue. The symbol changed, became a red flame on a white background. The flame seemed to spark to a life of its own and engulfed the background, burning it away to reveal the silvery waters of a vast expanse of water . . . a sea . . .

. . . Something was roiling just beneath the ocean's surface. The hitherto-smooth surface began to churn wildly, seething, as if from a storm, although the day was clear. A horrible sound that Arthas only dimly recognized as laughter assaulted his ears, along with the screaming of a world wrenched from its proper place, hauled upward to face the light of day it had not seen in uncounted centuries. . . .

Green—all was green, shadowy and nightmarish, grotesque images dancing at the corner of Arthas's mind only to dart away before they could be firmly grasped. There was a brief glimpse, gone now—antlers? A deer? A man? It was hard to tell. Hope hung about the figure, but there were forces bent on destroying it. . . .

The mountains themselves came to life, taking giant strides, crushing everything luckless enough to cross their paths. With each mammoth footfall, the world seemed to tremble and shake.

Frostmourne. This at least he knew, and intimately. The sword whirled end over end, as if Arthas has tossed it into the air. A second sword rose to meet it—long, inelegant but powerful, with the symbol of a skull embedded in its fearsome blade. A name—"Ashbringer," a sword and yet more than a sword, as was Frostmourne. The two clashed—

Arthas blinked and shook his head. The visions, tumbled, chaotic, heartening, and disturbing—were gone.

The orc chuckled, the painted skull on his face stretching with the gesture. He had once been named Ner'zhul, had once had the gift of true visioning. Arthas did not doubt that all he had seen, though imperfectly understood, would indeed come to pass.

"So much more," the orc repeated, "but only if you continue to walk this path fully."

Slowly, the death knight turned his white head to the boy. The ill child met him with a gaze that was astonishingly clear, and for a moment, Arthas felt something inside him stir. Despite everything—the boy would not die.

And that meant . . .

The boy smiled a little, and some of the sickness dissipated as Arthas struggled for words. "You . . . are me. You are both . . . me. But you . . ." His voice was soft, tinged with wonder and disbelief. "You are the little flame that burns inside me still, that resists the ice. You are the last vestiges of humanity—of compassion, of my ability to love, to grieve . . . to care. You are my love for Jaina, my love for my father . . . for all the things that made me what I once was. Somehow Frostmourne didn't take it all. I tried to turn away from you . . . and I couldn't. I—can't."

The boy's sea-green eyes brightened and he gave his other self a tremulous smile. His color improved, and before Arthas's eyes, some of the pustules on his skin disappeared.

"You understand, now. Despite all, Arthas, you have not abandoned me." Tears of hope stood in those eyes and his voice, though stronger now than it had been, quavered with emotion. "There must be a reason. Arthas Menethil . . . much harm have you done, but there is goodness in you yet. If there was none . . . I would not exist, not even in your dreams."

He slipped off the chair and slowly walked toward the death knight. Arthas stood as he approached. For a moment, they regarded each other, the child and the man he had become.

The boy extended his arms, as if he were a living, breathing child asking to be picked up and held by a loving father. "It doesn't have to be too late," he said quietly.

"No," Arthas said quietly, staring raptly at the boy. "It doesn't."

He touched the curve of the boy's cheek, slipped a hand beneath the small chin and tilted up the shining face. He smiled into his own eyes.

"But it is."

Frostmourne descended. The boy cried out, his shocked, betrayed, anguished cry—that of the wind raging outside—and for a moment Arthas saw him standing there, the blade buried in his chest almost as big as he was, and felt one final tremor of remorse as he met his own eyes.

Then the boy was gone. All that remained of him was the bitter keening of the wind scouring the tormented land.

It felt . . . marvelous. It was only with the boy's passing that Arthas truly realized how dreadful a burden this last struggling scrap of humanity had been. He felt light, powerful, purged. Scoured clean, as Azeroth would soon be. All his weakness, his softness, everything that had ever made him hesitate or second-guess himself—it was all gone, now.

There was only Arthas, Frostmourne, all but singing at having claimed the final piece of Arthas's soul, and the orc, whose skull-face was split with triumphant laughter.

"Yes!" the orc exhilarated, laughing almost maniacally. "I knew you would make this choice. For so long you have wrestled with the last dregs of goodness, of humanity in you, but no longer. The boy held you back, and now you are free." He now got to his feet, his body still that of an old orc, but moving with the ease and fluidity of the young.

"We are one, Arthas. Together, we are the Lich King. No more Ner'zhul, no more Arthas—only this one glorious being. With my knowledge, we can—"

His eyes bulged as the sword impaled him.

Arthas stepped forward, plunging the glittering, hungering Frostmourne ever deeper into the dream-being that had once been Ner'zhul, then the Lich King, and was soon to be nothing, nothing at all. He slipped his other arm around the body, pressing his lips so close to the green ear that the gesture was almost intimate, as intimate as the act of taking a life always was and always would be.

"No," Arthas whispered. "No *we*. No one tells me what to do. I've got everything I need from you—now the power is mine and mine alone. Now there is only I. I am the Lich King. And I am ready."

The orc shuddered in his arms, stunned by the betrayal, and vanished.

★ ★ ★

The teacup shattered as it fell from Jaina's suddenly nerveless hands. She gasped, momentarily unable to breathe, the cold of the damp, gray day knifing through her. Aegwynn was there, her gnarled hands closing on Jaina's.

"Aegwynn—I—what happened?" Her voice was thick, anguished, and tears suddenly filled her eyes as if she was grieving terribly for the loss of . . . *something*. . . .

"It's not your imagination," Aegwynn said grimly. "I felt it, too. As for what—well, I'm sure we'll find out."

Sylvanas started as if the mammoth demon in front of her had struck her. Which, of course, he would never dare do. Varimathras narrowed his glowing eyes.

"My lady? What is it?"

Him.

It was *always* him.

Sylvanas's gloved hands clenched and unclenched. "Something has happened. Something to do with the Lich King. I—felt it." There was no longer a link between them, at least not one in which she was under his control. But perhaps something lingered. Something that warned her.

"We need to step up our plans," she told Varimathras. "I believe that time has suddenly become a precious commodity."

For so long, he had felt nothing. He had stayed on the throne, immobile, waiting, dreaming. The ice had come to cover him as he sat still as stone, but not a prison, no, a second skin.

He had not known then what he was waiting for, but now he did. He had taken the final steps on a journey begun so long ago, begun the day that darkness had first brushed his world in the form of a weeping, young Stormwind prince mourning his father. The path had led across Azeroth, to Northrend, to this Frozen Throne and open sky. To the searching of his deepest self, and the choices to murder both the innocent that held him back and the parts of himself that had shaped him.

Arthas, the Lich King, alone in his glory and power, slowly opened his eyes. Ice cracked from them at the gesture and fell in small shards, like frozen tears. A smile formed beneath the ornate helm that covered his white hair and pale skin, and more ice fell from his awakening, slowly shifting form, fragments of an icy chrysalis that was no longer needed. He was awake.

"It's begun."

ABOUT THE AUTHOR

New York Times bestselling and award-winning author Christie Golden has written over thirty novels and several short stories in the fields of science fiction, fantasy, and horror.

Golden launched the TSR Ravenloft line in 1991 with her first novel, the highly successful *Vampire of the Mists*, which introduced elven vampire Jander Sunstar. To the best of her knowledge, she is the creator of the elven vampire archetype in fantasy fiction.

She is the author of several original fantasy novels, including *On Fire's Wings, In Stone's Clasp,* and *Under Sea's Shadow* (currently available only as an eBook), the first three in her multi-book fantasy series The Final Dance from LUNA Books. *In Stone's Clasp* won the Colorado Author's League Award for Best Genre Novel of 2005, the second of Golden's novels to win the award.

Among Golden's other projects are over a dozen Star Trek novels and the well-received StarCraft Dark Templar trilogy, *Firstborn, Shadow Hunters,* and *Twilight.* An avid player of Blizzard's MMORPG *World of Warcraft,*

Golden has written several novels in that world (*Lord of the Clans, Rise of the Horde*) with more in the works. She has also written two Warcraft manga stories for Tokyopop, "I Got What Yule Need" and "A Warrior Made."

Golden is currently hard at work on three books in the major nine-book *Star Wars* series Fate of the Jedi, in collaboration with Aaron Allston and Troy Denning. Her first book in the series, *Omen*, hit shelves in June of 2009, and her second, *Allies*, is slated for publication in early summer of 2010.

Golden welcomes visitors to her website, www. christiegolden.com.

NOTES

The story you've just read is based in part on Blizzard Entertainment's computer game *Warcraft III: Reign of Chaos* and its expansion pack, *Warcraft III: The Frozen Throne.* Released in July 2002 and July 2003 respectively, these titles topped sales charts and were praised by critics, picking up "Editor's Choice," "Strategy Game of the Year," "Game of the Year," and other awards from numerous publications.

Over five years later, *Warcraft III* is still a popular choice for online multiplayer matches, and is a staple of professional gaming tournaments around the world. The single-player campaigns allow players to command and interact with some of the most powerful and interesting characters in Warcraft lore and to experience a pivotal time in Azeroth's history firsthand.

FURTHER READING:

If you'd like to read more about the characters, situations, and settings featured in this novel, the books listed below each offer another piece of the story of Azeroth:

- Thrall's story (along with more on Taretha Foxton, Aedelas Blackmoore, Durnholde Keep, and the orc internment camps) can be found in *Warcraft: Lord of the Clans* by Christie Golden.

- Jaina Proudmoore plays a central role in *World of Warcraft: Cycle of Hatred* by Keith R.A. DeCandido as well as the monthly *World of Warcraft* comic book by Walter Simonson and Ludo Lullabi, Jon Buran, and Mike Bowden.

- Kel'Thuzad's reprimand by the Kirin Tor can be seen in detail in "Warcraft: Road to Damnation" by Evelyn Fredericksen (on worldofwarcraft.com).

- The further fate of the Sunwell is revealed in *Warcraft: The Sunwell Trilogy* by Richard A. Knaak and Jae-Hwan Kim (hardcover ultimate edition available).

- Prince Varian Wrynn of Stormwind is a young refugee in this volume, but his adventures continue in the monthly *World of Warcraft* comic by Walter Simonson and Ludo Lullabi, Jon Buran, and Mike Bowden (hardcover collected edition available).

- The magical city of Dalaran will also appear in *Warcraft: Mage,* a manga written by Richard A. Knaak and scheduled for release in February 2010.

- The story behind the mysterious prophet who warned Terenas, Antonidas, Arthas, and Jaina is revealed in *Warcraft: The Last Guardian* by Jeff Grubb.

- Further information about Ner'zhul's life and undeath has been recounted in *World of Warcraft: Rise of the Horde* by Christie Golden, *World of Warcraft: Beyond the Dark Portal* by Aaron Rosenberg and Christie Golden, and "Warcraft: Road to Damnation" by Evelyn Fredericksen (on worldofwarcraft.com).

- Sylvanas Windrunner and the Scourge attack on Silvermoon are both featured in *Warcraft: The Sunwell Trilogy volume 3—Ghostlands* by Richard A. Knaak and Jae-Hwan Kim.

- Illidan Stormrage, Archimonde, and the demonic forces of the Burning Legion all wrought havoc on Azeroth in the *Warcraft: War of the Ancients Trilogy* by Richard A. Knaak.

- Like most demons, Kil'jaeden was originally a mortal. His people, the eredar, largely decide to give themselves over to corruption in *World of Warcraft: Rise of the Horde* by Christie Golden.

- Anduin Lothar is forced to kill one of his oldest friends in *Warcraft: The Last Guardian* by Jeff Grubb. Lothar goes on to pit himself against Orgrim Doomhammer in *World of Warcraft: Tides of Darkness* by Aaron Rosenberg.

- Terenas, Uther the Lightbringer, and the Alliance of Lordaeron manage to drive back the Horde in *World of Warcraft: Tides of Darkness* by Aaron Rosenberg.

- Orgrim Doomhammer grows to adulthood just as the orcish clans of Draenor are forged into a single savage Horde in *World of Warcraft: Rise of the Horde* by Christie Golden. Later, during the Second War, Doomhammer faces unexpected defeat in *World of Warcraft: Tides of Darkness* by Aaron Rosenberg.

- The Knights of the Silver Hand are first formed in *World of Warcraft: Tides of Darkness* by Aaron Rosenberg. One of their most famous members goes into exile during the events of *Warcraft: Of Blood and Honor* by Chris Metzen and later reappears in *World of Warcraft: Ashbringer* by Micky Neilson and Ludo Lullabi.

- Khadgar's adventures are explored in detail by *Warcraft: The Last Guardian* by Jeff Grubb, *World of Warcraft: Tides of Darkness* by Aaron Rosenberg, and *World of Warcraft: Beyond the Dark Portal* by Aaron Rosenberg and Christie Golden.

- Aegwynn led a challenging and largely solitary existence until she met Jaina in *World of Warcraft: Cycle of Hatred* by Keith R.A. DeCandido. Aegwynn continues to advise and assist Jaina in the monthly *World of Warcraft* comic book by Walter Simonson and Ludo Lullabi, Jon Buran, and Mike Bowden.

- The pit lord Anub'arak reveals the Lich King's grim plans for Azeroth in "Warcraft: Road to Damnation" by Evelyn Fredericksen (on worldofwarcraft.com).

- Lord Prestor's betrothal to Princess Calia and his secret ambitions come under suspicion from the red dragon Korialstrasz in *Warcraft: Day of the Dragon* by Richard A. Knaak.

THE BATTLE RAGES ON

You've met Arthas. You've seen his youth, his greatest love, his greatest loss, and his greatest challenge. You've witnessed his most desperate hour, his brutal rise to power, and finally his reawakening. But that's just the beginning. Now you can challenge him yourself in *World of Warcraft: Wrath of the Lich King.*

World of Warcraft is an online role-playing experience set in the award-winning Warcraft universe. In it, players create their own heroes and explore, adventure, and quest across a vast world shared with thousands of other players. Whether adventuring together or fighting against each other in epic battles, they form friendships, forge alliances, and compete with enemies for power and glory.

World of Warcraft is the most popular massively multiplayer online role-playing game of all time, with more than 11.5 million active subscribers worldwide—if it were a country, that population would be larger than 135 real-world nations. Its second expansion pack, *Wrath of the Lich King,* was released in November 2008 and set a new record as the fastest-selling PC game of all time, with more than 2.8 million copies sold in its first 24 hours of availability and more than 4 million in its first month.

To discover the ever-expanding world that has captivated millions around the globe, go to worldofwarcraft. com and download the free trial version. Live the story.

With her hippogryph, Jai, trailing her, Tyrande led Broll to the nearest of the dwellings. She then shocked the druid by entering the domicile without any hesitation, a sign that things were even worse than he had imagined. He was filled with a sense of dread over what they would find inside.

The interior had some of the trappings of a night-elven home, but the plant life within looked sick, weak. The mist that covered Auberdine permeated even inside the dwelling, adding to the feeling of imminent disaster.

Jai, too large to fit through the entrance, peered uneasily inside. Broll watched as Tyrande glanced into the sleeping quarters. Withdrawing, she indicated that Broll should look as well.

With much wariness, the druid complied. His eyes widened at the scene within.

Two night elves—a male and a female—lay on woven

mats. The female's arm was draped over the male's chest. They were utterly motionless, which told Broll the worst.

"It is the same in the other places I have looked," his companion solemnly remarked.

The druid wanted to approach the pair but held back out of respect. "Do you know how they perished?"

"They are not dead."

He looked back at her. When Tyrande added nothing more, the druid finally knelt by the two. His eyes widened.

Quiet but steady breathing escaped from both.

"They're . . . asleep?"

"Yes—and I could not awaken the ones I found earlier."

Despite what she said, Broll could not resist gently prodding the male's shoulder. When that failed to wake him, he did the same to the female. As a last attempt, Broll took hold of an arm from each and shook. Backing away, the druid growled, "We must find the source of the spell! There must be some mad mage at work here!"

"It would take a powerful one indeed to do all this," said the high priestess. She indicated the door. "Come with me. I want to show you one more thing."

They left the home, and with Jai in tow, Tyrande led Broll over a bridge that connected to the more commercial areas of Auberdine. The mist kept many of the details of the village hidden, but Broll spotted a sign written in both Darnassian and Common that read, LAST HAVEN TAVERN.

Broll knew that the tavern, of all places, should have been lit and alive. Along with the local inn, the tavern was one of the few public gathering places in the town.

Jai took up a position outside the entrance, the hippogryph peering into the mists in search of any potential foe. The high priestess strode inside without a word, her silence again warning Broll of what was to come.

The tavern was not like the home, which had been in order despite the bizarre scene inside. Chairs were scattered over the wooden floor, and some of the tables had been overturned. The bar at the end was stained not just from years of inebriated patrons, but also from several smashed bottles and barrels.

And all over the tavern lay sprawled the bodies of night elves, a handful of gnomes and humans, and a singular dwarf.

"I landed not far from this area and was disturbed when I saw no life or lights," the high priestess explained. "This was the most immediate public place, and so I entered."

"Are they also . . . asleep?"

Tyrande bent down by one human. He was slumped over a table and looked as if he had fallen there from sheer exhaustion. His hair and beard were disheveled, but his garments, despite some dust, were clearly of a person of some means. Next to him lay a night elf, a local. Although the night elf lay on his side on the floor, his hands were still stretched forth toward the human. Like the human, the night elf looked oddly unkempt. They were the worst in appearance, though all of the sleepers in the tavern looked as if they had been through some struggle.

"A fight broke out here," Broll decided.

Tyrande stood. "A very polite fight, if that was truly the case. The only bruises I found were caused by their falls. I think these two collapsed." She gestured at the dwarf and a few of the other patrons. "See how these others are positioned?"

After a moment's study, Broll scowled. "They look like they're taking a rest. All of them!"

"They are all asleep now, even this first desperate pair. Look around. The tavern looks as if it was set up for defense."

"I should've seen that myself." Indeed, the druid noted now that the tables and chairs created a wall of sorts that faced both the entrance and the windows. "But a defense from what?"

Tyrande had no answer for him.

Broll squinted. In fact, he had been compelled to squint more often for the past few minutes despite the fact that, with the sun down, his vision should have been sharper. "The mist is getting thicker . . . and darker."

Outside, Jai let out a low warning squawk.

Tyrande and Broll hurried to the entrance. Outside, the hippogryph moved anxiously about. However, there was no sign of anything in the vicinity, as more and more the deepening mist limited the distance that could be seen.

A moan came from inside, and Broll brushed past

the high priestess to investigate its source among the slouched figures near the back end of the tavern. Then another moan arose from a different direction. Broll identified it as coming from the night elf near the human. He bent down next to the figure.

Tyrande joined him. "What is it? Is he awake?"

"No . . ." Broll turned the sleeper's head slightly. "I think he's dreaming . . ."

A third moan joined the previous. Suddenly, all around them, the slumbering figures wailed. The hair on the back of Broll's neck stiffened as he detected the thing all the voices had in common: fear. "Not dreams," he corrected himself, rising and glancing back at the entrance. "They're having nightmares. All of them."

Jai again made a warning sound. Returning to the hippogryph, the pair saw nothing . . . but heard much.

There were moans arising from all over Auberdine.

"This is tied to Malfurion," Tyrande stated with utter confidence.

"But how?"

Jai stepped forward, the beast's head cocking to the side, listening.

A murky figure briefly passed into and out of sight. It was shorter than a night elf, more the height of a human. The hippogryph started after it, but Tyrande quietly called his name. The animal paused.

The high priestess took the lead again. Broll quickly moved to her side, ready to use his arts to aid her. Jai kept pace behind them.

"There!" she hissed, pointing to the left.

Broll scarcely had time to view the figure before it again vanished in the fog. "It looks as though it's stumbling. May be a survivor."

"The mist seems to thicken most around our quarry." Tyrande put her hands together. "Perhaps the Mother Moon can remedy that."

From the shrouded sky directly above the high priestess, a silver glow descended in the direction of the mysterious figure. It burned through the fog, revealing everything in its path. Broll's brow rose as he watched the glow veer like a living thing stretching out to find the stranger.

And there he suddenly stood: a male human. His clothing bespoke of better times but he had clearly been put through a long decline of station. He stared back at them with eyes hollow from what seemed to be a lack of sleep. The human was more haggard looking than any of the group they had found in the tavern. Somehow, though, he kept moving.

"By Nordrassil!" blurted Broll.

The human had not only kept moving, but before the eyes of both night elves, he had also just *vanished*.

"A mage," Tyrande snarled. "He is the cause, then, not a victim . . ."

"I don't know, my lady." Broll could explain no further, but there had been something in the manner of the man's disappearance that had felt . . . familiar.

The druid focused on what he had seen. The human had looked at them, then he had started to take a step . . .

"He walked *through* something . . . walked *into* something," Broll muttered to himself. And when it had happened, the druid had sensed . . . what?

"Vanished, walked into or through some portal—what does it matter?" argued Tyrande, her aspect even grimmer. She quickly stepped back to the hippogryph and seized from the side of the saddle her glaive. "He may be the key to Malfurion . . ."

Before Broll could stop her, the high priestess darted toward the spot where the human had stood. Broll could not deny that perhaps the stranger was the culprit, as Tyrande had said, but even he knew that more caution was needed, especially if their quarry was indeed a spellcaster.

Arriving at the human's last location, Tyrande held the glaive ready while murmuring a prayer. The light of Elune surrounded her, then spread for several yards in every direction.

But of the human, there was no sign.

Broll joined her. "Great lady, I—"

She grimaced at him. "I am not Queen Azshara. Please do not call me by such titles as 'great' and such—"

More moans—the fright in them so very distinct—pierced the thick mist as sharply as the light of Elune had.

"We must wake them somehow!" Broll growled. "There must be some way . . ."

Jai let out a warning. Suspecting that the human had reappeared, both night elves turned at the sound—

And there, obscured by the mysterious fog, several figures lurched toward them as the mist carried forth a haunting, collective moan.

Broll experienced a rising anxiety. He suddenly felt the need to run or cower. He wanted to roll into a ball and pray that the shadowy figures would not hurt him. A nervous sweat covered the druid.

What's happening to me? he managed to ask himself. Broll was not prone to fear, but the urge to surrender was powerful. He looked to Tyrande and saw that the hand in which she held the glaive was shaking, and not due to the weapon's weight. The high priestess's mouth was set tight. Even Jai revealed hints of stress, the powerful hippogryph's breathing growing more and more rapid.

Tyrande looked to the left. "They are over there, too!"

"And to our right," Broll added. "If we look behind us, I'll wager they'll be there as well."

"I will not be sent to my knees crying like some frightened child!" Tyrande abruptly declared to the half-seen shapes. Her hands shook harder despite her words and served to fuel Broll's own swelling anxiety.

From above the high priestess emanated a silver light that wrapped over both night elves and the hippogryph. It spread toward the shadows, illuminating the first staggering shape.

And in the moonlit glow, they beheld a thing that was rotted and decayed. It stared with blank, unseeing eyes and a face twisted in pain even in undeath—a face that Broll suddenly registered as identical to the night elf lying on the tavern floor.

But if the face was that of the sleeper, the form was not. Rather, it was the shadowy outline of a thing Broll hoped never to see again. The night elf wore in body the semblance of a demon of the Burning Legion.

As the mob closed in, a second being was revealed, bearing the tormented face of the human, but his form, too, was otherwise that of a demon.

"They've—" Broll muttered. "They've returned . . ."

"No . . . it cannot be them!" Tyrande murmured. "No satyrs . . . please . . . no satyrs . . ."

The two night elves remained frozen. They wanted to defend themselves, but the monstrous figures converging on them had left the pair with minds in such turmoil that their bodies were paralyzed.

At that moment, a new figure stepped out right in front of the druid and his companions—the ragged human they had been chasing. He stumbled toward them, his eyes looking past.

Broll blinked his eyes, trying to adjust them, but it seemed the mist had thickened—or had his eyes gone out of focus? The fiendish forms with the faces of Auberdine's unfortunate inhabitants were once again simply murky shapes. Suddenly, the druid had the sensation of being near to the ground . . . and, feeling around with his hands, discovered he was on his knees.

"By the Mother Moon!" he heard Tyrande growl, but only as a faint echo. "What—?"

The hollow-eyed human who had stepped out of nothing finally spoke through the unnatural darkness. "Don't fall asleep again. . . . Don't sleep . . ." he whispered. Broll felt an arm drape over his shoulder and then he and Tyrande, kneeling alongside one another, were held together weakly by the haggard human who crouched behind them.

The world faded. It did not vanish. It *faded,* as if it were more memory than substance.

And in addition, it took on a deep green hue.